W9-BAU-372

CHEROKEE AMERICA

BOOKS BY MARGARET VERBLE

Maud's Line

Cherokee America

PRAISE FOR

CHEROKEE AMERICA

AND MARGARET VERBLE

"Verble has given historical fiction lovers a real gift: *Cherokee America* is an excellent illustration of how diverse books enrich literature, and the minds of those who read them."

— *New York Times Book Review*

"*Cherokee America* does what all the best historical fiction does — it vividly captures its particular time and place, yet simultaneously offers valuable insights about our own era. Margaret Verble is an exceptional storyteller, and this novel will enhance her already considerable literary reputation."

— Ron Rash, author of *Serena*

"An impressive historical saga of Native American life in the mid-nineteenth century."

— *BookPage*

"Highly recommended for readers of literary historical fiction in the vein of Lalita Tademy's *Citizens Creek* and Paulette Jiles's *News of the World*."

— *Library Journal*, starred review

"[Margaret Verble] gives careful consideration to place, having spent a lot of time on these lands, rivers, and streams, and through direct encounters with all the inhabitants of this place — both people and animals, their natures and behaviors. This is all rich source material that informs her writing."

— *American Indian* magazine

"In Verble's hands, this tale of a mother's love and her gritty resolve in a shameful era of false promises and broken treaties makes for a rich, propulsive novel."

— *Publishers Weekly*

"In clean, spare prose, Margaret Verble describes a people's struggle to maintain a culture and an identity that both sustains and imprisons them."

— Historical Novel Society

"Margaret Verble's voice is utterly authentic, tender and funny, vivid and smart, and she creates a living community . . . [in] the big landscape of the bottoms—the land given to the Cherokees after the Trail of Tears."

— Roxana Robinson, author of *Sparta*

"[Margaret Verble writes] as though Daniel Woodrell nods over one shoulder and the spirit of Willa Cather over the other."

— Malcolm Brooks, author of *Painted Horses*

CHEROKEE AMERICA

MARGARET VERBLE

MARINER BOOKS

HOUGHTON MIFFLIN HARCOURT

BOSTON   NEW YORK

First Mariner Books edition 2020

Copyright © 2019 by Margaret Verble

Q&A with the author © 2019 by Margaret Verble

All rights reserved

For information about permission to reproduce selections from this book,
write to trade.permissions@hmhco.com or to Permissions, Houghton Mifflin Harcourt
Publishing Company, 3 Park Avenue, 19th Floor, New York, New York 10016.

hmhbooks.com

Library of Congress Cataloging-in-Publication Data

Names: Verble, Margaret, author.

Title: Cherokee America / Margaret Verble.

Description: Boston : Houghton Mifflin Harcourt, 2019.

Identifiers: LCCN 2018006352 (print) | LCCN 2018011255 (ebook) |
ISBN 9781328494238 (ebook) | ISBN 9781328494221 (hardcover) |
ISBN 9780358116691 (paperback)

Subjects: LCSH: Cherokee Indians — History — 19th century — Fiction. |
Cherokee women — Fiction. | BISAC: FICTION / Historical. | FICTION / Literary. |
GSAFD: Historical fiction. | Epic fiction.

Classification: LCC PS3622.E733 (ebook) | LCC PS3622.E733 C48 2019 (print) |
DDC 813/.6 — DC23

LC record available at https://lccn.loc.gov/2018006352

Book design by Michaela Sullivan

Printed in the United States of America

DOC 10 9 8 7 6 5 4 3 2 1

For Fannie Anderson Haworth, my grandmother,
who loved me unconditionally, slipped her culture
to me indirectly, and who, on a hot summer's
evening in the kitchen, told me
about Aunt Check.

Cast of Characters

THE SINGERS

    CHECK, *family matriarch*

    ANDREW, *Check's husband*

    Their children

        CONNELL

        HUGH

        CLIFFORD

        OTTER

        PAUL

    Hired help

        PUNY AND EZELL TOWER

        LIZZIE, *daughter of Check's mother's cook*

        BERT AND AME VANN, *orphans from Arkansas*

        COWBOY AND BOB BENGE, *cousins to the Singers*

THE CORDERYS

    SANDERS, *Check's (more) Indian neighbor*

    NANNIE, *his wife in the bottoms*

    Sanders' children

        TOMAHAWK, *married to Mannypack*

        COOP

        JENNY

        JOE

    GEORGE SIXKILLER, *child of Sanders' best friend*

    SHERIFF BELL ROGERS, *Sanders' first cousin*

    FOX, *Creek medicine man*

THE BUSHYHEADS

DENNIS, *National Treasurer of the Cherokee Nation*

ALABAMA, *his wife*

GRANNY SCHRIMSHER, *Alabama's mother*

JOHNNY ADAIR, *Alabama's son by Lafayette Adair*

MAY GOSS, *Lafayette Adair's first cousin and Sanders' aunt by marriage*

DOVE, *Alabama's cook*

OTHER CHARACTERS

NASH TAYLOR, *town merchant*

JIM MURRAY, *Nash's assistant*

SUZANNE TAYLOR, *Nash's wife*

FLORENCE TAYLOR, *Nash and Suzanne's daughter, and Connell Singer's girlfriend*

SAM GARRETT, *postmaster*

JAKE PERKINS, *whiskey seller*

CROW COLBERT, *rowdy Indian*

CLAUDETTE, *lady of the bawdy house*

DOC HOWARD

ROB FORECASTER, *janitor turned preacher*

WILLOW STARR WATSON, *friend of Hugh Singer's*

TURTLE SMITH, *well-witcher*

COX, *saddlery owner*

LOUIE GLAD, *carpenter*

HANK, *Ross family hired hand*

JUDGE ISAAC PARKER, *US District Court for the Western District of Arkansas*

TOM RUSK AND BILL BOWDEN, *deputy marshals*

1

THE COMING OF THE OWL

More Than She Came For

C HECK HAD BOUGHT EVERYTHING SHE'D come for, but
frowned at her list and pursed her lips. She glanced at the
scales on the counter. "I'll take another three pounds of coffee, Mr. Taylor." She folded her paper to a square and slipped it into her
skirt pocket. Focused on bolts of cloth over the merchant's head while he
scooped the beans. The plinking of her purchase against the brass of the
scales reminded her of hard rain on her tin roof. The sound provided
some relief.

Mr. Taylor tipped the scale. Slid the beans into a burlap sack atop ten
pounds already purchased. He retied the string and set his hand on a
large spool of twine. "What else, Mrs. Singer?"

Check moved towards a barrel of nails. She should've brought Puny
in with her. He'd know if they had enough. But she didn't want to take
chances. She plucked a nail from the quarter circle holding the longest.
"Give me five pounds of these, please." She looked into the dark back
of the store to avoid Mr. Taylor's eyes. He was a close friend of her husband's, and there wasn't anything to say about Andrew that hadn't already been said.

Mr. Taylor came from behind his counter, scoop in one hand, burlap
sack in the other. "If you need anything else, I'll have Jim bring it out to
you."

"Yes, I know, thank you." Check moved away from the barrel and
back to the counter. She ran her fingers over ridges of wear. Was thinking she'd never noticed them before when she caught a streak of light in

the sides of her eyes. She turned as sunlight and a young man in a blue shirt burst into the store together.

"She's loaded, Aunt Check," he said.

Check Singer was related to many people in the Nation. But not to that particular youth. His people, she thought, were from somewhere like Maryland, or maybe Vermont. Being called "aunt" by anyone other than kin made her feel old. She responded, "Thank you. But I'm not your aunt, Jim."

"No ma'am, Mrs. Singer. But she's loaded anyways." Jim pressed his hands down the front of his pants. "I didn't mean disrespect."

Check shook her head. She knew she was irritable. But words to tamp her reactions were dammed off inside her. She tried to soften her face with her eyes. She liked Jim. He was long-legged and a worker. His lopsided smile and sandy hair would soon catch the eye of a girl. But not one of Mr. Taylor's. His eldest, Florence, was being sparked by her oldest, Connell. How that would develop, Check didn't know. And didn't have time to think on. But all three of the Taylor daughters would marry improved land. Jim, a white, couldn't improve any land without stealing it. And Suzanne Taylor would never condone that. Check turned back to Mr. Taylor. "I'll send Puny if I need anything. And either Connell or Hugh will be around with a checkbook at the end of the month." She hesitated, then added, "No matter what."

"Don't worry about sending Puny. Get me word, and I'll get it there. We want to help as much as we can." Taylor hoped Florence would marry Connell. The Singers paid with money drawn on an Ohio bank, not with produce or specie certificates. And Check Singer was a Lowrey, and the daughter of Colonel Gideon Morgan.

"I know. Thank you, Mr. Taylor." Check turned towards the door and Jim.

"Mrs. Singer?"

She turned back around.

"He's in good hands, Check." The storeowner's stubble of new beard made him look more like a drunk than an affluent merchant. His head bobbed awkwardly, but the informality of address was an attempt to convey the depth of his feelings.

"Yes, Nash. I know. Thank you." Check turned again, nodded, not directly at Jim but at the blue shirtsleeve holding the door. She walked towards the bright morning. Behind her, Nash barked, "Pack Mrs. Singer's coffee and nails."

Check staggered, overwhelmed with sunshine. It was still early in the planting season. The front of the store faced south and west, where the weather came from. She looked at the planks to get her bearings. Her ribcage was penned to a funnel by her corset; she feared for a moment she wouldn't be able to breathe. She gulped, and reminded herself to take deeper breaths. That winter was over, and bodies need fresh air like houses and rugs. Jim slipped past her and was putting her last purchases into her wagon when she heard steps on the planks behind her. Words came in a shout before she turned. "You through, Mama?" Clifford was on her.

Check stepped back. "Yes, get the reins."

The boy pulled himself to full height. He hopped towards the hitching bar. Helping his mother was a treat.

Check glanced at Cliff. His hair needed a wash. Children get dirty. She reminded herself that's their nature. "Clifford, where's Puny?" she asked.

"Visiting in niggertown." Talk about Puny wasn't what Clifford wanted. He wanted to show off for his mama. He unwrapped the reins.

Check thanked Jim as he went back into the store. She said to Cliff, "Don't say 'nigger.' Your father and I don't like that."

"Yes, ma'am." Cliff looked at his shoes.

"Yes, ma'am, what?"

"Yes, ma'am. Negro."

"That's good, Clifford." Check smiled with only her lips. She grabbed the side of the wagon. "We'll ride down and get him. He's been quiet lately. Maybe visiting will've cheered him up."

After they settled on the bench, Check tapped her boot against a quilt hiding a rifle on the floor. She flapped the reins and made a clucking noise behind her teeth. The wagon needed turning to the right to get to the Negro part of Fort Gibson, but mules don't like right, so Check turned them left and circled wide in the middle of the street.

The wagon rode better loaded than empty, and Check, who normally used a buggy and who was tired deep in her bones, gave silent thanks for the difference. She engaged Cliff in conversation above the clop of the mules. Talk was a good way to find out what he'd been up to, and had the added advantage of occupying her line of vision, reducing the likelihood of anyone calling to her.

Clifford was full of things to tell. He could recall minute physical details of any animal, wild or kept. He was focused on roosters that morning, and that was fine with Check. She listened to a description of green tail feathers sprouting from a Leghorn and steered the mules towards a distant group of dark children who were silent and still. They all wore feed sack shirts, but only the tallest wore pants. The garb wasn't unusual. But that Negro children should be quiet at a distance didn't seem natural to Check. As she grew nearer, she cocked her head as though that would help her hear words that weren't being said.

When the wagon got to within fifty feet of the clump of children, they scattered like buckeyes spilled from a sack. It occurred to Check they'd used a wiser strategy than the one used by quail, which fly up in the same direction before spreading. She reined in the mules before a row of shacks and looked at each one. There was no perceptible difference; all were unpainted wood with tar tops and a single door in the middle. Puny was inside one, but she couldn't tell which. They were all still, empty-looking, and cave-like.

While she was trying to decide whether to order Clifford to go inspect, Puny emerged from a shack to the left of the mules. He was tall, muscular, and broad-shouldered. Darker than a fullblood, but not completely black. Check's parents had owned slaves. She'd known Negroes all of her life. But she'd been taught they were people, not chattel; and she understood why her cook chose Puny over other suitors. A small child crept up and hid behind Puny's leg. He didn't seem to notice. But Check was already suspicious. She felt the slump in Puny's shoulders match the slump in her own. "We'll be leaving now," she said.

The child ran, and Puny turned his head towards the door he'd come from. Then he looked back towards the wagon.

"Puny, please come here. I don't like shouting."

Puny walked slowly towards the mules. He stopped at the head of the left one. His gaze fell on a fly on that mule's flank. The mule whipped its tail.

Trouble breeds trouble, Check thought. "What's the matter, Puny?" she asked.

"Don't know, Miz Singer. The child's bad sick."

"What child?"

"The one inside."

"Is that all you're going say? Am I going to have to come down off this wagon?"

"Yes, ma'am. I believe so."

Check let out an audible sigh. "Puny, this child better be sick if I get off this wagon. I'm not out here on a Sunday go-to-visiting ride."

"Yes'um. I know. She's awful sick." Puny looked squarely at Check's face. Tears tracked down his cheeks.

Check stiffened, surprised. "Hold these reins." She added, "Clifford, you stay where you are." She lifted her skirt and climbed out.

Inside the shack, Check couldn't at first see anything past the shaft of light framing her shadow on dirt. She did feel movement in the room at two or three different spots, but stench gave her eyes direction. There was blood in the room, dried and foul-smelling. Underneath that, the sweeter odor of unwashed Negroes. Check turned towards the blood. A small bundle on a mat of straw and rags came into focus. She sniffed deeply, hoping to smell movement there, if not actually see it. Her eyes let in more light. She saw the gray face of a baby in a bundle of rags.

Check squatted next to the bundle. Put her fingertips to the baby's face. It moved a little, twitched. She put her smallest finger in its mouth. It sucked. Check took a breath, and felt deep relief.

But, suddenly, she sensed movement behind her left shoulder. She turned in her crouch. Her ribcage contracted, leaving a space between her undershirt and stays. The movement was huddled in a corner. A whimper was followed by a wail: "My baby! It's dead, Miz Singer!" A small head emerged from the darkness. The shaft of sun fell over half a face. The features were wild and contorted.

Check, still startled, said, "Hush! This baby's not dead. Don't kill it with commotion. Who are you, child?" She rose.

"I'z Lizzie, Miz Singer. You know me. My mama was Beth. After the hard times, your mama brung us visiting to Tennessee."

Check studied the girl. She did look like her mother's cook. She said gently, "Lizzie, what're you doing here? I thought your family was farming in the Canadian District?" The Cherokee Nation was divided into districts. Part of the southernmost one had been set aside for the Freedmen after the War. It and the Illinois District, where the Singers lived, were named after rivers.

"I come back, Miz Singer. I been here in niggertown two winters." Lizzie's voice sounded like a tight banjo string. It was clear she was frantic.

Check put a hand on her shoulder to calm her. She shook her head. "You should've come to the bottoms. We've got a big place. Plenty of work." Check looked away from Lizzie's face. Her eyes had fully adjusted to the dark. She saw a broken chair. A few pots and pans. A squat black kettle in the corner. The mat where the child lay. "Lizzie, I'm going to pick this baby up. Take it outside to get a good look at it. You understand what I'm doing?"

"Yes, Miz Singer. I jist don't know what to do. It jist came on me. I got no milk. Got no food it can eat."

Check, long used to making lists and decisions, thought, *First the baby. Then the father. Then the mother.* With that, she picked up the bundle, straightened her back, and stepped into the sun. She shaded the baby's face with her hand.

Clifford stood up in the wagon and peered over the flanks of the mules. His eyes grew at the sight of his mother. And Check, once hers adjusted again, noted her son looked like a goose craning its neck. She marched past the mules, Puny, and Clifford to the back of the wagon. She stood between the bed and the sun. Laid the baby on a sack of flour that was flat. Then she again put her finger in its mouth.

She made a soft clucking noise and pulled the cloth back. A girl. A little mass of gray wrinkles, dirty and stinky. Her suck was weak. Check turned her with her left hand, right little finger still in her mouth. She peered at the base of her spine. No mark there. Then she wrapped the baby back up, and stood so that her shadow shielded its eyes from the sun. She turned her head. "Puny, come here," she demanded.

Puny pursed his lips. He slowly approached the back of the wagon. His eyes stayed on the little bundle.

"Is there something you want to tell me?"

Puny kept his eyes on the baby. "Yes, ma'am. She's mine. I don't have any problem claiming her. She gonna make it, ya think?"

Check shook her head. "I don't know, Puny. She needs milk. Is there a fresh woman in this part of town?"

"No, ma'am. I don't think so. I been asking around."

"With all these little children" — Check nodded towards vanished children as though they were still in sight — "you'd think there'd be a Negro mama somewhere."

"No. I done checked while you was in Taylor's."

"How about the Claymakers? They have Negro blood. Their oldest girl delivered last fall."

"They've done moved out to Manard. Not many folks left in town. Nothing to do."

Check felt irritated both by the sick baby and, irrationally, by the migration of the Negro population. "Well, this is a fine pot of soup. This baby needs something in her before I take her to the bottoms."

"You gonna take her? I don't think Lizzie'll be wanting to give her up."

Check sighed. "I'm not taking her for good. I'm talking about getting her something to eat. There're cows in the bottoms."

"I knows that. But Lizzie, she's attached to her already. And I can't be wagging no baby home. Ezell'll skin me alive."

"Ah, yes, Ezell. Well, Puny, you've got yourself in the fire, I'll say that. And we've got a dying baby on our hands, and . . ." Check then remembered her own child in the wagon not ten feet away. Watching every living thing he could see; his eyes, mouth, and ears wide open. Only eleven years old. The day didn't start out well, and it was ending up worse.

"Clifford, get down off the wagon. I want to see how fast you can run." Cliff jumped to the ground before his mother could finish. "You run back up to the store and tell Mr. Taylor I want a couple of baby bottles outfitted with nipples. And don't tell him what for." Check added quietly, "If he asks you, tell him I forgot we have puppies whose mama was killed by wolves."

Cliff hesitated. His head bobbled first one way and then another. His eyes were twice their normal size. Check could tell he was either trying to absorb the story or worried that Booty really had been eaten. And she was afraid he might tell the truth. She said, "Booty's just fine. But we don't have to tell the whole Nation our business. Run now. Scoot."

Cliff took a deep breath. "Yes, ma'am!" He darted away with his elbows pumping.

Check watched him run. That was a little window of relief. But not as much as she needed. To Puny, she said, "Do you want to tell Lizzie, or do you want me to?"

"Tell her what?"

"Tell her we're taking the baby for milk."

"She'll wanta come."

"She can, as far as I'm concerned."

Puny looked off into the distance, beyond the mules, to the horizon. He winced and shook his head.

Check cleared her throat. "Well, I'm not cleaning up that part of this mess. You go in there and tell her she can't come. That we'll bring the baby back as soon as we can get it some milk. And tell her quick. That's got to be done before Clifford comes back."

THE WAGON ROLLED DOWN THE road towards fields of potatoes with Check propped on feed and flour sacks, holding the baby in the crook of her arm. She wasn't uncomfortable, but she felt undignified, and the baby was weak. It couldn't suck the nipple Cliff had procured off Mr. Taylor. Check dipped her finger in a canteen and stuck it in the baby's mouth. Over and over. She was facing the back of the wagon and, after a while, felt nauseated. But talking to Puny or Clifford would've been worse. She turned to glance at them. They sat side by side on the wagon seat. Clifford was brown-headed, his hair splayed over his collar. Puny's hair was close-cropped. A large sweat stain ran across his shoulders and down his shirt in a V that disappeared in the middle of his back.

Check harrumphed and turned back around. Puny would eventually tell her how he got in such a mess, and Check didn't want to hear it. She didn't approve of carnal relations with girls that young. Even though her own mother had married at fourteen. And mere slips of girls were commonly wedded all over the Nation. All over the West. No matter, it would hurt Ezell. And then there was Clifford. All ears, and too observant. The further she rode, the worse Check felt. She held a dying baby in her arms, and her husband was dying at home. When she got in, she'd have to lie to her cook and hope she didn't find out. That pitiful scarecrow of a girl back in town was probably bleeding between her legs as well as wailing in the street like a wolf in a thicket. Check turned her head and barked, "Go to Mr. Cordery's."

SANDERS CORDERY SPOTTED THE WAGON long before it turned towards him. Everything in the bottoms could be seen at a distance. The land was flat, the potato plants only inches out of their mounds, the corn fluttering in a breeze close to the ground. The trees hadn't grown back between the fields from where they'd been cut for houses after the War. Sanders held his hand above his eyes to create a shade. Check Singer should be in that wagon. She was when it went to town. But Puny was holding the reins, and the boy was on the bench beside him. Sanders leaned on his hoe. When the wagon got within fifty yards, he tilted his chin up. Puny did the same. The sound of the hooves and the squeak of the axle rose like waves knocking a boat hull against a bank. The left mule was slew-footed on his front right leg. Sanders stood still, but reckoned some kind of trouble was coming.

Puny pulled the mules up about twenty feet in front of Sanders. He jerked his head towards the back of the wagon, rolled his eyes wide. Sanders saw all the whites and dropped his hoe. He slid a hand to the small of his back. Touched a gun held by his belt. Puny shook his head.

Sanders relaxed and strode through corn rows towards the wagon. He said, "Where's Miz Singer?"

Check called, "I'm back here, Sanders."

Clifford smiled. His freckles jumped up his cheeks like little bugs. One of the mules snorted. They both flicked their tails. A shimmy ran up the foreleg and withers of the slew-footed one. Sanders went around that mule. Cliff turned to watch his reaction when he saw the baby. Sanders laid his hand on the side of the wagon and looked at his neighbor. He raised both eyebrows.

"We've got a little problem, Sanders." Check shifted the baby onto her shoulder.

Sanders ran his hand over his throat. There was something wrong with the child, but he wasn't sure what. He glanced up at Puny, who was also turned around in the seat. Puny winced.

Sanders looked at the side of the wagon and winced, too. "You worried 'bout getting some vittles, Check?"

Check didn't know if that referred to feeding the infant or the problem she'd have with Ezell if she found out about it. She said "Yes" and covered them both. Then she said, "Can Nannie take care of this child?"

Sanders shifted his weight and looked down. He raised a finger to his cheek.

Check waited. She moved the baby to the other shoulder. Puny had stopped the wagon in the shade of one of the few new trees standing between the fields. It was a scrub, planted by wind. Clifford said, "Puny's the daddy." Puny groaned, and one of the mules whinnied.

Check said, "Clifford, be quiet." She didn't turn around, look at the baby, her son, or her neighbor. She looked at the road they'd just traveled. Ran her tongue around the outside of her teeth. Shifted the baby again, and thought of the green hills of her old home in Tennessee.

Sanders looked into the branches of the tree. "It's puny," he said.

That, Check thought, was just like him, to take forever to talk and then keep saying things that could be taken in more than one way. She wondered if Sanders didn't sometimes just think things up to confuse people. Although he couldn't have foreseen a baby showing up. Or maybe he had. Anyone with a hoot of foresight could've predicted it. Puny was as randy as a bull in a spring pasture. And Ezell raised a skillet when anybody crossed her. Check said, "We've got to get milk in this baby. We can't stand out here swatting flies."

Sanders rolled his eyes. His hair was as black as crow feathers, and long.

"You know I can't take this baby home, Sanders."

Sanders pulled at a strand of that hair and rolled his eyes again. He smiled at Check.

She slowly smiled back. "How's Nannie?"

Sanders said, "They're fine."

Sanders had two wives, both named Nancy and called Nannie. He stood six foot four, was dark brown, had a hairless chest, and was in his mid-fifties. He'd walked the Trail of Tears. And then to, and back from, the southern Cherokee refugee camp deep in the Choctaw Nation. But he was still as handsome as an unsliced pecan pie. Check didn't approve of him entirely, but liked him. And when he smiled, she, a mother of five living boys and winding like a river towards widowhood, understood exactly how he got two wives with nothing left after the War, except a stack of quilts, an ax, some cooking utensils, and clothes handed out in the camp. Sanders had a dead wife named Nancy, too. A lot of Cherokee women were named Nancy; but still, Check thought three Nancy wives were too many. She wished one had been named something else.

She said, "Please take her, Sanders. Puny'll come around later and bring you a quilt for her. Maybe a little cradle, if we can sneak it out of the house." She took the baby off her shoulder and held it with a palm under its neck.

Sanders took the infant in both hands. He looked at her wrinkled face and said, "Not gonna live."

Puny said, "Oh, Lord," and looked hard at the back of Check's head.

She felt the stare. She turned and said, "Puny, we'll do the best we can. She's in the Lord's hands. He'll see her through." Check feared lingering spirits would see the baby straight through to the next world. But she didn't add that. Puny believed in the Christian Lord, and Check wanted Clifford to believe in Him, too. She looked back at Sanders.

Sanders nestled the infant in the crook of his arm like a woman. He swiped the inside of his cheek with his finger, brought it out wet, and stuck it to the baby's lips. She didn't try to suck, but her little jaw dropped. Sanders pushed his finger in. He glanced over at Check. She had her elbow in the air, twisting her arm in a stretch.

"Please take her to Nannie. Or Jenny." Jenny, Sanders' daughter, worked for Check in the afternoons. Check handed him the single bottle and nipple Clifford had gotten off of Nash. She said, "Thank you," and added to Puny, "Take us home."

At the Edge of the Swale

SANDERS WALKED THROUGH HIS CORN towards his cabin using shorter strides than usual. He held the bottle between the baby's head and the sun. Muttered soft words under his breath. Mostly, "Yer gonna make it" and "Don't give out, yer a strong'un." But the baby turned cold in his crooked arm; grew blue on her lips before he was far out of the field. He tried tapping her cheek, but she didn't respond. He squatted, laid her on the ground, and tore off a small blade of grass. He set the blade beneath her nose. It didn't move. He pulled back the rag she was wrapped in. Laid his palm on her chest. Encased her ribs with his fingers. He was afraid to squeeze; he waited without breathing. But nothing moved under his hand.

So instead of taking the baby to the garden to Nannie, or to the cow lot where Jenny and her brother Coop were repairing a gate, he picked her back up and walked to his cabin, cradling her in his arm. He sat the bottle on top of a plank covering a rainwater barrel, and pulled his spade off the wall where it hung between pegs. He walked back towards the cornfield. There, not far from a swale, he laid the child on the ground again and commenced to digging a hole.

The soil was sandy, the digging easy. Early in, he picked a broken arrowhead out of the dirt. It was Osage. He ran his finger along the edge to the break, and then slung it sidearm like he was trying to make it skip over water. He dug two more feet. Hit hard dirt and stopped. Then he picked up the baby, laid her in the hole, and leaned on his spade. The wolves would dig that child out in only one night. Sanders thought about digging deeper. Then he laid the spade over the hole. Took long strides down the side of the field to the edge of the swale. There was brown water in the center, and green weeds encircling it. Sanders scanned the ground for cottonmouths. It was early in the season, but warm enough for them to be stirring. About twenty feet into the grass, he found a sandstone the size of a newborn calf. It was what he wanted, but too big to carry. He walked on, his eyes on the ground. He found two smaller stones, picked one up in each hand, and walked back to the baby and the hole. There, he sat one rock on the ground and the other on top of the infant. Then he shoveled dirt in. When the hole was filled nearly to the top, he placed the second rock and scraped dirt around it. That rock stuck out just in its center. It was light brown with a golden streak through the middle. Sanders packed the dirt hard with the back of the spade. Then he leaned on his tool and glanced at the sun. He'd buried two of his own children the same way. He remembered each one in a spot over his left nipple. He said, "You go on now, child. Get outta here."

But then an owl hooted. Sanders' body went stiff. He scanned the clump of scrubs at the south end of the swale. They weren't as tall as Coop. And at first he thought he'd imagined that hoot. An owl wouldn't rest that close to the ground. But the hoot came again. Quick, and so near it seemed overhead. Sanders' heart leapt. Thumped like a drum. He felt so alarmed he jogged towards his cabin in almost a run. He carried his spade like a spear. Left his hoe behind in the corn.

The Painted Door

WHILE CHECK HAD BEEN TALKING to Sanders, on her own front porch, the next farm over, a tall boy she'd never seen said to a shorter one, "Wipe yer boots."

The shorter one was the younger brother, but also short for his age. He said, "Ain't nothing on 'em."

"Wipe 'em anyways."

The short boy cocked his head. Looked at his brother with a stare he might've first seen a bird use on a worm. But he slid one boot and then the other over the brush beside the door. When finished, he stepped back and turned towards flat fields of tiny potato plants bowing before the wind. He looked at them blankly. Like he was thinking about where he'd been, rather than taking in the ripples before him.

The taller boy, still facing the house, studied the paint on the door. He hadn't, in recent memory, been through a painted door. He tried to see through the wood. Were there pictures on walls? Washbowls? Rugs? Food? His stomach growled. On the outside, faint under the paint, about an inch over his head, was a round knot in the wood. It looked like the eye of an owl. That might be a bad omen. His stomach growled again. He shied away from the door. Moved towards the edge of the porch closer to his brother.

The short brother was still looking towards the rows of tender potato plants bent east in the wind. He said more to them than to his sibling, "Ya gitting yeller?"

The tall boy sucked in his breath. "Jist need to chew on it more." He turned and jumped off the porch like a long-legged rabbit. He flew over steps. But landed in dirt. Fell sideways on his hip. "Shit!" he grumbled.

The short boy grinned. "Wipe yer butt."

"Ain't funny, Ame!" The tall boy, embarrassed and hungry, scrambled out of the dirt. Up two steps. Grabbed his brother by the shins. Brought him down on the planks. Climbed on top of him. They rolled over, one, two, three times, until they heard "Stop that!" from outside their scuffle.

Ame, muffled by his brother's chest, stuttered, "G-g-gun, Bert."

Bert spread his arms and legs over Ame. Sprawled like a girl widening her skirt in a curtsy. Ame flinched, drew his head into his shoulders. Made like a turtle.

"What're ya thinking you're doing?" The voice with the gun was holding the painted door open.

Bert twisted, looked up, winced. "Jist visiting."

"Visiting who? Each other?" The man stepped out onto the porch. He let go of the door. Dropped the gun to his side.

Bert rolled off his brother. "We was looking fer Mr. Singer." He sat up, brushed his hair from his eyes, draped his arms around his knees. He figured sitting he was less likely to get shot than if he scrambled up.

Ame followed his lead. They looked like a pair of mongrels hoping for morsels of food, hoping not to be kicked.

Connell Singer tucked his gun between his belt and his pants. He stretched, closed the door softly, kept an eye on his catch. Straight hair hung to the boys' shoulders. Their wrists and ankles were bony. Connell knew that was from hunger, not sudden growth. The small one's clothes were too big, worn ragged. He was dark; clearly some kind of Indian. The taller one was mud-colored, and dressed in clothes too short for his frame. Some time in a tub with soap and a brush might lighten him up. Or not. Connell couldn't really tell skin from dirt. He said, "Mr. Singer can't see you. He's busy."

The boys sagged in their middles, closed up like flowers beginning to fade. Connell saw their wilt and winced. He'd dealt with hunger some, and with hands all the time. But these were just children. He wished he'd gone into town with his mother and Puny. He said, "We'll give you some vittles. Where ya from?"

Christianity

BY MIDAFTERNOON, CHECK WAS WHERE she wanted to be. Seated by Andrew's bed in the front parlor turned sickroom. He asked her to read him a psalm. She turned to 81. Read a plot that, whittled down, says the Lord takes care of people who put away strange gods; He smites their enemies, blesses them with wheat and honey. Andrew, positioned so he could look out the front window towards his crops, liked to think of potatoes as wheat and honey. And himself, even dying, as blessed. The 81st psalm was his favorite.

When Check closed the Bible, she handed Andrew a glass of water and watched his throat as he swallowed. His neck was as wrinkled as that of a much older man. And he needed a shave. When he handed the glass back, she said, "Would you like more reading?"

He shook his head and raised his arm. "The Lord has given us all this." His hand floated in air, then fell to his chest. The gesture signified both the land that made them the wealthiest farmers in the area and their five healthy sons.

"Yes, we're mighty fortunate," Check agreed. Like Andrew, she was a baptized Presbyterian. But whereas his faith had descended from John Knox through Scottish ancestors, Check's family had knelt to Christianity with the conversion of a great-uncle, Chief Lowrey. She remembered the chief clearly. Although she didn't actually recall his nose plug and stretched ears, except through a portrait painted before his conversion. The chief had argued that adopting Christianity would protect their family against white aggression. He'd corralled his kin into church pews. And when they'd wiggled, poked them with sticks. That was before Check was born. But the chief had lived long enough to see his theory proven wrong. Check could recall the day she last saw her uncle. It was in Tennessee, as he and most of their family started out on the trail to Indian Territory. That recollection had settled somewhere in the center of Check's body. It went all the way to her backbone. She considered the Bible a prop and a betrayal.

But she held her tongue. And believed instead that the key to prosperity and healthy children was marrying well. Her grandmother, Chief Lowrey's sister, married the son of John Sevier, the first Tennessee governor. Her own mother married Colonel Gideon Morgan, a white ally of Andrew Jackson's and a friend of Tennessee's fourth governor, Joe McMinn. High connections allowed Check's immediate family to remain in the state when the rest of the tribe was removed.

When her turn at marriage came, she followed the family tradition. Married well and married the enemy. Her father had wanted a planter or soldier for her, but she chose Andrew, a merchant and Yankee. He was also an abolitionist. Colonel Morgan thought that was naïve, and would lead to unnecessary killing and starvation. And it caused more than one dinner disagreement. However, her father was dead when war broke out, and when Andrew and Check quickly moved with their children to his parents' home in Columbus, Ohio. They lived there in comfort, escaping the death and ruin that devastated Tennessee.

Check's thoughts drifted to her mother. By Andrew's bed, she felt especially drawn to her. Mary Margaret Sevier had married as a girl, unable (or unwilling) to speak English. On the surface, she'd conformed to her husband's strict, white ways. But over the course of their union, she'd molded the colonel as much as he had bent her. Through her influence, he broke with Andrew Jackson. And campaigned to hold off whites and their law from Cherokee land in Tennessee. But Gideon Morgan was a complex man, and hard by Indian standards. When he died, Mary Margaret joined her extended family in Indian Territory. She remarried, and reverted completely to her new husband's full-blooded Cherokee ways.

Andrew was an easier man than Colonel Morgan. And Check had always taken what was useful from both of her cultures. She'd as soon chop off one of her arms as give either of them up. She also didn't plan to move after Andrew's death. She had a huge farm to run, and sons to raise. The oldest was twenty, the youngest only two. She felt almost as overwhelmed by the practical and domestic tasks ahead as she did by the approach of death. But neither did Check see another marriage in her future. No other man was as interesting as Andrew, let alone as loving. Nor, on a more practical level, could she imagine explaining a new husband to five boys.

Andrew said, "How about number sixteen?"

Check realized her mind had been wandering. It did a lot lately. She lifted the Bible again and pushed her reading glasses further up on her nose. She thumbed with her tongue to the corner of her lip, her habit when turning delicate pages, sewing, or examining children for fleas, lice, or ticks.

Before she located the passage, Andrew said, "Did you get the supplies from Nash?"

Check took a deep breath and squinted at the Bible. She confided in Andrew, but wanted, if she could, to avoid the subject of town. She'd decided not to tell him about Puny's baby. Wayward activity distressed Andrew. Even when he wasn't ill. And he'd cared for Ezell all of her life. And for Puny for a decade. Check said, "I got what we needed. Connell says two new boys showed up here."

"They made a commotion on the porch. Woke me up. But we can use hands if they want work."

"I suspect they do. They were hungry. Although Connell couldn't tell if they're Cherokees."

Andrew's breath rasped like a saw crossing a chain. Check had said the wrong thing. She laid the Bible on the bedside table and patted her husband's arm. "I'm not saying they're not. Connell said they could be." It was against tribal law to hire non-Cherokees without paying a fee.

Andrew looked past the curtains flapping in the breeze off the river. The shade from the porch roof softened the light, and the thin white cotton reached out to him like the ghosts of his ancestors. He didn't much appreciate being caught in a moral bind while he was dying. He understood he'd spent his life as a rich man in the midst of other people's poverty. And he knew that some of that had to do with being white. And a lot of it with being from the North, which had the Lord on its side. But still, it seemed that God had given him, in particular, advantages and wealth as a sign that he was one of His blessed. If the Lord wanted other people to be rich, He would've made them that way. Andrew said, "We should be able to hire men who want to work."

Check patted his arm again. "How's the pain?"

Andrew shook his head. "It's tolerable."

She picked up the Bible again and thumbed to Psalm 16. Poetry wasn't as mesmerizing to Check as Cherokee chants. But it was a comfort to Andrew. And chants would just drive him crazy.

Marital Relations

PUNY LEANED AGAINST A BACK porch post next to the steps of the house. A cat was sleeping in a dust hole a few yards from his feet. Chickens and guineas pecked in the grass between the steps and the summer kitchen. The sun rested on the tops of trees to the west, but was out of Puny's line of vision. The Singers' farm sat on a large bend in the Arkansas River, and the house was built so that the breeze blew in the front windows. But Puny was comfortable in the back. That early in the planting season, the midday heat didn't linger.

Ezell stepped from the kitchen carrying a tin plate of food and a cup of buttermilk. She was a tall, strapping woman, firm in bosom and butt. Her hair was long, and when she worked, she secured it in a bright-colored scarf that hung down her back like the tail of an exotic animal. When she wasn't working, her hair was freed. It did whatever it damn well pleased. And Puny, in spite of worrying over his baby and its mother, couldn't look at his wife without wanting to undo her scarf, hold on to her mane, and ride her. He smiled. Ezell held out a supper of cornbread and venison. She said, "Here ya go. What's cooking in town?"

Puny grabbed the plate in his right hand, the cornbread in his left. He stuffed his mouth, garbled some words, and nodded. His fingers wiggled for the cup.

Ezell pushed it into his hand. "What?"

Puny chewed slowly and swallowed. Then he took a long drink of buttermilk and handed the cup back. "I said, Youse the best-looking woman in the Nation." He stuck more bread in his mouth, grabbed Ezell's skirt, and pulled her closer. His cheeks were puffed out, his mouth full of cornbread. His eyes were smiling.

"Don't mess with me in broad daylight." Ezell tilted her head and squinted. She was suspicious by nature; didn't miss much.

"When can I mess with you? I can't wait 'til dark."

"I can't be fooling with you. I gotta get supper on the table." Ezell brushed Puny's leg. Her thigh rested on his for a moment. "Eat yer vittles. I'll deal with ya later."

Puny hung his head. Picked a piece of venison off the plate. Said, "Later, I gots ta meet Connell at the ferry."

"What fer?"

Puny clamped down hard on the meat and talked while chewing. "We're about to get that thing up and running." He licked his thumb. "How's the dying going?"

Ezell set the cup on the porch planks. She leaned against the boards, shoulder to shoulder with her husband. Her voice lowered. "'Bout the same. She's feeding him morphine. Won't take whiskey now. Says he dudn't want liquor on his breath when he meets his maker."

Puny shook his head. "Make it whiskey fer me." He snagged another bite of cornbread. Poked Ezell with his elbow.

Puny genuinely loved his wife. She and her mother were working for Andrew's parents when he'd arrived in Columbus from Cleveland, avoiding the War and overseeing the laying of railroad tracks. He'd spied her close to the station. Fallen for her in a flash. Quickly concluded that after the hostilities, traveling work would be too lonely to tolerate. Luckily, the peace was on the heels of their meeting. Puny quit railroad work and took on a job painting the Singers' house. A month or so later, he and Ezell married on the porch. A few months into their marriage, they moved with Andrew and Check when they returned to Tennessee.

That move came as a shock. Puny and Ezell watched the white people in Tennessee like they were watching wolves. But the Negroes didn't seem familiar either; more like chickens running in circles. Or like catfish sleeping at the edges of ledges in shallow rivers. The couple spent the first few weeks looking at their southern brothers and sisters like house Negroes in the South looked at field hands. But soon they recognized that the former slaves were scared to death. And that their ways were strategies for staying alive that it might be best to remember.

But when Check Singer's mother visited from Indian Territory bringing a fullblood husband, a Negro cook of her own, and relatives of every degree of color and kin, Puny and Ezell saw things they'd never seen people of any race do. Men and women both sat where they wanted; sometimes in chairs, sometimes not. They made sounds like animals and birds; delighted in playing and tricking. Some went to church on Sunday. Stayed long into the day like Christians. But when they returned, instead of being quiet, reading, or singing hymns, they gambled right out on the front porch with their stay-at-home kin.

During that visit, Puny and Ezell learned from the cook that Check Singer was actually christened "Cherokee America." And it became abundantly clear that their female employer enjoyed her relatives. And could, with ease, fall straight in with their ways. She giggled, joked, and gambled. And when she played ball in the front yard, the neighbors fled from their porches. All that activity made Andrew Singer as nervous as a man with a bad case of fleas. He was normally mild-mannered, but he stayed away from the house a lot, and brooded when he stayed in. Puny and Ezell knew most everything that transpired between their employers. And at night they lay in bed figuring the odds for a big bang the next day. Betting on who would ultimately win. But no eruption ever came. The Indians didn't seem to pay any mind to Andrew. And the cook said they wouldn't fight him head-on anyway. So after an extended stay, the mother took her family back to the Cherokee Nation. Cherokee America Singer stayed in Tennessee. Acted like a regular white woman. Catered to her husband. And, to some extent, mended relations with her neighbors. But somehow, slowly, over the course of half a decade, she convinced Andrew to give up his store, move to Indian Territory, and take up planting potatoes. The decision was shocking to Puny and Ezell.

After-Supper Interviews

CHECK'S POLICY WAS TO HAVE a daily one-on-one conversation with each of her children. Before Andrew grew ill, she used the parlor. Now she had her after-supper conferences in the study. She commonly used a reverse-birth-order schedule so as not to delay the bedtimes of the younger ones, and, usually, a private time during the day excluded a boy from the rotation. However, when they'd returned from town, Check had immediately sent Clifford away from the house to search for medicinal plants. And she had not, by evening, had a chance to thoroughly impress upon him the absolute necessity of total silence on the subject of the day's events. If the extra baby lived, she'd be as welcomed by Ezell as a new hawk is among chickens. Check wanted to keep the child's existence secret until the situation became less murky. Or until she could find a way to obscure it completely.

"Clifford," she said.

"Yes, Mama?" He sat forward on the edge of his chair.

"What did you find in your exploration?"

"Some cherry bark. And dogwood. And broomweed."

"And what are they used for?"

"You ground the cherry bark and dogwood together to treat the chills. You have to heat 'em first."

Check listened carefully to Clifford's recitation of other medicinal uses of his finds, to hear anything indicating he hadn't gone directly to the canebrake and brush and to ensure he was learning. Clifford would grow up to be a doctor, Check had recently determined. As part of that plan, while he was home for the school planting break, she was sending him out every day to hunt for the barks and weeds of traditional Cherokee medicine. Not that she was preparing him to be some sort of shaman. No, when this school year was over, Clifford would go next to the Cherokee Male Seminary, and then on to Princeton. With two older brothers to run the potato business, and with a curious mind and an interest in detail, doctoring would be the perfect profession. Check was molding Cliff's interests.

But after a tedious description of his search for broomweed, she said, "There's something else I want to discuss."

"Yes, ma'am?"

Check clasped her hands on top of her husband's desk. "Clifford, I trust you understand that a man keeps his mouth shut on matters that aren't his direct business. This is one of the things that distinguishes a man from a boy. Or from a woman, for that matter. Most women don't have sense enough to do that. When you marry, look for a girl who's not a gossip." Clifford hadn't reached puberty, but Check tried not to miss an opportunity.

"Yes ma'am."

"So, I know you'll understand there's no reason to discuss the baby that has shown up over at the Corderys."

Clifford frowned, trying to appear genuinely perplexed. "The baby showed up in town."

Check lifted her right forefinger. She wagged it. "Cliff, there's no reason to be precise about where the baby first showed up. She's over at the

Corderys' now. She'll remain over there until she's healthy and goes back to her mother."

"Yes, ma'am." Clifford had gotten his poke in. He knew not to push.

Check released a breath, relaxed the mid-part of her body. "Clifford, you're getting old enough to understand that extra babies show up from time to time. There's nothing to be done about this. Nevertheless, some people — for instance, Ezell — are likely to be distressed by that fact. We love Ezell, and don't want her upset. Besides, she has quite a temper, and none of the food around here tastes very good when she's in a stew. Your father's ill and needs good nourishment. We can't have anything happen that would interfere with that."

Clifford looked perplexed again. Check hoped she'd spoken long enough to confuse him into complying without question. But not so long that he was confounded to the point of missing her meaning. She thought maybe she'd gone too far. She added, "So, what do you make of this?"

"The baby oughta stay over at the Corderys'?"

That was close enough. "Smart boy. You may go now. Come kiss me. Then kiss your father good night. But if he's sleeping, don't wake him. And wash your hair first thing in the morning."

Check had talked to Clifford first, out of rotation. Otter, her next to youngest, should have been first. Paul was too little for a nightly interview. He was being prepared for bed by Jenny Cordery, who minded him in the afternoons and evenings while Ezell cooked and cleaned up. Check was confident Jenny wouldn't mention the baby; Indian children gossiped only among themselves, and Sanders wouldn't have told her where he'd gotten the child anyway. He was too closed-mouthed to spill any beans. As he should be. But Check wished her neighbor were a little more forthcoming with her. And she hoped that would improve in the future. She'd known Sanders for only five years. But he'd served with her little brother, Ruff, in the Confederate Army. And he'd been in the removal party with most of her family. That walk bound families together as closely as husks held corn.

Check talked with Otter next. He was her strange child. She thought

every family had one. And although Andrew worried about Otter's pe-
culiarity, she didn't mind it as much. The boy had corrupted his own
name when he'd first learned to talk, and his brothers had ensured the
corruption stuck. It seemed appropriate. And it was better than "Otto,"
foisted upon the baby as Andrew's father's dying wish. Nevertheless,
Check occasionally wondered if Otter's development was being marked
by his nickname. He was a small, sleek child, darker than the rest of her
boys. He tended, on most days, to trail Ezell. He said he'd played under
the kitchen table in the morning. And played with the puppies in the afternoon. The puppies were old enough to be handled. And Booty would
soon weary of them. Check understood how the dog felt with every litter, and experienced some guilt about that. But with five boys to moni-
tor, she couldn't dwell in remorse. She asked Otter a few questions about
the puppies. Then she realized Otter probably didn't anticipate they'd
have to be drowned. She needed to steer him away from the litter, and
ask a hand to attend to the task. She added that to a mental list of things
to do the next day. Then Otter told her he'd named one of the puppies
"Boo." Check's lips parted. She almost said, "Don't name animals you
have to kill." But the child's eyes were big and dark, and his cheeks soft
and smooth. His father was dying in the next room. She said instead,
"Come give me a hug and a kiss."

After sending Otter upstairs, Check turned the lamps up and called
in Hugh. He was her second-born and, really, most infuriating son. He
looked like her: small-boned and dark-haired, with an aristocratic nose
and intense dark eyes. But he was also frivolous, unfocused, smooth-
talking, risk-taking, and prone to fun. Check, though recognizing a few
of those tendencies in herself when young, found Hugh's behavior un-
becoming. He said he'd spent his day in the fields. Check hoped he'd
not forgotten to supervise the hands. Not wasted his time jabbering and
gambling.

She didn't say that. They talked mostly about a horse Hugh wanted
to buy. And a racetrack he wanted to build. Check's father had raced
horses; she didn't, on principle, think a track was a terrible idea. That is,
if it wasn't built on land that could be used for growing potatoes. Hugh

assured her the course would go by some trees they'd never fell. He laid a sketch of the track out on the desk.

Check looked at the drawing. It was a straight course, and did run next to a line of trees that, with more growth, would provide afternoon shade for bettors. It wasn't like Hugh to plan things out very well. But he'd found a good spot. However, Check had reservations about building a track while Andrew was dying. She said so to Hugh. He quickly responded that he'd already talked to his papa. That he approved. That answer ruffled Check's feathers, though she didn't immediately recognize why. Hugh had done what she'd loosely suggested in a previous conversation, when her mind wasn't on the subject of a track and when she'd thought it was a theoretical fancy. She removed her reading glasses. Now the endeavor was so far along she couldn't impede it. That was it. She felt she was being brought in after the decision was made. She rolled up the drawing and handed it to Hugh. Took a handkerchief from her pocket and wiped a lens. She held her glasses towards the coal oil lamp, buying time. Andrew, of course, wouldn't object. Hugh was telling the truth. The love of horses was the only thing her husband and her father ever really shared. She enjoyed a good horse race herself. She wiped a second lens and inspected it by lamplight. She told Hugh to go ahead with his plans.

Hugh left with his sketch, and Check followed him upstairs. She told Jenny to have some vittles, and to be careful going home. She tucked in Paul, Otter, and Clifford. Kissed them good night. She came back down and peeked into Andrew's room. He was sleeping peacefully. She tiptoed away from the door feeling weighed down and sad. When she entered the study, Connell was seated with a book in his hand. Jiggers of whiskey were poured for them both. The whiskey was darkly golden from the glow of the lamps.

Connell closed the book and put it on the desk. He was, in Check's estimation, growing into the task of taking over the family business. She herself was in charge of a lot of the farm, but, beyond Puny, didn't deal much with the hands. Connell was doing a good job of directing the rest. As well as making sure the potatoes were tended, the contracts drawn up and signed, the buyers reassured. He was stepping into his father's boots. He had a literature habit, but also had Andrew's mind for commerce. She approved of the former, within limits, and felt certain the latter would make Connell a lot of money in the future.

She was also aware that he had some piece of his attention on romance. That, too, was entirely appropriate; at twenty, he was plenty old enough. He'd never been around girls. Had gone to a boys' academy in Ohio. Been privately tutored at a schoolmaster's home in Tennessee. Gone to the Cherokee Male Seminary in Tahlequah. It was time, Check thought, for interest in the opposite gender to creep in. But she also assumed most of Connell's attention still stayed either in a book or on business. She was depending on his diligence to compensate for Andrew's illness.

And, mostly, she was right. Connell was indeed managing the hands, the contracts, and the buyers. He was conscientiously fulfilling his new role. But lately, in spite of his father's illness, his mind had been playing, his thoughts straying to the potato shape in his pants. He'd fallen for Florence Taylor over the winter. She was returning his interest. However, Florence had gone to the Female Seminary in Tahlequah; and she wasn't allowing him to make much progress. So Connell was slowly (or rapidly, on some days) going crazy. He couldn't keep his mind off of Florence, or his hand out of his trousers. To get through the conversation with his mother without a lump coming up, he'd jerked off in the barn while she'd been talking to Hugh. Then he'd grabbed a book from the shelf and opened it to the middle as soon as he'd poured the whiskey. He looked at the spine for the title, in case he was asked what he was reading. Emerson's *The Conduct of Life*. He could answer a question on that if he had to. He crossed his legs. "I put those new boys to work. One in the fields and one on the ferry. The older one said he'd worked on a ferry in Arkansas."

"Are they Cherokees?"

"They're some kind of Indian by looks. But not officially. They're orphans. Their father was a miller. Killed when the War got to Arkansas. Sometime later, the mother took care of a sick soldier. He infected her, and she died. The boys were taken in by neighbors when they were little."

Check had heard a lot of those stories. If she dwelt on them, she'd sink under the weight. She let herself dip only into feeling it was a shame the boys had been orphaned so young. And she quickly moved to finding it inconvenient that they didn't know their heritage. She wanted certified Cherokee hands. She wouldn't have to fill out papers on those or pay any fees. "There were plenty Cherokees over in Arkansas," she said. "Not all of Chief Jolly's people moved on in '28. There're stragglers everywhere." She swirled her whiskey. Fine Kentucky bourbon, not cheap barrel whiskey smuggled up the river, unloaded at the mouth of the bayou.

Connell smiled. "Mama, it wouldn't make any difference if they were fullbloods."

Check cleared her throat. That was true. She'd detoured down the path of wishful thinking. Tribal membership was based on recognized kinship, living with the tribe, and being enrolled. Not just on blood. Generally, that worked in Check's favor. She was mostly white, but from a large, influential Cherokee family. However, the system also meant that Cherokees who lived in Arkansas or Texas often weren't tallied in any of the many US government counts. If not, they weren't considered tribal members. Fine with Check, usually, but sometimes — like when it came to hiring — irritating.

"What are their names?"

Connell smiled again. "Their surname is Vann."

Check felt cheered. She tapped the desk with a finger. "They're surely Cherokees."

"Mama, remember there were Vanns on our street in Ohio. I think Vann is a Dutch name."

Check didn't know, or care, if Vann was a Dutch name. It was evening, she was tired, and she liked a good story. She launched into the history of the Vann family in Georgia. James Vann had been the richest man in the tribe. One of the wealthiest in the whole of the South. But he'd shot a man just to try out a new gun. Had beaten his wife on a regular basis. Burned a slave at the stake. Even by the standards of the day, he was completely out of control. His best friend, Alexander Sanders, shot him as a civic duty. Check said, "Nobody, not even the State of Georgia, pressed charges. And his clan didn't avenge his death."

She moved on to the story of James's son, Rich Joe Vann. His descendants lived not twenty miles away, but Rich Joe himself had been blown sky high in a steamboat race on the Ohio River near Louisville. Check said, "Connell, they were firing those engines by throwing bacon slabs in 'em." She shook her head and sipped whiskey. Rich Joe's remains were never found. His death made good end-of-the-evening talk. Check continued on with details that survived only because one of Rich Joe's slaves had somehow managed not to be blown to bits or drowned either one.

Connell swirled his whiskey while he listened. He was tired, but sexually assuaged. And he enjoyed the stories his mother had only recently begun telling. He thought they were prompted by his father's illness. By his withdrawal from active family life. But he didn't quite understand how. However, that made no difference. They distracted him from his fears about his future, from his sexual energy, and from his grief about his papa's situation. He recognized, also, that his mother was passing on not only interesting tales, but valuable political information. The clans were a thing of the past. But time didn't always move forward in the Cherokee mind. Kinship and shared history shaped the politics of the Nation. Connell was eager to be a full adult. To play his part in the tribe.

Gone Visiting

WHILE CHECK AND CONNELL WERE talking and Ezell was cleaning the kitchen, Puny slipped off to the cow barn. There, he squeezed out a half bucket of milk. Then he trod a footpath to the river, carrying the bucket and also a cane, even though he was so strong in the legs that, in Tennessee, he'd shortened his stride to look humble. He'd carved his cane as a weapon when he'd gotten to the Nation and discovered that nearly all white people and most Indians carried guns. But it was dangerous for a Negro to carry one. The Cherokees, who'd fought for both the Confederacy and the Federals, were bitter about the treaty at the end of the War. It'd been forced upon them for ultimately siding with the

South after President Lincoln had withdrawn forces from Indian Territory, and left them undefended against the Osage, other Wild Indians, and the Confederates, who were sweeping in as an army and making sweet promises. The 1866 treaty took even more Cherokee land. And it gave freed slaves the rights of tribal citizens. All Cherokees saw it as unfair. And it was certainly harsher punishment than what was dealt to the southern states. After 1866, Cherokee resentment against Freedmen put down deep roots and sprouted tall shoots. And anybody who didn't know Puny couldn't tell by looking that he'd never been a slave.

But on Puny's secluded path, it was unlikely he'd run across another human, Indian or white. Still, it was wise to take a weapon. The snakes were coming out. And could still be moving near the river, where the sandbar held the heat of the day. Some of those snakes were harmless. But most were cottonmouths and a few were rattlers. Puny's cane was carved from a well-chosen branch of oak that divided into a fork at the top. With the fork, he could pen a snake's head, grab its tail, and sling its body against a tree. Sanders was always trying to win his cane off of Puny, but he wouldn't wager it. Sanders could carry a gun.

When Puny got to the river, he walked around the bend to the sandbar and, eventually, to the eastern boundary of the Singers' land. There, he turned north and took a path through cane towards Sanders' place. As it was dusk, and the moon only a sliver, he commenced to whistle. Puny didn't want to come upon Sanders' home site unannounced. Anywhere in the Nation, a person appearing by surprise was likely to be shot. Puny chose a fiddler's tune he'd heard most of his life. He whistled it merrily. He didn't intend to get killed; he intended to see his baby. And he hoped the whistling would settle his nerves. He'd had a distressing day. And the path he'd chosen was through wild, swampy land. There was no telling what kinds of critters and creatures were lurking. Now and then Puny poked his cane at the ground to be sure it was firm. And he waved it in the air just to feel like he was claiming a space inside of which he was safe from attack. In addition to snakes, there were wild boars out there, lots of wolves, and occasionally cougars and bears.

At the top of the ridge, the cane gave way to flat bottomland rimmed in new-growth woods and sown in corn and potatoes. Puny felt better as soon as the swampy wild was behind him, and, calmer, walked a semi-circle in front of the trees. Just ahead, Sanders' home site was situated on level, cleared ground. It consisted of a one-room log cabin, a milking pen, a drying rack, a tree stump with its center hollowed out as a bowl, a black kettle, and, west at a distance of about nine strides, a double stone chimney not attached to the house. The chimney was more substantial than the cabin. And when Puny had first visited, he'd asked Sanders why he'd built his chimney in one place and his cabin in another. It was an unusual arrangement, he thought, even for Indians.

Sanders had answered only, "Like it thaterway." But Puny subsequently picked up from various sources that Sanders had been burned out twice. Once by Federals and once by somebody unknown. He concluded that Sanders thought the spot in front of the chimney was an unlucky place to raise a third house, but didn't have the heart to abandon the smokestack. Nannie cooked in its fireplace, as well as in a kettle. And the wooden foundation of the old houses still formed a square that protected people sleeping under the stars from the intrusion of snakes.

As Puny approached, Nannie looked up from her work, recognized him, and hollered, "ᏙᏈᏥ!" Her little boy, tottering inside the foundation, lifted his head. A yellow dog rose from the dirt and sniffed the air. Sanders' son, Coop, came out of the cabin and stood in its doorway. Coop was wearing long, tattered pants held up by a rope. His hair touched his shoulders; his arms were crossed over his chest. Nannie said something to him in Cherokee. He went back in the cabin, and came out with a gourd. He handed it to Nannie at the stump. Puny realized Nannie'd been grinding corn, and he felt embarrassed. He wished he'd brought her some flour.

Nannie, Coop, the dog, and the tot were tickled to see Puny. And after he was refreshed with a swig of water, he and Nannie fell into an exchange about the weather and the progress of crops. Coop joined in the talk when it turned to the new ferry. But neither Nannie nor Coop said anything about the baby. Or the bucket of milk Puny brought. And Puny, though he looked around and towards the cabin door, didn't ask any questions. He'd learned since coming to the Nation that questioning Indians was usually a fruitless way to get information.

After a short while, Nannie again said something to Coop in Cherokee. He went back in the cabin, and brought out a deer-horn pipe and
a pouch. He handed those to her. She handed them to Puny, then sat
down on the ground inside the foundation. Coop sat down nearby.
Puny stuffed the pipe bowl with a tobacco and sumac mix, walked to the
chimney, poked beneath the ashes, and exposed an ember. He picked up
a twig, touched it to the ember, and tried to light the pipe, unsuccess-
fully. Nannie and Coop giggled. Puny glanced over, squinted at them,
and searched around for more suitable tinder. He finally found a stray
feather, got the pipe lit, and sat in the dirt with his hosts. The sliced logs
inside the foundation were, Puny thought, benches. But as many times
as he'd visited, he'd never seen anybody use one for anything other than
a backrest. Indians liked to sit on the ground. He thought it was strange,
but wasn't going to sit above them.

While they smoked and talked, Puny listened for any sounds from
his baby. Maybe, he thought, she was asleep in the cabin, or Sanders
hadn't told them who she belonged to. Or maybe he'd told them to keep
the baby a secret. Or maybe Lizzie had come from town and taken her
away. As Puny sifted possibilities, he began to feel twitchy. He wished he
wasn't sitting on the ground, wished he was up higher, where he could
look around. He tried to think of a reason to walk towards the cabin, to
peek in the door. He could say he needed to see a man about a dog. But
that would take him towards the woods or the cow lot, and he didn't
actually feel a need to pee. He couldn't think of a reason to walk to the
cabin door. He was stuck. And he was beginning to fear Jenny might arrive home any minute. He couldn't risk her carrying tales to Ezell.

Finally, Puny realized that the worries in his stomach were tangled
like a ball of night crawlers, and that thought sparked, "Sanders and me
talked about going fishing in the morning."

Nannie's little boy grabbed her shirt. She moved his hand away from
her breast, passed the pipe to Coop, and tickled the baby. She said, "Joe,
Joe, Joe." The tot giggled and swatted at Nannie's hands. His little manhood bobbled. Coop sucked in smoke and passed the pipe to Puny.
Puny took a long, deep draw and thought, *Lord, calm me down. Why
won't Indians talk when ya want 'em to?*

At last Coop said, "I'll go fishing with ya."

Puny thought, *O Lord Jesus, where's my baby?* He took a second long draw and passed the pipe to Nannie. He said, "You and me'll go another time, Coop. I come over to tell Sanders I can't make it. Connell wants me to help on the ferry. I best be gitting back now. Long day tomorrow." He put his hand on a log, stood, and looked around for any sign of Sanders. He said, "Tell yer daddy Connell gots me tied up."

Coop nodded. Nannie said, "Gone visiting his grown chil'run."

Puny felt his knees going weak. He squatted back down. Put a hand on a log to steady himself. He said, "Lord, help me. Why'd he do that?"

Nannie said, "Twas jumpy."

Puny stood back up with a grunt. Thought about asking another question. Nannie had answered that one; maybe he'd get lucky. But maybe Sanders hadn't shown her the baby? Maybe he had taken the child with him without Nannie knowing it? Would he do that to keep Jenny from telling Ezell? Probably not. But why go? And why take his baby? Puny wanted to ask more. But if he did, he'd turn over the pot on himself. And Jenny would be prancing in any minute. Puny ran his hand over his face. He mumbled goodbye, grabbed his cane, and disappeared into the dark in almost a run. He knew "Gone visiting his grown chil'run" was how the Corderys referred to Sanders going off to his other Nannie's cabin. It was several miles away, up on Braggs Mountain. Puny couldn't imagine why Sanders would take his baby up there. By the time he hit the canebrake, his legs shook so that the earth under his feet felt like the ground rumbling before a train.

Improving the Younger Generation

BY THE TIME THE SUN was an orange ball in the east, Check had fed, washed, and shaved Andrew, given Ezell ideas for dinner, and told Hugh to keep his boots off the chair rungs or go sock-footed in the house. She'd also draped a quilt over a porch rocker for Puny to take to the

Corderys'. As she left for the river, she decided to ask Sanders or Nannie if she could have Jenny in the mornings, as well as in the afternoons and evenings. Andrew had grown so ill that she wanted and needed to spend more time with him. Connell, Hugh, and Puny had hired the hands for the season, gotten the earth turned, the crops and garden into the ground, and the ferry up and finally running. But none of the three were any help around the house. She needed an extra pair of hands that weren't male and dirt-covered.

But, as was frequently the case with Check, behind that thought stood several others. She missed having a daughter. And liked Jenny Cordery. But, also, the child was beginning to bud. Jenny's flowering around Clifford called for monitoring. And for some civilizing as well. Andrew and the Academy and Seminary instructors had made respectable men out of Connell and Hugh; and though Cliff was set to go to the Seminary in the fall, he'd be home for breaks. Andrew, Check knew, wouldn't be around. Clifford and Jenny were already friends. There was no telling where that could lead to.

When Check hit the path through the weeds, she began scanning where she stepped, and put her hand on the pistol in her pocket. Her thoughts skipped briefly to her own childhood. Half-clothed Indian boys had been everywhere. Her mother hadn't objected. But her father — well, he'd kept his girls close to the house. Check knew now that wasn't just to ensure they learned to play the piano, read, write, figure, and sew. It was to keep them away from boys who wore only shirts (or less) until their manhood protruded like a cornstalk out of spring ground.

When Check heard rustling in the weeds, her mind snapped back to the present. She looked around at the ground to be sure she didn't step on a snake. She kept her eyes alert. But soon her mind returned to wandering. Sanders and Nannie had never, to her knowledge, allowed Jenny to run naked. But she'd been born in the southern refugee camp, and clothing there had been so rare that even many of the adults were bare. The girl also swung her arms freely, ran, and roamed at will. She did exactly what Check had wanted to do as a girl. And hadn't been allowed to. But Check didn't see civilizing Jenny as a replication of the rules she'd resented as a child; she saw it as refinement that would improve Jenny's chances. But not enough to hook one of her boys. Check liked Sanders and Nannie as neighbors, but didn't plan on sharing grandchildren with them.

Check thought she'd begin taming Jenny by teaching her to read and write English. The child was bright. And already read and wrote Cherokee. Check saw slates and chalk in Jenny's future. The ABCs. She saw herself giving instruction. The girl reading books, almanacs, newspapers, and recipes. That vision gave Check satisfaction. She needed growing and progress to offset the fading and dying.

Check had told Andrew she was going to the river to inspect the new ferry. But she really wanted to inspect the new boy. To get a better hold on his origins. She'd have to pay a dollar a head a month if the pair turned out not to be Cherokees. But work permits were temporary, and tribal authorities cranky about white intruders. Check agreed with everybody else — the intruders were a problem. But they weren't a new one.

The weeds along the path turned to tall cane. The cane gave way to a short span of large, smooth rocks that stretched to the water. Connell had decided to name the ferry Frozen Rock after those stones, and Check liked the ring of the name. It sounded substantial. The other ferries around — the Harris, the McMakin, and the Nevins — were named after their owners. And Jim Bow McMakin was already dead. Check thought his murder was senseless, and hoped his killer would be apprehended, but harbored a practical wish that his ferry would go out of business.

The Arkansas River was loud. Check had been raised on a tranquil tributary of the Hiwassee River in Tennessee. And had lived near the quiet Olentangy in Columbus. The noise and power of the Arkansas had come to her as a shock. But she'd taken to the river immediately. It was a force of nature she could feel in her bones and veins. Every time she heard the water, or saw it, she sucked comfort from the river's strength. When Andrew, she, and the boys were dust, she envisioned the Arkansas still going around the bend with a roar, running full force, rolling and swirling, all the way to the Mississippi and the Gulf.

Check was meditating on the movement of all life towards eternity when a tall boy, punching a barge pole at rocks in shallow water, came into her line of vision. He was shirtless, poor in the ribs, and long-legged. The hair on his head was about the color of hers. His chest was entirely hairless — a hopeful sign. Check stopped, crossed her arms over her bosom, and watched him test the rocks. His rear was flat, but a lot of white boys' rears were, too. She tried to determine if he had much hair in his pits. She couldn't tell. But clearly saw he possessed curiosity. That, she thought, could serve them both well.

She was still watching when Bert looked up and, startled, stopped poking the rocks. The woman on the bank was wearing a white blouse with ruffles up to her neck, a long dark skirt, and an apron. He figured her to be Miz Singer, but she was smaller than he'd imagined. He was swallowing that when she moved her fingers towards herself in a beckoning wave. He threw his pole onto the ferry. Wiped his hands down the sides of his pants. Searched for a good place to leap onto the bank.

Bert hopped from rock to rock, watching his feet, and finally stopping about ten paces away from Check. He said, "Howdy, ma'am."

"Howdy, son. I'm Mrs. Singer. What's your name?"

"Albert Vann. Friends call me Bert."

Check squinted at sunlight sparking on water. She'd hoped for a first name like Duck. She said, "Where're you from, Bert?"

"Malvern, Arkansas, ma'am."

"What brings you to Indian Territory?"

"Looking fer my folks."

That was a better sign. Check glanced at him. "Who would they be?"

"Don't know exactly. I was told they lived in the big bend of the Arkansas, so that's where we come."

Check squinted again. "Don't know their name?"

"I'm guessing now it's Singer."

Check put her hand in her apron's pocket. Touched her gun. Shook her head. "Mr. Singer's from Ohio."

Bert's shoulders fell. And instantly, he looked so forlorn that Check took her hand from her apron and fingered a locket that rested on her blouse. "You don't know who you're looking for?"

Bert turned and glanced towards the bend of the river. The sun on the water blinded him. He turned again and looked at the ground. "Raised up by neighbors. Parents died during the War."

"When was that?"

"'Sixty-two or -three. Mama died in the winter. Ame, my little brother, can't hardly 'member Daddy at all."

Check slumped also. Half of the country was orphaned. A whole generation was raising itself. Images, both imagined and remembered, arose from her breast: Her brother George, dead on a field in Kentucky. His grave by their cousin's in a cemetery in Lexington, Kentucky. Her brother Ruff, dead on another field in Indian Territory. His body lost to the ground. Confederate soldiers dying on cots in the Federal prison in Columbus. Bandaged and bloodied Federal soldiers unloaded on stretchers from railway cars. She stiffened her shoulders. Swallowed to close down the visions. She said, "What was your father's name?"

"Greely Vann."

"Maybe you're looking for Rich Joe Vann's grandchildren. They're about a half day's ride up the road."

Bert shook his head. "Mama said our folks was on the bend of the Arkansas, below where the rivers come in."

Check looked down at a rock. That was their bend. But she'd never heard of a Vann named Greely. The boy was lost. "Do you know where your parents came from? Maybe Georgia or Tennessee?"

"I think Daddy's folks waz from Virginia."

That wasn't good. "How about your mama? Was she from Virginia, too?"

Bert shook his head. "Arkansas." A lump came up in his chest. He'd taken Ame and walked away from the only place they'd ever lived, from everybody they ever knew. Hoping to find their family. Some blood to settle down with. Somebody who claimed them. And now they were lost among strangers, probably in the wrong place. A white egret rose from a hidden spot on the bank, its long wings flapping with effort.

Check felt the boy's desolation. She'd pay the fee on him, and on his brother. But they needed more than work. She said, "Were your parents Indians?"

"Daddy were white. Mama were Choctaw and Cherokee."

That was better. Although Choctaw and Cherokee was an odd combination in Check's estimation. To determine which tribe he belonged to, she asked, "Your mother's mother — was she a Cherokee or a Choctaw?"

Bert looked down at the ground. Check looked out at the Arkansas again, hoping his maternal grandmother had been the Cherokee. But the boy didn't speak. And after a while she said, "Let's go at this another way. Do you know your mother's name before she was married?"

"Yes, ma'am. It were Sanders."

The answer didn't entirely please Check. But the corners of her mouth turned up. His maternal grandfather being a Sanders probably wasn't a coincidence. The boys were Choctaw, but had likely come to the right place. Or near enough. But that wasn't for her to say. She said instead, "That might be of some help. You get back to your work. I'll ask around."

Remembering Dead Warriors

WHEN CHECK RETURNED TO THE house, she dug into a bag of medicines she kept in her bedroom, and, at her dressing table, concocted an ointment to doctor the eye of one of her oxen. She took that in a little jar to one of her hands for the actual application. Then she returned to the house, read Milton's poetry to Andrew, and brought Paul and Otter in to see their father while she fed him biscuits left over from breakfast, the only food he would take. She ate her own meal in the summer kitchen with her little boys. Ezell wasn't there. Check assumed she was taking food to the hands. She sent her three youngest sons to the pump to watch toads when she went back to the house. Andrew was sleeping. She did paperwork until Hugh came in to lobby for a loan against his wages, to make up the difference between his horse in trade and the new horse's cost. As he laid out a repayment plan, Check thought, not for the first time, that he was the image of her first cousin John Hunt Morgan, leader of Morgan's Raiders, a Confederate hell on a horse.

Check told Hugh she'd think on the loan, and shooed him out of the room, back to his work. Her mind returned to the Federal prison in Columbus. She'd last seen John locked in that filthy place. She could smell the stink of the walls. Hear the wailing. She pinched an earlobe, shook her head. She called up, instead, John's infectious smile and childhood daredevil ways. Hugh had her cousin's charm and temperament both. Check shook her head again. She found reckless behavior easier to tolerate in her peers than in her boys.

She put her papers away in a drawer and went to the sickroom. When she closed the curtains against the heat, she saw the quilt, still lying on the back of the rocker. She realized she hadn't seen Puny all day. She sat down by Andrew's bed with the intention of talking over with him the loan Hugh wanted. And, if he had the energy, explaining who she thought the new boys were. But Andrew nodded off almost immediately. So she lay down on a little cot set up for her to sleep on, rested an arm on her forehead, and let her mind move like bees over clover.

Since visiting the ferry, she'd had memories of her father. Check hadn't retained much affection for him. He'd favored her brothers, run the family like a regiment, and, she'd learned as an adult, engaged in double dealings regarding Cherokee land. Nevertheless, she wished she could raise him from the grave to ask him some questions. Gideon Morgan had led the Cherokees against the Creeks at the Battle of Horseshoe Bend. He'd ensured Andrew Jackson's victory and fame. And though her father had grown to despise the future president, his own battle experiences had been the topic of conversations throughout her girlhood.

Hearing the same tales told repeatedly had bored her at the time. But it'd also pinned details in her memory like nails driven by hammers. She recalled well her father's stories of his warriors fighting in headdresses of feathers and deer tails. Tales of his officers, her own great-uncles, John and George Lowrey. And tales of their good friend Captain Alexander Sanders. Alex Sanders had not only killed James Vann; he, along with The Ridge and Hellfire Jack Rogers, had executed Chief Doublehead.

When just shooting the chief had been ineffective, Sanders had driven a tomahawk through his treacherous head.

Doublehead's assassination ensured Captain Sanders' fame, even before he fought at the Horseshoe. But Check also recalled her father saying that the captain later converted to Christianity. And, in a Christian fervor, burned the council house at Etowah to the ground. That so enraged the tribe that Sanders had to flee with his wife and children to the Cherokee encampment in the Arkansas Territory. But he came back to Tennessee at least once afterwards. And he stayed at their house on that visit. Check had been an infant at the time, but her father told his stories for years. She clearly recalled him talking about hiding Alex Sanders from men angry about the council house fire. But she couldn't remember what happened to the captain and his family after that. Did they return to Arkansas? Probably, but she didn't know for sure. That's where her father would've been helpful. However, in his absence, Sanders Cordery would do just as well. He was named after his uncle by marriage. Check was almost certain the boys were looking for the Corderys. When she and her family had arrived, they'd been the only people living on the bend.

Dried Apricots

WHEN CHECK DETERMINED ANDREW WOULD remain asleep, she got up from her cot, slipped to the curtains, and checked the rocker again. The quilt was still there. She turned from the window resolving to visit her neighbors. Even under normal conditions, Check couldn't stay inactive for long. And she had multiple motivations propelling her on — finding Puny, checking on the baby, confirming the Vann boys' identities, and securing Jenny's employment full time. She thought about making the trip in her buggy. Riding sidesaddle was dangerous, and Check not particularly skilled. But the journey was short, and a buggy pretentious. She left the room and located Clifford playing with his boats in the winter kitchen tub. She told him to saddle her horse quickly. To get a hand to tighten the girth.

She planned to go to the summer kitchen next, to measure out a small sack of flour for Nannie. But at the doorframe she saw Ezell in the yard, kicking a pie pan. While the pan was in the air, Check reversed course and went to the study to think. After deliberating there, she went to the dining room and picked up an old bowl from the sideboard. After checking that Andrew was still asleep, she gathered her rifle from the corner by the front door. On the porch, she wrapped the bowl in the quilt. She walked to the horse lot thinking about why Ezell was as mad as the devil.

Clifford had her horse, 'Wassee, waiting. Check handed him her rifle. Asked if he'd seen Puny.

"No, ma'am."

"What's he supposed to be doing?" She rubbed 'Wassee's nose.

Clifford looked at his mother sideways. "Don't know, Mama."

"You need to keep up with things, Clifford." She regretted that statement immediately: he noticed too much as it was. She stuffed the bowl and an end of the quilt into a saddlebag. Tossed the rest over the back of the horse. Tested the girth. Led 'Wassee to the block and mounted. Leg hooked, she took her gun from Clifford. She holstered it at the front of the saddle. Said, "I'll be back shortly. Look in on your papa."

Check wouldn't have been an accomplished rider even in a western saddle. Her father kept a stable, but not horses for girls. So she rode slowly around the curve of cane and trees that separated her land from the river. She kept to the space next to cultivated fields, and stayed, when she could, in the shade. She inspected the potatoes, and watched for wild hogs that roamed in the cane and could dart out and frighten her horse. The hogs were so plentiful that even poor Indians ate side meat and ham all year long. And, though Check found the taste strong, she ate it, too. But if a pig ran out in her path, 'Wassee would rear and throw her.

Even with that concern and her mind in its usual spin, eventually the mare's clop-clop lulled Check away from hog-patrolling and potato-admiring. The sound produced a hypnotic effect that settled her into a feeling of melancholy. She tried, most days, not to dwell on Andrew's dying. She could only care for him and her boys and steel herself. No telling how long the sickness would last. Or how much Andrew would suffer. The disease had moved into his bones. Had, recently, developed an odor. Andrew's mind was still mostly clear; but, though she sat with him several hours a day and was otherwise busy, Check missed him already. Her thoughts wandered to their first years together.

Andrew arrived in Tennessee as a traveling merchant with a wagon of the finest cloth Check had ever seen. His ability to supply it from up north secured him a job at a nearby trading post — and the favor of her mother, who liked to shop when she could, and admired anything beautiful and exotic. But her father had other values. When she and Andrew fell for each other, he forbade her to leave their land. Forbade Andrew to come on it. But Check was high-tempered, and descended from two lines of fighting stock. Besides, her mother was cooperative, and their land surrounded by woods. Her mother lied for her by omission, and Check snuck around. Overtly, she waged a battle against her father until she won.

She and Andrew were married in her parents' front parlor. A year later, their babies began coming. But their only girl had, at three months, succumbed to a fever. The child's death was a blow from which Check didn't expect to recover. And her pain had been refurbished by Puny's baby. She didn't suppose it'd survive, but hoped it would, even if it caused a heap of trouble. She thought about Lizzie crying in the street in town. She couldn't bring her to the farm to work under Ezell's nose. But maybe she could convince her cousin, Alabama, to give her employment. Check thought about how to put that to Alabama to help keep her mind off the baby's pitiful face. And off Andrew's dying back at home.

Check was lost in thought and rocking in the saddle when 'Wassee startled. A covey of quail flew up and spread out. 'Wassee shied towards the potatoes. Check jerked the reins with one hand. Grabbed the saddle's cantle with the other. She steadied the mare. Brought her to an even pace. Patted her. Talked to her. Eventually settled them both. A breeze rustled the trees. A formation of ducks flew over the potatoes. The world was alive and immediate. Check started weeping.

Andrew had been a wonderful husband. A good provider. He genuinely cared for others. Was always an honorable man. In Columbus, he'd steadfastly proclaimed to Federal authorities, to his parents, and to their neighbors that it was merely a coincidence that John Hunt Morgan had escaped prison the very evening of his wife's visit. Andrew believed that. He was not much of a liar.

But Check didn't have the luxury of crying. She banished those thoughts. Called up her determination. Turned into the woods and dismounted. Searched her pockets for a handkerchief. Not finding one, she picked a new leaf off a low-hanging branch and dabbed her eyes. She stopped weeping. But to avoid being seen red-faced by her neighbors, she looked around and found a log to rest on. She calmed her mind by naming each bush, weed, and tree within sight. Her eyes were resting on a small elm strangled with a wild vine when movement caught her attention. She refocused past the tree. Saw two eyes in a face the color of bark. Check stopped breathing. Looked towards her rifle. It was holstered on 'Wassee's far side. She looked back. The eyes had vanished. She peered deep into the foliage. Nothing. She stood slowly. Untied her reins. Guided 'Wassee next to the log.

When she neared Sanders' cabin, Nannie was setting wood for a fire. She looked up and smiled. But she greeted Check with "Hello," not "ᎣᏏᏲ." Check understood slow Cherokee, but Nannie knew she preferred English.

By the time Check had tied 'Wassee to a tree, Nannie had gone into the cabin and brought out a gourd of water and a terrapin bowl of dried fruit. Check drank, and the two sat on a log, munched, and watched Joe totter. They spoke first of the crops. The spring was bringing the right amount of rain. The heat was rising as it should. The plants were growing fast. But, mindful of how quickly that could turn, neither wanted to dwell on the subject. So shortly, Check rose and unpacked the bowl and the quilt. She handed Nannie the bowl first. As Nannie held it up to admire, Check looked around for signs of the baby. The child could be in the cabin, asleep in a drawer. Check took the bull by the horns when she held out the quilt. "This is for the baby Sanders brought in."

Nannie glanced at her blankly. Then quickly away. She didn't reach for the quilt. Or speak. Check realized then no baby was there. She breathed in sharply. In the next motion, she pressed the quilt closer to Nannie. She said, "Yesterday, I gave Sanders a baby to bring here."

Nannie shook her head. And at that moment, a gunshot fired in the woods. Check jerked and turned. Nannie looked towards the kettle.

Check looked back to Nannie. "Please take the quilt."

She took it. "Ain't no baby here 'cept Joe."

"Apparently not." Check sighed. "But use it for him." She turned, gathered her skirt, and sat back down on the log.

Nannie smoothed her hand along the top of the cloth. Pinched up a little red swatch. Said, "This is mighty nice." Asked about patches of material used in the making. Check said the quilt had come from Tennessee. Had been one of her mother's. She couldn't say for sure where her mother had come by it. The material wasn't from any dresses she remembered anybody wearing. She thought it was from the Moravian missionaries. The stitching was unusual. And the missionaries sometimes bartered in quilts.

Nannie laid the quilt on the drying rack and sat down, too. She pinched dried fruit from the terrapin bowl and chewed slowly. After a while, she said, "Sanders come in yesterday saying he heared an owl hoot with the sun up. He's gone visiting his grown chil'run."

Check knew then the baby was dead. Her heart rose into her throat. She felt like crying again. She reached for more fruit. It was bits of dried apricot, both bitter and sweet. After she thought her voice was under control, she told Nannie the events of the previous day. And Nannie told her about Puny's visit. Check asked for, and got, Nannie's permission to give her daughter full-time work. But she forgot to mention the new boys.

Brooding

ON THE SLOW RIDE HOME, 'Wassee's every clip-clop jarred Check's tender heart. One of her Cherokee hands removed her saddle at the door to the barn, but Check brushed her horse herself. She wanted the comfort of the animal's warmth and breath. She'd seen a lot of death. Hardened herself to most of it. But the death of a child — before it'd seen a spring, felt the wind on its face, seen the sky at night — seemed especially cruel. And deeply sad; not just for the baby, but for her parents. Check put muscle into long, hard strokes to feel an animal connection to life. To set her mind on her practical problems at hand.

Check didn't know where Puny was, what he knew, or how he felt. Was he with Lizzie? Wanting a younger wife? Planning to leave Ezell? Or just being male? All would cause anguish. And turn the farm upside down. She wouldn't be able to employ Puny and Ezell both. But losing either would be like losing an arm. Brooding on the worst, Check moved to 'Wassee's right side. With her first long strokes, Lizzie's crying in the street, screaming really, invaded her mind. Made Check even more miserable. Remorse for taking the baby knotted her stomach. She bore down on the brush. Replayed her decision.

But while prone to regret, Check wasn't overly disposed towards guilt. As a girl, she'd been around too many fullbloods to take on the emotion properly. As an adult, she considered the twisting feeling as an unfortunate element of a harsh religion. Found it useful only for disciplining children. And besides, she'd tried to keep the baby alive. Had been thrown into the middle of a mess on a day cluttered with chores and sadness. She'd been short of options. And the infant could've died no matter what. That was a common outcome of pregnancy.

So Check moved on, resolving to visit Alabama as soon as she could. She'd also go to the Negro section of town to see how Lizzie was doing. And, if the child didn't already know, to tell her of the death of her baby. That'd be a tough visit; she'd have to endure the girl's grief and wrath. But she grew up on Beth's cooking. She couldn't abandon her daughter. If Alabama couldn't take Lizzie on, she'd find a way to return her to her parents in the Canadian District.

By the time 'Wassee was cooled and content, Check was soothed by having a piece of a plan. But she still had the problem of Ezell. Her cook was obviously in a stew. No doubt over the disappearance of her husband. Or maybe she knew the whole thing? There was really no telling.

And Check felt approaching Ezell without knowing the lay of that land might be like stepping into a nest of snakes. Ezell's temper was fierce. Check had learned to avoid it for the sake of the food, and for their bond, which was tangled, but true.

So when Check went up to the house, she surrounded herself with her boys. Had them take supper around Andrew's bed, both to draw life into the sickroom and to skirt Ezell as well. While Hugh spun a tale for his papa that Check felt sure was more fib than fact, she settled on the conclusion that Puny knew the baby had died. From that, she reasoned he was off comforting Lizzie, probably in town. She could escape breaking the bad news, and the emotions that would ensue. But ultimately, it'd all come out at the farm. On every acre, there'd be hell to pay. She waited to leave Andrew's side until she was certain Ezell had retired to her cabin.

Turkey Talk

CHECK HAD BEEN GONE LONG enough for Nannie to have a kettle of water rolling when Coop appeared with his rifle over his shoulder, dragging a dead turkey by its feet. He plucked a hatchet from the cabin wall, cut the turkey's head off, and lifted the body by its legs. Blood from the butchered neck streamed onto the ground. The dog, ᎣᎥ ᎠᎰᏃᎬᎯᎥ, got up from her hole. She tried to lick the wound. Coop jerked the turkey, slinging blood. Swore at the dog in English. Moved away until he held the bird over a stone. He bled it there. ᎣᎥ ᎠᎰᏃᎬᎯᎥ lapped from the rock.

Nannie stuffed a shirt into the kettle with a pole. She said, "Know why he run off." She punched the shirt with the stick. "Dead baby."

Coop's eyebrows rose. He shook his head all the way to his shoulders. Couldn't bear to imagine a dead baby. He lifted the turkey higher and dripped some blood onto the dog's back. She turned her head, shook, shimmied, and threw a suspicious glance at Coop. Coop wagged his head at his pet. To Nannie, he said, "Accounts fer the bottle and pail of milk."

After the blood slowed to drops and the wash was spread on the rack, Nannie took one of the turkey's legs from Coop. They held the bird between them and dipped it in the boiling water. When they pulled it out, Nannie said, "Phoowee, wet birds stink."

They set the bird on the stone, pulled at its feathers, and threw them in a pile to bury in the garden for fertilizer. They didn't talk, saving the conversation to savor. It was later when Coop said, "Miz Singer were crying in the woods today."

The turkey was roasting. They were drinking coffee cut with okra. Passing the pipe. Nannie took it and said, "She's gotta heart like ever'body else." They chewed on Mr. Singer's dying. On Puny's dead baby. And on the trouble likely ahead for their neighbors.

Guns and Gold

IN THE STUDY ALONE WITH Connell, Check didn't directly go to the problem of Puny. She'd realized she'd forgotten to ask Nannie about the new boys, and told Connell her theory based on her conversation with Bert: the two new hands were probably Sanders' kin, and might, or might not, be able to prove tribal status.

Connell tapped the ash off the end of his cigar. He liked the feel of the tube in his fingers; larger and harder than a cigarette or a pipe. He fondled cigars even unlit, and had recently taken them up as a substitute for sticking his hand down below. He figured if he couldn't stop, jerking off would sap his strength. As it was, he was sinking with relief about three times a day. He wished he had a cold tub of ice to slide into. But in the absence of that, a cigar would do. He said, "We're hard up for hands. We can just pay the fee." Then he realized that "hard up" and "hand" were words on his mind. He blushed down to his boots.

His mother didn't notice. The conversation was turning down a path she had plotted. But she sighed like a thought just occurred to her. "I can't locate the hands we have."

Connell knew she was referring to Puny; he was worried about him, too. He bit his lower lip. Then said, "My Smith and Wesson's gone."

Check rose from her chair like it'd pinched her rear. She moved to a cherry sideboard. Poured herself a half jigger of brandy. "You think Puny took it?"

"Don't know. Have you talked to Ezell?"

"Ezell's in a state. She's kicking pie pans."

Connell picked a piece of tobacco off his tongue. Ezell's temper could explain why Puny was gone. But it didn't explain the gun going missing.

Check thought Connell knew more than he was telling. But maybe not; he looked genuinely concerned. She offered him a jigger of brandy, and kept her teeth clamped as a gate for her tongue to prevent from mentioning the baby. She'd tried to impress on her boys that extra children shouldn't sprout like wild onions in spring. And Connell might not know about the infant's existence. She'd like to keep him from finding out. He'd met Puny when he was at an impressionable age. And Andrew and she had encouraged their closeness, to inoculate him, and Hugh, too, against the hatefulness towards Negroes they would see when they returned from Ohio to Tennessee. Puny had taken the boys under his wing. Andrew didn't have brothers. And hers were already dead. Puny had filled a hole in her sons' lives, and she thought they had filled one in his. She added, "Maybe one of the new hands took your gun."

"Maybe. But Puny knows where I keep it." Connell tossed back his jigger.

"Well, he's not a thief." Check downed her brandy, too. She trimmed the lamp on the sideboard and moved to the one on the desk. She wanted to be off to bed, to figure more on the situation.

Connell knew Puny wasn't a thief. He looked into the bottom of his jigger. Hoped to see something he didn't already know. "Maybe he borrowed it."

Check sighed. "I hate to think of Puny out there with a gun. Somebody could kill him."

Connell winced. His mother had named his worst fear. He'd been loaning Puny that gun to carry when they were off the farm together. Not only was every male Indian and white in the Nation armed, so were most of the women and boys. It was dangerous not to carry a weapon. Connell had reasoned that nobody who knew Puny would shoot him. And it embarrassed him that he could carry a gun and Puny couldn't. But maybe he'd promoted a dangerous habit. He probably had. If Puny got killed, it'd be on his conscience for the rest of his life. He said, "He's just been missing a day. Maybe he went to town. Or maybe he found the gold at the fort and is floating downriver on a big boat." He got up from his chair and set his jigger on the silver tray on the sideboard. Connell, too, wanted to be alone with his thoughts.

Check said, "What gold?"

"The coins that Indian buried at the fort."

"What are you talking about?" Check's right eyebrow rose.

Connell realized he knew something his mother didn't. That was rare. And having the upper hand was more pleasant than thinking about Puny's disappearance. He feigned a frown. "You don't know there's a big pot of gold coin buried somewhere around the old headquarters building?"

"Whose gold is it?"

"Supposedly a Confederate Indian's. Hid it before the Federals captured the fort."

Check was amazed. Not by the story—there were stashes all over the Nation—but by the fact she hadn't heard it. She considered herself informed on all things worth knowing. For something that interesting to have escaped her attention momentarily knocked her back. Then she wondered if Connell was making it up. However, his imagination didn't usually run very wild. Hugh or Clifford would concoct a story, but not Connell. "Humph. Probably just a legend," she said, irritated.

"Probably. Although I did hear it from Puny."

Mention of Puny shot Check's mind back to her worries. She said, "Let's go to bed."

Kitchen Poker

CHECK AWOKE THE NEXT MORNING with the realization that a missing gun didn't jibe with the theory that Puny had gone into town to comfort Lizzie. She felt a strong urge to find out for sure where he was. And, straightaway, what-all Ezell knew. She strategized about how to do that as she washed and dressed. By the time she was ready to talk with her cook, she'd cobbled together a plan. It was a gamble. But Check had the mind of a poker player, knew that about herself, and considered it a virtue. She walked out to the summer kitchen completely composed.

When Ezell sensed a shadow fall across her threshold, she turned from the sink. She held up both hands, soapy water running to her elbows. She looked at her employer directly. "You know where he is?"

Check had planned on speaking first. And she didn't necessarily enjoy answering questions. She said, "Are you talking about Puny?"

Ezell glared. She slung soap from her right arm and hand onto the stone floor. She did the same with the left.

Check stepped deeper into the kitchen. Light streamed in through the door behind her, and in through windows high overhead. The center of the room was taken by a large rectangular table. The sink behind Ezell had a pump hooked over it. On the north wall was a huge fireplace. The west wall held shelves, cabinets, an icebox, and a wood stove. Pots, pans, skillets, and cleavers hung from the ceiling on chains and hooks. Check placed a hand on the table and stood quite still. She said, "Contrary to popular belief, I don't know everything that goes on around here." She tapped the table like she was laying a poker chip. "I thought you might have some idea where Puny is. Did y'all have a fight?"

Ezell had wanted somebody to talk to. She felt some relief that Check had finally come around. She dried her hands and arms on her apron. "Said Connell wanted him on the ferry. Took outta here night 'fore last, headed towards the river. Shoulda been back yesterday morning. Didn't show."

It seemed Ezell didn't know anything about the baby. That would've been the first thing out of her lips. Check upped her bet. "Did you go looking for him?"

"Went to the ferry midmorning. New hand said he hadn't seen any Negroes."

"What about his horse?"

"She were in the field. I looked for her 'fore I went to the ferry."

The fear that Puny could be dead again entered Check's mind and heart. He could've been bitten by a cottonmouth concealed in the weeds. Or shot by a hateful fool. She calculated the odds of the second fate. The only shot she'd recently heard was the one in the woods near the Corderys'. Single shots were usually for game. A gunfight generally required at least two. She moved back to the first alternative. If Puny had been snakebit, he would've hollered. Somebody would've heard him. The owl hooting in the middle of the day was probably related to the dead baby, not Puny. Check landed on that conclusion before she recalled she didn't really believe daylight hoots signified death. But Sanders did; that's what had spooked him. Nowhere in that hand of cards did Puny look dead. She said, "Connell said he thought maybe Puny had gone off hunting buried gold."

Ezell's eyes grew round. She took a deep breath. "Now that ya mention it, Puny's been talking 'bout hunting that gold. He was gonna scout it the other day whiles you was in town."

Check relaxed in her stays. "He did go out and about while I was in Mr. Taylor's store." More was on the tip of her tongue, so she bit it.

"Lands a'mighty," Ezell said, "I hadn't even reckoned on that gold."

The Legend of the Gold

EZELL WAS AS SMART AS a bee sting. Though susceptible to the winds of emotion. She'd been as mad as a crossed cougar when Check came to the kitchen. But felt tamer after Check left. If Puny had found that gold, he might need extra time to hide it somewhere else. But he'd be back. In Ezell's calculation, their marriage was solid. And, in front of many fires, they'd talked about what they'd do if they got rich enough to return to Ohio. Ezell churned all that as she finished the dishes and started the noon dinner, the Nation's big spread. She also turned over and over a conversation she and Puny had had six weeks earlier.

He was at the washbowl in their cabin, cleaning his hands, arms, and face. She was in a rocker, her feet propped on a stool in front of the fire. Puny said, "Heared something interesting in town." He and Connell had ridden in on errands. He'd carried a saddlebag, and gone to the post office alone. The building was double-logged, with two main rooms, a smaller one, and a trot in the center. It was part of old Fort Gibson, and had been a barracks in the past. Puny'd given the postmaster some letters and asked for the Singer mail.

The postmaster handed him three envelopes and said, "Watch fer the spot."

"What spot?"

"Yer standing on blood."

Puny looked to his feet. Dark wings of stain spread from beneath the sides of his left boot. He stepped sideways and back. "Somebody kilt here?"

"I reckon. Can't get her up."

Puny peered at the blot and shivered. "Anybody ya know?"

The postmaster shook his head. "Naw. Probably died long ago."

Puny breathed deeply. He slapped the envelopes against his hand. "These walls seen some death."

The postmaster cackled. "Yeah. And that ain't all."

Puny put the envelopes in the saddlebag. "I guess those guys had a hard time." He was referring to the first soldiers of the fort who, in the 1820s, had died from cholera and malaria in droves.

The postmaster lowered his voice. "Hear tell there's a stash somewheres. Been looking for a loose board, but ain't found none."

Puny looked at the floor again. He pressed a boot against the puncheon in a couple of spots. Then he looked out the door and beyond the trot. Connell was on the lawn, looking like he was in a serious talk. Puny said, "Stash in the building?"

"Can't say. Maybe. Maybe not." The postmaster pursed his lips like he'd said too much. He had a white stubble and rheumy blue eyes.

Puny said, "I was thinking about a little drink."

The man smacked his lips.

Puny said, "Can't drink alone in the middle of the day."

The man shook his head. "No. That'd be wrong."

Puny's bag was stuffed with old clothes he planned to take to Lizzie when Connell went to Taylor's to settle up for the month. Lizzie was full with child, and had nothing to wear. Ezell was a much larger woman, and had laid by an old skirt and blouse for a quilt. Puny intended to sneak them back after Lizzie delivered. He set the bag on the table and said, "I believe I may have a little liquor." He opened the buckle, reached under the clothes and below Connell's gun. He brought out a flask he'd won off Hugh a couple of nights earlier.

The man's mouth began to move like a carp's.

Puny said, "Course, I always like a story to go with my liquor." He unscrewed the top, held the bore to his lips, and threw his head back. He pretended to drink. Wiped his mouth with his hand. "Mighty good."

The postmaster's fingers twitched. "Confederate Indian. Hid solid-gold coin. That's the story. Not really in here. Out under a tree."

Puny studied the flask like he was praying over a problem. The postmaster said, "That's all I knowed. Supposed to be around the headquarters building. Or 'tween it and the river." His fingers wiggled like worms turned up in spring.

Puny said, "Take a swig." He held the flask out.

The man said, "Hold on. Can't drink after a nigger." He turned to a cubbyhole in the wall and pulled out a tin cup. Puny poured him a drink, but not much.

The postmaster drained his cup. He wiped his mouth with the back of his hand. "I started looking down by the rocks. Been working my way up. Got a pick left over from the fort." He held his cup out.

Puny poured him a little more. "Who told ya that story?"

The man took a gulp, shook his head, and wiped his mouth on his sleeve. "Common knowledge. The Singers probably the only people that don't know it. Y'alls got money enough."

Puny thought about saying, "I ain't a Singer," but said instead, "That's right. We's rich." He laughed and walked out.

The post office sat on lawn spotted with trees and grazed by horses. Next to it was another double-log building, which formerly had been the fort's headquarters. Now it was the home of Dennis Wolf Bushyhead and his wife, Alabama. Dennis was who Connell was talking with. Both buildings overlooked the Grand River at a point just northeast of where it flowed into the Arkansas. Puny stood in the post office trot, looked at the smooth lawn and the tall trees clothed in new growth. He thought about the gold, wondered where it could be hidden.

Later that night, he told the story to Ezell. He left out the part about taking her clothes to Lizzie.

The Calm Before

CHECK WASN'T PROUD OF HER conversation with Ezell. Her cook was the only other female she saw on a daily basis. They knew each other well, tolerated each other's moods, and colluded against the men when they needed to. Check was especially worried Ezell would find out she'd lied to her. Well, not really lied, just concealed the truth. Well, not concealed the truth, actually. Just not said what Puny had been up to. That was merely an omission due entirely to affection, to not wanting to bear bad news, to minding her own business. By the time Check entered the parlor turned sickroom, she'd worked all of that through.

The bed was a mahogany four-poster. Andrew was resting against the headboard, his gown and face made even paler framed by dark wood. His eyelids seemed transparent except for spidery veins. Check took his hand, asked if he wanted a pillow. He shook his head. A breeze fluttered the curtains. It refreshed the air. But Check decided pine candles were needed.

Andrew's voice rasped, "What's your day like, my love?"

Check took her chair. "Just the usual. Nothing happening except work. Shall I read from the Bible?"

"You pick this time."

Check lifted the Bible from the table and turned to Ecclesiastes. The only part she really cared for at all.

After Andrew fell asleep, Check quietly left for the dining room. She rummaged through the hutch. Found the candles she needed, unwrapped them from cloth, and tiptoed back to the sickroom. She removed the candles they'd been using from their holders and stuck the two new ones in. She lit both, and hoped, when Andrew awoke, he wouldn't notice they were burning during daylight. He'd understand what they were for. That would embarrass him, and make him melancholy.

After the first blow of the diagnosis, Andrew had stayed even-keeled. Or so Check reckoned. They hadn't discussed his sickness directly; only the changes it would bring, what Andrew could or couldn't do for himself, who would pick up what tasks. The name of the disease wasn't mentioned. But it didn't have to be. They'd seen it in Andrew's mother, and in others. Its effects were awful. Its conclusion certain.

When Check felt sure Andrew wouldn't wake, she left for the back porch. Otter, Clifford, and Jenny were playing on the planks and minding Paul. Check settled Paul into a cradle and took a seat. She sent Clifford for the writing slates and chalk. When he returned, she told the children they were going to write out the names of animals. From where they were seated, they could see several. Clifford would write a name in English, Jenny in Cherokee. Then they would write each other's words and supervise Otter's writing them both.

Check felt smug with her system. It would give Otter a head start. Strengthen Jenny's English skills. And, in one fell swoop, keep Clifford engaged in learning during his break. Cliff didn't need to be in the fields; he wasn't going to be a farmer. She wasn't yet sure how to direct Otter; he was too young and strange to decipher. But time and close observation would reveal his nature. She'd take his natural abilities and hone them.

Jenny would pick up writing English quickly. The skill would channel her mind into a more confined course. Check congratulated herself. One thing, at least, was going correctly.

She pointed to a chicken. Clifford scratched "chicken" on his slate. Jenny wrote "ɦWS."

The children showed their slates to each other. They all started writing again. When Otter was finished, Check directed Clifford and Jenny to look at his letters. When they agreed he'd produced them correctly, she pointed to Booty. Jenny wrote "ꮯ." Clifford wrote "dog." Jenny put down "dog," too, as did Otto. Then Clifford chalked "ꮯ." Things were progressing nicely. Ezell came out of the kitchen and said she was cooking. She was civil. Check decided there was a chance Puny had gone searching for the stash. She sighed, expelling some of her worry into the air.

She was contemplating dusting off her own Cherokee language skills when she gazed off into the fields. It was a fine spring day. A breeze rippled the potato leaves. The horizon was clear. A small, dark dot was moving towards the house. Check's distance eyesight wasn't what it'd been. She squinted. The dot was bigger than a wolf or a dog. It looked like a bear. But bears stayed on the mountain. Or down by the river. And the dark dot didn't move like a bear. It moved on two legs. It was getting closer.

Check sat up straight in her chair. "Clifford, take Otter and Jenny to the barn. Play horseshoes. Don't leave the lot."

Clifford looked up at his mother, startled. So did the other two children. Cliff said, "What about dinner?"

Check rose abruptly and headed for the door. "Do it now, Clifford! Have a good time. Watch for snakes. I'll bring your food." She shut the door behind her. Walked the hall in a hurry. Scampered up the stairs to the bedroom she'd shared with Andrew. There was an empty spot where their bed had been removed. She stood in that spot, to the side of the window, to look out. A dark brown girl was striding over mounds of potatoes. She was headed straight towards the house.

Panic and Prevarication

CHECK RECOGNIZED DANGER WAS COMING. The last time she'd felt real panic had been the morning of a loud banging of the knocker at her in-laws' house in Columbus. She'd heard Andrew answer the door. Heard low tones of strange voices in the foyer. Her mother-in-law's quick steps, the swish of her skirt. Heard unusually high tones of familiar voices. Heard her own name. Check had been at her mirror. She jumped back into bed, took her dressing robe off under the covers, pushed it with her feet to the footboard. She waited, one ear on a pillow, the other as alert as a dog's. Andrew eventually climbed the stairs and opened the bedroom door. He said, "Darling, soldiers are here. It seems John has escaped."

She lifted her head slowly. Her lids were half closed. "What? I've gone back to bed feeling woozy. I may be in a family way again."

Andrew's eyebrows unfurrowed. His frown spread to a grin. "That's wonderful!" He stepped towards the bed, temporarily forgetting the officers in the foyer. Then he remembered. Grasped the knob again. "I'll tell them you're indisposed. But you'll have to talk to them later. They're quite unpleasant and official."

"Did you say John escaped? He wasn't shot, was he?"

He hadn't been. Not then.

The Federal authorities searched the entire house, the basement and attic, and then the cellar. They found nothing of interest beyond jars of plum jelly, which Mrs. Singer pressed upon them. In the late afternoon, when they came back for questioning, Andrew's father provided them brandy. He wanted to stay. The officers forbade that, but allowed Andrew to remain with her. John Hunt Morgan had escaped, two men with him. Their guards had been asleep, or drugged, or something. The questioning had been a grilling for Check. But Andrew's family were well-known abolitionists. That protected her from being removed from the house.

This time, however, Andrew's parents were dead, and Andrew

couldn't be a buffer. Or could he? Check turned from the bedroom window. Flew from the room. Held her skirt high, sped down the stairs, and checked the back porch to be certain the older children were gone and Paul was asleep. Then she slipped into the study, pulled a revolver from the desk, and came out again. She took an apron off a peg in the winter kitchen and flew into the parlor where Andrew was napping. She drew the apron on, tucked the gun in its pocket, and sat down by the bed. She was winded. She touched Andrew's arm.

He stirred and smiled. He realized his wife was at his side. Check was a comfort. He couldn't've asked for a better spouse. She was feminine and small. But strong enough to bear healthy children. And brighter than any woman he'd ever met. The Lord had provided him a wonderful mate. He was a man blessed among many. He said, "You're my angel."

That heightened Check's alarm. Was Andrew seeing angels? Then she realized that as a silly fear, brought on, no doubt, by the panic she already felt. She said, "Andrew, I want you to know that whatever happens, I've been perfectly happy with you."

Tears welled in Andrew's eyes. They weren't hard to come by. He was in pain and knew he was dying.

Things Get Sloppy

LIZZIE CAME INTO THE YARD from the fields just as Ezell stepped from the summer kitchen carrying a bucket of slop for the chickens. The girl looked at Ezell and said, "I'z here fer my baby."

Ezell said, "Whose blouse has you got on?"

Lizzie looked down at her breasts. Back up at the woman with the bucket. "My own."

Ezell stepped closer. She looked Lizzie over head to toe, toe to head. "Who is you?"

Lizzie straightened up as tall as she could get. "Puny's wife."

Ezell stepped back. Her eyes widened. Her mouth flew open. She took a deep breath, then clenched her jaw. Her eyes narrowed to slits. She put a hand to the bottom of the pail. She swung her arm back.

Check heard the screams clear in the parlor. Andrew did, too. He said, "What —?" Check interrupted, "It's one of the children. I'll be back." By the time she got to the porch, the women were on the ground rolling over each other. Check fired a shot in the air. Paul woke up screaming.

BY HER NIGHTLY MEETING WITH Connell, Check had had a difficult day. Connell handed her a small glass of whiskey. He said, "Or would you rather have brandy?"

"I'd rather drown myself in the river."

Connell chuckled. He'd run to the house when he'd heard the shot, Hugh close on his heels. They hadn't gotten there in time to see the two women wrestling, just growling at each other. Connell said, "It was the best standoff I've ever seen."

Check grunted. Drummed her fingers on the desk. Lizzie's mother had remained with hers until her death. She couldn't send Lizzie away now, not even to Alabama. But the bunkhouse was full of men, and she couldn't keep the girl on the back porch, either. Ezell could attack her in the night without anybody hearing. Until she could come up with a better solution, she'd have to put Lizzie on a pallet on the front porch under Andrew's windows. The weather was warm enough, and in the height of summer, when the heat was unbearable, often they all slept out there.

Connell said, "What're you gonna do?"

"You are going to find Puny." Check emphasized "you." She wasn't about to do the finding, or leave it up to Hugh. He'd lately taken any excuse to leave the farm. He was up to something.

"You should've told me about this sooner, Mama." Connell scrunched his face to appear pained.

Check grunted again. She wasn't accustomed to being corrected by her grown children. And didn't think she could get used to it. "You know his haunts," she said.

"I don't know where he is now."

"I thought you said he was hunting for gold." She looked directly at Connell. Cocked an eyebrow.

"I made that up."

"Lying to your mother?" Her voice pitched low.

"I wasn't lying. Puny did tell me that."

"You misled me into thinking you knew what he was up to. That's a deception. You're supposed to honor your father and mother."

"Imitation is an honor." Connell raised his eyebrows. Smiled without parting his lips.

Check smiled back. She didn't think Connell had any way of knowing about her conversation with Ezell about Puny. But she recognized he was old enough to have insight into her ways. That wouldn't do him any harm; she'd gotten along well enough in the world, and intended for him to do the same. But at the moment, that was neither here nor there. She shook her head. "Maybe Puny took off to Braggs Mountain, looking for Sanders and his baby. If he's carrying your gun, somebody could kill him."

Connell knew that only too well. "I can go up there. Or Hugh can."

"No. I need you and Hugh here. Get Coop to do it. Lend him The Bay to ride. He'll know exactly where to go."

"The Bay?" That was his father's horse.

"Yes. He needs to be ridden. He's lonesome and restless. I saw him in the lot yesterday."

Connell shook his head. He winced.

"I know," Check said. "But somebody needs to ride him. He'll go into mourning. You can ride him yourself. Give Coop your horse."

Connell considered that. The Bay, a gelding, was sixteen hands high, the finest horse on the farm, and the only thoroughbred close around. Connell admired him every day. But wasn't ready to take his father's horse to ride. Not yet. He bit his lip.

Check saw Connell fighting tears. She said, "You decide."

Connell composed himself, changed the subject. "Do you think Coop can get Puny to come home?"

Check sighed. "I don't know he's up there for sure. But tell Coop to tell Puny we need him to come home. But don't tell anybody Lizzie's here. If Puny finds out, he'll lay out even longer. Or not come back at all. And ask Coop to find out what Sanders did with the baby. Lizzie has a right to know. I worry about telling her the baby's dead without knowing for certain."

Having Studied the Ways of Animals

IN THE GRAY DAWN OF the next morning, Check, awake on her cot, was listening to Andrew's breathing when Lizzie screamed from the porch. Assuming the yell was provoked by Ezell, Check shot up, rushed to the door, and flung it open. Lizzie was jumping on the planks, shouting, pointing to the lawn. Ezell was nowhere around. But three yards from the porch, a polecat was dancing on its hind legs. It lurched forward and backward. Dropped to four feet. Twisted its rump, raised, and shimmied its tail. Check grabbed for Lizzie's arm. But Lizzie weaved and darted. Check reached again, but then got a whiff of the skunk following its nature. Check turned and slammed the door in time to escape the spray. Like sunlight without shades, the smell invaded the house through the windows.

The boys pounded down the stairs. Hugh scrambling first, carrying Paul, who was crying. He handed Paul to Clifford. Then he and Connell — at Check's direction, while stretching her arms through her robe — lifted Andrew from his bed and carried him out the back door to the porch rocker. The boys, in various states of undress around their papa, shifted from foot to foot and yelled about the smell. Ezell, in the kitchen brewing coffee, saw the family group and caught a whiff of the odor. She said, "Good riddance," and closed the door.

Check was the last to leave the house. She counted heads on the porch, and realized Lizzie wasn't with them. She started to go back in. But instead, turned again and walked down the steps and around the house to the front. There, she found Lizzie running in a circle, screaming. Check used a voice her father would've admired. "Stand still!"

Lizzie stopped, stunned. Then fell to the ground in a heap. She buried her face in her skirt. Started sobbing. Check shouted, "Lizzie, we've gotta get you out of those clothes!" Lizzie raised her head. Check said again, "We've gotta get you out of those clothes!" Lizzie jumped to her feet. Started pulling her blouse off over her head.

Check waved both hands in the air. "No! Not yet! The men'll see ya!"

Lizzie stood stock-still. Tightened her fingers into fists and bawled.

Check didn't really want to get closer. She took tentative steps and tried to breathe through her mouth. When she got to Lizzie, she gulped in air and mustered her sternest voice. "Stop that noise, Lizzie! Follow me." She turned and marched, her dressing robe swishing.

Check led Lizzie to a tub behind Puny and Ezell's cabin. It was surrounded by a small clump of saplings, and next to it was a large, flat sandstone. In front was a bucket and a round sandstone hearth, circling ashes. Check told Lizzie to get in the tub and throw her clothes out. Then she picked up the bucket and walked to a pump close to the kitchen. She was pumping water with vigor when Clifford wandered over and stood too close to her shoulder. He said, "I feel sick. Do we have'ta do lessons today?"

"Get out of my way, Clifford. It's no time for discussion." The water spilled over the lip of the bucket.

"What's gonna happen to her? Where's the baby?"

Check straightened up. Brushed her hair back from her face. "Clifford! I'm warning you. Don't mess with me."

Clifford said, "I was just trying to help." He hung his head. Slumped away.

Check hauled buckets of water to the tub, muttering under her breath, "ᎩᎶᏯᎢᏴ ᏬᏰᏚᏓᏅᏓ ᎢᏕ ᎠᎩᏄᏭ," something she'd often heard her mother say when dealing with skunks. Once she got Lizzie bathed and into different clothes, she carried the skunk-sprayed ones on the end of a pole to the trash-burning can. She stood downwind and set them on fire. Gave herself the luxury of watching them burn. They were her own clothes; she'd given them to Lizzie after Ezell had doused her in slop. They didn't make a big fire. But as Check watched the flames, she plotted.

She'd studied the ways of animals. Every day, she saw hawks patrolling their territories. Knew that creatures, even in packs, fiercely defend their space. But when pulled away, they're thrown off balance. Check knew, too, it's possible — she'd done it with dogs, horses, and boys — to force animals into getting along. So she didn't go to the summer kitchen to talk with Ezell. She asked Otter to bring Ezell to the study. And she was at the desk, writing in a ledger, her glasses perched low on her nose, her hair pulled tightly into a bun, when Ezell stopped in the doorframe. She said, "Got something on your mind, Miz Singer?"

Check looked up from her books and sighed. She was wearing a blouse with a high collar. Her locket lay between her breasts. Her sleeves were rolled up. She said, "I'm afraid so. Come have a seat." She gestured with her pen towards a chair in front of the desk.

Ezell said, "I'd rather stand. I got work to do." She patted the scarf that held her hair.

Check smiled. "Don't worry about your work. I'll put in a word with your employer."

Ezell expelled an audible breath. She walked to the chair and took a seat.

Check stuck her quill in its holder. "Ezell, we have a situation here. Puny got Lizzie in a family way, and now he's gone. Do you have any idea where he went?"

Ezell shook her head.

"Well, we're sending Coop off looking for him. And for the baseborn baby. But in the meantime, we've got dying going on. Mr. Singer's the only reason any of us have a roof over our heads. He can't get a moment's peace in the middle of a big ruckus. Do you catch my drift?"

"Send her away," Ezell said.

Check had anticipated that. "I wish I could. But she's sort of family. And if I did, she'd come creeping back. Any woman has a right to know about her baby, no matter how it got here."

Ezell shrugged.

"I can't leave her on the porch, either."

Ezell's eyes went to slits.

"The way I see it, there's only one place to put her for now." Check leaned forward in her chair. Clasped her hands on the desk. Furrowed her brow. "We're going to have to lodge her with you."

Ezell popped out of her chair. She pulled herself to full height. "I'll leave if ya do."

"So be it. I'll put her in your cabin. She'll be there alone when Puny shows up. Her mother was an excellent cook. I'm sure she's learned something from her."

Ezell pursed her lips like she had eaten a persimmon.

Check said, "Think about it. You decide."

Later, after more wrangling, and when Ezell was finally out of the house, Clifford led Lizzie down the hall. Her head twisted, taking in the wonders of the pictures on the walls. When she got to the study's threshold, she saw the big desk, the sideboard, bookshelves, and mounted antlers over the hearth. The whites of her eyes expanded to egg size. She stopped in the doorframe.

Check said, "Thank you, Clifford. Go see if Jenny needs help minding Paul." Cliff made no effort to move. She added, "Now!"

Lizzie stepped aside to let Cliff slip out, but didn't budge past the doorway. Check said, "Lizzie, I want you to come into the room."

"I'z all right here, Miz Singer."

Check pinched the bridge of her nose. "I'd like to speak softly, Lizzie. Mr. Singer is trying to rest. He's ill, you know."

"Yes'um. I'z sorry."

"Come in, then. And take a seat. I'm not going to bite you."

Lizzie said, "No, ma'am," but did as she was told. She sat, dropped her head, and looked at her hands.

Check felt tender towards the girl. She couldn't be over fourteen, and was, no doubt, still weak from giving birth. Her baby was surely dead, and she'd been attacked by both Ezell and a skunk in the past twenty-four hours. Check said, "Did the vinegar help?"

Lizzie raised her right arm and sniffed it. "Yes'um. I think so."

"Did you have any trouble with the porch?"

"No'um. I wrenched it twice."

"Well, we can always open some stewed tomatoes and throw them on there if we have to."

Lizzie nodded.

Check took a handkerchief from her pocket and patted her brow. It was the hot part of the day and warm in the room. "We can't leave you out on the porch tonight. Ezell has agreed to let you sleep with her."

Lizzie started shaking. That unsettled Check. She blinked several times and went on. "She's promised me she won't hurt you. But you have to do your part. Ezell's legally married to Puny in a Christian marriage. I was at the ceremony myself. Naturally, she's upset."

Lizzie raised her head. Her eyes brimmed over. Tears rolled down her cheeks. She nodded.

"I want you to help her with her work. She's a busy woman. And I'll pay you like I do the rest of our hands."

Lizzie nodded again.

"You do what Ezell tells you to do, and mind her."

Lizzie pursed her lips.

"Do you understand?"

Lizzie didn't say anything for a moment. Then she sat up straight and said in a fairly loud voice, "Where's my baby, Miz Singer?"

Check had anticipated that. And felt guilty for not having an answer. She'd turned her actions over in her mind, examined them carefully many times. If she'd left the child with Lizzie in town, she would've surely starved there. If she'd brought her to the farm, it would've been over Puny's protest. And, on top of Andrew's dying, there would've been the baby to tend to under Ezell's nose. If she'd brought Lizzie, too, Ezell would've . . . well, no telling what.

Check had also mulled over her own dead infant daughter. Her child's little fingers and hands. Her soft, smooth skin. She thought of her again. Her breath knotted in her chest. The heat in the room closed in. Check said, "Lizzie, your little girl was at heaven's door when I found you. You must understand, it's most likely she's dead and buried."

Lizzie started sobbing. She hid her face in her hands. Shook from her head through her body.

A hollow space opened in Check's chest. Spread to her shoulders. Her breath fled through that hole into a past that she didn't want coming back. She opened her mouth for more air. Fingered her locket. When her breathing steadied so she could move without crying, she got up, walked around her desk, and stopped at the arm of Lizzie's chair. She held the girl's head against her skirt. Rubbed her shoulders. Let her sob.

An Uneasy Evening

THAT NIGHT, EZELL POINTED TO the maple table Puny had built back in Tennessee. She said, "Girl, get under there."

Lizzie murmured, "Ain't no dog." But pulled a quilt closer to her shoulders, dropped to her knees, and sat. The cabin was nice by her standards. It had a puncheon floor, a sandstone fireplace, and two glass windows. A spinning wheel sat close to one window; a feather mattress and rope bed was pushed against a wall. Next to the bed was a coal oil lamp and a small table. At its foot was a large trunk with a curved top. Two rocking chairs and two straight-backed ones provided places to sit. Bowls, plates, and eating utensils lay on the shelves of an open-faced cabinet, and clothes hung on pegs on the wall. Lizzie looked to the bed and said, "Can I have a piller?"

Ezell's eyes narrowed. "Be thankful for what ya got."

"Can't sleep with my head on wood." Lizzie's lip trembled.

Ezell was in her rocker. "Get it yer own self. I ain't waiting on ya."

Lizzie rose from the floor, went to the bed, and grabbed a pillow. She went back to the table, got down on the floor again, put the pillow under her head, and pulled the quilt over it. She rolled over and faced the wall.

Ezell kept rocking. Her chair faced the fireplace, and an oil lamp on the mantel provided more light to sew by. Her hair was loosened, and sprang thick from her head. She bent over a blouse and listened to the girl's breathing. But she'd run out of steam thinking about Puny being with her. To get some relief from her torment, she turned her thoughts to their life before the girl had appeared. Puny had been a good husband. Wasn't one to lay out. Normally, not one to chase a skirt. He drank only when work was done. And was pleasant, not mean, in his cups.

They had dreams. They'd talked about finding the gold, about leaving together, going back to Ohio. To Cleveland, where their people had schools of their own, lived in neighborhoods, and owned businesses. The newness of the Nation had worn off for them both. They recognized that in it, life was dangerous for people of every color. The food was plentiful, and the air filled with the aroma of turned dirt and bloom, but there was no law for anybody at all who wasn't an Indian. The federal judges appointed to oversee Indian Territory had, everybody knew, been a series of drunkards and thieves. And Indian law applied only when the parties were of the same tribe. The US government was trying to fix that by setting up a new judge at Fort Smith. But he probably wouldn't be any better than the previous ones, and the Cherokees were trying to block him. Ezell wasn't in the right circles to even guess who'd win that fight, and thought it probably didn't matter. She did know, though, that killings were as common as yellow dogs; and criminals and adventurers were streaming into the Nation, squatting on Cherokee land, carrying out meanness. Her greatest fear at the moment was that Puny had come to a bad end at the hands of one of them.

She tried to work her mind away from that. Told herself Puny was big and could take care of himself. But she didn't think he'd found the gold and run off; he would've returned, even a rich man, and stayed until Mr. Singer died. He was beholding to him, and he was a man who paid his debts. Ezell looked over at Lizzie, asleep, or pretending to be, on the floor. Puny had run off because of that girl and her baby. That was it.

That he didn't take the girl with him gave Ezell hope. However, if he showed up again, which was likely, she would lay claim to him. She could bear children. And the question Ezell had held in her bosom for years was answered: it was her fault they were childless, not Puny's. That realization burned into her soul. A tear fell onto the blouse she was making. Not wanting to cry in front of the intruder, she laid her sewing aside, got up, and went out the door.

OUT IN THE DARK, BERT was alone on the ferry, studying the milky arch of stars over his head. He saw them as cornmeal dropped from a dog's jaw, and felt his mother's arms around him. He was holding on to that memory, feeling the rare comfort of it, when he was bitten by an insect. He slapped the back of his neck. Got the villain. But, startled and irritated, he couldn't conjure his mother again. He lay back and turned his thoughts to his brother. Ame was working the fields and sleeping in the bunkhouse with the rest of the hands. The two weren't used to being apart, but it'd made them better friends, and the rest of their arrangement was pleasing to them. They were going to get wages; and Bert had already pocketed tips from three wealthy people appreciative of his care with their cargo. At night the ferry was stopped, but he slept on it to make sure it wasn't sunk or stolen. Mr. Connell had given him a tick of feathers, a quilt to sleep under, and a rifle to discharge if he needed help. The ferry was tied securely, but not directly, against the bank, in a little cove that protected it from the current. Because of the cove, the roar of the river sounded more distant than elsewhere on the shore. Bert listened to the lap of the waves hitting the wood, and drifted on their beat almost to sleep until a large fish jumped and slapped back into the water.

Bert rose up and looked around. On shore, he saw the light of a lantern and, in it, a woman's skirt. At first he thought Miz Singer was coming to give him an order. But, on a closer look, the woman was too tall to be her, and her head appeared gigantic. It was the darkie who'd been around asking after her husband. The lantern light rocked closer to the water and then stopped. The woman sat down on one of the rocks. She pulled her knees to her chin and, in the circle of light, buried her head and giant ring of hair in her skirt. Her shoulders shook.

Bert had seen a lot of misery. And had felt a lot himself. He didn't like anybody seeing his. And didn't feel that he should be looking at hers. He lay back down on his tick and pulled the quilt over his shoulders and head. He knew crying was catching. Didn't want to be infected. He had a lot to be thankful for. He started counting—a tick, a quilt, a job, coins in his pocket. He didn't have much more than that. So he counted the same things over and over until he counted himself to sleep.

Coop's Mission, Indian-Style

COOP COULDN'T BELIEVE HIS GOOD fortune. He was riding atop a real saddle, astride Mr. Singer's bay horse. The horse was admired all over the bottoms, and was the tallest he'd ever ridden. The smoothest, too. He rode at a canter down the Military Road, hoping to run into everybody he knew. And he did see a few. Stopped and chatted, but held his tongue on his task. Connell had told him to, and he wanted a job, like Jenny, with the Singers. But not in the fields, which were bad enough at home, and not any better when planted in potatoes. Coop wanted work with horses, or ferries, or anything that moved in a wider arc than a hoe.

After jawing with a man searching for a lost, or stolen, cow, Coop rode on. A rabbit sprung from the weeds and crossed the road at such a distance The Bay didn't notice. A moment later, the rabbit scampered back to the weeds he'd come from. Coop whooped. He didn't believe luck was made by hard labor or bestowed by gods; he believed it blew in on the winds of fate. The zigzag of a rabbit in his path was a fortuitous sign not lost on his mind.

Coop was headed towards Braggs Mountain. His mission was to find his father, the fate of the baby, and Puny. But his brother's cabin sat on the bayou between the bottoms and the mountain, inland a bit from the river. It was directly in Coop's course — well, almost. Maybe a little to the side. A straight line as the closest distance between two points never crossed Coop's mind. However, he was familiar with the idea of making Tomahawk Cordery's mouth water with envy. So Coop detoured off the beaten road to stop by his brother's place to show off The Bay.

He crossed a creek at its shallows and rode the tree line next to the stream, watching the ground carefully. The land was rockier than in the bottoms; he didn't want The Bay to misstep. Past the rocks, he turned into a meadow and approached his brother's home site in the open, so he'd be seen from a long way away. Ahead in the distance, a deer carcass hung from the limb of the tree shading the cabin. Tomahawk and Mannypack, his wife, were skinning it.

Tomahawk heard the hooves coming, peeked around the deer, and spied the fine steed. He dropped his knife to his side, appreciating its prance. Mannypack said in Cherokee, *"Rich man's horse coming our way."* But when The Bay got a little closer, Tomahawk recognized Coop and whooped. Mannypack screeched. Their baby, Minnie, imitated her mother. And out of the cabin and into that racket stepped Sanders.

A lot of horse talk followed. After that, some horse riding ensued. Then there were the matters of finishing dressing the deer, cooking, eating venison steaks, smoking a pipe, teasing, and giggling. The stars were over the family around the fire when Coop finally meandered towards the point of his visit. He said in English, "Pot's hot the Singers'."

Mannypack said, "Aunt Check's the boss over there."

Tomahawk laughed. "Manny, you're the boss over here." He was shorter than his father, but muscular. Black-headed, his hair was cut at his ears.

Mannypack said, "Runs in my family." She tilted her head and touched her braid. She was a Lowrey, too.

Coop said, "Saw yer aunt crying the woods."

Mannypack said, "She has good reason."

Sanders, who'd been sitting up, lay back with his head on his hands, face to the stars. He cogitated on why Coop would be riding The Bay. The boy had said no more than "Doing Connell a favor." Sanders figured the rest would trickle out, and hoped it wasn't to do with the hole he'd dug in the field. That made him twitchy to think about. He turned his attention outwards. Listened while the young'uns bet on when Andrew Singer would die. That annoyed Sanders; but they were too green not to be foolish, so he didn't bother to grunt disapproval. And after a while they, too, fell into silence. Sanders hoped that was brought on by a respect for the darkness, and for all that lived and died in it. The night was mild. Insects, attracted by the fire, buzzed and fluttered. Minnie slept in Mannypack's lap. Wolves howled in the hills to the east and down on the river.

Coop wanted to have The Bay to ride for as long as he could. And was no more direct in conversation than he was in moving from one point to another. He'd whittled away the day without mentioning a precise word about either Puny or the baby, and he wasn't entirely sure from his instructions if he could say anything in front of his brother and sister-in-law. But eventually, he did say, "Going up the mountain, Pa? Maybe I'll ride along."

Sanders' mind turned again to why Connell would give Coop The Bay to ride. Maybe it was to do with Singer's dying? Some kind of errand? While he thought about that, he beat his fingers on his belly. His stomach was so hard it sounded like a drum when he got to thumping it fast. But he beat only slowly and softly, trying to tap out the mystery. Finally, he said, "I'm purty comfortable here." He rolled over to go to sleep.

Coop didn't mind that a bit. And by the next morning, he'd decided he'd hang around until his father mentioned the baby. That way, he could ride The Bay every day.

Coop's Detour Continues

ABOUT FOUR EVENINGS LATER, COOP, Sanders, and Tomahawk were throwing knives at a knot in the tree next to the cabin. They were jawing in general and making unflattering predictions about each other's throws when, behind them, a *gobble gobble gobble* arose. They twisted around towards the sound. Peered into a thicket of dense bushes and cane. Another piercing *gobble gobble gobble* followed. They looked at each other, narrowed their eyes to slits, gripped their knives tighter. Sanders shouted, *"Show yer face or get scalped!"* They crept towards the sounds like cats slipping up on a bird.

Gobble gobble gobble shrieked from the thicket again. Tomahawk threw his knife into a tree trunk close to the sound. A bush shook. A boy fell out. He rolled around on the ground. Yelled, "ᏍᏊᏯᎻᏍ!" Thrashed in the grass.

Coop and Tomahawk jumped up and down, whooped, and threw their arms around. Sanders' shoulders rose and fell. He covered his mouth with his hand. Mannypack came out of the cabin. She said, *"What're ya crazy men doing?"*

Tomahawk shouted, *"Wez killed a Wild Indian!"*

Coop pounced on the body. The corpse grabbed him tight. Arms and legs tangled. The two rolled over and over.

Mannypack giggled. "George Sixkiller, Coop Cordery, *y'all got less sense than chickens!"* She shook her head. The boys started tickling each other. Before either could win, Tomahawk and Sanders each grabbed an elbow, pulled them apart and up to their feet. After a lot of backslapping and rib-poking and a little dusting off, the four meandered back to Mannypack, who'd been watching with a glint in her eye and a flicker of a smile on her lips.

George Sixkiller was dark. His teeth were strong and white, his mouth frequently fixed in a grin. His nose had been broken in a fall off a horse, and healed in a knot that strengthened his expression. He was vain regarding his looks, and occasionally wove a feather into his hair. His shoulders rippled with muscles; his chest was bare. His father, Robert, was Sanders' best friend.

In the summer of '62, Sanders and Robert had heard reports that the Federals were headed towards them, killing every man in their way. They rushed to Fort Davis and enlisted in the Confederate Army. The fort was built on the mound of a lost civilization, directly across the Arkansas River from Fort Gibson. Three days later, Sanders and Robert exchanged fire with Federal soldiers over the water. Those skirmishes went on for weeks. When the Federals moved to another position, Sanders went home. He found his wife in a grave, his six children living in his cabin's ashes. He put Coop and his sister on a mule, his two younger boys on his horse. He, Tomahawk, and his oldest boy, Lovely, walked. Robert's wife, Sallie, had survived. When they arrived, she was packing utensils, quilts, and chickens to take to the Cherokee refugee camp on the Red River. So Sallie led two broods of kids to the south edge of the Choctaw Nation, and Sanders and Robert went back to fighting.

Two years later, they, too, walked through the Choctaws' land, bony and barely clothed. When they arrived at the camp, Sanders' younger children were under the wing of Sallie's friend Nancy, whose husband, Jumper, had been killed in the War. Sanders got to know that Nancy, as well as the other one, the widow of a Creek. He and Robert told their kids stories about ambushing Federal soldiers. They shouted the *gobble gobble gobble* war cry of Cherokee warriors. Their boys shrieked with delight. They imitated their fathers.

So after everybody had eaten and was seated in front of Tomahawk's cabin, Sanders saw George Sixkiller as a much younger boy: gaunt in the face and naked, his ribs well defined, his bowed legs thin, streaked with dirt. He said to George, "Yer pa still a strong'un?"

George nodded. "What about the copperhead story?"

Sanders cleared his throat, settled his back against a log and his butt deeper in the dirt. He looked up, calling the memory from clouds. Then he looked into the middle distance, somewhere in the air shared by the group. "We was camped in a cave, waiting fer Colonel Adair to bring in reinforcements. A rock outcrop twer over our heads. It come out 'bout this far." He stretched his arms wide. "Yer pa and me waz sitting under that cropping, tending a fire, while the other fellers waz down bathing at a stream. We waz jist talking, poking the kindling, and gitting her going. And all of er sudden, a copperhead, long as my arm, dropped off that cropping. He hit the fire and popped. Wiggled and sizzled all tw'once. Robert and me, we got up a-dancing. That snake started crawling out. But yer daddy shoved 'im back in the fire with a stick. He did that over and over 'til he weren't going nowhere. We roasted him good, and chopped him in bits. When the other fellers got back, we fed them fried copperhead. Swore it were chicken."

Sanders — and everybody else — laughed. A silence followed. Quail called back and forth in the twilight. Minnie put something in her mouth. Her mother took it out. Tomahawk said, "Found a brass belt buckle over yonder." He puckered his lips and raised his chin towards the meadow.

Sanders looked into the distance and cocked his head. He closed his eyes and waved his arm. "Through here, we drove five hundred head of Federal horses and mules we stole from Fort Gibson. Moved them thaterway, crossing the river at Hildebrand Ford. The Federals was following us hot. They's a lotter men kilt near here."

Tomahawk said, "You kill any of 'em?"

Sanders plucked a pebble from the ground and slung it towards the stream. He rolled his tongue over his teeth. "Thomas, I'm gitting dry. I need a gourd of water."

Tomahawk unfolded his legs and got up. He wasn't surprised by his father's reaction. But Coop hung his head. He wanted more stories. He'd been too young to remember the ones told in the camp. But his father calling his brother "Thomas" was a sure sign the storytelling was over. Tomahawk's given name was "Thomas Clark," after a white soldier who'd given their grandmother a blanket on the Trail Where They Cried. "Thomas," used by his father, meant "Stop."

Meanwhile, Back to the Gold

LATE THAT SAME NIGHT, DENNIS Wolf Bushyhead was hunched at his desk in his study in the house next to the post office. Dennis had a barrel chest, a thick mustache, and a goatee. When standing, he was well over six feet tall, and he was the national treasurer of the Cherokee Nation. He was poring over maps — some large and etched on yellow paper, others small and scratched in delicate wisps of quill, two or three more drawn with stubby lead pencils. Dennis held a map up close to the light of a coal oil lamp and squinted.

Dennis's wife was Check's cousin, Alabama. And his father had been the Reverend Jesse Bushyhead, the only man, Indian or white, who could ride alone and unarmed in both the old Cherokee Nation East and the new Nation in Indian Territory. Jesse Bushyhead had been a Baptist with deep moral convictions. He helped John Ross lobby President Jackson against stealing Indian land by appealing to the love of fellow man that Jackson turned out not to possess. Later he appealed to practical considerations that couldn't trump the president's greed and that of his friends. So Reverend Bushyhead led one of the detachments on the Trail Where They Cried.

Dennis had been a boy when they walked. In the new Nation, he was schooled by a private tutor in Chief Ross's home, and later attended the Cherokee Male Seminary. He was in his second year at Princeton when his father suddenly died. Dennis then returned to Indian Territory to earn a living. He stayed in I.T., working as a merchant, for five years. But in 1849, when gold fever hit the United States, it didn't bypass the tribe. Dennis went west and spent the next nineteen years selling wares to miners, buying up their stakes for their debts, and hiring grubbers to work in the dirt. He made some money, but not a lot. So he was sorely afflicted by gold deprivation, and had been studying his maps since sundown.

When Alabama entered the study, she said, "It's late. Don't you want to come to bed?" Dennis looked up and shook his head. She stepped closer to the yellow cast by the lamp on the desk. "It's been there for over a decade. Nobody'll find it tonight."

Dennis removed his glasses and pinched the bridge of his nose. "If only these maps made sense."

Alabama moved to stand over her husband. She was descended from successful Cherokee families. Wealthy in her own right, educated, and widowed young by the War. She didn't share her second husband's gold lust, but understood it. "Do you think the well you're looking for would be on a map?"

Dennis shrugged. "Other wells are. Look here." He pointed with his glasses. "See." He tapped three X's. "These are wells. I can take you out and show 'em to you."

Alabama peered at the map. "The one you're looking for wasn't really a well."

"But they didn't know that for nearly a year and a half."

Alabama knew the hole's story. Forty years earlier, Fort Gibson's commander, General Arbuckle, had ordered a new well to be dug outside the fort's walls, closer to the Grand River. The task was assigned to prisoners. Picks flew, and the hole grew so deep that the workers' heads disappeared below the rim. In the evenings, they came in and reported their progress. However, after months of digging, they still hadn't hit water. Eventually, General Arbuckle asked for an inspection. When an officer was lowered into the hole, he discovered a room that was cool in the summer and warmer in the winter than the air above. The prisoners had been playing cards in it.

Dennis thought the gold stash was in that pit. A deep, cozy hole in the ground would be a valuable resource in a locale characterized by warfare, bloody feuds, and a good deal of sneaking around. He figured the hole hadn't been filled in, only covered with planks and sodded over.

Alabama said, "If you find the stash, I want to go to New York. I hear it's wonderful."

Dennis withdrew an arm from the table and looped it around Alabama's waist. He'd married late in life. Felt thankful for every day he woke up with his wife. "If I do, I'll take you. And I'll buy you a carriage."

Same Night at the Singers'

THE ONLY LIGHT IN THE front parlor was that of the moon through sheer curtains and the dim yellow flicker of the two pine candles burned to stubs. Check and Andrew were in bed together, propped against the headboard, holding hands. They saw each other in outline, their features and coloring sketched in by memories of a long, happy marriage. They were taking advantage of one of Andrew's "good spots," times when the pain and medicine drained away and his true personality rose to the surface and lingered for an hour or two. These respites were unpredictable, and came, more often than not, in the middle of the night. Check didn't want to miss one. She knew that soon everything she knew of her husband would float away and settle like silt in the bed of a river.

She'd tried at times to envision Andrew lifted high into heaven, fully alive, perhaps robed in white. But her mind never advanced beyond that vision. The ancient Cherokees didn't have words for "heaven," "hell," "sin," "guilt," or "salvation." And although Check had been schooled in Christianity all her life, its concepts hadn't nestled in her mind as they had in Andrew's. He believed in eternal bliss with the Lord. Had notions of light, praying, singing, and angels. Check figured heaven was boring. She hoped her husband wasn't going there, but instead to the Smoky Mountains. Her vision of paradise was dawn scattered over the sacred, foggy hills where her ancestors were buried.

Andrew said, "Tell me about the boys."

Check's mind jerked away from the mists of mountains. She sniffed the odor of pine before she answered. "Well, you've heard Paul's jabbering. And he's taken to throwing things. He's male all over. Otter's still following Ezell. I've encouraged that. He's her favorite, and it's harder for her to be ugly to Lizzie with a child underfoot."

"Who's Lizzie?"

Check had made a misstep. She felt thankful the room was dark. She cleared her throat. "The new hired help. You remember, I told you. Her mother and father worked for Mama."

"Your mother owned them."

Check shifted slightly. Andrew and his family had no tolerance for slavery. They were complete abolitionists, in both opinion and charity. But her family had been painfully split over the grave question. All, including her parents, agreed slavery was a flawed and inhumane institution. But several hadn't seen any workable way out. And all thought the North was hypocritical by insisting upon the South's moral inferiority while they benefited economically from the same institution they condemned. Check's father had argued slavery one way and then the other, in much the same way he'd argued for and against Removal. Her two grown brothers had died for the Confederacy, one of her brothers-in-law for the Federals. Her sisters had split in their views. She'd easily agreed with Andrew about the equality of all people, but never with the harsh rhetoric used in the North. And she found it impossible to think of her mother as a brutal woman. Check had seen brutality—Indians driven from their homes at gunpoint, herded like animals, penned up, dying of disease, starving, forced to start a long walk in winter weather. She'd never seen her mother threaten a Negro, let alone raise a hand to one. Still, she was ashamed that her parents had owned slaves. She said, "Beth and Hancock stayed with Mama after the War."

Andrew was familiar with his wife's evasions. He didn't want to waste his lucidity chasing them. He cleared his throat. "Go on with the boys."

She was relieved. "I've been sending Clifford out to hunt for birds' nests. He's reporting back as many different species as he can find in the bottoms."

"Careful he doesn't grow up to be a naturalist. They're invariably peculiar and don't make a lot of money."

"I just don't want him to grow up with silly superstitions."

Andrew shifted his weight to his other hip. Cherokees were distrustful of birds. Most believed that songbirds, like robins, mockingbirds, and larks, were enemy spirits. It wouldn't hurt to inoculate Cliff against that idiocy. Andrew approved of his wife's good sense. He said, "And Hugh?"

"He doesn't want to do a thing but ride his new horse into town and lure people into betting on races." Check's voice rose a little too loud for a middle-of-the-night conversation.

Andrew squeezed her hand. "He's high-spirited. You didn't object to that when you were his age."

"I didn't know any better." She sounded grumpy, but smiled in the dark.

And Andrew wasn't fooled by her tone. He smiled, too. But instead of asking after Connell, he lowered his head to Check's shoulder, put his arm over her waist, and snuggled. She didn't speak anymore, and her thoughts didn't stray. She kissed Andrew's head. His bones protruded from frail shoulders. His legs grew thinner each day. She clutched him to her. To fuel her strength for the coming weeks, she took in every sensation of his body against hers. She wanted to remember it for years. Her cheeks became wet with tears.

Keeping Order in the Kitchen

SHORTLY AFTER BREAKFAST THE NEXT morning, Ezell turned from the sink and barked, "Bring me a bucket of water."

"Youse got a pump right at ya," Lizzie whined back.

Ezell put both fists on her hips. "They's dishes in this sink up to my chin. I can't git a bucket under this pump."

Lizzie wrinkled her mouth and nose into a formation that caused her face to resemble a walnut shell. She grabbed a bucket and stomped out the door. Ezell crossed the kitchen, took a kettle off the stove, and brought it back to the sink. She poured hot water in, tested the result with her fingers, and poured in a little more. Then she pumped in a splash of cold water. It was, she had to admit, convenient to have more help. Puny didn't know how to do woman's work, and was too big of a pain to train. But Lizzie took to work well; and, as predicted, knew something about cooking. Not much, but a little.

Ezell was still washing dishes when Lizzie returned and said, "Where ya want this?"

Ezell didn't look up from the sink. "Put it down by the stove."

Lizzie trudged across the room, grunting. She set the bucket on the floor and said, "Whew, that were heavy."

"You ain't bigger than a mite. Yer'll blow away come winter. We'll look up, and yer'll be caught in a tree." Ezell looked to the ceiling and giggled.

Lizzie frowned and stared at the floor. "Can't fatten. Bleeding bad."

The water suddenly seemed hot to Ezell's hands. She pulled them out, let them drip over the sink while she got her bearings. She dried them on her apron as she turned. "How long since you had that baby?"

Lizzie shrugged. "Hard to keep track o' time."

Ezell leaned against the sink and crossed her arms. "How long was it between the time it was born and you give it to Miz Singer?"

Lizzie shrugged again. "Maybe a couple of days. I waz in and out of it." She sucked in her cheeks.

The kitchen was silent while Ezell tried to decide exactly how she felt in her body. She was getting a little sinking feeling in her right side; but in her left side, she was feeling a flutter. "How bad's the bleeding?"

"I gots to git more rags. These don't dry 'fore I have'ta put 'em on again. I'z getting real chafed."

Ezell crossed to Lizzie. "Look at me. I ain't gonna bite cha." She took the child's head in her hands, turned it to the light, and pulled down a lower eyelid. She said, "Yer eyelid's 'bout the color of an eggshell."

Lizzie pulled away. "I feels faint all the time."

Ezell put her fists to her hips again, but sighed deep in her body. "When ya get well, I'm gonna whip ya. I wanta make that clear right cher. But for now, I'm putting ya in bed. Come on." She grabbed Lizzie's hand.

LATER, AROUND NOON, EZELL SET some side meat and a large piece of cornbread into a feed sack. She said to Jenny, "Tell that ferry boy I want this poke back." She'd used Jenny to pack food back and forth to the ferry on several occasions. If the ferry was on the near side of the river, she always got her sack back. But once it'd been leaving for the far side, and getting that sack back had been a chore.

Jenny said, "He might want some pie."

"Would that be pie fer him? Or pie fer you?"

Jenny dropped her chin to her breast and picked up the hem of her dress in the pinch of her fingers. She cut her eyes at Ezell. Pushed her lower lip out a little. "Both."

"It ain't pie season. Wash yer hands. I'll give ya some sugar."

Jenny did as told, and Ezell plucked two lumps of brown sugar from a bowl. She put them in the child's open palm. "Give him one." Then she added, "How old is you?"

Jenny shrugged. She put one sugar lump in her mouth and set the other in the sack on top of the cornbread.

Ezell took Jenny's chin in her hand. "Here, let me see."

Jenny cuddled the sugar lump in her tongue and parted her lips. Her teeth sat atop each other without a bite. She had four second ones above, six second ones below. The rest were milk teeth or holes. Ezell said, "Yer about eleven or twelve." She squinted. "You be careful." She let her chin go.

Otter, who was on the floor scooting a little wooden wagon, looked up at Ezell. "Can I go?"

"If ya don't go near the water."

Jenny said, "No!"

"Take him wit'chu."

Jenny stuck out the tip of her tongue.

Ezell raised her hand. "Don't mess with me, child. You'll be sorry. And take that little boy. You don't need to be going to the ferry by yer-self."

Jenny pulled her tongue back in. "I do all the time." But after that flash of defiance, the lingering sweet lump in her mouth won. She said to Otter, "Come on." She picked up the sack from the table. Put a hand to the door.

"Watch them snakes," Ezell cautioned. To herself, she said, "Snakes like little girls." She shook her head. She turned to the stove and her mind returned to Puny. It did that whenever she was alone. She was going to beat him with his own snake cane as soon as he got home.

Gone Missing

THAT AFTERNOON, CHECK WALKED OUT to a field close to the river. She stopped a little away from where Connell, Hugh, and some hands were unloading split rails off a wagon. The ground for the race-track was already measured and marked. The rails were for keeping the horses from straying into the bettors. Check was both avoiding the dust and signaling Connell that she wanted a private conversation.

He saw her, walked over, and pulled off his gloves. "Come to inspect?"

Check had, in part. She wasn't quite convinced Hugh would run the rails where she'd told him to. But he seemed to be following the plan, and she didn't appreciate Connell implying she wasn't minding her own business. But instead of saying that, she named the things beyond Andrew's illness that occupied her mind: "We've lost a hired hand, a baby, a gun, a horse, and two neighbors. Do you have any news?"

"Haven't heard a word. But Coop'll eventually show." Connell was irritated Coop hadn't returned, but knew he would. He hoped he'd bring Puny with him. Running the farm without Puny's help meant more work, and was cutting into his sexual fantasies and his actual courting. He patted his pocket in the irrational hope of locating a cigar.

"I wish he'd show soon," Check said. "Can anything else go missing?"

Connell looked towards the men unloading the rails. He'd come by gossip that had ignited his imagination. But had also convinced him he was the only man in the Nation not getting his needs met. He felt crazier with each passing day. He patted his pocket again. "As a matter of fact, it can."

Check's chin jerked in. "What now?"

Connell moved his hand to his brow and scratched it. He planned on telling his mother what he'd heard. But didn't want to in an open field, and was afraid his dick would squirm as he told it. "Mama, we gotta unload this wagon. It'll take some explaining."

"If you think I'm leaving before you tell me what's going on, you're mistaken."

Connell was overly familiar with his mother's determination. And didn't want a squabble in public. He looked towards the unloading. Hooked a thumb in a belt loop in case he needed to adjust his pants. "The preacher's gone missing."

Check's head jerked again. "Where to?"

"Some say Kansas. Mrs. Bets is gone, too. Rob Forecaster is taking up the preaching."

Check looked at Connell wide-eyed. He ducked his head, grinned, and held up the hand gripping his gloves. "I'm not saying it's true. I'm just reporting."

Hugh yelled, "We could use some help over here." He was standing by a line of rails and next to a man using a posthole digger.

Connell said, "I better get back to work. We can talk about this later."

"We'll talk about it when I want to talk about it."

"Yes, ma'am." A show of compliance often worked with his mother.

Check said, "Good. We'll talk about it later." She turned towards the house holding her skirt out of the dirt.

THEY WERE TALKING ABOUT IT later in the study when Connell said, "If you have a headache, I can fetch a wet rag."

The heels of Check's hands were pressed to her eyes. "No need. I'm just trying not to envision your father prayed over by Rob Forecaster." She leaned back, laid her palms on the desk, and patted the wood with her fingers.

Connell's face scrunched to a frown. "No, we can't have that."

"Who would've thought Dan Stoddard and Henrietta Bets? . . ." Check shook her head.

"Evidently, not Mr. Bets."

"Did they take the children?"

"Only his." The preacher was a widower.

"And Forecaster is taking up the preaching for certain?" Forecaster was the church's janitor.

"Maybe he thinks he has the name for it. I don't know."

"Maybe I should take up singing."

Connell smiled. His mother kept her mouth shut during hymns. He assumed her ear was tin. "He's the church's only other employee. It figures, I guess."

That was followed by a silence. Then Connell added, "Could we send for Reverend Braun when the time comes?" He was the Moravian minister over in Tahlequah. The white Baptist preacher in Fort Gibson had fallen off a roof, and was making even less sense than usual. The Methodist preacher was off east at some sort of convention. The only other preachers close by were the Negroes'.

"We hardly know him. Besides, we'll have to be quick. It's not winter."

"We've still got river ice," Connell supplied, but winced. Laying his father in the springhouse wasn't appealing. If they did that, he didn't think he'd be able to take ice in his drinks for the rest of the hot season.

Visiting Alabama

AFTER CHORES THE NEXT MORNING, Check headed towards town in her buggy, click-click-clicking 'Wassee and jangling the reins. The sun was up, but not high enough to raise the heat, and a rain the night before had settled the dust without making mud. Although Andrew was dying, multiple people were missing, and Check didn't have answers to any questions that plagued her directly, she was enjoying being alone away from the farm. Between her buggy and the Grand River was a field planted in corn. The stalks were dark green and nearly knee high. Check was pleased the crop had gotten a good start. She rode contemplating the favorable weather, and soon guided 'Wassee past the fort quadrangle and pulled up at the back of the Bushyheads' house. As she got out of her buggy, she was sniffed by a couple of dogs and eyed by a horse hitched to a post. On the back porch, she called in the open door, "Alabama? Dennis?"

From the dark of the house, a voice returned, "Aunt Check?"

Johnny Adair, Alabama's son by her first husband, Lafayette, wasn't Check's nephew, but was close enough. She smiled when she heard his voice. Alabama and she were fourth cousins, and since most everybody around was related, Check found it almost incomprehensible that the Adairs and Lowreys hadn't also married into each other. She wondered if they might be of the same clan, and wished her mother were alive to ask about that. Johnny came to the door. She said, "How tall you've grown!" The boy was short, but the Adairs were tall people. Check was sure Johnny would soon shoot up like cane.

He allowed himself to be hugged. "Are you looking for Mama?"

"For her and Dennis both."

"Mama's on the front porch. Dennis is out somewhere."

Check stepped inside as Alabama came in the front door and down the hall. The two greeted with a hug. They'd been acquainted for only five years, but were family, and with few other educated women within a day's ride, had quickly become true friends. After they saw Johnny off on his horse, they settled with coffee in rockers on a porch that over-looked the large, green, shaded lawn and the Grand River.

As was the custom, they first talked about the weather. Then they talked about their common kin. Check's uncle John had married Dennis's aunt Nannie. They lived up in the Cooweescoowee District, so Check didn't see them often. But Alabama did. Her sister Mary had married Dennis's close friend Clem Rogers, who had a ranch up there. Clem was a cousin of Sanders Cordery. But Check asked about the Rogers family without mentioning Sanders laying out with his other Nannie. Alabama paid even less attention to that arrangement than Check did. Alabama's mother, Granny Schrimsher, owned an inn; there wasn't much Alabama hadn't seen.

Slowly, the conversation turned to the topic of Andrew's health. Check said, "You know I love him. But I hope he dies before the pain tortures him."

Alabama looked out at the river. She often saw the water flowing by as reassurance they all were going in the same direction, even if that direction was to sea. "I know it's hard to watch him suffer. It's easier for everybody when it happens quickly." She was recalling, at the moment, her first husband's death.

Check also looked towards the Grand. She knew where Alabama's mind had gone. She said, "Lafayette's death was a shock. At least I've had time to prepare."

Alabama hadn't really been shocked by Lafayette's death. He was a soldier; men shot at him all the time. But she appreciated Check's sympathy. And it brought her back to the porch, and to the circumstances at hand. She said, "How can Dennis and I help?"

While a few days back Check had wanted Alabama to take Lizzie in, the arrangement at the farm had settled into a truce. She'd decided she could keep Lizzie there, at least until Puny returned. Her mind was on the newer, pressing problem of the preacher's disappearance. She said, "I guess you've heard about Reverend Stoddard and Mrs. Bets."

Alabama had. And she didn't approve of idle gossip any more than Check did. But that news was astonishing because those people were white. And Alabama hadn't had anyone to discuss it with except Dennis.

Unfortunately, Dennis didn't enjoy speculation about people, or dwell on details as much as she would've liked. So she and Check spent several minutes and much wonder on the events. Then Check got to the point. "I can't have Rob Forecaster praying over Andrew's burial." She frowned into her cup.

Alabama lifted the pot and poured her more coffee. "No, of course not."

"I'd like Dennis to speak the service when it's time."

Alabama poured herself more coffee and settled the pot on the table between their chairs. "I'm sure he'd be honored. But you understand, he's not a real preacher."

"Yes. But Andrew likes him, and he's family."

"Andrew won't care he's a Baptist?"

Check winced. She twisted in her chair and looked into her cup. "I don't plan on Andrew finding out that the preacher's run off."

Alabama patted her mouth with her kerchief and waited for more information. Check took another sip. She set her cup down carefully in its saucer. "Andrew would never object to anything Dennis does." She looked up at Alabama and arched an eyebrow. "But he'll haunt me over a janitor."

At Granny Schrimsher's Inn

WHILE CHECK AND ALABAMA WERE sipping coffee, Coop and George were riding towards Granny Schrimsher's inn. Coop was afraid he didn't look as good on The Bay with George behind him as he did mounted alone. But he was happy riding without the saddle, which, however handsome, rubbed him wrong. They were detouring towards Granny's both to use the good road and to be seen on the horse, but their ultimate destination was the Sixkillers' cabin near Tahlequah. Coop planned to drop George at his parents', return to Tomahawk's to pick up the saddle, and go home to the bottoms. He needed to get back before people started thinking he'd stolen The Bay, even though he hadn't pried a word from his father about Puny or the baby. Once he'd tried, "Puny brung a bucket o' milk to the site," hoping for a reaction. Sanders had merely grunted. When he'd said, "Puny's laying out. The Singers are fretting over him," Sanders had said, "He's a growed-up man." Asking a direct question hadn't occurred to Coop as a way to get information from his father. And wouldn't have been successful if it had.

So as they rode, Coop said over his shoulder to George, "I set out to find me a darkie, but I ain't located him."

George said, "Just any darkie?"

"Naw. The Singers'. Laying out. Got woman trouble."

"I done a woman good at the bawdy house."

Coop pulled up on the reins. Stopped The Bay and looked over his shoulder. His nose was about a foot from George's. "Is that where you waz?"

George nodded and grinned.

"Tell me 'bout her." Coop thought about sex even more than he thought about horses. He turned back around and stared at The Bay's mane. Tried to picture a woman's long tresses.

"Screwed her standing up. A white woman."

Coop got a mental picture of that. It was pleasing. A nature-made twitch ran up through his body. And, as the boys were sitting pelvis to rump, George felt the spasm. He said, "Done her hard," and thrust his privates against Coop's butt.

Coop leaned sideways so fast he fell off the horse. He landed on his hip and tumbled onto his shoulder. He jumped to his feet. "Damn you, George. Don't be messing with me." He rubbed his flank. Put his hand over his pants to hide a condition he'd rather not have at the moment.

George raised his eyebrows and grinned. Shook his head so hard his hair slung around. He moved up on The Bay, kicked his sides, and yelled, "Gitty-up!"

Coop started yelling. But George keep riding. When he was clearly not coming back, Coop sat down on the ground. He wrapped his arms around his knees, hung his head, and stared at the dirt in the shadow of his body. He was in a full heap of trouble. He'd failed on his mission. And needed to get back to the Singers'. But he couldn't return without their horse. And there was no telling where George was off to. Coop thought of, and discarded, a couple of possibilities. But George did ride in the direction they were headed. So Coop got up, dusted his britches, and tightened the rope that held them up. He started off walking.

He kept going until he was within sight of Granny's inn, a giant two-story building of square-cut oak logs. A porch ran along the entire south side, and four hitching rails stood in the front. A stagecoach team and three other horses (none The Bay) were tied to the rails. Scattered in the yard were chickens, a few dogs, and some Indians. Two of the Indians were pitching pebbles into a circle drawn in the dust; another was resting against the trunk of a tree, his face under his hat. A woman was sitting on the ground nursing a baby.

Coop was parched from his walk. He approached the pebble pitchers and said, *"Where's the well?"*

One of them raised his chin. Pointed with his lips to the side of the building. *"Back there. You wanta play?"*

Coop shook his head. *"Don't have no money. You see a* GWY *ride by here on a bay?"*

"Big, good-looking horse?" the second Indian said.

Coop had been sagging. He perked up. *"ii. Which way did he go?"*

The other Indian said, *"He started out that way."* He glanced east. Then the two Indians looked at each other and shook their heads.

Coop said, *"And?"*

One said, *"It was bad."*

The other said, *"Waz the worst thing I ever seen."*

Coop said, *"What're ya talking about?"*

One Indian looked at the other and said, *"That waz the best-looking horse I'd seen in a long time."*

"Yeah. It's a crying shame," the other Indian said.

"What are ya talking about?" Coop said again, in a louder voice.

One of the Indians raised his hand to his temple, held his trigger finger to his head, said in English, *"Bang."*

"What'd ya mean he shot the horse? Why would he do that?" Coop

yelled. The man who'd been resting against the tree got up, threw a look of disgust, and headed off to behind the inn.

The second pebble-throwing Indian said, *"Leg broke."* He shook his head and hung it.

The noise Coop made started low in his belly. It worked its way up, not quite a human sound. By the time it came out of his mouth, it resembled the cry of a wolf. His face contorted.

One of the Indians gripped his shoulder. *"Hold on to yourself."*

Coop wailed and dropped to the ground. He squatted and held his head in his hands. *"My whole life is burnt wood."* He rocked back and forth.

The two Indians looked down at Coop's crown and giggled. The woman nursing the baby laughed out loud. Coop stopped rocking and looked up. His eyes narrowed. But then, coming from behind the inn, he saw, all in a clump, the disgusted-looking Indian, The Bay, and George riding him.

"ᏍᏬᏏ!" George yelled. Then he said something that had to do with sitting in the dust like a toad. The Bay pranced a little. George threw his chest out like a warrior. The formerly disgusted-looking Indian bent over laughing.

Coop moved like a blacksnake. He grabbed for the reins. George pulled The Bay to the right. Coop fell in the dirt on his stomach. He scrambled up. Lunged again. George danced the horse around in a circle. The other Indians kept laughing. After the third skid on his belly, Coop quit trying. And he was dusting off his pants when a double-holstered white man came out of the inn onto the porch. Coop recognized the stagecoach driver. He switched to English and yelled, "Horse thief!" Employed a white gesture by pointing to George.

Stealing a horse was a serious crime in the Nation. People who killed horse thieves were commended for public service rather than jailed. So when the stagecoach driver pulled his gun, George hopped off The Bay, ran to Coop, and slung his arm around his shoulders. He shouted in English, "He's my little brother!"

The stagecoach driver scratched his chin, scrunched his face, and holstered his weapon. Coop and George started pushing and shoving each other. Their insults were so loud Granny came out on the porch. She wiped her hands on her apron, placed both palms on a rail, and cocked an eyebrow. That sparked some rapid-fire Cherokee from the woman with the baby. The two parties to the argument stopped in mid-fight. Stood stock-still. Looked at the ground.

Granny didn't move for over a minute. Then she rolled her tongue around in her cheek, patted the gun in her apron, and went back inside. Coop spat in the dirt. George turned his back, hunkered down on his heels, and propped his elbows on his knees. The formerly disgusted-looking Indian walked off behind the inn again. Coop walked over to The Bay. Inspected him for signs of wear. The Indian returned with a gourd of water. He said, "GSℙᏂ D♦," and stuck it under George's nose first. George drank his fill and handed it back. The Indian stuck it under Coop's chin. He told him to drink, to cool himself off. Coop did. Shortly after, he mounted The Bay. He hadn't even looked at George sideways. And George was beginning to feel deep remorse. Coop was turning The Bay towards Tomahawk's when George said, "Hey, Coop, I know where yer darkie is."

Where Puny's Been

AFTER LEAVING NANNIE AND COOP, Puny had walked fast and hard along the sandbar of the Arkansas River, puffing and panting with effort and fear. The exertion calmed him a little. He'd told Ezell he was spending the night at the ferry, so he headed in that direction. Close to the water, the sand was packed, easy to tread, but the roar of the river was loud. Puny began to worry that something he couldn't hear would sneak up on him. He recalled Sanders' story of his aunt back in Georgia. She was in the woods, carrying her baby, when a wildcat jumped from a tree onto her back, grabbing her neck in its jaw. She hit the ground. Her baby flew from her blanket. The animal went for the child. But the aunt scrambled up and threw the blanket over the cat's head. Jerked it off the baby, and kept its eyes blinded by cloth. They struggled. It clawed her bloody, both her arms and her body. But she managed to loosen her apron from her waist. And she choked the cat to death with its strings. Sanders said his aunt showed off her scars for the rest of her life. People came from far and wide to see them and to hear her tale.

Puny didn't have a blanket and apron. And he knew wildcats, wolves, and bears came to the river at night. His cane couldn't slow a big cat in its tracks, couldn't stop a bear or a wolf pack on the attack. So by the time he got to the rocks at the river's bend, he was full of fear again. And clouds were covering the moon; he didn't think he could make it through the rocks to the ferry without breaking an ankle. So he picked the largest and highest stone he could see. He lay down on it. Still, he was so worried about being attacked that he didn't sleep until the first gray of day. Then he pulled his hat over his eyes and was out for most of the morning.

When he woke, he started towards the ferry, but not around the bend, which would get him there sooner. He took a wandering path through the woods and cane, a slow course that gave him time to think. He was still muddling on what to say and do next when he saw Hugh astride his horse at the edge of the potatoes. He seemed to be studying the ground. Puny yelled to him.

Hugh waved him over, took his hat off, and pointed it towards an irrigation ditch. He said, "Lookee there."

A wild boar was in the ditch. Legs stiff, belly busted open, body covered with flies. Puny took a single glance. Turned his eyes away. Hugh said, "What d'ya think happened to him?"

Puny winced. "I'd say it's a her. Got tits."

"Her, then."

Puny scratched his head. He said, "Could be anything." But his mind flashed on Sanders' aunt and the wildcat. A shiver shimmied up his back. He said, "Ya wanta leave her there? Or do we have ta get her outta the ditch?"

Hugh slumped in his saddle and rested his hands on the horn. "Getting her out seems a little like work to me. Maybe we'll just leave her in. What're ya doing out here, anyway?"

Puny shook his head. Squinted towards the sun. "Woman trouble."

Hugh dismounted. They sat on a log away from the hog. First Puny spilled the story. Then they sorted his options. They couldn't think of anything convincing to say to Ezell. And Puny couldn't go back into town and face Lizzie without taking the baby. But he couldn't find the child under Ezell's suspicious eye. He needed to find Sanders. He apparently was on Braggs Mountain with his other Nancy. But Puny couldn't make that trip without a gun. So Hugh offered to lift Connell's spare one.

Hugh left Puny and went to the house for the noon dinner. After he ate, he walked up to his and Connell's room, took his own gun out of his holster, and slipped it in his dresser. Then he opened Connell's top drawer, lifted his extra gun, and holstered it. He jerked the pillowcase off his pillow, went back downstairs to the dining room, and stuffed the leftover food in it. He hid the pillowcase behind the bathtub in the winter kitchen and went to the summer kitchen. Not finding Ezell there, he breathed some relief and quickly jammed jerky, biscuits, and coffee grounds into an old sugar sack. He took that back to the house and set it next to the pillowcase. He waited until his mother was at a backyard rainwater barrel, then slipped out the front door. He took the food and the gun to Puny in the woods.

After that, Hugh went to the field and led Puny's horse to the stable. He distracted a hand with an errand, saddled the horse alone, and rode it to the woods. He and Puny sat again on the log and plotted. By that time, it was late afternoon. They decided Puny had better hide a while longer; avoid anyone coming to the river to fish for their evening meal. When they parted, Hugh told Puny to be careful, and pledged his silence. He was glad to help. Was returning favors. Puny helped him with Willow Starr Watson, his woman on a farm north of town. Lied for him regularly. Also kept an eye on the barbershop, in case Willow's husband, the owner, suddenly hankered for a noon meal at home. Puny could outride the barber easily, and had.

So according to plan, Puny waited until twilight descended. Then he left the woods and rode east on the sandbar. Braggs Mountain sat on the horizon, clearly in sight. But Puny'd been in the Nation for only five years. He rarely rode alone. Didn't know his way entirely. He slowed to get better bearings. An early moon cut a path on the river. He turned away from the water to avoid the threads of quicksand that jutted into the bar. Crossed the point on the sand where the roar of the water abruptly disappeared. Heard other sounds — bird calls he didn't recognize, a cow mooing in the distance, something crashing through a thicket.

After a ride of a comfortable length, Puny crossed a stream of the bayou and heard human voices. But he couldn't hear them well. He got off his horse, tethered him to a scrub, and climbed the side of a sand dune. He peeked over its top. A huge flatboat was tied at the bayou dock. Both the boat and the landing were lit with lanterns. Men were unloading barrels. Puny assumed they contained whiskey. The Nation was dry. With liquor so dangerous to Indians, it had to be run up the river illegally.

Puny slid down and leaned back against the sand to think through his choices. Inland, beyond the bayou's mouth, was a bawdy house where white men and Indians with money bought fun. He and Connell had once gone there together to gather Hugh home. But Puny couldn't go up to the house without an Indian protector. And the bayou spread out at the river. Crossing it at night would be dangerous, unless he went inland as far as the house. He thought through that again. Everybody there would be white or Indian and drunk and armed.

So Puny made camp next to the dune. He figured Indians would bathe in the river come morning. He could ask them the best route to the mountain. He ate biscuits and jerky. Then gathered driftwood by the light of the moon. He laid out the wood in a square to guard against snakes while sleeping. He hoped his horse would neigh if anything bigger came creeping. He was exhausted. Slept better than he thought he would.

At dawn, he was awakened by the sound of children laughing. He sat up, wiggled the stiffness from his muscles, and peered over the bank of sand. Five Indian children stopped short of the river. The two oldest ones were wearing clothes. They slipped them off. All waited beside the water until an Indian woman joined them. She said something in Cherokee. The children headed towards a pool cut off from the current by the shifting of sand. The woman pulled her dress off over her head.

Puny slid down behind the dune and turned his back to the scene. He was in enough woman trouble already.

But, suddenly, he heard shrill, childish voices talking Cherokee. The voices got nearer, closer to his horse. Puny couldn't understand what was being said. He muttered under his breath about being so unlucky as to live in an English-speaking country where people spoke something else. He pushed up, popped his head over the top of the dune, and smiled. One of the children saw him, and said something to the others. They all turned to look at Puny. Then they ran off screaming towards the woman. She ran for her clothes and held them to her breasts. They all fled.

So Puny's day started off on the wrong foot. And by the time the sun was full up, he realized he'd made a mistake. After two nights away, Ezell would know for sure he was up to trouble. Miz Singer and Connell would worry where he was. And if he was going after his baby, he should've brought Lizzie. He didn't know anything about babies. But after eating a couple of biscuits and drinking bayou-water coffee, he realized he couldn't be carrying one back in his arms on a horse.

So he broke camp, turned up the bayou, and rode until it narrowed. He crossed there and rode on until he spied the bawdy house. He splashed through a stream near it. Dismounted, walked over to a stump, and sat down out in the open. He put his hat on the ground. After a while, an Indian came out of the house into the dogtrot and walked around on the porch. The Indian moved to two or three different positions, looking mostly towards a big tree. But Puny knew the Indian was watching him; he'd learned that when Miz Singer's mother had come visiting to Tennessee.

Eventually, the Indian went inside. He came back out carrying a tin cup. He then walked directly towards Puny and stopped at a distance of about seven feet. He held the cup down to show it was empty. Puny smiled, pulled a coin out of his pocket, and held it up. The Indian smiled back. Puny figured if he was going to lay out, he might as well have a little fun.

The Indian who supplied him with his first cup supplied him all morning. After bringing the second cup, he squatted about six feet from the stump. Puny drank more. The Indian brought over three friends to squat with him. In his cups, Puny felt friendlier and friendlier towards the Natives hunkered around. They'd had hard times, been moved from pillar to post, robbed, and marched across the country by white people who'd cheated them every way to and from kingdom come. Puny felt sorry for them. And he had a big heart. He got to sharing his liquor. And his new friends got to enjoying his generosity. By midday, the four Indians were drunk, and Puny was still sitting on the stump. He was singing a hymn his mama was particularly fond of.

About the third time Puny sang the chorus, a white man came out of the bawdy house and stood on the porch with his fists on his hips. He yelled, "Come here, nigger."

Puny's eyebrows condensed into a V over his nose. He forced his eyes to focus. The man was dressed in a long-sleeved underwear shirt. His pants were held by suspenders. A kerchief was knotted around his neck, a holster slung low on his trousers. Puny didn't want to be on the business end of that gun. He got up from the stump and put his cup down on his seat. He picked up his hat, but didn't put it on his head. He walked across the yard saying, "Yassir, yassir." He stopped about fifteen feet from the porch.

The man said, "Ya got my goddamn Injuns drunk, ya son of a bitch."

"Yassir. I didn't reckon it'd be so easy." Puny hung his head like he felt some remorse.

The man said, "I need help. Come in here. I'm trying to move a broke table." He turned into the dogtrot.

Puny climbed the steps and followed the man into the room on the left. In it were several barrels, some turned on end and some on their sides. Three tables with chairs stood around, but in front of the fireplace, a table with broken legs was split in two. An ax was sticking out of it.

Puny said, "That table oak?"

"Shore is. Busted up like it twer pine."

"Goddamn. What happened?"

"Crow Colbert done busted her last night. Or maybe sometime this morning. I can't quite recollect."

"How come?"

"Drunk. And mad that another customer were with the entertainment." He tilted his chin towards the ladder to the loft. "Help me git the table out the back. We'll turn it into firewood. Can ya swing an ax, or are ya a house nigger?"

Puny scratched the back of his head. "I'm a house nigger. But I'm a little short on the house part. Give me a place to sleep and I'll bust her up fer ya."

The man said, "That's a deal. We're the only sober ones here."

The Boys Scout Out

WHEN COOP AND GEORGE RETURNED from the inn, they told Sanders a big Negro was at the bawdy house and that he was probably Puny. Sanders said, "It's his own bizness if it is." So the boys told everybody they were going fishing. They mounted The Bay, carrying their poles and a bucket with them. Trotted off talking about where to find grubs for bait and trying to look innocent. But when they got to a spot not far from the bawdy house, they dismounted, tied the horse to a tree, set the bucket by its trunk, and stuck the poles in it. Coop was still licking his wound from George tricking him, and wanted to glimpse the Negro to be sure he was Puny before they barged in. Sanders had also said, "That bawdy house ain't no place fer young'uns." So Coop was disobeying his father and wary about his mission.

The boys entered a thicket, bent over low, and skirted along silently. When they saw the bawdy house, they moved closer in and stopped at a spot near the back. They squatted among saplings, broke off twigs, sharpened them, and applied them to their teeth. To help pass time, Coop concentrated on a line of ants. George kept an eye on birds that flitted between branches. Their breaths evened out. They waited.

Eventually, the white man in the long-sleeved undershirt came out into the trot, pulled out his pecker, and took a piss off the edge. Coop and George exchanged glances. Coop held up his thumb and trigger finger spread out about an inch. The man went back in. Nothing happened for a while after that. The sun sank below the roof of the house. Still nothing happened. The boys changed their positions to relieve their haunches. Darkness descended. Then the sound of horses arose in the distance. The hooves got nearer and stopped. Voices carried. But not well enough for them to hear what was said. Coop poked George's arm with a stick. He brought his hand to his face and tapped his teeth together. George undid his belt and pulled a bull's balls pouch off it. He pinched dried meat from the pouch, cut it in two with his knife, and handed a piece to Coop. They chewed in silence. Darkness grew thicker. More horse noises and voices floated over.

Finally, George said, *"This might not be the best plan."*

Coop said, *"You got a better?"*

"I could go in and try to bring him out. But it's so dark you couldn't see him if I do."

Coop looked towards the bawdy house. It was swallowed by night. An owl hooted. The boys shivered and stood.

Meanwhile, Back at the Farm

CHECK WAS STRETCHED OUT ON her cot in the sickroom, listening to Andrew's breathing. She tried to erase how shallow it seemed by rolling over onto her side and facing the wall. For a moment, she considered praying. That petered out before she could figure who to. Her mind floated to her boys. It being a Saturday night, she hadn't had her usual conferences with the oldest two. Connell was in town at the Taylors' home, sparking Florence. Check pictured them on the front porch swing. Nash's house was the finest anywhere around. Its double porches floated across Check's mind, followed by its French doors, high ceilings, and circular staircase. Then Florence's mother, Suzanne, floated in. Check's forehead crinkled. She moved back to musing on the stairs. Pictured Connell and Florence at their foot, posing for pictures.

Check next reviewed the afternoon. Hugh had run his first races. Had attracted a crowd. The men stood in clumps and wagered. The ladies visited each other's buggies. Nash and Suzanne had come. Check's mind briefly strayed to Nash's new beard, to Suzanne's voice. She twitched and turned to musing on Dr. Howard's wife. She was kind and plump. They were a good match.

The Benge, Gulager, and Martin families had also attended the races. As had three of Hellfire Jack Rogers' descendants and several of the Starrs. Major Percival had ridden. So had Cowboy and Bob Benge, cousins to her and her boys. Hugh had ridden his new horse. Won one race. Placed in another. Check had mingled with the crowd. Assured everyone Andrew wanted the races run. Brought a few people up to the house to look in on him. He wanted the company, and his friends wanted to see him. But the excitement had worn him down after a couple of rounds. Still, Check was glad some folks heard straight from Andrew that Hugh was following his wishes.

Hugh floated into her mind next. He, Cowboy, and Bob had stopped by the kitchen after the races. She'd eaten with them. Then they'd left for the cockfights at the fort. The smell of dust and the feathers arose in Check's nose. She sniffed, and whiffed pine. Her thoughts drifted to Connell and Hugh riding home. They'd promised to meet up and come together. Outlaws were streaming into the Nation. The road between town and the bottoms was too dangerous to ride at night alone.

Check jerked her mind off that by thinking about Clifford. He'd thrown a fit about going back to school. Complained so loudly that Andrew had heard him. Cliff liked school; he didn't want to leave because his papa was dying. But Check had whipped him for upsetting Andrew. Sent him to his room crying. She didn't feel much remorse about that because she'd also given in to letting him stay home. Her mind moved to Otter and Paul. Their days had been perfectly untroubled. She imagined their sweet faces and drifted off to sleep.

EZELL AND LIZZIE WERE UP later than usual, in rockers, bent over sewing. Ezell's hair was unsheathed. She looked at Lizzie's stitches and said, "Didn't nobody teach ya nothing?"

"Gives me the heebies." Lizzie flexed her fingers.

"S'posed'ta be relaxing."

"I gets my relaxation a different way."

"Hum, hum. I guess you do."

Lizzie frowned and jabbed her needle into a cushion. "I didn't mean that. I want some excitement."

"Yer still sick." Ezell kept sewing. A quilt top was draped over her lap. Behind her shoulders the coal oil lamp gave out warm yellow light.

Lizzie was taking a blouse down to her size. She rocked back. "I ain't never gonna be a sewer."

"Yer is if ya gonna wear clothes."

Lizzie rocked forward, got up, and set her sewing on the table next to the cushion. She stretched. "Someday I'z gonna have me a seamstress."

"Yeah, someday I'z gonna be the Queen of England."

Lizzie pinched up her skirt between her fingers and thumbs. She danced in a little circle, dipped and glided. Sang, "Ain't chopping any cotton no more. Don't hav'ta, 'cause I ain't poor."

Ezell shook her head. "Yer always gonna be poor." She examined her stitches.

Lizzie stopped dancing. "Not if I find that stash."

Ezell looked up. "How do ya know 'bout that stash? Did Puny tell ya?" She squinted. She intended to lick his hide as soon as he got his sorry tail home.

"I knowed it 'fore I ever run into Puny."

"What d'ya know about it?"

"Ain't telling." Lizzie sat down on the bed with a bounce.

"Fine. I won't tell you what I know about it neither." Ezell bent over her sewing again.

Lizzie was too much of a child to have patience for secrets, even her own. She said, "I heared where the gold is."

"You don't know where that stash is. Yer making that up."

Lizzy stood. "I'll tell ya what I knows ifin you'll tell me what you knows."

"How do I know I can trust ya?" Ezell didn't look up. She knew more about playing hard to get than Lizzie did.

Lizzie frowned. Then she went to the table, took her needle out of the cushion, and pricked her ring finger with it. A bright drop of blood grew from the tip. "I'll make a vow on my blood to tell the truth ifin ya do, too." She looked directly at Ezell.

Ezell stopped sewing. She licked her lips. She was growing attached to the girl. She wanted to trust her. Wanted a friend of her own color. Wanted a daughter, too. Lizzie wasn't any of those things, really. But maybe, just maybe, she would do. Ezell set her quilt aside. She stood up directly across from Lizzie and looked down at her. She raised her hand. Used her needle to prick her ring finger. She touched its tip to Lizzie's. She said, "I swear." Blood ran down to her first knuckle.

Big Trouble at the Bawdy House

IN THE WEEK AND A half Puny had been at the bawdy house, he'd taken to wearing the long-sleeved undershirts favored by his employer, Jake Perkins. The shirts came off steamboats running dry goods on deck and whiskey below, and Puny bought two with the specie certificates Jake paid him for his work. Puny missed the real money he earned at the Singers', but he wasn't ready to return to the bottoms. And Jake was glad of that; the big man fit in nicely, even if he was a darkie, and was making a contribution to the orderly running of the house. Jake didn't want to risk any public killing going on, and didn't want to break up fights himself. He was tired of his Indian enforcers getting drunk, and didn't see how he could provide illegal whiskey and a little prostitution in a safe environment without sober help.

Claudette, the woman of the house who'd so charmed George, also considered Puny a welcome addition. She was blond and sallow-skinned. Her eyes were set a little too close together. She'd come to the Nation by steamboat, and had been left at the bayou dock by her husband, who'd tricked her into going ashore and paid the captain to push off without her. Claudette hadn't cared that her mister skedaddled; he'd given her a shiner every few weeks, and once thrown her so hard he'd busted her collarbone. But she wished he'd left her someplace where there were other women to talk to, a sewing machine, some material, and fewer mosquitoes. She'd taken up with Jake as an alternative to boredom, savages, and starvation, but Jake was too liquor-logged to have a sustainable interest in women.

He had not, however, lost his eye for money. He soon talked Claudette into tricking by paying her fifty percent of the take. She was competent at her job. Turned as many tricks a night as men could buy, and mostly didn't even lie down to do it. All she required was a dark corner, a rag, and a bucket of lard that she, through a mixture of misinformation and good luck, had found to be a surefire pregnancy preventer. Since Puny had arrived, he'd persuaded her to abandon the corner for her work, and instead take her clients up the ladder to the loft. Claudette considered that advice evidence that Puny was a gentleman, but found the new arrangement had disadvantages. Between screws, she got bored in the dark doing nothing except staring at the rafters, and twice already customers had fallen off the ladder while going back down. Too, it was hard to solicit new attention while hidden away overhead. She was thinking she needed to return to servicing in the shadows of the corners, but didn't know how to break that to Puny. He was nice for a darkie, and seemed genuinely upset by fucking in public.

About three hours into Saturday night, the bawdy house was filled with its usual crowd. The room on the left no longer held tables, but did have a couple of oil lamps and several barrels, one to dip liquor from and the rest to set drinks on. Puny poured spirits into tin cups left over from the War, and pocketed money and certificates in his trousers. Jake liked Puny holding the money because, with his sleeves rolled up, his undershirts showed off his muscles, and he was so brawny that nobody bothered him. Jake gave him a holster so he could protect the wad in his pocket under his gun, and kept a close enough eye that he could tell Puny wasn't cheating him or going to run.

In the room across the trot, men played cards on wooden tables. On the front porch, others leaned against posts and told stories. It was a warm night; all the doors were open. The lamps were low, so bugs were nibbling but not swarming. A local salve made of bark and applied to necks, wrists, and ankles provided some protection against the bites and the shaking fevers they carried. And so did the liquor and cigarettes. Everybody was taking those remedies, and Claudette was servicing a customer upstairs, when Crow Colbert first strode into the room on the left.

Crow was single-holstered. He wore a black hat with a feather in the band, black trousers, and suspenders. He was a fat Indian (but not tall), round-headed, and dark. One scar ran from below his left eye to the corner of his mouth. Another zagged down his left shoulder and over that nipple to the top of a belly that resembled a bullfrog's throat in full croak. He looked around for the lady of the house, peered into the back corners, didn't see anybody in them. He said to Jake, "Where's my whore?"

Jake said, "Minding her bizness," and went back to lying to some white fellows about fishing.

Crow walked over to the open barrel, held out a certificate, and said to Puny, "Gi'me some liquor."

Puny dipped up whiskey with a clean tin cup and handed it to Crow. Crow grunted, turned, and walked through the front door, out to the porch.

A few minutes later, Claudette descended the ladder on the east wall of the room. A white boy of about nineteen followed her. He pecked her on the left cheek, tapped the same cheek on her bottom with his hand, and left through the dogtrot door. Claudette sidled over and asked Puny for a drink. A white man came up and engaged her in conversation.

With the exception of Crow, most of Claudette's clientele were of the white persuasion. The concept of whores hadn't ever fully taken hold in the Nation because the citizens indulged their inclinations so freely that paying for sex seemed the height of stupidity. However, occasionally Claudette would take on a young Indian like George, who'd never had a white woman and wanted to find out if they were made the same way a regular female was. Occasionally, too, she took on a young one who just had a stiff on so hard he needed somewhere to stick it. She had a tender spot in her heart for kids, and could get them off quicker than seasoned men, who were sometimes so soaked that their pricks were as pliable as pincushions.

Puny had capped a barrel and was crowbarring open another one when Hugh stepped through the front door with Cowboy and Bob at his shoulders. Hugh said, "Drinks, partner," and grinned.

Puny grinned, too, popped the lid on his new barrel, and said, "How'd the racing go?" He lifted cups off the mantel and dipped up whiskey for Hugh and both Benges. They fell into jawing, bragging, and disparaging other men's horses.

Hugh had discovered Puny at the bawdy house just a couple of nights after they'd parted. And he'd been filling him in on developments at the farm. Puny appreciated knowing that Lizzie had showed up and was living with Ezell. And he was sure as hell glad he'd missed the slop-throwing and the skunk. Hugh, for his part, enjoyed keeping a secret from his mother and brother, and whenever either one of them said, "Wonder where the dickens Puny's laying out?," he shook his head and answered, "No telling." He also pretended to be sorely perplexed about the location of Connell's missing weapon.

Hugh was shorter than either of the Benge boys, and lighter in color. Only his black hair, dark eyes, and high cheekbones belied his Indian blood. He was well dressed in a white shirt, snakeskin boots, and a holster with brass finishings on it. His hat sat on his head at an angle. And his arrival didn't escape Claudette. She found Hugh as handsome as blood is red, but had never been able to get his attention. She unwound herself from the conversation she was in, walked over, and knocked her left breast against Hugh's chest. She said, "Ya sure never act it, but I hear tell yer friendly."

Hugh had a taste for women. But was getting his needs met by Willow, who was dark enough to look several years younger than she really was and irritated enough with her white husband to find Hugh a real diversion. The arrangement worked well. Willow had aspired to be a schoolteacher when she was younger, and considered Hugh a willing pupil. She enjoyed showing him various ways to give and take pleasure. Hugh, for his part, enjoyed learning every nook, cranny, and angle of Willow's lessons, and knew she was preparing him for a life with other women, or maybe with one. He hadn't thought that detail out completely. But he did have some standards, and wasn't desperate, so the thought of poking Claudette made him squeamish. Nevertheless, Hugh liked to think he could tease with a whore any day. He said, "Who told you that?"

Claudette cut her eyes up to Puny. "Yer darkie friend."

"You trust that man?" Hugh's eyes widened.

Puny rolled his. "I'm the only trustworthy person here."

That jack-jawing went on for a while. And all were engaged in such mutual amusement that they didn't pay much attention to anybody else. None of them, including Cowboy and Bob, saw two young Indians peek in the front porch door and disappear again into the dark.

The night wore on. More drinks were consumed. And eventually, Claudette, by running her hands over Hugh's trousers, convinced him that a little hand job in the corner wouldn't do him any harm. In fact, the idea that he might come in a room full of men heightened Hugh's interest some. So Claudette led him into the northeast corner. She dampened the lamp there to darkness, fluttered her eyelids, and licked her lips. She dished some dirt into Hugh's ear. Pretty quickly, he unbuckled his gun belt, laid it on the top of a barrel, and covered it with his hat. Then he unbuckled his pants' belt, and unbuttoned his trousers with Claudette's help. His dick was stiff before they got it out, and he had to shove his pants down around his hips to give himself room to wiggle a bit. Claudette was stroking Hugh's member with a regular motion and thinking about getting on her knees when Crow staggered into the room.

Crow focused on Puny, who was still serving drinks, so he didn't see the couple at first. But once his cup was filled, he saw, over Puny's shoulder, Claudette's elbow pumping up and down. He noticed her neck bent back in a curved position. Hugh's head also seemed set at an angle too cockeyed for a man just carrying on conversation. Crow put his cup down so hard his whiskey splashed out on a barrel. He took three long strides and pulled his gun. He lodged its tip under Hugh's ear before anybody knew what was happening. Said, "Get your dick outta my whore's hand." That stopped the jerking.

Hugh had started pulling his pants up with one hand, his shirt down with the other, when Crow said, "Let ever'body see what'cha got." He slung his left arm around Hugh's neck. Whirled him around to face the room, gun still pressed to his earlobe. He mashed Claudette into the corner with his butt and his back.

Puny put his hand on his gun. Crow said, "Don't anybody move. Put yer hands up or I'll shoot him. We're gonna see what this white boy has. Show 'em, kid. Stick it out." He pulled back his gun's hammer. Tightened his grip on Hugh's neck.

Every man in the room raised his hands. Crow nudged Hugh's neck with his gun. He said, "Show yer bizness."

Hugh slipped his dick out from behind his shirttail. Claudette groaned. But was pinned so tightly she could barely breathe, and her arm with the mended collarbone was trapped behind her back. Crow said, "Git it all the way out. Let's have a good look."

Hugh said, "It's out, goddamn it." His neck was clamped in Crow's elbow. He was shaking and red in the face.

Crow looked down. "Don't look out to me. Git it out more." He belched. The gun bobbled.

Hugh's pants were open to his hips. His dick in his fist. But it wasn't any firmer than dough, and its head had ducked into its hood.

Puny's hands were in the air with everybody else's. He said, "He's a Cherokee. You better leave 'im alone."

Crow belched again. "Don't look Indian to me. Don't have a dick worth noticing." To Hugh, he said, "Pump it up more." He adjusted the angle of his gun.

The room was so silent the mosquitoes sounded like fiddles. Nobody moved except Hugh. He squeezed himself hard and pumped. He pumped some more. Tried to imagine Willow, going into her. Fucking her hard. His eyes were closed in a squint. He loosened his squeeze just a little. Got another grip and pumped harder. But the pumping didn't have any swelling effect. Hugh's knees started shaking. Crow snorted. He said, "That ain't as big as a worm. Couldn't even fish with it."

Hugh tried not to pay that any attention. But he was scared, and he could feel the cold steel against the side of his neck. He started crying. Once he started, he couldn't stop. His sobs rose over the sounds of the insects. It punctured the bawdy house silence. Not a plank creaked; nobody coughed. Hugh cried, and pumped. Most men turned to look away. Crow said, "Everybody watch 'im. Anybody who takes his eyes off his pitiful little dick gets shot." The men turned their heads back towards Hugh. Hugh kept pumping. His trousers fell down to the tops of his boots. He sobbed.

Suddenly, a tall man strode through the dogtrot door like nothing was happening. He wasn't wearing a gun or a hat. He laid a coin on top of a barrel. Said, "Puny, can ya give a friend a drink?" He looked around and said, "Fine night." Smiled like he was glad to be there. Said, "Howdy, Crow. Ya taken up with boys?"

Crow's eyes widened to the size of silver dollars. His jaw sagged open. He tightened his elbow around Hugh's neck, extended his gun arm, and pointed his weapon at the man. He said, "Sanders, ya son of a bitch!"

A gun fired. The only lamp still lit exploded. The room snapped to darkness. Yelling, bumping, grunting, and thumping filled the air. The planks of the floor rattled. Barrels shook. Somebody fired another shot. Somebody screamed. Men cussed. Another shot was fired. Claudette shrieked and several men shouted. A ripping sound was followed by a yell like a panther's.

Dragging Home

CHECK'S EYES POPPED OPEN. SHE'D either dreamed a thud or heard one. She caught moaning, down low, towards the floor. She called, "Andrew," listened, and heard another moan. The room was black. The wind had blown the candles out; the curtains floated in and around the windows like ghosts. Check sat up on the side of her cot. She looked to the four-poster bed. When her eyes adjusted, she saw it was empty. She said, "Andrew" again. She paused. "Darling?"

Another groan came from close to the floor.

Check rose, gripped a bedpost, ran her hand along the footboard, and gripped another post. Andrew was on the rug. She knelt beside him, put her hand on his chest. "Sweetheart, you've fallen. Can you get up?"

Andrew shifted and groaned.

Check stood. Andrew was frail, but she was a small woman. She said, "Hold on," and went to the hall. At the newel, she thought about calling. But that would wake Clifford, Otter, and Paul. She gathered her gown and carefully climbed the stairs in the dark. At the door of Connell and Hugh's room, she knocked.

Connell was startled awake. "What?"

Check opened the door. "Connell. Hugh. I need help. Your father's fallen out of bed. I can't lift him." Her eyes adjusted. Hugh's bed was empty and made.

Connell sat up. "Is he okay?"

"Where's your brother?"

Connell was groggy. And hadn't expected to be interrogated by his mother in the middle of the night. He said, "Damned if I know."

"Exactly what do you mean by that?"

Connell woke fully up. "Nothing, Mama. We better tend to Papa. Hugh's out with Cowboy and Bob. He's probably spending the night."

Check said, "He's never around when you need him. And you shouldn't have ridden home by yourself."

THE NEXT MORNING WAS EASTER. Before Andrew grew ill, the men of the house rode horses to church on Sundays. The hands without horses and the children rode in the wagon, and Check drove it with Ezell on the bench beside her until they reached the Negro Baptist church. After Andrew became too sick for services, he insisted they go without him. But that morning, looking to avoid the janitor's preaching, Check declared the whole farm would stay home and share Easter together. They'd eat a big breakfast, then sit in the front yard while Connell read from the Bible. If Andrew took to the plan, she thought it would work for as many more Sundays as he was with them.

The service had concluded. The hands were pitching horseshoes at the bunkhouse. And Connell had taken Clifford and Otter fishing at the cove where the ferry was docked. Check was at Andrew's bedside,

Paul napping on her cot. Ezell and Lizzie were weeding a small garden behind the summer kitchen, where Ezell grew tomatoes, onions, lettuce, and a few other vegetables and herbs for her and Puny's personal consumption. She was the first to spot horses on the horizon. She said, "Lizzie, yer sight is better'n mine. Who's that riding thiserway?"

Lizzie shaded her eyes with her hand. "Hard to tell. It's five horses. They's hauling sompthing."

Ezell pointed with a trowel. "Is that Puny's horse?" Since she'd finally discovered it was missing, she'd seen it in her imagination every day.

"There's sure a big darkie on one of 'em," Lizzie responded.

Both women commenced to shouting. Check heard them in the sickroom, where she was reading a paper. She said, "Excuse me, Andrew. There's a commotion." She closed the door behind her. By the time she got to the back porch, Ezell and Lizzie had taken off through the potatoes, yelling and waving their arms. In the lane between the Corderys' land and the Singers' were five horses, four riders, and a litter. By his paint horse, Check first recognized Sanders. Then she made out Puny. They were riding slow. They turned west and rode in a straight line on a lane between rows of potatoes. Check recognized The Bay. A shirtless Indian was riding him. On another horse, a bundle stuck out on both sides like the steed had sprouted the wings of a mythical creature. The litter was behind Sanders' horse. And Coop was riding Hugh's new one.

Ezell and Lizzie met up with the riders. Everybody stopped. Then the women fell in beside the horses and jogged at their pace. Check had counted horses and riders three times. She'd determined Hugh wasn't upright. He had to be either on the litter or in the bundle. One or the other. But which? She wanted to fly off the porch and run to the horses. Instead, she prayed to her ancestors for strength. Stepped to the ground and walked to the hitching rail. She stood in the yard with her arms at her sides, her head held high. She waited until the riders and horses, the whole party, were on her.

Sanders looked in Check's direction, but well over her head. "We'll need us some rags and some of that painkiller yer feeding Mr. Singer." He pulled his underlip in between his teeth. He moved only with his horse's breath going up and down. His absolute stillness helped Check hold her composure. She stepped past him to the litter. Hugh was on it. He was pasty-colored. Tied down by ropes, but breathing. His chest was bare and his left trouser leg missing. That thigh was wrapped with his shirt, pink with blood. Check nearly collapsed with relief. She fell to the side of the litter. Gripped its edge. Examined Hugh's thigh, and then his face. She touched his hair and his cheek. He opened his eyes and said, "Mama." His eyes closed again.

Check pulled in a deep breath and stood. "Lizzie, get Paul off my cot. Puny, you and Coop move that cot to the hallway. Don't wake Mr. Singer if you can help it." She looked at George Sixkiller. She didn't know him. He slid off The Bay. She said, "Young man, head to the ferry." She pointed the direction. "Bring the grown man there back to the house. If you can, get the young boys to stay with the ferryman. I appreciate it."

George got back on The Bay and rode off. Coop handed the reins of the horse with the bundle to Sanders. Check said, "Ezell, we need hot water." She walked around the litter and took a good look at the bundle. It was a deerskin stained dark with blood. Two boots pointing up stuck out of one end. Check turned to where she could see Sanders' face from the side. His hat was tilted back on his head. His muscles were brown and rippled. A pistol and hunting knife were wedged in his belt. He stared straight ahead. Check said, "Seems like you had a long night."

Sanders nodded.

Check waited. Nothing came. She said, "Thank you for bringing Hugh home."

"Tweren't no problem."

Check didn't exactly know where to go from there. Felt she could've pried more information from a tree. If she hadn't been so grateful, she would've wanted to shoot Sanders off his horse. Instead, she said, "I'd like to do something for you."

Sanders said, "Gotta get this body acrost the river. Need to use yer ferry."

The practicality of that request settled Check's feelings some. "That won't be a problem. Anybody I know?"

"I doubt it" was Sanders' reply.

Check turned her attention back to Hugh. She bent over him again and murmured what mothers do to hurt children, no matter their age.

When Puny and Coop returned, Sanders looked at his son, jerked his head, and said, "Tell Nannie to git food ready." Coop reached for Hugh's horse's reins. Sanders said, "Run to it."

Coop said, "ᎡᏪ" in a pitiful voice. Sanders flexed his thigh muscles and pulled his stomach further in.

After Coop ran off, Sanders dismounted. He secured the horses to the hitching rail and helped Puny untie the litter from his horse. He and Puny carried Hugh into the house and laid him on the cot. When George returned from the river, Sanders said to Check, "We'll need to borry The Bay." Then he and George rode towards his home site, leading the horse carrying the body.

Clifford and Otter hadn't stayed at the river. Check said to Lizzie, "Mind them. And don't let them in the house." She sent Connell and Puny to dismantle Hugh's bed and to take it downstairs to the hall. Check and Ezell unwrapped Hugh's thigh. The hole in it was the size of a thumb. The bullet had entered at a downward angle, traveled through the front of the leg, and exited above the back of the knee. The exit wound was large, but away from the bone. When Puny returned, he said Sanders had poured liquor down Hugh's throat and cauterized the wounds with a hot poker. By the smell, Check began to believe that Hugh wasn't so much unconscious as drunk. She asked Puny, "How'd he get shot?"

"Don't rightly know. The lights waz out. I gotta get a hammer to put this bed back together." Puny sprung out the back door.

But Lizzie was on the back porch. She moved suddenly, blocking him. She said, "You sorry-ass sucker, what'd'chu do with my baby?"

Puny looked this way and that. Thought of turning back. Said, "Shuuuu, Lizzie. They's little children around." He frowned towards Clifford and Otter.

Lizzie said, "I don't care if they is. I want an answer."

Puny sighed. Took Lizzie by the elbow. Led her into the yard. Bent over her low and whispered, "The baby died. Sanders buried her. He'll show us where she is."

Lizzie started wailing.

A moment later, Ezell came out of the house with a bucket of bloody water. She walked down the steps, over to Puny. She said, "Where ya been laying out?"

"Down on the bayou."

She threw the water all over him. He jumped back and shook. She said, "Jist get back on down there," and marched off.

SO PUNY WAS IN HIS cabin, changing his clothes, when Connell stopped in the open door. He said, "I got the bed together without the hammer. Not perfect, but she'll hold."

Puny slipped his arm through a sleeve. "That's good. Hammering would've awaked yer daddy."

"I've got to get Doc Howard after we get Hugh in his own bed."

Puny nodded. "I'll help ya move 'im."

Connell stepped into the room and stopped. Puny shook his head. "I'd invite ya to take a chair, but it ain't my cabin no more."

"You can use the bunkhouse. I'll tell the men to let you in."

Puny let out a deep breath. "Hard to sleep in a room with white men."

Connell looked to the beams overhead. "If you aren't safe there, I'll run 'em all out. They can sleep under the stars."

Puny buttoned his last button. Tucked his shirttail in. He lifted his holster from the bed. "I'd like ta buy this gun off ya."

Connell shook his head. "Can't sell it to you. But don't get killed carrying it."

"Thank ya. I'll work at it." Puny buckled his gun belt on and took a couple of steps towards the door. Connell didn't back away. He said, "I need to know."

Puny said, "I know ya do. Ask the Benges. They'll tell ya."

Connell spread his feet and tried to look larger. "Mama'll want answers before I can round 'em up. You know how she is."

Puny ran a hand over his mouth. "Tell her Sanders kilt Crow Colbert for threatening Hugh's life."

Connell shook his head. "Colbert's a huge man. That can't be him in that skin."

"It's him all right. He's thin 'cause we had'ta gut 'im."

Carrying the Corpse

IN FULL RIGOR MORTIS, CROW Colbert's body sat on the back of his horse like a plank. It was secured by a rope and stuck out about a foot and a half on both sides. George didn't like keeping company with a corpse; didn't like anything dead. He frowned at the top of Colbert's head. Turned his back. But a dead man behind him wasn't comforting either. He turned sideways. Watched the bundle out of the side of his eye. Sniffed, thinking he'd smell the sickening odor of Crow's open gut, but got only a thin whiff of it. The smell of horse butt was stronger.

George and the body were in a thicket southwest of Sanders' cabin. The horses didn't need watching, but Crow's corpse would attract wolves, even in daylight. George had Sanders' gun for protection; so after standing guard for a while, he lay down on the ground, his palm on the weapon. Exhaustion took him over. He nodded off. After a while, he woke with a start and sat up. Talking was coming towards him. He recognized the voices. He'd scampered into the saddle by the time Sanders and Coop were on him.

Sanders held out a feed sack to George. He extended his other hand for his weapon.

Coop said, "Pa, I could ride behind 'im. He wouldn't mind."

Sanders checked Colbert's body on both ends of the bundle. Then he mounted his horse. Coop looked to George with hungry dog eyes.

George said, "Coop and me ride together all the time."

Sanders shook his head. Tapped his horse with his heels.

George didn't know what to do. His own father would've treated him the same way for disobeying. And for having to track him down.

He turned The Bay around in a circle. Looked from his friend on the ground to Sanders riding away, leading the horse with the corpse. He did that two or three times.

Finally, Coop picked up a stick and threw it. Then he picked up another and beat the ground. By that time, he was crying. George figured the best thing he could do was ride away and pretend like that wasn't happening. He turned The Bay north and jabbed his heels into the horse's sides. When he caught up with Sanders, to keep from looking back, he opened the sack of food, pulled out a hunk of jerky, and bit off a chew. He followed Sanders and the corpse through the potatoes to the Singers' yard and, through it, to the river.

There, Bert was waiting on the ferry. Clifford had warned him somebody was coming, but he didn't recognize either Indian riding towards him. When the horses got near, Sanders called, "We're needing to get acrost." Bert saw the boots sticking out of the bundle. He rubbed his hands down his pants and licked his lips. He said, "Miz Singer send ya?"

Sanders said, "Swing her 'round to the rock." He turned his horse and the one with the body towards the landing, watching the ground to avoid the rocks. George followed.

Bert didn't know what to do but to obey the order. He guessed these were the people Miz Singer was sending, but Clifford hadn't mentioned a body. Bert had seen some dying, and he didn't like being around any dead people at all. Now he was going to have to take one across on the ferry. He wondered if crossing water with a corpse would bring on a special kind of bad luck. He was just beginning to feel better from settling down and didn't want to do anything to turn that around. However, the big man on the horse was clearly nobody to cross. And, no matter what, he had to do what Miz Singer wanted. Bert grabbed his pole and, with no little muscle, guided the ferry into place and hooked it to the rigging.

After Sanders and George boarded, they helped with the ropes and pulleys. The river was slower at the crossing than it was above or below, but the sand moved every hour, and the ferry could get stuck and stay that way until the grains shifted again. As they crossed, they all scanned the water for sandbars and alligator gars. Gars wouldn't stop the ferry;

but no one wanted to get thrown off near one, and all three of them, like everybody else, wanted a big gar story whenever they could get one.

Finally, when the ferry steadied against the west bank, Sanders said to Bert, "Thank ya fer yer help. What's yer name?"

Bert thought about lying. The tall man had been a lot of help with the rope, but he wasn't sure he wanted to make friends with anybody carrying a body. On the other hand, Miz Singer had probably sent the man. And Cliff had said not to charge him. "Bert Vann," he said.

"Kin to Rich Joe Vann?"

Bert shrugged. "Don't know. Orphaned."

"Where?"

"Arkansas. 'Round Malvern."

Sanders looked over Bert's head and squinted into the sun. He ran his tongue over his teeth. Then he turned to George and said, "We gotta go." He took up his horse's reins and mounted. He rode off the ferry, stringing the horse with the corpse behind him.

George followed on The Bay, up the bank to level ground. After that, they wandered, single file, Sanders leading, through brambles and bushes, sidestepping young trees, until George wondered if they were lost. Then Sanders' horse came to a halt. So did the horse with the corpse. George pulled The Bay up. He could see something in front of Sanders, but couldn't tell what it was. He pulled The Bay to the south, rode in an arc past the body, and came up even with Sanders' horse. An iron pole was standing alone, stuck out of the ground. It was head high on a tall man and engraved with numbers. Sanders dismounted. George slid off The Bay. Sanders stepped to the pole and hit it with a knuckle. "This here's the boundary."

George pulled his chin in. He squinted.

"'Tween the Nations. I'm standing in the Creek Nation. Yer in ours. We got the river." Sanders patted the pole with his hand.

George crossed his arms in front of his chest, his hands under his pits. He straightened his back and tried to look perky. He said, "You reckon the horses need a rest?"

Sanders snorted and smiled. He squatted, picked up a stick, and drew a straight line in the dirt from the pole to the river. Then he straightened back up and took a couple of steps, bent over, and drew another line north from the pole. He studied the angle and the horizon.

George pulled his hair up in his hand, twisted his neck, and yawned. "Can ya tell the time of day with that pole?"

"Not so's I can reckon." Sanders looked at the sun. "Two hours 'til sundown. We'll camp by the Hitichi ford."

George was about to ask how far that was when Sanders remounted, goaded his horse, and jerked the rope of the horse with the corpse. George had had the most exciting night of his life, but it hadn't involved any sleep; and he was of an age when sleep was as important to him as food and sex. He'd never been in the Creek Nation before, but it looked pretty scraggly. He hoped the ford was close. He didn't feel like he could stay awake until sundown. It was an effort to grab the horn and hoist himself onto The Bay.

When The Bay picked up Sanders' horse's rhythm, George slumped in his saddle and fell to dozing. But shortly, the horses hit a wide, shallow gully of dust pocked with hoof marks and cattle patties. George perked up. The path was so famous that, though he'd never seen it, he knew what it was. He yelled, "Texas Road!" and expected Sanders to yell the same back to him. But Sanders only nodded. Or George thought he did. It's hard to tell a nod from the usual bobbing up and down of a head over a horse.

They rode on north on the cattle road. But the going was slow because of the body. George got to watching it seesawing up and down, and pretty soon found it so mesmerizing that he dozed off again. He was sound asleep in the saddle when a buzzard picked them up. Sanders yelled, "We got company fer supper." George jerked awake and saw Sanders' arm up flapping.

The buzzard was gliding in a lazy circle on air beyond the range of a revolver. George watched it warily until they came to a hill marked by low weeds, a few saplings, and charred lumber. They climbed that hill. Sanders stopped his horse and the one with the corpse. George stopped behind him. He asked, "What happened here?"

Sanders turned his horse half a circle and faced George. He puckered his lips and pointed his chin east towards the Grand, flowing into the Arkansas in the distance. "See Bushyhead's house over yonder? In '61, Fort Gibson waz run down. Colonel Pike built a new fort here atop an old mound. Used soldiers from Arkansas and Texas. Two days after Christmas the next year, Colonel Phillips brought the Union's Third Indian Regiment into Fort Gibson. It waz deserted. This'un waz about empty, too. It waz too cold to fight. Snow waz on the ground to midcalf. But yer daddy, me, and a few others waz here, trying to stay warm. Phillips crossed the Arkansas on ice there above the Singers' ferry. Had four cannons. We had only rifles and muskets. He fired on us at sunset. Set the whole fort to burning. Burnt all night. The next morning, he chased us deep into the Creek Nation. Burnt ever'thing standing for miles around trying to catch us."

George said, "I didn't know Pa waz here."

Sanders nodded. "Yer pa were a fighter, yessiree. But we shoulda never been in that mess in the first place. Twern't our fight."

George was slumped in his saddle. He straightened his back and shoulders. "I thought ya liked the War?"

"Don't like war a'tall. Fought 'cause we had to. Picked the Confederates 'cause Mr. Lincoln cut off our removal payments and pulled the troops outta Fort Gibson. Left us with no defense against the Osage. Then the Federals headed straight fer us."

George didn't like the Osage one bit. He said, "Damn the Osage," and spit.

Sanders nodded. "They waz purty bad. Never fought 'em myself, but heared tell. Best to avoid the Osage and war both when ya can." He glanced at the deerskin-wrapped body and winced. He'd hoped to get the younger ones raised up without killing.

George looked around at the charred foundations of buildings and then up at the vulture. "I wished we had us a rifle. I'd shoot that buzzard outta the sky."

Sanders shook his head. "Jist bring more of 'em in." He turned in his saddle and pulled Colbert's horse to him. He tried to wiggle Crow's boot. He said, "Still stiff. He'll soften up towards morning."

Sibling Rivalry

CONNELL HANDED HIS MOTHER A tumbler of whiskey. The glass felt warm. Check figured the liquor couldn't touch her thirst. She set it on the desk without a sip. They'd used a lot of ice on Hugh's leg during the day, and had packed on more for the night. But Check had felt hot all along. She didn't know if that was a result of the weather, the events, or her stays. Or maybe it was the beginning of the change. It could be all of that together. But she was inclined to think it was entirely Hugh's fault. She said, "Who is this Colbert, anyway?"

Connell poured his own drink. "Just an Indian. I didn't know him. Just seen him around." He took more than a sip and sat down.

"Do you reckon your brother knew him?" Except to ask for food, Hugh had managed to stay incoherent or asleep since being brought in.

"Hard to tell. But not to my knowledge." That was sort of true. Connell knew Hugh frequented the bawdy house. Figured Colbert was a regular customer, too. He didn't need to tell his mother that at the moment. But he was thinking about telling her in the future. Hugh had no business getting himself shot. He was out running loose, doing things decent people oughtn't to do. Connell was sure of that. Though he didn't have the details. But Hugh disappeared too much during the day to be up to any good. And he was happy all the time. Also, he'd stopped using a towel at night. That was something Connell had never discussed with his brother, except to say "Stop that" every so often. He had the decency to use his towel when nobody was around, not in the bed next to Hugh's.

Check could tell Connell's mind had wandered off. She guessed he knew more than he was telling. "And you don't know how Colbert came to threaten your brother's life? Or in what way? Really, Connell?"

Connell's brow wrinkled. He tried to look serious and cooperative. "No, ma'am, I was here asleep, as you know. And I've told you everything Puny told me. I'll ride over to the Benges' tomorrow. Talk to Cowboy and Bob. Puny was awful tight-lipped."

Check wiped her brow with her handkerchief. "Generally, that's a good thing. But it's aggravating when taken to extremes." She wished she could take a bath in a tub of ice. "Where'd Puny go, anyway?"

"Back to the bawdy house. Ezell wouldn't let him stay."

"I don't blame her. We've been worried to death about him, and all along he's been down there serving up liquor." Check cleared her throat and glanced at her own glass. She wondered if there was a way to get her whiskey back in the bottle without going to the kitchen for a funnel.

Connell was quiet. He wanted to defend Puny. But he was mad at Hugh for getting himself in a position to need his life saved. It was clear as the nose on his face that Hugh had done something to get himself shot. Connell was determined to find out what. He could feel anger rising in his throat. Figured his face was turning red. He didn't want his mother to think he was mad at Puny. He said, "Puny helped Hugh. Let's don't forget that. And he came back with him. And faced up to Ezell and Lizzie. He's had *his* punishment." Connell hoped Hugh would get his, too. It slipped his mind that a bullet had gone through his brother's leg.

Check could read Connell's thoughts fairly clearly when it came to Hugh. The two were near in age, but not much alike. They'd never been close, but she held out hope for that to change. She knew from her own growing up that sibling rivalry could fade with a few years of maturity. But she wished, maybe for the thousandth time, that her own brothers and sisters hadn't been split by the War. Wished her brothers hadn't died so young and so needlessly. She said, "Well, Hugh's been punished. Let's go to bed." She looked again at her whiskey. She opened a desk drawer, brought out a small notebook, and set it on top of the glass.

Hugh's Dream

AT THE HITICHI FORD, GEORGE and Sanders were too exhausted to dream. Check, fretting over Andrew and Hugh, never fell into sleep deeply enough for phantoms to arise. Connell had his usual erotic visions. But, in the middle of the night, Hugh had an uncommon dream, or maybe a hallucination. Four hooded horsemen rode through the potatoes towards him. In front of them was fire. Behind them, wind. They stopped in front of Hugh and addressed him.

The first horseman was faceless. From somewhere around his head came a voice: "Hugh Singer, the Lord doesn't like whoring. It's filled with worms and rot." He extended his arm. Pointed his trigger finger straight at Hugh's heart.

The second horseman's body was as wavy as water. But fire shot from his mouth. He said, "There's many a dead man in the bayou. You could be food for catfish and carp."

The third horseman had the face of a crow. His eyes were beady, his shoulders hunched, his beak sharp. He leaned back in his saddle. Turned his face to the sky. Cawed three times.

The fourth horseman wore a hood. He ripped it off. Underneath was the face of a rabbit. Its eyes blinked, its nose twitched, its mouth made soft, smacking noises. Hugh couldn't distinguish words, and yelled, "What?" But the rabbit turned its horse, and they hopped away through the potatoes. Puffs of dust that rose in the air behind them drifted onto the other three horsemen. They disappeared into the ground. The wind whipped the fire into the sky.

Hugh woke up in a sweat. A figure in white was at the foot of his bed. Hugh screamed. The figure said, "Don't try to stand. And don't wake your father."

Alabama Dishes

CHECK DIDN'T GET MUCH SLEEP. But early the next morning, she drove her buggy towards the Bushyheads' house. Although Alabama was a Lowrey cousin, her branch of the family had married into Germans for two generations. That dilution left her with auburn hair, lighter skin than most of her neighbors', and a need to cover up in the sun. When Check found her, she was in her flowerbed in long sleeves and a bonnet. But by the time Check disembarked, Alabama was bareheaded. They embraced and brushed cheeks. Alabama noted that Check looked tired. She asked after Andrew. Then she took Check to the kitchen and offered refreshments. They settled on coffee, and Alabama poured some from a kettle into a silver pot. Check carried the pot, and Alabama carried china cups on a silver tray to the front porch.

After they took rockers, Check said, "I guess you've heard the news about Hugh."

"Some of it. How is he?"

"Restless. And in pain. But he'll mend. I need to know what happened. And who was involved. Everybody at the farm is as buttoned up as winter coats." She didn't ask a question, but it hung in the air.

Alabama poured into Check's cup and then into hers. She set the pot down before she spoke. "I'm not sure Dennis will want me to tell you."

Check looked at her over her glasses.

Alabama picked her cup up. "Martin Benge says Sanders killed that Colbert man with a knife to the stomach. When his intestines spilled out, according to Martin, they found three rocks the size of goose eggs. And some undigested bones and feathers." She took a sip and wrinkled her nose like the coffee tasted bitter. "I don't believe that part."

"I don't believe that either. Intestines eat feathers up."

Alabama nodded. "Although Creeks do have peculiar eating habits."

"Was he a Creek?" Check leaned forward.

"Yes. You didn't know that?"

"No." Check set her cup down. She leaned back. Put a hand to her chest. "Thank goodness."

"I'm sorry. I should've told that first. That was stupid of me." The Cherokee courts didn't have jurisdiction over the death of a Creek. When the parties were of different tribes, the federal judge in Fort Smith took jurisdiction. But random killings of people who weren't white or of means never interested those judges.

Check blew out hard. "It's not stupid. It's a stroke of luck. I can't face a trial. I'm sure Hugh was up to no good." She picked her coffee cup up. She felt relieved, but was also fishing for more information.

Alabama knew Hugh had been up to no good. But she was Cherokee enough not to have led with that information. She took another sip before she said, "I heard the woman was killed, too."

"What woman?"

Alabama winced.

Check had tamped her temper as she'd matured. But it could still flare like a kerosene torch. And she'd envisioned an argument over cards. Or anger fueled by alcohol. She hadn't reckoned on a woman. She set her cup on its saucer with a clatter. "I'll skin him alive! I swear I will!"

Alabama reached for Check's arm. "Check, you know how boys are. It's perfectly natural." Her mind shot to her own son. The Cherokee seminaries forbade even kissing. She hoped Johnny was bent over his studies. Hoped he wouldn't develop an interest in girls for another couple of years.

Alabama withdrew her hand. Check stood and moved to the edge of the porch. She could feel herself trembling, but didn't know if it was from fear or anger. Hugh could just as easily be dead. That possibility loomed large in her head. But a new thought crept up like a shadow: Andrew knew only that Hugh had hurt his leg. She'd tried to imply it was from a fall off his horse. It might be difficult to keep Andrew from finding out that a woman had been killed. There could be an investigation. Before Check, the Grand River ran muddy from rain farther north.

Alabama rose and stood beside Check. They watched the river without speaking. Eventually, Check said, "I don't guess we're lucky enough for the woman to be a Creek, too?"

"No." Alabama sighed. "She was a white."

"Good Lord. That's terrible." Check didn't consider the loss of a white life worse than the loss of an Indian one. But she, like Ezell, didn't know anything about the new judge who'd just taken the bench in Fort Smith. If the news reached him, the killing of a white woman could well perk up his ears.

"Dennis has gone to visit Bell Rogers," Alabama said. Bell was the sheriff for the Illinois District.

Check said, "I know him just to speak."

Alabama was younger than Check, and had never been in the old Eastern Nation. But, though the clans had been abandoned before her birth, she could recall who belonged to which, and the all-important Cherokee kinships were crocheted in her mind. She embraced Check's shoulders. "He's Sanders' first cousin."

Check sighed. "That'll help. Did Sanders knife the woman, too?"

Alabama shook her head. "She was shot. Let's take a walk."

The two left the china and silver behind on the porch. They crossed the lawn and went towards the river.

Bell Begins His Investigation

BY THE SPRING OF 1875, Bell Rogers was an old man. But he was over six feet tall and still black-headed. His hair was cut short for an Indian, and his face, particularly his eyes and jaw, resembled Sanders'. Standing in front of the bawdy house, he was wearing black trousers, a blue shirt, and suspenders. His holster sat close to his waist, and he held a cowboy hat in one hand. In answer to his question, Puny pointed to a mound of dirt about twenty feet from the bayou stream. "That's her there."

"And you fellas buried her yerselves?"

Puny and Jake Perkins both said, "Yes, sir."

"Well, dig her up."

Jake said, "We jist buried her this morning."

Puny said, "The shovel's in the house." He jerked a thumb that direction.

Bell looked at the stump Puny had previously favored. "I'll wait right'cher." He put his hat on his head and a hand on the wood. He eased onto the seat, extended his legs, and crossed them at the ankles.

Puny had brought the shovel from the farm the previous evening. He'd found Jake alone on the porch, and Claudette's body inside where it'd fallen. Rather than dig the hole while they were exhausted, they left the body where it was, dragged pallets down from the loft, and shut the doors to the room. They bedded down on the porch, not expecting visitors because everybody for miles around knew the house would be closed. But in the middle of the night, Puny awakened to sounds. Not human ones. Four pairs of yellow eyes glared at him from the dark. He fumbled his gun from his holster. Fired a shot that jarred Jake awake. But the proprietor had taken on so much liquor for his grief that he rolled over and went back to sleep. Puny stayed sitting up until he was sure the wolves weren't creeping back.

When Puny returned with the shovel, Bell was whittling a stick and Jake was sitting on a clump of weeds, staring at the trees of the bayou, spitting tobacco. Puny went straight to the grave and pushed the blade into the dirt.

Bell said, "Hold her right'cher."

Puny stopped with his foot on the shovel. "I thought ya wanted her dug up?"

"I wanted to see if she waz in that grave. If somebody else waz in there, ya would've run off."

Puny moved his foot to the ground and scratched his chin. He'd never understand Indians.

Bell threw his stick away and drew a foot up close to the stump. He rested an elbow on that thigh and waved his knife as he talked. "Now, you say this here Sanders Cordery waz defending this young fella, Singer?"

Puny said, "Yes, sir." Jake nodded and spat again.

"And this Colbert had a gun to Singer's throat?"

"More to his head, or maybe his ear, I reckon," Puny said.

"And Cordery, he jist walked in and said, 'Gi'me some liquor'?"

Puny nodded. "Sompthing like that."

"Then Crow pointed his gun at Cordery," Jake interjected. He pushed himself up.

"And Cordery didn't have a gun?" Bell scratched his cheek with his knife.

"No, sir. He done give his to George Sixkiller to shoot out the lamp." Puny hung an elbow over the shovel's shaft.

Bell ducked his head to hide his smile. When his face was straight, he looked up. "Well, who shot this woman?"

Jake said, "We reckon Colbert did."

Puny said, "Yes, sir. Colbert done it."

"And y'all know that with the lights out?" Bell looked perplexed.

Puny ran his hands down the front of his pants. "Only one shot gone from Mr. Cordery's gun."

"And George Sixkiller had it all the time?"

"Yes, sir. As far as I know. I wasn't really paying him much attention."

"Who else had a gun?"

"Ever'body," Jake said.

Bell tapped his teeth together. Then he said, "And the only gunless man in the room saved Singer's life and killed Colbert?" He rubbed his neck with his knife like he was shaving. Puny and Jake looked at each other. Neither said anything. Eventually, Bell took his knife from his neck and said, "Well, did ever'body else have their guns up their butt-holes?"

Puny and Jake both looked at the ground. Didn't know whether to laugh or not. Puny spoke first. "Well, sir, we waz all afraid Colbert would shoot Hugh Singer if anybody moved."

Bell looked off into the trees. He studied them like he was preparing for a test. Then he looked at his suspects. "Well, I can feature that . . . if Colbert caught Singer fucking his woman."

"Weren't his woman," Jake quickly interjected. He spat again.

"She were the woman of the house. That right, Jake?" Bell cleaned under his thumbnail with his knife.

"Yeah. Claudette. You knowed her."

Bell shook his head. "Well, I don't rightly know her. I'm a little old for that. But I heared tell of her." Bell cleaned another nail. "So Singer was giving her the bizness?"

Puny and Jake looked at each other again. Puny said, "Yes, sir." Jake coughed and spat.

Bell looked up. "Yer sure? I got other sources I can ask."

Puny said, "Yes, sir. I'm sure." He jutted his jaw.

Bell looked towards Jake. Jake swung his leg back and kicked a small rock into the air. He said, "Damn it all to hell."

Bell stuck his knife in a sheath on his belt, put both hands on his knees, and stood up. He sighed, took off his hat, and tapped his thigh with it. He looked at Puny. "Where'd Cordery go with Colbert's body?"

Puny jerked his head. "Over to the Creek Nation."

"To the Berryhills?" Bell asked.

Puny frowned. He looked to Jake. Jake said, "I don't know what he done. I stayed here, by myself, with Claudette's body. I couldn't have did it without liquor." He flapped a hand in the air. "They all went away."

Puny shook his head. When Jake was sober enough to talk, he whined about being left with Claudette's body. Puny was tired of hearing it, but didn't think he could get Jake to stop. He was hoping to get away from him. Puny said to Bell, "Mr. Cordery didn't say where he waz going. He ain't high on explaining hisself."

Bell looked off towards the bayou and nodded. He tapped his thigh with his hat again. Then he said, "Either one of you suckers got a drop of Cherokee blood in ya?"

They both shook their heads.

Bell looked at Puny. "You ain't even a Freedman, are ya?" The freed slaves of the Cherokees were officially citizens of the Nation.

Puny said, "I ain't never been a slave."

"Ya work fer the Singers, that right?"

"Yes, sir. I come here with them."

Bell looked at Jake. "And you, Mr. Perkins, are trespassing here, and selling illegal liquor to Indians?"

Jake shifted his weight from one scrawny leg to the other. He opened his mouth, then clamped his teeth tight.

Bell put his hat on with one hand and pulled his gun out with the other. He drew its hammer back slowly. "Both of ya. Put yer hands up. Let's go." He jerked his head towards the bawdy house.

Puny had figured he'd get arrested before the questioning was over. He just hoped he wouldn't be thrown in jail with Jake. His employer's character, which had been middling mean, had taken a turn for the worse since the shootings. Puny had seen some goodness in Jake, and he hoped it would come back; but he didn't want to still be around when it did. He was filled to the gills with the whole situation. If he had anywhere to go, he'd be headed in that direction. As it was, it looked like he'd be spending time in jail. He hoped he'd have a decent bed. One night of sleeping in the dogtrot, bitten by mosquitoes and looking out at wolves, was enough. He raised his hands, and so did Jake.

Bell marched them up the bawdy house steps onto the porch. Both doors to the left room were open. When Puny and Jake got to the front one, Bell said, "Hold her right'cher." He came up behind them and took their guns. He put Puny's in the front of his pants, holstered his own, and held Jake's. He said, "Move over there towards the trot. If ya so much as scratch yer balls, I'll shoot ya. Indians watch out of the sides of their eyes. Don't ferget that."

Puny and Jake stepped towards the trot, and Bell looked into the room. He counted fifteen barrels, some stacked on top of others. He said, "Are they all full?"

Jake said, "I can tell ya, if ya let me come closer."

Bell jerked his gun, turned its nose to the spot he'd let Jake move to. When Jake could see into the room, he lowered one of his hands and pointed. "They's full, except fer that one, and that one, and that one." He pointed to another. "That'un's about half full."

Bell said, "That's good to know. Step back." He raised Jake's gun, aimed towards the bottom of one of the barrels, and shot. Liquor spurted out. He aimed at another, and another. The shots were loud and bounced off the walls. The smell of burnt lead and whiskey drifted out onto the porch. Bell changed guns and shot some more. Jake squatted and put his hands over his ears. He jerked with each shot. Finally, he lowered his butt to the boards, hunkered into a ball, and whimpered.

Hugh Revives

WHEN CHECK RETURNED FROM ALABAMA'S, she unhooked 'Wassee from the buggy, slapped her flank, and sent her to the field. She walked to the house itching to slap Hugh's flank as well. She would've

MARGARET VERBLE

slammed the front door if Andrew hadn't been ill. Would've yelled "Hugh Morgan Singer!" at the top of her lungs. Instead, she peeked in the sickroom and got quite a shock. Hugh was in bed next to his father. His back was against the headboard, his legs over the covers. He was holding the Bible. Check sputtered.

Hugh said, "Good morning, Mama. It's still morning, isn't it?"

Andrew said, "Hugh's voice is strong, but he's hurt his leg." His fingers flickered over Hugh's thigh.

Check huffed three times. Then she said, "Don't tire your father."

"I won't, Mama. He has a longing to hear the Bible. It's pretty good, too, isn't it, Papa? Listen to this: 'Though I speak with the tongues of men and of angels . . .'"

Check reached far enough into the room to grab the doorknob. She shut the door. She was even more infuriated than she'd been before. She went to the study. Shut that door, too. She hoped deep breaths would help her regain her composure. She tried not to think about what she wanted to do to Hugh. She focused on Connell instead. Hoped he'd get home from the Benges' so she could hear what he'd learned.

She thumbed through ledgers while she waited. But Connell didn't show. So she steeled herself, turned the knob, and looked out. Almost directly across the hall, the door to the winter kitchen was open. Ezell was bent over a washtub. Her arms were soapy to the elbows. Lizzie was lifting a sheet from the rinsing tub. Steering it through a wringer. Check stopped in the doorway. "When did Hugh Singer get so perky?"

Ezell said, "Waked up thaterway. Ate six eggs fer breakfast. Begged extra biscuits outta me." She ran a forearm across her forehead. It left a white track.

"When is Connell coming back?"

Ezell found that question odd. Everybody knew Connell didn't report to her. But she saw Check was upset. She wished she could help. She said, "It oughta be soon."

Connell's Scouting

CONNELL WAS ON HIS WAY home. By the crow, the Benges lived less than six miles from the Singers, and not much more by the road. But Connell had heard things from Cowboy that had embarrassed and infuriated him in equal measure. So he was riding slow. For the first half of the trip, he pictured Hugh with his pants down around his boots, his penis in his hand, crying in front of a room of men. That sickened Connell to his core. He wouldn't be able to look any man in the face without wondering if he'd seen Hugh's floppy dick, heard him wail like a baby.

Then another image invaded: Claudette unbuttoning Hugh's pants, slipping her hand in, her fingertips touching his skin. Her palm closing around his shaft, squeezing and pulling, squeezing and pulling, squeezing and pulling. Connell's own penis started to pulse. It wiggled. Bulged against his buttons. Bumped his saddle horn. That infuriated him more. He focused on Florence; she wouldn't help him out, wouldn't touch him at all, barely pressed up against him. But she expected him to stay as pure as newly churned butter. The whole situation made Connell crazy, and miserable in his saddle.

He jerked his reins and rode off the road to behind a tree. He looked up and down the highway. He was alone out there. He stood in his stirrups, unbuttoned his pants, and pulled out his member. It was straight up. But he couldn't point it to where he wouldn't mess on himself or his saddle. And his pants were down around his hips. He tried stuffing his tool back in. But he was well hung and, by then, huge; he couldn't get it to fit. And he was in such a state of excitement, he was afraid, if he touched himself much more, he'd shoot off accidentally. He cupped his hand over his dick's head and tried picturing Nash Taylor's face. It usually dissolved his desire. But instead, an image of lace on a dress's sleeve invaded Connell's mind. The lace was delicate and delicious. Connell licked his lips. He licked them again. He couldn't stop licking. And he could feel the effect it was having. But by then, he didn't have control over his imagination, his lips, or his dick. He came quite fast in the cup of his hand.

At first, he felt enormous relief. But his palm was sticky. He wiped his mess on the horse's mane. The horse snorted. Connell pulled his trousers up in the back, but he was still too swollen to button them. He awkwardly dismounted, waddled over to a different tree, and pulled off some low-hanging leaves. He cleaned up with them and dropped them to the ground. He watched the road until his dick finally shrunk. He tucked it back in and buttoned up. But a spot on the front of his pants looked obvious. It made Connell mad all over again.

He was examining the spot and cussing his brother when he heard a rumble. He looked towards the road, grabbed his reins, and hid behind the tree. The rumble grew louder and louder, and then it passed. Connell peeked out and saw the stagecoach rolling down the road. Its whip waved in its stand like a banner. The coach receded in the distance, disappeared in a cloud of dust. He took a deep breath and checked his pants again. There was a stream not far away. He could ride over there and douse his whole front with water. He'd need a story. Or maybe a bigger spot would dry in an even, broad way that wouldn't be noticeable. Connell had never paid much attention to the problem of spots, and didn't know what his pants would look like when he got through with his plan. But he figured they'd look better with a wide spot than with a little one in its particular position. He remounted and headed towards the stream.

As he rode, his mind went back to the stagecoach's whip. He'd like to beat Hugh's back and rear end with it. Not only had his penis been out in public in the hands of a whore, he'd worked it in front of a whole room of men and bawled like an infant. Connell's mind went to the story being told all over the Nation. His parents — his little brothers — would be laughingstocks. Hugh had violated them all by showing himself like a fullblood who could walk around half naked, cock big, and laugh about it. Only worse, Hugh couldn't get swollen at the point of a gun. Every man in the Nation would think the Singer men had droopy dicks. Connell thought about the situation over and over. With each repetition, he felt more humiliated.

He hadn't gotten over his ire by the time he got back to the farm. And after visiting the stream, the spot on his trousers looked like he'd pissed himself. One of the hands gave him a puzzled expression. Connell said, "Turned a dipper of water over on me." The hand made a *sic* noise and went back to nailing a new board to a fence. That embarrassed and infuriated Connell even more. He turned back to the barn.

Only his horse, a cow, and a sickly calf were in there. He went to the furthest stall, near the back wall. In it, an old saddle was sitting on a sawhorse. At times, he'd favored in a sexual way. But Connell didn't feel sexy, just angry. Old reins and bits were hanging on the wall of the stall. He lifted a set from a hook. Unlatched the reins from the bit. He wrapped the ends of the bands around his hand. Took a few steps towards the saddle and swung the reins like a whip. Leather cracked against leather. It sounded good in his ears. He swung the reins again. That crack sounded even better.

Connell wore out his fury on the seat of the saddle, loitered in the barn until after supper, and ate leftovers in the kitchen. All the time, he was working on a story to tell his mother, and on getting his expression to match his words. When he and Check were finally conferring in the study, the house was quiet and Hugh was asleep in the hallway. Connell said, "All I know is that Colbert was drunk. He pointed a gun at Sanders. And that young Indian with Sanders shot the light out. Then Sanders attacked Colbert in the dark."

Check turned the lamp wick up to see Connell better. "That's all there was to it?" She'd gotten more information from Alabama.

"Yes, ma'am." Connell felt like his eyes were wide enough to look innocent.

Check studied his expression. His mouth looked like it had a bit in it. She sipped her brandy, sat the glass down, and drummed her fingers on the desk. There was no use letting Connell think she didn't know he was lying. On the other hand, she had five boys; she didn't necessarily want to know all of the truth all of the time. She was torn about how far to pursue the story. She said, "Do you think Cowboy told you everything?"

Connell's jaw muscles worked at the temples. "Yes, ma'am. I do."

"Well, I don't." Check hoped she sounded more suspicious and wise than annoyed and tired.

Connell upended his whiskey and wiped his mouth with the back of his hand. "Hard to say exactly what happened."

"I'd lay money on that."

Connell cocked his head. He turned towards the door. Check said, "What is it?" Connell turned back and whispered, "I thought I heard Hugh stirring, that's all." He frowned. "Maybe we should continue this conversation on another occasion." He rose from his chair. "I'm tired, anyway."

Check didn't know what to say. She hadn't heard a noise, and suspected Connell hadn't either. However, he was probably right about needing more privacy. Not that it seemed he was going to tell her anything. Check closed a ledger on the desk. It was just as well that they all went to bed. What she might hear that late could keep her awake. She was up four or five times a night as it was. She was tired in her bones. Tired in her heart.

Some Comfort

AS CONVERSATION IN THE BIG house's study concluded, in Ezell's cabin another continued. The lamp by the bed was lit. Ezell was in her nightgown. Lizzie in one of Ezell's that swallowed her. They were on the bed, and Lizzie's head was on Ezell's shoulder, nestled on her tresses. Ezell's arms encircled the girl. Lizzie whimpered and sniffled. Ezell said, "Hush now, ya hear? It's gonna be all right. Lots of women bleeds for a while. It's the Lord's way of protecting ya."

Lizzie raised her head. "Protecting me from what?"

"From men poking ya after ya give birth."

Lizzie shifted her weight. She wiped her tears with her sleeve. "Ain't never thought 'bout that."

Neither had Ezell. But it made sense as soon as she said it. Men couldn't think about anything but poking. Surely God had figured out a way to give women some relief. Ezell had faith in the Lord's goodness.

Nevertheless, rather than pray over it, she resolved to ask Check how to stop the bleeding. "It's the truth," she said.

Lizzie slid off the bed and blew her nose on a rag. "Well, when it stops, I'z going to the Canadian District."

Ezell studied the young woman. Then put a hand to her head and gathered up her hair. She pulled a ribbon from the bedside table and bound her tresses back. She didn't like the idea of Lizzie leaving, but would feel odd saying so. She said, "What's so special 'bout that district?"

Lizzie flopped down on the foot of the bed. Tucked her toes under her gown. Her eyes looked less miserable. Crinkles of smile crept into her cheeks. "My fambly's got a farm down there. We work fer ourselves. My mama's there. And my daddy. And my little sister and brother."

Ezell frowned. "Well, if it's so special, why'd ya leave?"

Lizzie rubbed the tip of her nose with her palm. She shook her head. "'Cause I waz young and stupid."

"Well, girl, you can say that again. What's his name?"

Lizzie's chin went in. "How'd ya knowed it waz a man?"

"Couldn't be nothing else. Girls don't leave their families to follow the cows. Only boys is dumb enough fer that."

Both women giggled. Lizzie fingered a button. "His name waz Ferdinand."

"Oh, girl, you're lying." Ezell giggled again and waved her hand. "Nobody's got that kinda name."

"He did, I'm telling ya." Lizzie sat up straight and tried to look proper. "He waz a Portuguese."

"A white man?" Ezell rolled her eyes.

"No!" Lizzie frowned. "A Portuguese from Africa."

"Portugal ain't in Africa. It's in Europe. That's where them white explorers came from. I learnt it in school."

"Well, he said he waz from Portugal."

Ezell felt sorry for the girl. But also felt relieved. At least Puny hadn't been her first. "Well, maybe they's Negro men in Portugal. We didn't read too much 'bout 'em."

Lizzie's eyes brightened. "Let's go to Portugal and find out."

Ezell laughed. "How we gonna get to Portugal, girl? That's crazy."

Lizzie laughed, too. "We'll find the gold at the fort. We'll go together. Dress in fine clothes. Have Indians wait on us."

Ezell leaned against the headboard and smiled. She saw what attracted Puny to Lizzie. She reminded her of herself, but younger. She wondered how Lizzie had gotten off to such a bad start. But decided that was none of her business. And asking would just open sores. The future was important, not the past. Ezell said, "We ain't going nowhere but to bed. We gotta get up with the dang rooster. Dampen that light and lie down. And don't be rolling to my side in yer sleep."

Reckonings the Next Morning

CHECK WAS CARRYING ANDREW'S TRAY out the back door as Hugh was hobbling from the outhouse on Dr. Howard's crutches. Booty was with him, tail wagging and whining. She squeezed between his leg and a crutch. Hugh hopped once, twice, then fell over. Check set down the tray with a clang. When she got to Hugh, he was pulling himself up by a crutch. She said, "Just stay where you are, Hugh Morgan Singer."

"Mama, how are ya?" Hugh let go of the crutch and lay with his forearms on the ground.

"I've been better."

Hugh smiled. "Could ya move a bit, Mama? The sun's right behind ya. You look like a big bear."

Booty sniffed Hugh's bandage. Check didn't budge. "I want to know why Sanders killed that man."

Hugh lowered his eyes. He'd known this was coming. Connell had already said he wasn't doing his dirty work for him. Those were the only few words they'd spoken since he'd been shot. Hugh shook his head and looked up. "Mama, Colbert pointed a gun at him. He was defending himself."

"That's not what I'm asking, and you know it."

Hugh reclined completely. Crossed his good leg over the hurt one at the ankle, spread out both arms, and looked up at the sky. His chest was in Check's shadow. His head in the sun. He closed his eyes. "Mama, I've confessed my sins to the Lord. Please spare me from burdening my mother."

Check tapped her foot. Hugh could wiggle his way out of a snake hole. She was used to his tricks. On the other hand, she expected her boys to grow up to be men. And there was something about Hugh's evasions that was deeply familiar. She said, "You could've been killed."

"Life's fleeting, Mama."

Check harrumphed and looked towards the river. She lived that truth every day. She hoped her sons wouldn't. She wished she could protect them more, felt like she hadn't done enough. That feeling of failure nestled tight in her throat. She touched her locket. At least so far, the lives of her living children had been easier than hers. She hoped they'd remain that way; that fresh earth and good crops would be their inheritance, that killing and war would stay far away. She looked down at Hugh. "That may be, but I want you to have a good run."

At that moment, a shadow crossed Hugh's face. He sensed it, and opened his eyes. Check looked up. A hawk was gliding over. The sky was bright, light, and blue. Check looked again towards the river. She felt its flow in her body. Thought she heard its roar. She bent and extended her hand. "Here, let me help you up."

"I'll topple you, Mama. Hold a crutch steady." Hugh held one up to her. She steadied it while he climbed upright.

Hugh felt better, but couldn't go anywhere, ride, or work, and he hoped to avoid Ezell. He hobbled behind his mother, watching the ground between his legs as he walked. When he got to the porch, he sat down on a step and called Booty to him. He scratched her head hard.

RIDING ON THE LANE THROUGH the potatoes, Bell felt every one of his sixty-eight years. His rear end hurt all the way up to his shoulders, and his horse, in his mind, wasn't easing that any. Bell wished he'd taken his buggy. But a sheriff riding around like a woman wasn't all that impressive. Ahead, on the back porch, the Singer boy's leg was stuck out on a straight-backed chair, and Miz Singer was surrounded by young ones. Clothes were flapping on the line. A dog was in the yard looking his way, two puppies around her. Chickens were pecking the ground. Smoke curling from the kitchen's chimney. It was a peaceful-looking setting. A sharp pain spiked up the sheriff's back. He shifted in his saddle and slowed his horse.

"Who's that coming, Mama?" Hugh's hurt leg was pointed towards the road. He picked up Paul and set him on his good one.

Check turned around in her seat. "Can't make it out." She hoped it wasn't Puny. Lizzie was in the cabin with ice packed between her legs. Ezell was fixing dinner. Puny would stir her up like a nest of hornets. The hands wouldn't get their food on time.

Clifford laid his slate down and jumped to the porch's edge. Jenny and Otter stopped counting pebbles. When the rider got closer, Jenny said, "It's Bell."

"Bell who?" Cliff asked.

Jenny glanced towards Hugh, suddenly embarrassed. When Bell visited with them, it was to gossip or fish with her father. But even she knew Hugh had been in trouble down at the bad place on the bayou. Coop had told her all about it. "Sheriff Rogers," she mumbled.

Hugh ducked his head. Paul's fingers pulled on his buttons. Check stood. She said, "Jenny, greet Mr. Rogers and bring him up here. Then you and Clifford take Otter and Paul to the front porch."

Clifford said, "But Mama . . ."

"Do as I say, Clifford, or I'll send you back to school in the morning." Check stepped off the porch. She headed to the summer kitchen, not looking back nor towards the sheriff. The two puppies followed her.

After Bell was seated with Hugh and the children had disappeared, Check emerged from the kitchen, carrying a tray holding a pitcher of buttermilk and some glasses. She crossed the yard carefully and stopped at the bottom of the steps. "Good morning, Sheriff. I have some refreshments."

"Morning, Miz Singer. Don't mind if I do."

With first sips, they talked about the weather. They agreed the crops needed more rain. After that, Bell commented on the puppies. They were marked by nature, not breeding; but cute and roly-poly. Two had disappeared, and Check was planning to give one to Bert, to keep at the ferry. So she still had a spare, and drowning was beginning to seem inconvenient. She asked Bell if he knew anybody who needed a dog. Bell said he'd keep his eye open for prospects, and asked about Andrew's health. Check said he was ill enough that she was letting Clifford miss school, but that he'd had a good night, though he was concerned about Hugh. Hugh adjusted his leg, looked at his toes, and bent them. Bell took a long drink of buttermilk and let out a sigh of appreciation. He sat his glass down. "Now, Miz Singer, normally I wouldn't question a feller in front of his mother."

Hugh said, "She doesn't mind leaving. Do ya, Mama?"

"But in this case," Bell continued, "it's about one of your employees, name of Puny Tower."

Check and Hugh both started. Almost in unison, they said, "What about him?"

"Well, I've got him and Jake Perkins in jail. Jake's here illegally, and has been engaged in an illegal trade. I'm gonna run him out of the Nation when I git back to town. But I'm not sure what to do with Puny. He sez he's been working for you, Miz Singer. But seems to me he's been tending bar at the bawdy house."

"He came with Mr. Singer and me to the Nation. We pay the fee on him. But he's had a patch of trouble lately."

"What kind of trouble?"

Check cleared her throat. "Woman trouble. The usual kind."

Bell frowned. "Seems like woman trouble's going around." He looked off into the potatoes.

After a pause, Check said, "It does seem that way, Sheriff. Have some more buttermilk." She filled Bell's glass. She turned the pitcher Hugh's way, but he was examining his toes and his glass had hardly been touched.

Bell took a long drink. Then both he and Check rocked for a while. Hugh watched clothes flap in the breeze. A rooster came near the porch, made a run at a chicken, and scared the puppies away. A large toad hopped onto the lowest step.

Finally, Hugh said, "Puny didn't do anything. He was just an inno-cent bystander."

Bell studied the potatoes more. Check took an interest in the toad.

Hugh moved his leg with his hands. "He held me down while Sand-ers burned my wound. And he helped Sanders clean up the mess and gut Colbert's body. I'll come get him myself as soon as I can ride in a wagon."

Bell sighed. In his time, he'd seen a lot of friendship and a lot of be-trayal. He'd lost count of murders he'd probed, and had a pain migrating up his back to his head. He said, "He's been a good friend to ya, Mr. Singer?"

"Yes, sir, the best."

Bell studied the potatoes again. They were young plants, waving in the wind, hopeful and tender. He said, "I been looking fer a way to close that bawdy house without making ever' man in the Nation mad. You've been right helpful to me, young man. But I don't ever want any more killing 'cause of ya. Ya understand?"

"Yes, sir, I do." Hugh felt hot all the way to his uncovered toes.

Bell looked at Check. "Reckon when Sanders is coming back thiser-way?"

"He didn't say. But he'll probably cross on the ferry. I can have the new ferryman tell him to come see you."

Bell drained his glass, picked up his hat from the porch, and stood. "I'd be much obliged if you do. I'll let yer hand outta jail."

Check said, "Thank you, Sheriff. Won't you stay for dinner?"

"No, thank you. My daughter overfed me this morning."

Check then asked Bell to stay twice more. Nobody in the Nation would accept until the third invitation. But Bell turned those down, too, and Check walked him to his horse.

On the way, Bell said, "I admired DSϴᎶW, Miz Singer." Bell had been an Old Settler. He left the East before Check was born. But he fought in the War with her brother Ruff, and, like everyone, knew she was Gideon Morgan's daughter. He'd used her father's Indian name.

"Thank you, Mr. Rogers. He was certainly a warrior. But we're in your family's debt. I understand Sanders is your first cousin."

"We claim each other. He's the son of one of my mother's baby brothers. Came to us at the end of the Trail. Hunkered fer a couple of years."

Check looked into Bell's lean face. Saw what Sanders would look like in a decade or so. She said, "Would you also be kin to a friend of my father's, Captain Alexander Sanders?"

Bell's face broke into a smile. "Yes, ma'am. I would. Uncle Alex taught me how to use a gun and a tomahawk, both." He shook his head. "Course, he was the best man in the tribe to do it. Not ever'body could use a tomahawk like he could."

Both Check and Bell had given recent thought to the death of Chief Doublehead. And each knew the other one had, too. The manner of the chief's death was known all over the Nation, handed down generation to generation. They smiled an understanding without exchanging a word. Then Check said, "Your uncle removed early, I recall."

"Yes, ma'am. He came to us in the Arkansas Territory. He were married to my mother's sister, Peggy. I waz living with my aunt Lucy and uncle Robert then. They waz full sister and brother to my own parents, and I liked them better. My own pa were somehow a Methodist, and I were jist wild. Aunt Peggy and Uncle Alex joined us fer many a year, next farm over. Then we all got ran out under the '28 treaty."

"What happened to your uncle Alex?"

"Well, course, he died. Would be 'bout a hundred if he twer alive today. Aunt Peggy were about the same age. They lived in Westville, here, and Tahlequah."

"What about their children?"

"They waz all grown. Most farming their own land. Some came with 'em. Later, moved over to Tahlequah with Aunt Peggy. Some stayed back in Arkansas. You know that treaty waz writ so that only Cherokees living north of the Arkansas River got land here. The ones living south didn't get nothing. The usual kind of gypping."

"So some of their children stayed in Arkansas?"

"Yeah, it were a wild time. Whites came in and kept ever'body drunk. Stole orchards, land, cattle, and houses. Lotta folks living south of the river moved on down into Arkansas or went to Texas. Those of us that lived on the north bank came on."

Check shook her head. "It's a miracle this tribe has stayed together."

Bell nodded. "A tribeless Indian is a miserable creature. No reason to live." He looked off to the east and the mountains. Loneliness overtook him.

Check saw the softness in Bell's face from the sides of her eyes. And she well knew how it felt to be an Indian without a tribe. She said, "If you don't mind, before you leave, I'd like to introduce you to our new ferryman and ask your opinion on him."

BERT HAD BEEN WATCHING FOR Jenny to bring food when he saw Miz Singer and a tall, lean old man walking down the bank towards him. He felt disappointed, but forced a smile.

When they got to the landing, Check said, "How's business today, Bert?"

"Ain't been too good, Miz Singer. Only took one trip acrost."

"You haven't seen Mr. Cordery, Jenny's father, have you?"

"Wouldn't knowed him if I had. Never met him."

"Didn't he come by here a couple of days ago with an Indian boy and a body?"

Bert's head jerked. "Yes, ma'am. A man with a body crossed here on Sunday. Didn't know he were Jenny's father."

Check said to Bell, "Mr. Rogers, our ferryman is new to the Nation. He doesn't know many people. Name of Bert Vann." Then to Bert, she said, "This is Sheriff Rogers, Mr. Cordery's cousin."

Bert was startled to meet a sheriff. It made him nervous, even though he hadn't done any wrong. He wondered if the sheriff was hunting Jenny's father. But Miz Singer had just said they were cousins, and she was talking about a body like it was a calf. He said, "Howdy, sir. Do ya want to go across?"

Check said, "Come on up here, Bert."

Bert walked a plank from the ferry to the rocks, watching his steps until he got to within five feet of the adults. Then he turned his head and gazed off upriver.

Bell looked the boy over like he was a horse for sale. His memory shot back to his boyhood. To a cousin he'd often hunted with. Ellis. This boy was Ellis's spitting image. He smiled. "I ain't going anywhere today, son, but you can take me acrost some other day. You ain't kin to Rich Joe Vann, are ya?"

Bert glanced towards the sheriff, ducked his head, and smiled. "Don't think so. But I oughta be. Ever'body asks me about him."

"Where you from, boy?"

"Arkansas. 'Round Malvern. Orphaned in the War."

Bell looked over Bert's head, downriver. He took a long breath. "I'm sorry to hear that, son. What brings ya to the Nation?"

"Jist looking for my mama's folks. She told me to find 'em. Said they waz in a couple of different places. The nearest one were in the bend of the Arkansas River, below the three forks."

"What's their names, son?"

"I'm thinking now it's Sanders. That were Mama's maiden name. The ones farther up north carry yer name, Rogers."

"That's interesting. But there's a lotta Rogers in the Cherokee Nation. What waz yer mama's first name?"

"Her first name were Margaret."

Jailbird Talk

THE NATION HAD A NICE jail. But it was over in Tahlequah. Bell made do with the abandoned powder magazine at the fort. It was a square, sandstone block, twelve feet on a side. A hole in its wooden door was two feet off the ground and about an inch wide. Puny and Jake were in the magazine with the rheumy-eyed postmaster. They were sitting on the stones of the floor with their backs against the wall so they could see the ray of light coming in the hole.

The postmaster, Sam Garrett, was in jail for digging for gold beneath the foundation of the Bushyheads' house. It was the third time he'd done it, and Dennis and Alabama were fed up. Alabama's brother-in-law, Clem Rogers, was the son of Bell's double first cousin, so the Bushyheads were family to Bell — and he, too, had had more than enough of Garrett. Sam was an intruder in the Nation, and the sheriff figured they could find someone who could read and sort mail to replace him. He didn't completely understand how Sam had gotten the job in the first place. He blamed it on the army.

Sam said to his jail mates, "That damn Bushyhead's sitting right on that gold. I knowed it."

Jake said, "I heared there waz gold and silver both hid 'neath an old stump somewhere on the bayou. I dug up a bunch of stumps between them four forks. Never did find it." He shook his head.

Sam said, "There's an Injun at Manard who has a stick that can find stashes."

Puny said, "I don't believe that."

"Got it on high authority. Houston Benge told me." The Cherokees' government was based on the US model. Houston was one of the senators from the Illinois District.

"What'd he say 'bout him?" asked Jake.

"Why should I tell you? I don't even know ya." Sam had had the cell to himself for the first night he was in. He'd been happy to get company. But when the last drops of liquor left his bloodstream, he'd gotten grumpy.

"I was jist trying to have a little conversation. Ya don't have to be so touchy." Jake was sober himself, and sobriety didn't agree with his disposition any more than it did with Sam's. He didn't even have any tobacco on him. And the piss bucket in the corner was smelling just exactly like what it was.

Puny put a hand to a stone and got up. "Could you two stop acting like chil'run?"

Jake pushed himself up, too. He stumbled a bit in the dark, got his balance, and then put his eye to the peephole. After a moment, he said, "Well, I'll be damned. Look at that."

Sam said, "What're ya talking about?" He pushed up, fell against a wall, then tried to look out over Jake's shoulder.

Jake poked Sam's stomach with an elbow and pushed him back. "None of yer bizness. Dang! I ain't never seen nothing like it."

Sam shoved Jake and dislodged him from the hole. Jake shoved him back. The two white men got into a pushing match, though they could barely see one another. They cussed, and threw and missed a couple of punches. Puny didn't care if they beat each other to death. He didn't like Sam; he remembered the "Can't drink after a nigger" remark. And he'd had a gutful of Jake. He reached out towards both of them in the dark. He grabbed Sam by the collar and jerked him up. His other palm found Jake's chest. He said, "I'm gonna butt yer two heads together if ya don't sit down and shut up. We're trapped in here like moles in a tunnel. Try to have some consideration."

Sam said, "He started it, trying to hog the hole. Git your hand off my shirt, nigger."

Puny thought for an instant about Sanders' aunt strangling that wildcat. He could use his shirt. But that would get him hanged. And Sam wasn't worth losing his life for. He let him go with a push.

Jake said to Sam, "You started it by being so secretive 'bout the Injun. I don't believe a word ya have to say anyway." He turned his back to Sam. But the postmaster couldn't see well enough in the dark for that to have any effect.

They all sat back down. Jake first, in a corner, then Sam, against the back wall, and Puny between them. They were as far away from the piss bucket as they could get, and they were quiet for several minutes, each brooding on his own misfortune. Then Sam said, "Oh, all right, I'll tell it. But ya can't tell nobody I told ya."

Jake said, "Well, spit it out. Let's hear if it's worth telling."

Sam said, "Mr. Benge said Turtle Smith, the well-witcher, has a stick that'll witch stashes. Said he's witched up three or four. That's where he gets his money."

Puny said, "He gets his money from witching wells. He's witched ever' one in the bottoms and the bayou."

Sam said, "I don't care if ya don't believe me. But he uses that stick on stashes. Holds the single end, rather than the two ends."

Jake said, "That don't make no sense."

"Sure it do," Sam said. "One of them forks is fer gold, the other fer silver."

There was a silence after that. Then Jake said, "I wonder if it's the stick or the holder."

"Wonder if what's the stick or the holder? Yer talking in circles," Sam said.

"No, I ain't. Ya ain't listening. I'm a-wondering if the stick in somebody else's hands would find a stash, or if you'd have to have Turtle Smith a-holding it."

"Hum," Sam said. "That's a good question."

They settled back into the darkness after that. Sam and Jake thought about the well-witcher. Puny thought about how the hell he'd gotten himself in such a pickle.

Driving Nannie Crazy

NANNIE CORDERY COULDN'T SAY WHAT year she was born. What she could say was that both of her parents fell sick and died. She didn't know what of. After their bodies were buried, a man who'd been around during the dying, but who she didn't recall as kin, had come to the cabin. He'd picked up her and her brother and taken them away in a wagon. They'd sat in the back on a quilt with two hams. They rode like that for a while, and then they came to a stop under some trees at a fork in the road. They stayed in the wagon for some time. The detail of how long, Nannie never knew. And, grown, she saw that children reckoned time different from adults, and white people reckoned it different from Indians.

The man had given her, her brother, and the two hams to a man and a woman in a long line of walking people. He'd given the man a piece of paper to go with them. This was somewhere in Arkansas, and Nannie later understood that she and her brother had been given to the Cherokees when they were being moved. She guessed the hams were payment to take them. The paper had her parents' names, and her and her brother's names, on it. She'd seen it many times before it was burnt up. She couldn't read English, but somebody smart had once come to the house where they settled, and read the paper out loud to everybody around the table. Her name had been Susie. But the people who had taken her couldn't read English either, and she reckoned that's why they'd called her Nancy. They called her brother David. Nannie couldn't recall his written-down name, and for a while forgot the English talking she knew. The people around her were speaking Cherokee only. She didn't think she was Indian by blood, but she easily got dark in the sun and didn't know for sure.

Her childhood had coincided with the tribe's civil war between the Ross Party and the Treaty Party. People got shot in revenge by posses, by lone gunmen in ambush, and, occasionally, by stray bullets while walking in the street. The couple who'd taken David and her were murdered during that war. She and her brother were raised up afterwards by the woman's mother, who taught them to keep undercover.

Her first husband was a fullblood named Jumper. They lived in the Flint District. But when Jumper was killed in the big war, Nannie fled to the refugee camp. David ran off west to avoid taking sides in a conflict that he didn't care about one way or the other. Nannie didn't know if David was alive or not. But she reckoned she'd never see him again. He didn't know where she was now. So she was just thankful to be alive at all, and thankful for what she had. She wanted to slide by unnoticed. To stay in harmony, to keep an even keel, her nose to her work. She tended to the home site, milked her cow, ground corn, and watched animals and humans from the sides of her eyes. Just letting things be was her primary policy. But Coop — well, Coop was driving her wild. "Yer giving me a bad case of chiggers," she said.

Coop raised his head. "Huh?" He'd been beating a stick against a log.

"Why don'tcha jist go on over to the Singers' and wait at the ferry? They'll be coming back thaterway."

"I don't care if they never come back."

Nannie picked her teeth with a chicken quill. "I can see that."

Neither of them spoke again for a while. But Coop did quit beating the log. He threw the stick, and ᏅᏓ ᎪᏃᎦᎥ fetched it. They did that about four hundred times. Nannie finally said, "Yer gonna make that dog sick."

"What's it to ya?"

"Nothing. Never liked the dog anyway." Nannie took Joe by the hand, turned, and walked off.

Coop yelled to their backs, "Where ya going?"

"To visit the Singers," Nannie yelled over her shoulder.

"Why ya going over there?"

"One of us has to."

"I'll go. You don't hav'ta."

"Okay. You go and do it."

"I will." Coop put his fists on his hips. "What am I going fer?"

"See if yer pa's on his way home."

"Okay. I can do her." His head bobbled. He ran with the stick, threw it in the air, and caught it while jogging.

Nannie breathed a sigh of relief. Since his daddy had gone, Coop had been as crazy as a calf eyeing a branding iron. He just couldn't swallow the injustice of Sanders taking George and leaving him behind. He'd complained night and day. Worked himself speechless. Nannie had kept her thoughts inside. But understood why Sanders punished Coop. He'd told him not to go to that bawdy house. And he'd had to go after him. She was just glad Sanders got there when he did, and didn't get shot.

Freeing the Prisoners

BUT SANDERS AND GEORGE DIDN'T come back by the Singers' ferry. They used a ferry closer to Fort Gibson because Sanders knew he needed to talk to Bell. He told George to take The Bay to the bottoms and to get on home. He was certain George's parents had heard about the killings. They'd be worried about their son. Boys laid out; everybody expected that. But they didn't lay out forever.

Bell heard Sanders was in town almost as soon as his horse was sighted. He cleared his office of two dominoes players and of a man mad at his neighbor for sneaking a cow into his bull's pasture. Then he picked up his whittling project, came out from behind his desk, and sat in a comfortable chair, on a cushion his daughter had made for him. When Sanders walked in, Bell's tongue was at the corner of his mouth and he was shaving on a whistle.

Sanders went to the dipping pan and plucked the dipper off its nail on the wall. After throwing back two helpings of water, he hung the dipper up and wiped his mouth with the back of his hand. He said, "How's bizness?"

Bell studied the blowing end of his toy. "Slow, since ya've been gone."

Sanders grunted, took a seat at the dominoes table, and summed up the ends of the arms.

Bell continued to whittle. Pretty soon he said, "You git him buried?"

"Sorta. Give him to Mac Berryhill. One of his boys took him on to the Colberts."

"What kinda shape were he in?"

"Drawing flies."

Bell winced. In his line of work, he couldn't avoid dead bodies. But, like most of the tribe, could hardly tolerate one. He said, "That won't bother them Creeks."

Both men snorted. Sanders set the double nickel on its edge. "I guess ya got the story?"

"Benge boys told it."

"They tell it all over town?" Sanders balanced another domino on top of the double nickel.

"Nope. Somebody else done that. Yer a hero. But Hugh Singer don't look too good fer a young feller."

Sanders balanced dominoes until they fell more than once. He and Bell swapped information. Then Bell left Sanders building a dominoes house and walked to the jail. He unlocked the door and said, "Get yer butts out here."

Jake and Sam scrambled into the daylight. Puny followed. All three ducked their heads and raised their hands to shade their eyes. They took deep breaths. Jake said, "I gotta see a man about a dog."

Bell said, "Go behind the jail. But come back here when yer through. I got bizness with ya." To Puny, he said, "I'm gonna let ya go free. Go on to my office 'til I get through with these here men. Ya got a friend waiting on ya there."

"Not my wife?" Puny asked.

Sanders had supplied Bell the details of Puny's woman trouble. He said, "Probably not."

Puny left as Jake came back around the wall of the jail, buttoning his pants. Bell said to him, "Perkins, who owns that bawdy house?"

Jake fumbled with his top button. "I don't rightly know. Some Injun."

"Who hired ya?"

Jake straightened up. "Hired myself. When I come there, I come by the river. On a boat that was transporting whis — cotton."

"And you jist stayed put?"

"Didn't mean to. Twern't my fault. They went off and left me."

"And?"

"Well, ya know, Sheriff. Things jist developed. Trying to earn a living. Support my widowed mama in Mississippi."

"Did ya ever pay any rent?"

"Naw." Jake shook his head. "Other than the Injuns already there, nobody never come 'round but customers."

"Did it ever occur to ya that ya were squatting in somebody's house?"

"I figured if somebody owned it, they'd show up. If they didn't, they waz probably kilt in the War."

Bell scratched his chin. "So ya got no information?"

"No, sir. That's it. Are we free?"

Bell dropped his hand to his gun. Spread his legs and cleared his throat before he spoke. "I'm giving ya and yer buddy Sam, here, 'til sundown tomorrow to leave the boundaries of the Cherokee Nation." He spoke to them both. "Ya can go to Arkansas, ya can go to the Creeks, to the Choctaws, or to hell. But yer gitting out of the Nation. I've just made Sanders Cordery a deputy sheriff. His only official duty is to kill ya both if anybody ever sees ya again. He's my kin. I've told him if he has to kill ya, to go on and gut ya. We'll hang yer innards in the trees on the Grand where the eagles feed. I promise ya that on the heart of every Cherokee who ever died by a white hand. Do ya understand what I'm saying?"

Both men sucked in breath, glanced at each other, and said, "Yes, sir."

"Good. Jake, you can take yer horse. It's in the lot in town. But I'm keeping both of yer guns. Telegraph me when ya get to civilization. I'll send 'em on to ya. Now, git going. There's a rain a-coming up. I don't want ya bogged down in mud. It'll jist make killing ya messier."

The two white men turned and walked off without saying "Yes, sir." Bell watched them go for a bit, shook his head, and locked the jail's door. But instead of returning to his office directly, he walked to the Bushyheads' house. There, he had a conversation with Dennis. When he got back to his office, raindrops were starting to fall, and Sanders and Puny were surrounded by men asking questions. Bell parted the crowd with his hands, saying, "Y'all get on out of here. Yer interfering with the investigation."

Somebody said, "Oh, Bell. Don't git riled up. They was jist saying what were inside Colbert's stomach."

"Yeah? What were that?"

One of the men said, "A pearl ring." His eyes were wide.

Bell looked at Sanders. Sanders covered his mouth with his hand, coughed, and said, "I said not to tell that."

Bell said, "And what happened to that ring, Sanders?"

"It were slimy with gut. It slipped outta my hand into the bayou when we waz trying to warsh ourselves off."

"I see," said Bell. "Well, I'll enter that into the investigation." Then to the crowd, he said, "Now, y'all get on outta here. I got bizness to conclude with these men."

There was some grumbling during the leaving. And walking out into a shower didn't appeal to some. But eventually, the office cleared, and the door closed. Bell, Sanders, and Puny were left to themselves and the dominoes.

Bell said, "They'll be thick as spawning carp trying to find that ring in the bayou."

Sanders chuckled. "It got their curiosity offen Hugh Singer's troubles."

"Singer'll have as hard a time holding up his head as he had holding up his dick," Bell offered.

Puny looked gloomy. "How's he doing?" he asked Bell.

"Healing. But his mama's got him by the earlobes."

Puny shook his head. "She'll pin him to the clothesline if she finds out what happened."

"I doubt anybody'll tell her," Bell said. "Unless you do."

Puny's eyes widened. "I'm not telling her."

"Well, that leaves you to tell her, Sanders."

Sanders shook his head. "She won't ask me."

"That covers it, then. As officer of the law, I can't be discussing the facts except in open court. Fortunately, no court'll ever hear it." Bell turned to Puny. "Before you go anywhere else, Dennis Bushyhead wants to jaw at ya."

"I ain't in any more trouble?"

"I don't see how ya can git in any more trouble. Go see him. He may have some help fer ya."

SO IN THE POST OFFICE a few minutes later, Dennis said to Puny, "This room is where you'll sleep." He opened a door off the main room and stepped aside. "There's a little stove for cooking. It's not vented, but you can open that window. That's Sam's tick. We burned his quilt after Bell carted him off to jail. It was filthy. You got any bedding of your own?"

"There's some down at the bawdy house. I'll get it on Sunday."

Dennis nodded. "Now, you do read pretty well. Is that right?"

"Yes, sir. That's no problem. I can show ya, if you wanta test me. I'm beholding for the opportunity."

Dennis shook his head. "No test necessary. I take your word." He turned from the open doorway to the counter, stepped behind it, and pulled up a large sack. He turned it upside down. Envelopes tumbled out. "Just sort these and put 'em in the boxes." He nodded to the wall of pigeonholes behind him. "People'll come in and tell you their names, and you just give 'em their mail. That's all there is to it. Worse part is having to be here all the time. I'm not saying you can't go take a piss, but people'll be expecting to pick their mail up when they come into town."

Puny said, "That don't sound too bad. I jist appreciate the job."

Dennis smiled. "I don't expect it'll be as exciting as your last one. But it probably won't be as dangerous either. I'll leave you to it." He walked out into the trot and saw the rain had started again. When it became clear it wouldn't stop, he ducked back into the post office and picked up the mail sack. He jogged to the house holding it over his head.

After Dennis left, Puny picked up an envelope and studied the writing. The script was in English. He started sorting slowly, based only on which language the address was written in. But shortly he started putting the English ones into piles, using last names and then first. After that, he studied the boxes. None of them had first names scribbled under them, only last. He stuck all the Martins, Foremans, Starrs, Benges, and other big families' letters together in the holes marked by surnames.

As he worked, his mind turned to recent events. He wasn't particularly distressed over Hugh's hurt leg. It would mend. The memory of Hugh's screaming as Sanders cauterized his wound was worse. But what Puny could barely stand to think about was Hugh's crying out loud, pumping his dick. That was the kind of thing that could stick to a man for the rest of his life — and ruin it, if not the outside of him, then the inside of him. Puny didn't want that to happen to Hugh. He'd watched him grow up. He'd never seen Willow up close, but he'd known for months what Hugh had been doing. He hoped Hugh could get back to Willow again. That she could get his tallywhacker standing back up to attention.

Puny's mind slid to between his own legs. That territory had been unusually quiet. He figured that was, in part, nature's way; he was in his late thirties. But still, he was used to some stirrings at inconvenient moments, and those hadn't happened (that he could recall) since the night at the bawdy house. He tried to remember back. Naturally, he wouldn't get a bone-on in jail with those two turnipheads. If he had, it would've been distressing. And he hadn't felt anything but frightened when he'd been at the bawdy house with Jake, Claudette's body, and the wolves. To have gotten jacked up under those conditions would've also been alarming. But neither did he feel anything except remorse when he saw Lizzie on the Singers' back porch. Getting doused with a bucket of bloody water hadn't exactly been uplifting either. However, the image of Ezell wielding that bucket lingered in Puny's mind as he sorted mail. That woman, she had some spirit. And the thought of that spirit began to give Puny a tingle beneath his buttons. He put a hand to the front of his pants and patted his pecker. He reckoned maybe he was still alive in all the important aspects. As he slipped mail into pigeonholes, a fiddler's tune crept into his head.

Lickings

THE NIGHT WAS NEW, THE air refreshed by rain, the water high. The river was a loud, fast torrent, transporting tree limbs and debris further downstream. But the cove was protected. Cricket and frog calls ricocheted across the air. Bert and Ame dangled their legs off the ferry. Ripples of varying heat eddied around their feet and made them tingle. It was the first night since their arrival that Bert felt real peace. He clamped down on an urge to hug his brother. He'd told Ame that the man with the body was Jenny's father. That Jenny's brother, Coop, had visited all afternoon. That Coop had offered to teach them to fish like Indians.

Ame didn't know what fishing like Indians meant. Neither, really, did Bert. But both felt certain Indians knew more about fishing than white people did. And they were excited, and looking forward to it. To pull the fishing nearer, they bragged about big ones they would catch. Got into a disagreement about whether a grandfather catfish was larger and meaner than a grandfather carp.

When the dispute petered out, Bert said, "I met the sheriff. He's gonna look fer our family." He felt Ame's breath on his shoulder. It didn't waver. But Ame didn't say anything. After a long wait, Bert added, "Didja hear me?"

Ame's breath went away.

"Aren't ya happy 'bout that?"

"Sure. Jist thinking."

"'Bout what? It's what we come fer. Now we're here. We need to git on it." Bert pulled his feet out of the water, lay back on the boards, and cradled his head in his palms. He stared at the moon. The crickets carried a tune. Waves slapped the side of the ferry. Eventually, Ame said, "Can't really feature a family. Guess they're Cherokee."

"Probably. Or Choctaw. You was too little to remember. Mama was dark. Yer 'bout the color of a walnut yerself."

"No, I'm not."

"Course ya are."

"I'm colored like a pecan."

"I'm like a pecan. Yer a walnut. Or maybe a turd."

The boys kept on until they ran out of insults. Bert sat up, and they resorted to punching each other's arms until Ame said, "Ouch! That hurt."

Bert felt a pang of remorse. But instead of saying "I'm sorry, he said, "The sheriff said he had business to tend, but he'd be back around."

"Ya think he'll do it?" Ame rubbed his arm.

"He's the sheriff. I don't see why he'd lie."

"Hard to tell what people'll do." Ame was young, but had seen real meanness. And no matter how he tried to shake it, it stayed around like the shadow of a giant oak thrown on the ground. Bert had seen meanness, too. But was more cheerful by nature, and wanted to make up with his brother for hurting his arm. He said, "Look at the moon. See the rabbit in it? Ask fer something and you'll git it."

Ame lay back on the boards. He thought about making a wish, but didn't know what to ask for. He had an inside place to sleep, food three times a day. He had men around; one or two who'd seemed like a father once or twice. So he had more than he'd ever imagined even a year in the past.

The white people who had taken them in had been pretty mean. Bert had excused them, said they were tired and worn out, were grieving their boys, killed in the War. Ame reckoned that was true. But he didn't like the curl on the man's lip when he was wrapping his whip around his fist. And he hated the lickings. The woman wasn't much better. She cooked cabbage every day, and on cold winter nights spat tobacco juice into the fire. So Ame didn't make a wish. He was away from all that. There wasn't anything more he could wish for.

But Bert made a wish. He was worried about not having a shack for shelter when the weather turned. He wished for one. But didn't tell his wish for fear of not getting it. So both boys were silent. Bert lay back, too. They listened to frogs and crickets. An occasional jumping fish made a slapping sound. Bert was almost asleep when Ame said, "Saw something strange in the barn today."

"What?"

"Waz in the loft sleeping during the rain. Woked up by a crack. I thought it were lightning. But somebody waz down below. Then I heared another crack, and another."

"What waz it?"

"Well, there's this sawhorse in the barn with a saddle on it. Somebody waz whacking that saddle with a whip."

"You see 'im?"

"No. I waz peeking through a crack in the floor. I could jist see the saddle. But it waz taking a hell of a beating."

"I reckon somebody waz having a fit. It's good you stayed put. You don't wanta git in the way of a whip."

Ame said, "No. I'm tired of them lickings."

AS THAT CONVERSATION PROCEEDED, PUNY, restless from having been confined inside, was on the post office's front porch. The night there was also still, the air also cricket-filled. Puny was leaning against a post, smoking his pipe, watching the shadows of the trees on the lawn. He was beginning to feel sleepy when he heard a scraping sound. He heard another. And others. They were coming from the direction of the Bushyheads' house.

Puny put his pipe down. Listened carefully. The sounds definitely were scraping. But there was another noise, too. He couldn't quite make it out. He got up slowly, slipped to the wall of the trot, crept along its shadow to the back. At the edge, he stepped to the ground. He crossed the lawn bent over until he got to one of Alabama's flowerbeds. There, he stubbed his toe on a rock. He dropped to his hands and froze. The noise grew louder. Puny moved forward again, crouched low to the ground, creeping (he thought) like a panther. And, in truth, he was quiet. So quiet he was able to slip up unheard on the man with the shovel. When he was about five feet away, Puny pounced and yelled, "Ya sneaky bastard!"

If Puny had jumped Sam as he'd intended, he would've won that fight fast. Or had he been able to grab the shovel, maybe, he could've gotten the upper hand. But neither of those things happened. Instead, the smack across Puny's face was delivered with the back of a spade wielded by Dennis, a much larger man than Sam. And the single whack knocked Puny down and completely out.

New Alliances

THE NEXT MORNING, CONNELL CAME into town. He first went to Nash Taylor's store, looking for Florence. She wasn't around. So he bought supplies and settled the family's tab, and from there swung by the Taylors' house. He was told by their help that Mrs. Taylor and the girls were gone visiting. So he drove back through town to the fort and post office. He secured his mules to the rail, hopped onto the trot, and found the door closed and locked. A sign in both Cherokee and English said, MAIL AT THE BUSHYHEADS.

Connell stepped out of the trot and walked towards the Bushyheads' front porch. A man in a turban was seated on the steps. At first glance, Connell thought he was an important Indian. Cherokee men had worn turbans in the past, a fashion he was thankful had gone out of style. But on ceremonial occasions, chiefs, senators, and councilors still sometimes donned the colorful cloths. And Dennis did run with high mucketymucks. However, the man seemed too dark to be a Cherokee. Connell thought he must be Choctaw or Creek. But he couldn't recall if those tribes ever wore turbans. He was puzzling on that, coming closer, when he realized that the man was Puny and the turban was a bandage. Connell said, "What the hell happened?"

"Had a little accident." Puny's jaw was swollen on one side. He couldn't talk clearly. Connell said, "What?" Puny repeated himself.

Connell ran a thumb across his eyebrow, propped a boot on a step, and crossed his arms on his leg. "Well, at least you're out of jail."

Puny tried to smile, but that hurt his face.

"Mama's been worried about you. Sheriff Rogers told her he was letting you out, but we hadn't heard anything more. Thought maybe you'd gone back to the bawdy house."

Puny shook his head. He held up a letter.

"You've written a letter?"

Puny shook his head again. He pointed to the post office.

"You're the postmaster?"

Puny nodded.

Connell sat down on the step next to Puny. "Well, that's a good thing, I guess."

Puny said, "How's Ezell?" His locution was garbled, but Connell caught the meaning.

"Well, she and Lizzie have taken to each other. Every time you see one, you see the other. It's sort of mysterious. I don't understand women." Connell's mind flashed on Florence. He looked down at his crotch.

Puny nodded. "Hugh?"

A cloud came over Connell's face. The thought of Hugh made him angry to his core. He shook his head. "Don't understand him, either. Cowboy told me what happened. Hugh oughta have his head under the covers and never come out. But instead he's sitting in the middle of the family like he's the prodigal son." Connell waved a hand in the air. His voice rose in pitch. "He's always got that leg propped up, and Paul on his lap. I'd like to horsewhip him for embarrassing Mama and Papa." He turned red in the face.

Puny thought of Connell and Hugh like salt and pepper: different in taste, but good when sprinkled together. He'd seen them squabble all their lives; figured someday that would smooth out. He understood Connell was the straighter arrow. Could only be humiliated by Hugh's predicament. So instead of trying to defend Hugh, he said, "How's yer papa?"

Connell gripped the edge of the step with both hands. "Not doing any good. Getting weaker and weaker. But Hugh sits in the bed with him like they're just resting together." He spat onto the lawn.

Puny's head and face hurt. And he didn't know how to comfort Connell. He wasn't that good with words, even when his jaw was working. And he didn't want to have to answer questions about the night at the bawdy house. He tried to spit, to show agreement with Connell. But his mouth was swollen. His spittle dribbled onto his chin. He swiped it with his hand and slung it into the yard.

DENNIS HADN'T GOTTEN MUCH SLEEP after he'd hit Puny, and had been napping in the room over the porch until voices awakened him. Instead of continuing his nap, he stared at a knothole in the ceiling. He was a man with a conscience, raised by a preacher who truly believed in the word of the Lord. He felt bad about giving a shovel-smacking to someone who, in his wife's opinion, was trying to protect his property. But he tried not to dwell on that. Instead, he turned his mind to his future.

A feeling of destiny was calling Dennis. He'd had that feeling for months. Now the voice was getting stronger. It called him to reorganize the faltering Ross Party into a new one. He envisioned himself speaking to the greatness of the Cherokee people. Saw himself as chief, unifying the factions, leading the tribe into the future. He realized that some would be cynical, would point to his years in California, say he was merely ambitious. But he could rise above that. And he would — with enough money, and without having to waste his time and energy earning it. That's why he'd been digging under the foundation of his own house. And that's how he planned to make the best of the recent unfortunate mistake with the shovel.

So as soon as Dennis heard Connell leave, he crept downstairs. He found Alabama in her back flowerbed, and said to her it seemed that

Puny was able to carry on a conversation. She said, "I don't think he's ready to talk to you yet," picked a clod of dirt off her trowel, and dropped it. Dennis thought about questioning her remark. But decided he might not like her answer. It might be better to wait until later to talk to Puny about what he'd thought up. He let it rest. He left the house on business, and managed to stay away all day.

The next morning, after breakfast, coffee, and grooming, Dennis approached Alabama again in her back flowerbed. He said, "How's he doing?"

Alabama had her trowel in hand again, a row of newly dug holes at her feet. She didn't have her bonnet on, as the sun wasn't yet high and the air was still cool. But she was feeling flushed. "Well enough to go back over to the post office." She wiped her brow with her empty hand.

"Did he say anything?"

"You mean did I ask him how he got himself into a position to be viciously attacked?"

Dennis felt like his wife would eventually see his side. She knew he wasn't violent. He let that remark ride. "Well, yes, more or less. That's what I was wondering."

"I told you. He thought you were Sam Garrett sneaking back to dig up gold. I was right."

"That's what I figured, too." Dennis looked serious.

"Too bad you didn't figure it a little sooner."

"That couldn't be helped. It was dark." Dennis waved a hand to shoo away the subject.

"Dennis, we've got enough money. Why don't you attend to the affairs of the Nation? So much remains to be rebuilt." Alabama believed in public service, and the Nation was still in shambles from the War.

"I'm going to do that, Bamy. Don't you worry. I promise." Dennis puckered his lips like a carp.

Alabama squinted at her husband. Smacked her palm with the trowel. She knew he was ambitious, and she liked that about him. But he did have an impractical side that rubbed on her nerves. She guessed he got that from his daddy. She looked up into the trees. A breeze was blowing, but she felt hot.

Dennis saw he wasn't going to get any sympathy. He turned back into the house. He grabbed a box of cigars from the chest in his study, and went out the front door to avoid his wife. He walked over to the post office with the cigars in hand. He found Puny behind the counter, slotting letters into boxes.

When he saw who came in, Puny took a step back. Dennis said, "I made a mistake. Here, have some cigars." Puny eyed him with the same squint Alabama had used. His head was bare of the bandage, but a swollen knot and a scab were above his right eyebrow, and the side of his jaw was puffy. Dennis said, "Come on. It was dark. You were sneaking up on me."

"Thought ya was Sam Garrett." Puny's speech was some better.

Dennis put the cigar box on the counter and opened the top. "Mrs. Bushyhead told me that."

"Guess I scared ya," Puny mumbled.

"Well, it's over. Let's forgive and forget. I've got a proposition for you."

Puny picked up a cigar and sniffed it. He tried to smile, but his face hurt.

"Let's you and me go into business together. I've got a lot of things that need tending."

"What about my post office job?" Puny jerked a thumb towards the boxes, in case Mr. Bushyhead couldn't understand him.

"That's not a problem. The work I have for you is mostly after hours. Bell Rogers told me you're in a female situation. Can't go back to the Singers. But Mr. and Mrs. Singer think the world of you. They wouldn't be high on you if you weren't honest. Obviously, you already know I think there's a stash around here. I thought maybe it was under the house, because that's where Sam kept digging. But I'm not sure about that. What if we go in together, and I pay you a salary? Then, if we find anything, I'll give you a quarter of it. If we don't find anything, you'll still make money." Dennis, of course, wasn't thinking about doing much digging himself.

Puny knew who'd be doing the digging. Mr. Bushyhead was a man without calluses on his hands. But Puny wanted the extra money, and a chance to find the gold. He sort of garbled, "Ya gotcha a deal, Mr. Bushyhead."

So that evening, the Princeton-educated national treasurer and the Negro railroad man from Ohio smoked cigars together on the porch overlooking the river. Since Dennis didn't keep whiskey, they sipped buttermilk. It was a strange alliance, but in both of their estimations, perfect for the situation. Every Negro in the Nation needed a powerful Indian protector. And Dennis needed a confidant and strong-arm who could never be his rival. Beyond that, they were both smart men and, basically, honest. Puny told Dennis what Sam had said about the well-witcher, and Dennis showed Puny his maps. They thought they had as good a chance as any of finding that gold. Probably better.

A Surprising Turn in the Investigation

ON FRIDAY, BELL WALKED OVER to the Bushyheads' house. Dove, Alabama's help, invited him in, and Alabama greeted him with a squeeze on the arm. She told him, "Dennis is over in Tahlequah. He won't be back until tomorrow."

"That's fine. It's you I've come to talk to."

Alabama was surprised. Even men in the family usually didn't sit and talk to women unless they were eating. She turned to the kitchen and asked Dove to bring cake and coffee to the front porch. Then an alarming thought crossed her mind. The color drained from her face. "Nothing's happened to Mary, has it?"

Bell shook his head. "Not that I know of. Yer sister's made of granite."

Alabama put a hand to her chest. She blushed. They both smiled. At the start of the War, with her husband off fighting, Federal soldiers descended on Mary and Clem Rogers' farm. They started shooting cattle. Set fire to the house. Mary was inside. Alone, except for her infant. She fled out the back door. Ran to the barn, grabbed a horse. She rode bareback, holding her baby, seventy-five miles, mostly in rain, to the farm of the widow of Bell's double first cousin. The baby died the next night. But since that ride, Mary was considered indestructible.

Alabama and Bell settled on the front porch. Dove brought their refreshments, and, for Bell, a tin cup and a saucer. Bell said, "Thank ya. I'll use the cup today," and Dove took the saucer away. He picked up his cake, and, after complimenting its taste, he and Alabama swapped family news and a little town gossip. Then Bell said, "Spent most the week working on that bawdy house mess."

"How's Sanders doing?"

"He were totally wore out."

Alabama shook her head. "That wasn't just your routine kind of killing."

"No. Twaz bad."

Alabama didn't want to sound critical. But she didn't think the bawdy house needed reopening. She said, "I hope we won't have to worry about that place for a while."

Bell said, "I hope so, too."

Alabama felt reassured. She leaned back in her rocker. Let her mind wander over her years growing up in the inn. She said, "That bawdy house has been there for a long time. Old Mrs. Mackey owned it when I was a little girl."

Bell shook his head. "She could dance up a storm in her day." He looked out over the lawn. A smile crept along his lips. "The best I recall, she was a well-endowed woman." He held his cup to his mouth.

"She was a white, I believe."

"She were, yep. Don't recall how she got here. I waz living in the Going Snake District. Didn't git down here too often."

Alabama smiled. "I bet you enjoyed yourself when you did." Thinking back to her girlhood and seeing memories soften Bell's face, her disapproval of the bawdy house slipped away momentarily.

"Well, yeah. I were a young fella. It were only natural." Bell smiled more. "Maybe that's why I've been so poky 'bout closing the place down. That, and I wanta get reelected."

"That would certainly be a consideration." Alabama's mind shifted to her husband's political ambitions. When it shifted back, she said, "I heard you ran that Jake Perkins out of the Nation. I hope whoever buys that place turns it to something useful."

"Jake didn't own it. He were jist running it."

"Please run the owner out, too."

Bell frowned into his cup. "I wadn't really planning on doing that."

Alabama's voice pitched higher. "He'll open it again. Whites prey on Indians. That'll never change."

Bell looked up and out over the lawn. "I agree with you there. But that bawdy house ain't owned by a white."

"I thought Mrs. Mackey had a son. Uh . . ." Alabama hesitated. She frowned. "I can't recall his name."

"Me neither. But he died 'bout twenty years ago. Hit a branch of a tree riding his horse. Nearly took his head off."

"I don't remember that. I don't see how I could forget it. Maybe I never heard it."

"Happened up in Kansas. He'd already sold the house to a Cherokee anyway."

"So an Indian's owned it all this time?"

"Yeah. I had a hard time tracking it down. So many records burnt up in the War. But I'm pretty sure I know the owner. Ya wanta know who it is?"

"Well, of course I do!" Alabama chuckled.

"Yer gonna be shocked."

Alabama laughed like a schoolgirl. It felt particularly fun to gossip with a man. "Good! I like a surprise. Who is it?"

Bell took a long sip before saying, "It's you."

More Gossiping at the Inn

ON HIS WAY HOME FROM Tahlequah, Dennis stopped by his mother-in-law's. She was in the kitchen, supervising her cook, and he sat down at the table sensing an opportunity for food before the noon meal. Granny Schrimsher filled up a plate for him, but, with the flap of a hand, shooed him towards the main room. It was, at the time, empty. She sat Dennis's plate on the side of the big table there. Took the seat at the head, her eyes towards the front door. Granny was a businesswoman to her bones and soul, and Dennis had spent many a year trying to make money. So, rather than weather, they talked business. Then they talked politics and killings. That took up most of the meal, a cup of coffee, and a piece of cake. But finally, Dennis got to his main mission. "You ever see Turtle Smith around here?"

"See him ever' day when he ain't traveling fer witching."

"What's he up to?" Dennis ran his golly rag over his lips.

"Jist minding his business. Turtle's always pleasant. Never has a bad thing to say 'bout anybody."

"Well, he's a darn good well-witcher."

"That he is. I knowed Turtle since he waz young. Always could find water."

"He ever learn to talk English?"

"Talks English real plain. Just won't."

"Acts like he can't."

Granny chuckled. "That's to his advantage."

"Well, I'd like to see him. If you happen to run into him, tell him I'll make a trip to the fort worth his while."

"Gonna dig Bamy a new well? She's always complaining 'bout the sulfur in yer water."

"Been thinking about it. I aim to please Alabama as best I can." Dennis tried to stay on the right side of his mother-in-law. He was a believer in good family relations. And she was one of the most informative people in the Nation.

Granny squinted at Dennis. Tried to turn the squint into a smile. He hadn't been her son-in-law long. So she was still adjusting to him. And she'd been quite fond of Lafayette Adair.

In the Shadow of Death

A FEW DAYS EARLIER, ON the afternoon of Bell's visit, Clifford found a box turtle at the edge of the potatoes. When he picked it up, the turtle pulled into its shell. Clifford poked it with his finger. The turtle pulled in tighter. Cliff tapped his teeth together, thinking tapping was a sound turtles might find attractive. But that tortoise didn't. So Clifford decided to wait it out. He cradled the reptile under his arm and marched towards his mother, who was a short distance away in the field, patting the ground with her foot. Clifford was watching for the turtle's head to pop out, not looking where he was going. Just a few feet from Check, he tripped on a clod of dirt, dropped the turtle, and fell on a potato plant. He looked up instantly and said, "I'm sorry." He cringed to be more convincing. Crushing potato plants could cause a switching.

But Check said, "There're moles running here. They're difficult. Are you all right?" Clifford jumped up, dusted off his knickers, and looked down at the plant. Check said, "Don't worry about it."

Clifford's eyebrows contracted over his nose. His mother seemed strange for herself.

Check said, "You dropped your tortoise. Good he has a hard shell."

Clifford picked the turtle up and looked into the shell where its head was still tucked. He complained, "He's tight inside. I can't get him out."

"I want you to be kind to that turtle. Don't annoy him. His shell's his protection."

Clifford said, "Yes, ma'am." Which is what he usually said, whether he intended to mind or not. And to avoid the possibility he might have to set mole traps, or, at the least, carry them to the field, he tucked the tortoise under his arm and trotted away between rows of potatoes.

Check, watching her son's back, saw him clearly, not as the boy he still was, but as the old man he would be, receding into eternity. The vision startled her. She sucked in air. Suddenly, she'd entered that space where dying takes place. She recognized it from past deaths. And she didn't welcome it. She looked to the ground. Studied the dirt. Moved her left boot over a mole's tunnel. Kicked another one. The crust of earth crumbled into the hole below. Check raised her head and looked to the western horizon. She tried to hear the roar of the water. Thought she caught that. But maybe it was the blood flowing around in her body. However, she preferred to think the sound was the river. She imagined being carried by rushing water, rounding the bend, floating over Webber Falls, all the way to the Mississippi and out to sea. That fate both reassured and frightened Check. She wasn't prepared to leave this patch of earth. And not ready to give up another person she loved to eternity. She'd endured death after death. One after another. For over a decade. She was worn out with dying. But Check knew life wasn't for the weak. She stiffened her spine. Turned from the potatoes. Walked towards the house.

Their father looked much the same to the boys as he had for several days, but they recognized a change had come over their mother. However, Connell and Hugh were barely speaking, so they didn't discuss it. Clifford and Otter weren't old enough to put words to the difference; they got quiet and even more watchful. Only Paul was too young to be affected.

The boys usually came into the sickroom one at a time, and lowered their voices during their visits. Otter chose the corner between the cot and a window, and played with his blocks on the floor, his thumb in his mouth. Check had broken him of thumb-sucking three years back, but saw the comfort it gave him, and wished she could suck a thumb herself.

Clifford generally stopped at the door and slid to the floor. He often read a book in the threshold. Check thought it was just like Cliff to want to be in the middle of where people were stepping, but she approved of the reading. She also recognized Cliff was afraid of his father's sickness, but wanted to be near him. She understood, parked in the doorway, he was compromising.

Connell came in every couple of hours. He always took a seat in one of the windows. He looked out as much as he looked in, talked almost as loudly as he normally did, and escaped as soon as he'd said what he'd come for. Check could tell Connell was uncomfortable and restless. She knew that, in practical ways, Andrew's death would affect him more than the rest of their children. Beneath his grief, she figured he also must be feeling liberation — and the guilt that's always its wife. He would be the man of the farm, of the whole operation. That would soon involve the laying of a railway line, and the shipping of potatoes all the way to the East Coast of the United States. Connell was still young, and he was about to shoulder even bigger responsibilities. Check thought he couldn't help but be deeply worried. She was sorry his manhood was coming by way of his father's death, but she recalled her own brothers. One had died at seventeen; the other two became men through war. Andrew's death, at least, was a better route than that. And Connell, unlike George and Ruff, would survive it. She looked over at her husband. He was asleep. His cheeks dark and hollow.

Connell always skedaddled when Hugh visited. Hugh usually brought Paul with him. Paul liked to walk holding on to Hugh's crutch. The boys practiced by walking together around to the side of the bed away from the door. Andrew's eyes showed more life during those demonstrations than they did at other times. And Hugh's visits were lengthy enough that Check could leave the room and attend to chores. When she returned, she often found Hugh in the chair beside Andrew's bed, and Paul on the mattress next to his father. The odor didn't seem to bother either of those boys, and Hugh seemed content acting as an interpreter between Paul and his papa.

Check watched those conversations mostly in silence. Andrew, and for that matter everybody else, seemed to her like they were preserved inside quart jars. Check held them to the light, turned them around, and inspected them from bottom to top. She set them on shelves and watched them some more. She was distancing herself from the grief and fear that made her quake as though someone was shaking her by the shoulders, screaming in her ear.

Fishing Like Indians

SANDERS HAD BEEN SO WEARY when he returned from the Creek Nation that he slept for most of the next four days. But when he got up on Saturday afternoon, he went to the woods and pulled up some devil's shoestrings. He stuffed them into a sack and twisted the burlap ends into a knot. Then on Sunday morning, Coop went to the ferry and collected Bert and Ame. The three boys walked around the river's bend to meet Sanders, who was on the sandbar looking out at the water, holding the weed sack and other empty bags. In the distance, with the sun behind him, at first he looked to the boys like a small shadow. As the space between them shortened, he grew taller, but not lighter. Bert's fear of Sanders had been tamped by the knowledge that he was Jenny's father and the sheriff's cousin. But Ame had never seen Sanders. He'd heard the gossip, however, so his imagination had played, and by shouting distance to him, Sanders seemed seven feet tall. However, Ame was short for his age, and so bowlegged from rickets that it cost him a couple of inches. That warped his perspective.

Sanders said, "Ya boys ready to fish?" He handed each a sack. Then he stepped from the loose- to the harder-packed sand close to the river. Coop and Bert walked with Sanders. Ame tagged along like a hungry dog. Soon he started walking the line where the noise of the river suddenly ended. He listened to insects and birds with one ear, the roar of the water with the other.

They trod east until Sanders turned north into the cane and woods. The three boys followed. They walked a narrow path, single file, until they came upon a wide pool of the bayou. Sanders looked around on the ground. He picked up a stone that fit his hand nicely. "Find one like this. Be careful of the cottonmouths."

The boys spread out, looking for stones and worrying about snakes. They found rocks and brought them back. Sanders opened the sack and pulled out the weeds. He squatted, separated out three, and threw them to the boys. Coop hunkered on his heels like his father. Both raised their arms and brought them down. Pounded the roots with their rocks. A strong stink invaded their nostrils. Sanders turned his face away. He rubbed an eye with his shoulder. He said, "If it gits to ya, it'll make ya cry."

Bert and Ame hunkered also, and took to smashing roots. Soon the smell was bringing tears to everyone's eyes, and Sanders stopped beating. He pulled off his boots, and dropped his gun and his knife inside one. He stood up. Undid his belt and dropped his pants. Ame and Bert exchanged looks. Sanders said, "Ya can wear yer pants if ya wanta."

Coop stepped out of his pants, too. "But yer'll ruin 'em if ya do."

Bert and Ame had just gotten pants that fit. They took theirs off, folded them up, and set them on rocks.

Sanders said, "If I had a shirt on, I'd take it off." He sort of snorted.

The Vann boys put fingers to their buttons again. While they stripped, Sanders picked up the roots he'd smashed. He said, "Spread out." Then he stepped to the side of the pool. Swished the roots back and forth in the water. Coop picked up a tangle of roots and moved off a distance up the bank. He did the same thing. Bert and Ame had no idea what they were doing. But they, too, went to the edge of the bank. They swished their roots.

Shortly, a big perch popped to the surface of the water. It rolled over and bellied up. A drum and two fat carp appeared next. Three catfish followed. In less than ten minutes, fish were rolling around everywhere on top of the water. Sanders tossed his roots behind him. Plunged into the pool with his sack. He scooped up a drum in his hand, slid it into the burlap. He said, "Leave the carp. Let me handle the catfish. They'll cut ya."

Bawdy House Haints

PUNY ALSO HEADED TOWARDS THE bayou on Sunday morning. He didn't know the Singers had stopped coming into town for church; so out of Fort Gibson's horse lot, he chose a path parallel to the main road. After that, he took the Military Road east, and turned off it onto a path he thought would take him near the bawdy house. It carried him just west of Tomahawk and Mannypack's cabin.

Tomahawk was leaning against a log, whittling, and Mannypack was grinding corn and watching Minnie, when Puny appeared in the distance. Mannypack saw him first. She grunted. Tomahawk looked up. He said, "I bet that's that Puny Tower. Wonder if he's gonna open the bawdy house."

Mannypack said, "Haints down there." She stuck her arm out to block Minnie from the coals of the fire.

"Sez who?"

"I got secret sources."

"I don't believe 'em."

Mannypack went back to grinding corn. The bawdy house was a root of disagreement in the marriage.

Tomahawk could hear Mannypack's thinking. He said, "Women don't know what they're talking about."

Mannypack flicked a hard piece of corn off the mortar. "Know a lot more than men do."

"I may jist go down there with 'im."

"Go on. Liquor's drained out on the floor."

"Who told ya that?"

"Not saying." Mannypack went back to grinding.

"Yer jist making things up."

"Think what ya want. That dead woman's alive down there. I knowed somebody that's heared her."

Tomahawk couldn't decide whether to believe his wife or not. Women jabbered a lot of gibberish. But Mannypack had a disgusting habit of being right. "Well, I'll jist go down there and see," he said.

"Suit yerself. But don't say I didn't tell ya."

And a few minutes later, Puny heard a horse in the water behind him. He turned to see an Indian on a sorrel climbing the bank of a creek. Puny put his hand to the saddlebag that held his gun.

But Tomahawk smiled and waved. When he got close, he stopped. "Going to the bawdy house?"

"Might be."

"I'm Tomahawk Cordery."

Puny relaxed. Retracted his hand from the leather. "Puny Tower. Glad to meet ya."

As the two rode together, Puny gave Tomahawk an account of Sanders' bravery, the gutting, and the cleaning up. They were in animated conversation when the bawdy house came into view. It looked lonesome, silent, and shadowy. They stopped talking. Beyond the clop of the horses, the only loud sounds were from a couple of jaybirds. They rode on to near the front porch. They were about to dismount when, quite by surprise, they saw a rattlesnake coiled on the planks. Puny started fumbling for his gun, but Tomahawk said, "Can't shoot him." The rattler raised its head. The horses shied a step back. Puny grabbed his reins with both hands. Tomahawk said, "If we kill him, we'll have luck so bad we can't overcome it."

Puny's eyes grew. The snake shook its rattles.

Tomahawk said, "Follow me." He turned his sorrel and rode about twenty feet from the porch. He dismounted, tied his horse to a tree, and squatted. Puny dismounted and said, "What're we doing?"

Tomahawk said, "Sit."

Puny knew he was in Indian Territory. But he still felt surprised. He walked over to the stump he'd used before and sat down on it. Tomahawk watched the snake; he looked at the trees. The jaybirds kept fussing. Puny reckoned they were as distressed as he was. Soon he spotted a nest. Saw a head pop out. He focused on the nest to keep from looking towards the rattler. Eventually, Tomahawk said, "He's gone," and stood up.

Inside, the bawdy house smelled of liquor. The odor so strong that Puny felt like his shirt was soaked in it. Tomahawk wanted to fall on his knees and lick the floor. His nostrils flared. Maybe he could get drunk if he breathed in deep.

Puny said, "This place's a mess." The room seemed smaller than he remembered. It was still cluttered with barrels.

Tomahawk squatted, stuck his finger through a bullet hole in a keg, and felt something wet. He said, "We've struck gold."

Puny's head jerked. He thought Tomahawk was talking about the stash.

But Tomahawk said, "There's still a little liquor in this barrel." He stood up and twisted the top off.

They both agreed there was no use letting good liquor go to waste. In a few more days, it'd probably be completely dried up. If it didn't vanish, the squirrels, snakes, and frogs would get into it. There was no telling what could happen with a bunch of drunk animals that close to the bayou. There could be a mass drowning. That would be bad for the fish. They would swim off in search of better water. People wouldn't have anything left to eat except corn (if the weather held) and some game, which, after all, gets tired of being hunted. Or so the theory developed.

The barrels were fairly well drained when Puny remembered his cane and bedding. The more sober of the two, he said, "I gotta get my snake cane and sompthing to sleep on."

Tomahawk said, "Snucan?"

Puny thought he was talking Cherokee. He said, "Snake . . . Cane . . . Bedding . . . Upstairs." He pointed.

Tomahawk fell back and looked at the ceiling.

Puny grunted himself up off the floor. "Take a nap. I'll be back."

The ladder to the loft hadn't been moved since the night of the killings. But it did look to Puny like the ladder, at that second, might be shifting. He realized he was a little unstable. Grabbed a rung to make the ladder stop drifting. A couple of burps later, he grabbed another rung. He started climbing. The wall seemed taller than he remembered. The loft further off. When he got to the top, he leaned in on his stomach, caught ahold with a foot, and shoved himself in.

He didn't have room to stand without bending. He rested on the floor. The loft was dim; light filtered through holes in the eaves. The bedding and the sandstone rocks of the chimney stood out clearly. The cane was propped against the rocks, its two forks pointed up. Puny was on his hands and knees more than halfway to the stick when he heard a noise. He lunged. Grabbed the cane. Scooted on his rear until his back hit the chimney. He said, "Who's there?"

A hissing sound answered.

Puny turned towards the sound. Something moved in the rafters. The hiss came again. Puny'd never heard anything like it. He swung his cane. Shouted, "Don't ya come near me! Don't ya come near me! I'll kill ya!" He stopped and listened. Heard only his own panting and his own heart beating. He scrambled across the floor, threw a leg out of the hole, searched for a rung with his foot. His leg flailed in the air. He dropped the cane to the floor below. Put a shoulder against the side of the hole. But missed a rung or two with his feet. Broke his fall by grabbing one with his hand. Still, he slipped when he hit the floor. He landed on his back, on his cane. He yelled, "Tomahawk! Let's git outta here!" He rolled over, grabbed the rod, and stood up. He pulled Tomahawk up by the top of his pants.

Tomahawk said, "Wha'th'h'll?"

Puny still thought Tomahawk was talking Cherokee. He said, "Talk English! Come on! There's sompthing up there! It's hissing!"

Tomahawk sobered instantly. He said, "Oh, shit! It's the white woman's ghost!" He bolted out of the door. Puny followed fast, limping and putting his cane to good use.

They reached their horses. Managed to mount. Galloped off. After they were gone for a while, the barn owl quit moving its head back and forth. It ruffled its feathers. Settled into an uneasy repose in the rafters. Eventually, it nodded back to sleep.

The Call of Life at Death

CLOSELY CONFINED TO ANDREW'S BEDSIDE, Check couldn't oversee her boys as well as she commonly did. The older two were mostly off on their own. And coping with their father's dying in ways she (thankfully) couldn't imagine. Connell had, in the past, creatively used the saddle in the last stall of the barn to relieve his manly tensions. But lately he'd used it only for the beatings he couldn't give Hugh. Now he was in a terrible state. His penis was popping up all over the place. Connell was vaguely aware his erections were linked to his father's dying. Yet every time he made that connection, he hastily erased it from his mind. It felt appalling and disrespectful. Connell didn't know that yearning for sex is almost universally stronger in the face of death.

Wherever he went, he started positioning his hat in front of his pants. Finally, in a desperate state, he rode into town for a serious talk with Florence. He told her he was pining for her day and night. Told her he could get relief only from her. Said he didn't know how much longer he could wait. Said he would properly propose when he could talk it over with his parents. Said they were in difficult straits. He tried appealing to Florence's loving nature. To her full womanhood. To her compassion. He whined a bit.

Florence wasn't buying any of that. However, she did like hearing it. She asked for details. And they discussed them over and over. Really, they got to the point where they couldn't discuss anything else. That made it worse for Connell. And Florence, though she wouldn't admit it, began thinking of Connell's penis very possessively. Even tenderly. However, with Connell not proposing, she wasn't about to give in.

Hugh was in a bad way, too. His dick was like an eel he'd once reeled in and left on the bank to expire. Just a flop here and a roll there. He pulled back its hood, examined its top. Looked closely at its sides and bottom. He talked to it; called it Buckaroo in the same throaty way Willow did. When that didn't work, he called it Buckaroo in a commanding tone, like an officer ordering a soldier. He squeezed it, ran his hand up its shaft, held it to attention. When he let it go, it usually fell to the left, the same side his leg was shot on.

Hugh began to see some symbolism in that. He recalled the four horsemen of his dream; particularly the first one, faceless, speaking of whoring, worms, and rot. That horseman's blind, noseless, mouthless face looked to Hugh a little bit like Buckaroo. He knew he'd sinned by getting Claudette shot. And was afraid that rider foreshadowed his punishment. Afraid Buckaroo would never rise to the occasion again. Afraid he would rot.

Reading the Bible to his father didn't diminish those fears. And for the first time in his life, Hugh contemplated the meaning of his existence. It certainly wasn't to raise potatoes. But he'd known that before he got shot. And before Claudette had sacrificed her life to his lust. So Hugh left off playing with Buckaroo. He played with his little brothers, started toilet training Paul, and felt a general despair about his life. He was wallowing in the pit of misery when, late on Sunday afternoon, about the time Puny and Tomahawk were scrambling away from the bawdy house, his father's moaning pitched higher and lengthened. It took on the quality of the call of a calf stuck in a fence. Unable to go forwards or backwards. Hugh was pierced by every yell.

Alabama Investigates

ANDREW'S LAST PANGS OF DYING were not yet known beyond the farm, and life elsewhere was not yet suspended. Alabama, in particular, had her nose in her own affairs. It'd been two days since her conversation with Bell, and she'd not yet told Dennis that she owned the bawdy house. But she was going to do it; and she decided if he asked about the lag, she'd tell him she'd delayed because he was busy and didn't need to be bothered. However, the deeper truth was that the Cherokee Nation was one of the few places on the continent where a married woman, still more often than not, controlled her own property. Alabama was a great admirer of the old days, when the women owned all the crops, all the houses, and all the other improvements, and she'd been raised by Granny, who was shrewd about money. So, although Alabama had conjured an explanation because Dennis would have to know, she didn't feel guilty about not immediately laying her business out flat in front of her husband. She wasn't spreading dough with a rolling pin.

Besides, she wanted to check Bell's facts. She did that with a visit to May Goss, her first husband's first cousin. May was much older than Lafayette. But still had most of her mind, and knew all of the Adairs, both living and those dead for a long time. Though occasionally she did get those two categories of Adairs jumbled up. That Sunday afternoon,

May was in her rocker on her daughter's front porch. She was wearing a patchwork dress of blues and reds; her sleeves were long, her hair unbraided. May was blind, and her daughter off visiting their neighbors. Alabama announced who she was as soon as the dog started barking. May recalled her immediately, and was glad for her visit. During the War, they'd been in the refugee camp together.

Alabama handed May a jar of strawberry preserves. The old woman settled the gift on a little cane table next to her chair. Then Alabama pulled a rocker close to May's good ear, and turned down an offer of snuff. They talked about the weather and its effect on the joints. Then they talked about a hog that had run into May's daughter's house and was shot scampering out the back door. From there, they moved naturally to the recent killings at the bawdy house. May was Sanders' aunt by marriage. The old woman took some pride in the subject.

Eventually, Alabama said, partly in Cherokee, "May, *remember* Mrs. Mackey, *that white woman who owned that place?*"

May's wrinkles folded into a laugh. "Phewee! *Sure do! Haven't thought about her for some time.*"

"*I hear she's dead.*"

"*Who told you that?*"

Alabama reverted to English. "Bell Rogers, the sheriff."

May reverted to English, too. "He'd probably know."

"Well, ever since I heard about the killings, I've wondered who she sold that house to." In the Nation, land was held in common; ownership extended only to improvements, like houses, crops, barns, and fences.

May spit into a can. "Didn't sell it. Her boy inherited it. Guess she is dead, now that I think on it."

"I suppose so. Do you happen to know who her boy sold the house to?"

"Didn't sell it. Lost it in a poker game."

"You know that for sure?"

"Yep. Lost it to my brother."

"Which brother was that?"

"Wash. The one with the hook nose."

Except for the winning rather than selling, it was the same story Bell had told. But Alabama continued her questioning, trying to sound conversational for fear of May clamming up. "I guess Wash passed it on when he died," she said.

"Yep. Willy got it." She was referring to William Penn Adair. After being a commander, he'd become a diplomat to the US government and other tribes.

Alabama was so stunned she completely forgot about being clever. "And Willy allowed it to be used to sell whiskey! I don't understand that." She shook her head.

"Didn't sell whiskey there when Willy owned it. He rented it out."

"Had tenants in it?"

"Yep! Then, when the troops waz around, they used it as a headquarters. Least, that's what I heared."

Alabama thought her first husband must have gotten the house from Willy shortly before he was killed. But she and May had been in the camp on the Red River. Maybe May didn't know any more than she did. She rocked, trying to remember anybody saying anything about Willy selling the house to Lafayette.

May closed her eyes; her head dropped a little. Alabama was glad she dozed off. Took the opportunity to study the situation more. But soon a rooster crowed, and May awoke with a jerk. She wiped dribble off of her chin with her handkerchief. "Messy stuff," she said. "Don't ever take it up."

Alabama said, "No, I probably won't."

May felt around in her chair and pulled out her pouch. She pinched a little tobacco and tucked it in her lower lip. She said, "I guess you're wondering how Lafayette got the house offen Willy?"

Alabama was startled by the question. Felt like May had read her mind while dozing. And she wondered how many other people knew she owned the house now. She sat up straight in her rocker. Felt grateful the old woman was blind. "Well, yes," she said. "You wouldn't happen to know, would you?"

"Won it on a horse race. Twer right before the War, as best I recall."

Alabama shook her head. "Lafayette didn't bet on the horses."

May cackled. "That may be what he said. He'd bet on anything as a boy."

Alabama left shortly after that. When she got home, she asked Dove to serve their supper in the study, and let her go for the night. Towards the end of the meal, she told Dennis the story. Then she said, "You were Lafayette's best friend. Didn't you know any of this?"

Dennis was behind the desk. His maps had been moved aside to make room for their plates. "I was in California, Bamy." He leaned back, pushed his spectacles to his forehead, and frowned.

"I wasn't suggesting you knew it in California. I'm saying a horse race is an awful public place to win a house. You'd think somebody would've mentioned it sometime."

"Maybe everybody thought we already knew it. And why bring something like that up? 'How do ya like selling illegal whiskey?' is not something most people will say to your face."

"Well, it looks like they'd say it to yours. That's my point."

Dennis took his glasses off, laid them on the desk, but eyed his maps. He wished he could just think about the stash. Wished his wife didn't own the bawdy house. He usually liked property, but not this property. "Nobody's ever mentioned it to me, I can assure you of that. But they will just as soon as I start running for chief."

"I'm sorry, Dennis. I still can't believe it." Alabama was genuinely distressed. She brushed a strand of hair from her face and regretted her husband's ambition. Under less public circumstances, she'd dispose of the bawdy house without bringing it to his attention.

"Well, Willy's back from Washington. I'll see him in Tahlequah and ask him about it." Dennis spoke through his last chew of pork.

"In the meantime," Alabama said, "I'll sell it quietly."

"You won't have any luck." Dennis swallowed and frowned.

"I will too. I bet it's a fine house. As hard up as people are for places to live, somebody'll snap it up. I'll probably get a lot of money for it."

"I doubt it." The corners of Dennis's mouth turned further down.

Alabama suddenly felt the pride of ownership that most people feel when they're thinking about selling their assets for a good price. "And why not, Mr. know-it-all?"

"Well, Mrs. bawdy-house-owner, because it's haunted. That's why."

Alabama's eyes went from narrow to wide. "What makes you think that?"

"Puny was by before you came in. I gave him a quilt. He was down at that house today, hoping to get his bedding. But he and one of Sanders' boys were run out by a ghost."

"Whose ghost is it?"

"That dead woman's."

Alabama stood. She walked to the window and looked out over the lawn. The dark gave her no comfort. Dennis wiped a finger over his plate, sucked grease off it. The grease helped him some, but not much. The Bushyheads' fine minds and educations didn't preclude them from believing in ghosts. Everybody in the Nation believed in spirits. Educated white people in Boston, New York, and London believed in them, too. In those cities, the elite were holding séances around trembling tables. Asking dead people questions. Sometimes fainting outright. But Alabama was satisfied with dealing with one world at a time. That was trouble enough. She said, "Damn it to hell!"

No Fieldwork Tomorrow

CHECK FELT THE LINEN OVER Andrew's privates. It was dry. His thighs were gray and sunken. He moved a leg and let out a cry. Check covered him again. She said, "Let's give him more dope. Hold his head."

Ezell waited until Check had the spoon to the bottle. She put one palm on Andrew's temple, cupped his chin with her other. She said, "We ain't gonna hurt ya, Mr. Singer. This'll make ya feel better." She opened Andrew's jaw and turned her face away. Andrew's legs shuffled under the sheet. Check stuck the spoon over his mouth and turned it. His breath was rancid. She gagged and tried to conceal it.

Both women backed off. Andrew twisted and yelled. Hugh put a hand on his father's foot. Connell stood up from the sill. Moved to the bed to catch him if he rolled over. He said, "We're gonna need help."

"We've got it." Check nodded towards the windows. The hands were squatting in the yard. On the edge of the porch, one strummed a banjo softly. Twilight was falling.

"They need to be up early," Connell said.

"There won't be any fieldwork tomorrow," Check replied.

Connell left the room. He wanted to saddle his horse and ride. Maybe gallop down the Military Road. Maybe ride to see Florence. Ride anywhere to get away from the dying. To get away from Hugh. He couldn't fight him while he was still on crutches. But he'd give him the licking of his life when he was surefooted. Connell kicked Hugh's bed in the hallway. Felt thankful they currently weren't sharing a room. He walked out into the evening. Passed the hands on the porch and in the yard on his way to the barn.

The last dim light of day fell in the doors. Connell shut those behind him. He used the slivers of light streaming in between the boards to check the stalls. Found only a delinquent sitting hen. Looked up the ladder to the loft, but didn't climb it. No one went up there unless he had to. He turned to the last stall. It was dark, but his eyes had adjusted. He patted the horn of the saddle, cupped it in an affectionate squeeze. The other hand he used to unbutton his pants. He guided his penis into the space between the leather and the blanket. Felt immediate comfort. He sighed. His anger started draining away. He moved his penis just a little. Tears came to his eyes. He moved his member slightly more. He didn't want to come too soon. He just wanted some relief from the grief, anger, and fear that were filling his body. The muscles in his chest contracted, expanded, contracted again. He held on to the horn. His penis was wedged safely in. He didn't need to hold it. He put his right hand over his left on the horn. He moved a little more. Imagined the leather and soft wool as the dark recess between Florence's legs. He began to tremble. His breath was heavy and hot. He rocked back and forth. Began to pant. He wanted Florence so much, he didn't think he could stand it. And he wanted his father to live.

Connell started crying. His chest convulsed. He couldn't keep from making a noise. He sobbed. He kept on rocking. The sobbing delayed his coming, but relief oozed out of every pore of his body. He gasped for breath. His penis was bursting. It felt four times its natural size. Connell wanted to be so deep in Florence that he'd disappear. She'd be as wet as the river. He'd drown. He wouldn't care. He wanted to go that way. He wanted to come. He wanted to come. He wanted. He wanted. Wanted. Wanted. Then he wanted to get his breath. He bent over the saddle and sobbed.

The Scent of Pine Needles

BERT AND AME DIDN'T REALIZE it was late until Sanders rolled onto his side and started snoring. They took the hint, got up, and whispered their thanks. Nannie said, "Hold up," stepped into the dark, and stepped back with two sticks. She gave one to each boy and told them to beat the ground to scare the snakes on their walk. And she invited them back. She didn't know that Bell had told Sanders he was fairly sure the Vann boys were their aunt Peggy and uncle Alex's great-grandchildren. And that their cousin Ellis was probably the boys' grandfather. But Nannie had her own opinion on orphans. Caring for them evened things out.

So Bert and Ame left the Corderys' feeling full in their stomachs and hearts. They walked the lane in the dark contented, not talking. Ame thought first of their fishing. Then his mind drifted to carving a slingshot, becoming a better shot than Coop. Bert's thoughts were attached to Jenny. She'd caught his attention in the way girls will, and he enjoyed his mind roving into new fields. They walked on, each lost in his own thoughts, Ame in front, until they were close enough to the Singers' house for its outline to emerge from the dark. Ame said, "Look yonder, 'round the house." He pointed with his stick.

Bert said, "They're doing sompthing." He came even with Ame.

"Ya reckon?"

"Yeah, I reckon." Bert gave Ame an elbow to the shoulder.

Ame stepped back. "Yer a genius. Can ya predict the weather?"

Their conversation was about who could predict what, until they heard the banjo's low, lonesome sound. Bert's mind went to the ferry. He hoped the hand he'd ask to mind it was still on the job, not listening to the music. He imagined the ferry being cut loose and stolen. Ame said, "I bet Mr. Singer's dying."

When they got to the group, one of the hands confirmed Ame's suspicions. Bert took off towards the river. Ame found a place on the ground. He rested his head on his arms. After a short time, Bert rejoined him. He'd picked a Cherokee to watch the ferry, a man who'd rather be alone near water than with company near dying. They listened to the banjo with the rest of the men until Andrew started screaming so loudly that music didn't seem right. Ame took off to the ferry then, but Bert stayed with the men.

By dawn, Andrew was too worn out to yell anymore. His breathing turned to a rattle. Check was awake in a straight chair at the side of his bed. Hugh was curled against the footboard, Connell sitting on the windowsill, and Otter, Paul, and Clifford tangled in sleep on the cot. The hands, Bert included, had moved up onto the porch to sleep on the planks. Most had their hats pulled over their eyes. There was a chorus of snoring. Two hands sat up, scratched, and stretched.

Hugh suddenly lifted his head. "What's happening?"

"The fluid's built up in his lungs." Check got up and lit another pine candle. She extinguished a nub.

"Should we do anything?" Hugh asked.

"You could get off the bed and make it easier on him," Connell spoke from the window.

Check looked at each of her eldest boys. Her left eyelid closed slightly.

Hugh grabbed a bedpost, slid his good foot to the floor, and hopped to a crutch. He said, "I'm gonna relieve myself." After he left, Connell took a position at the foot of the bed. Wrapped his arm around a post. "Mama, let me get us some help. Doc Howard'll be up by now."

Check shook her head and sat back down.

"How 'bout Aunt Alabama?"

Check shook her head again. "No need to impose on folks. They're busy."

"She wouldn't mind coming. Neither would Doc."

"There's nothing to do but wait."

Connell hesitated, but turned back to the window. He'd waited in the barn until he thought there was no trace of tears on his face. And, except for lack of sleep, he felt better than he had in a while. However, he wanted to do something. His mother would try to do it all by herself.

Check folded her hands in her lap and closed her eyes. She tried to breathe in only the pine scent of the candles. The smell of the disease had grown sordid, but she'd tricked her nose into ignoring it by recalling the forest around her parents' home. It'd been filled with pine, cedar, and spruce. As a girl, the strong odor of evergreens had protected her against the cold of the winters. She recalled that smell and that feeling. Then she drifted into remembering, one by one, the faces of her mother, sisters, and brothers. Her mother had been so dark, she'd looked young even when she wasn't. Her three brothers were dead. So was her only sister west of the Mississippi. Her other two were in Tennessee. She hadn't planned on being widowed this far away from them. Really, once the War was over, she hadn't worried about being widowed at all. She wanted to cry, and would've if the boys hadn't been with her. She thought about going upstairs, closing the door, and sobbing at her dressing table. But if she did, she would be heard. And she didn't want to leave Andrew's side for a minute. She wouldn't have him much longer. She wouldn't have him again.

Preparing for the Dying

WHEN CONNELL FINALLY ESCAPED TO Fort Gibson, he first went to the carpenter's shop. In the doorway, trying to sound normal, he said, "Rain's on its way." The carpenter, Louie Glad, watched the weather as closely as anyone. "Hope so," he said, and wiped his hands on his apron. He added, "Ya look like ya been rode hard, Mr. Singer. Have we lost yer pa?"

Connell shook his head. "No, but it's not looking good."

Glad pursed his lips, folded his arms, and looked down. He was a burly man of medium height and undistinguished in appearance, except for a purple birthmark on his forehead that he covered with a shock of hair and a pleasant personality. He said, "How's yer mother doing?"

"She hasn't slept. I'm here to take care of her business."

Glad nodded. Nobody in the Nation would place a firm order for a burying box before a person actually died. Connell's comment edged up to that line. Coincidentally, Glad had recently finished a fine cherry coffin. He said, "How's yer brother?"

Connell bristled. He wanted to examine Glad's face to determine his motivation. But was afraid his eyes would be drawn to the mark. He looked instead at a wall of saws. The carpenter was white, a teetotaler, and a churchgoer. If any man in the district didn't know what Hugh had done, it would be Glad. Connell shook his head. "He's all right. Full of himself."

Glad recognized he'd offended Connell. But he didn't know how. He said, "I hear that crazy Creek shot him. It's a shame." He was trying to be pleasant.

Connell looked straight at him. "You wanta make something of it?"

Glad blushed almost to the hue of his mark. He showed his palms. "Mr. Singer. Ya don't seem like yerself. Yer upset about yer daddy. I know. We got ever'thing covered we can."

Connell realized his mistake. And knew he wasn't himself. He waved a hand to swipe the blunder away. "Sorry. I haven't slept." He turned on his heel, passed his tethered horse, and walked briskly towards Nash Taylor's store. He was as knotted up as a calf roped for branding. He needed to find Florence. To show her how miserable he was. To get some pity from her. He was so tired his dick wasn't standing up. He just wanted sympathy.

Nash was dipping sugar from a sack. Connell touched his fingers to his hat and walked to the back. There, he pretended to be interested in a wall of holsters. He didn't want to talk to a soul except Florence. Sometimes she helped women decide on cloth. Sometimes she showed them gloves or hats. He cut his eyes this way and that. But he saw only Jim Murray carrying a feed sack out the door. Connell suddenly felt grumpier. He was wallowing in irritation when Nash came up, put a hand on his shoulder, and asked, "How's it going?"

"Mama sent a list." Connell pulled a piece of paper from his pocket.

Nash looked the list over. It was four times what the Singers usually ordered. It included a length of black cotton. The paper shook slightly in Nash's hand. He read it again from the bottom up. He cleared his throat, turned away, and started gathering the items closest to where they were standing. Without looking back, Nash cleared his throat again. He said, "Miz Taylor's been wanting to go on out to the bottoms."

Connell lifted a holster off the wall. Mrs. Taylor was the last person his mother would welcome seeing. He rubbed his thumb over the leather. He rubbed it again.

"She thinks highly of your parents," Nash added. "She was thinking about taking Florence with her."

Connell put the holster back on the rack. Ducked his head and palmed the back of his neck. "Mama won't let me ask anybody for help. But I wouldn't wanta stymie Mrs. Taylor."

WHEN CONNELL GOT TO THE post office, he walked in on Puny and a fullblood sorting letters. The fullblood grunted and went back to poking envelopes into slots. Puny said, "Ya look like hell."

"I feel worse than that."

A sinking in Puny's chest slid all the way to his stomach. Other than Ezell, Mr. and Miz Singer were his oldest connections around. From the looks of Connell, Mr. Singer was about to be finished. Puny felt a flash of regret. The flash melted into guilt. As soon as he'd declared to Ezell, Mr. Singer's father had offered him good work. But it'd been Mr. Singer who'd taken him over, and who'd talked with him in the late afternoons about what everybody called "the Negro question." About how it would turn out. Mr. Singer had been the first white man Puny'd ever had a real conversation with; one about ideas and feelings, not just, "Do this, do that." Puny wanted to tell Connell. But the fullblood was there, and Puny didn't know how to explain it in a way that would convey how those talks made him feel. How they reassured him that white people had red blood, too. That there was a chance of a brighter future for all, no matter their color. That there was hope, someday, people would get along. Instead, he said, "I'd like to see your papa 'fore he passes." He handed Connell his mail.

Connell shuffled it. Two letters from his aunt Elizabeth in Tennessee. A bill from a store in St. Louis. He looked up. "You can risk it if you want. I don't know that Ezell'll even notice. She's awful busy."

Puny's mouth turned down. And Connell saw he'd made another mistake. He, too, was stabbed by guilt. He'd tell Puny he had female problems, that women were beyond understanding. But he couldn't admit he couldn't get laid. He kicked the counter with the toe of his boot. He had, in the past, told Puny he'd done the deed. Told him about a girl over in Tahlequah, at the Seminary. Described her in detail. But he'd made it all up. He wondered if Puny knew. He tapped the letters on the countertop to erase that thought from his head. And it went. He had bigger worries. He was in genuine grief, and he recognized the same in Puny. He said, "Come while Papa can still recognize you."

Puny wiped a hand over his mouth. "I'll ride out tonight."

From the post office, Connell walked to the Bushyheads' house. The back door was closed. He knocked below a knot he'd often thought of as the face of a raccoon. Nobody answered. He knocked again. He hadn't seen anyone on the front porch; Dennis and Alabama evidently were out. He waited, trying to decide what to do. He settled on telling Puny to ask Alabama to come out to the bottoms when she came back. As he turned, the door cracked. A strip of Alabama's face appeared in the opening. Connell took a step back. "I didn't mean to bother you, Aunt Alabama."

"You're never a bother, Connell." Alabama opened the door wide enough to reveal her whole head. But she didn't invite him in.

So he didn't know what to do next. He looked down at his feet and up again. "I was just at the post office." He waved his mail. "Thought I'd say howdy." Alabama looked paler than usual. And was in a robe rather than a dress. It suddenly crossed Connell's mind that Alabama and Dennis had been having relations. He took another step back. He held his mail to his forehead. He wished he could hide his entire face. He stammered.

Alabama said, "Are you feeling poorly, Connell?"

"No, no, not me! How 'bout you?"

Alabama shook her head. "Nothing to speak of. Is Check ready for me?"

"Mama won't say. You know how she is."

Alabama nodded. "Don't tell her you've been here. I'll be out after the rain."

RAIN BEAT HARD ON CONNELL'S hat and back by the time he crossed the Military Road. It also beat hard on Check's tin roof in the bottoms. It was so loud on the summer kitchen's roof that it sounded like Indian rattles. But neither the storm nor the deathwatch dampened Jenny Cordery's mood. In fact, the turbulence of the weather heightened it. She stood at the door and watched pools of water form in the grass, crater the path between the kitchen and house. Lightning cracked in the sky. The wind sounded like the river. Jenny's heart raced. The wild weather added to her belief that life had suddenly turned exciting, and was likely to stay that way. Bert was the best-looking, strongest, funniest boy on earth. Her parents and brother had taken to him like he was a colt with a star between its eyes. His little brother wasn't bad, either. He watched everything Coop and her father did. They could all be friends. When she married Bert, they could all live together. Jenny saw that vision in a puddle close to a steppingstone.

Lizzie said, "You better git away from that door."

Jenny turned only her head. "Huh?"

"Git away from the door. That lightning'll fry ya like fatback."

Jenny took a step back into the kitchen.

Ezell was at the fireplace, stirring stew in a hanging kettle. She dipped up a spoonful, blew, and tasted. She didn't know how word spread so fast in the Nation. When the rain let up, people would descend on the farm from all directions. And they'd roost just like big buzzards in trees. Even though most would bring baskets of food, they'd all expect to be fed. She looked towards the stove and said, "The cornbread's ready to come out. The skillet's heavy. Let's do that together. Get the gloves." She was talking to Lizzie.

They pulled a large skillet from the oven. Set it on an iron trivet on the table. They pulled out another. Set it next to the first one. Ezell said, "As soon as these cool, we'll use 'em for biscuits. Can't be slighting people."

Jenny smiled to herself. She loved biscuits and rarely got to eat them. Her mind leapt forward to sneaking one when nobody was looking.

CONNELL'S DEERSKIN PONCHO WAS TREATED with oil. But he was wet and muddy when he got to the barn. He led his horse to the stall next to his favorite saddle. He took his hat off first, slung it two or three times, and set it on a post. He pulled his poncho off over his head, also flapped it two or three times, and hung it on a hook to dry. Then he took his saddle, the blanket under it, and the bridle off his horse. He settled them apart, thinking he'd need to soap and oil the leather as soon as he could. He was exhausted, in need of some comfort, and aware of the other saddle on the sawhorse just beyond the partition wall.

He tried to shake it out of his mind like he'd shaken the rain out of his hat and poncho. He picked a brush off the ledge of the stall and commenced to stroking his horse. He talked to her. Tried to keep one part of his mind off his father's dying, the other part off the saddle in the next stall. During a storm, men sometimes hung around the barn; Connell knew that. He didn't want to get caught with his pecker hanging out, or lodged between the saddle and the blanket, or getting stroked in any way at all. He brushed and brushed, trying to rid himself of even the notion of looking over into the next stall. He tried to concentrate on the sound of the wind blowing through the boards of the barn, on the rain hitting the tin of the roof.

But though his ear was tuned to the storm, the longer the strokes he made on the side of his horse and the steadier the rhythm of his arm and his hand, the larger the bulge grew in his pants. He held the bulge against his horse's stifle. He rubbed it up and down, just a little. He was trying to reach the top of the rump to brush it, so it was only natural to be against his horse, he told himself. But the animal was warm and hairy, and, really, his friend and boon companion. If he just unbuttoned his pants and pulled out his pecker, he could get some relief without going over to the next stall, without being anywhere in the barn he didn't have a reason for. It could all be over in a flash. He was brushing with his left hand, so unbuttoning wasn't difficult. His dick sprung out. He took his hand off and let the movement of his brushing carry his penis through the short hairs of the horse. And that's what he was doing when Hugh said, "I didn't know you were so fond of that animal."

Connell lunged at him. Hugh tried to raise his crutch. But it caught in the leather of his poncho. Connell batted it down. Hugh stumbled, and swung his other crutch. It caught Connell on the back of the neck. Stunned him. Connell bent over, lunged, and tackled Hugh around the waist. Hugh tumbled to the ground, Connell still attached. Both crutches fell away. Connell climbed on top of Hugh so that he was sitting on his stomach. He drew his right fist back. But his pants were loose and his dick standing between them, over Hugh's chest. Connell looked down and saw it. He saw Hugh red in the face, struggling, his jaw clenched.

Had Connell been a different kind of man, he might've held Hugh's wrists to the ground and done something he would've regretted for the rest of his life. But Connell was a straight shooter all the way around. Instead, he crumpled and rolled off his brother. He lay on the floor, put his head in his hands. The first thing he said was "Don't tell Mama."

Hugh rubbed his left wrist. "Don't worry about that." He rubbed his right one. He took a deep breath. The underside of his brother's dick wasn't a picture he wanted lodged in his head. He replaced it with an image of Connell rubbing himself against his horse. Still, Hugh was fearful and mad. He said, "There's no good way to say 'Mama, yer firstborn's fucking a horse.'"

"I wasn't fucking her. I was just using her." Connell covered his eyes with an arm.

Hugh sat up and reached for a crutch. Gripping one, he felt safer. He looked down at his brother's privates. "Cover yourself up."

Connell was wilted by then. He raised his hips, tucked himself in, and buttoned his pants. He rested his buttocks on the ground again. He said, "Florence is driving me nuts."

Hugh breathed in deep. He breathed out and in again. His emotions passed with his breath. He and Connell had had many fights. Some even naked. This one was different only in that Connell had been so largely aroused. But that wasn't by him. And Connell hadn't finished off with him what he'd started with the horse. Hugh was powerfully thankful for that. He took another deep breath. He took in several more. His thoughts moved to the words Connell had just spoken. He didn't feel in any position to give advice. And he doubted Connell would take any from him. Hugh knew how Connell felt about the situation at the bawdy house, and he knew just as well that every man in the Nation had heard about his humiliation. His thoughts turned to that. He was glad his father wouldn't live to hear it. Or to have it said behind his back. He figured it would never reach his mother's ears. But he did expect to get taunted with it, himself. He thought maybe the only thing that could keep that from happening was the seriousness of Claudette getting killed. Crow wouldn't be missed. He was a Creek; a mean one at that. But Claudette hadn't ever really done any harm. Most men had either enjoyed her pleasures or felt sorry for her. Hugh chewed on his guilt day and night. He was chewing on it again when Connell said, "I can't even get a peek down her dress."

Hugh lay back and stared up to the floor of the hayloft. He couldn't see much hope for anything at all. He was tired of everything. That tiredness included fighting with Connell. He said, "It'll happen. Just give it time."

"Do you think?"

Hugh hadn't given Florence much thought. Nor had he spent any thought on Connell's advances towards her. He assumed they were doing what everybody did, as often as they could. He said, "Sure. She's got the eye for ya. Ya just gotta get her in the right circumstances."

Connell listened to the rain. It was letting up. Maybe Hugh was right. He hoped so. He relaxed some. The ground wasn't uncomfortable. He didn't want to go out in the weather or up to the house. He wanted to sleep. He was halfway to that when Hugh said, "Mama sent me out here to find you. Papa's asking for Puny."

"He's talking?"

"No. Just Puny's name. Mama wondered if you could go get him, since you're already wet."

"She saw me ride in?"

"Cliff did."

"That figures. I've already talked to Puny. He's coming tonight. Are you as tired as I am?"

"I got some sleep. But, yeah. I'm whipped." Hugh was lying on his poncho. It was wet on the side next to the ground, but dry on the inside next to his back. He said, "Why don't we just sleep here until the rain lets up?"

The Dying, and All Around It

BEFORE HE STRIPPED IN THE winter kitchen, Connell told Clifford to bring him clean clothes. He was soaking in the tub when people began to arrive. He got out, toweled off, and put on the trousers Cliff had brought. He discovered the shirt was missing a button, stuck his head out the door bare-chested, and called to Cliff, who was in the hall with Alabama, her hand on his shoulder. Cliff said, "Excuse me. Connell's naked."

As soon as he could reach him, Connell grabbed Cliff by the collar. Jerked him in the door. "I've got clothes on. Mind your mouth."

"How was I supposed to know?"

"Go upstairs and get me a shirt with all its buttons. Make sure it's a white one. And I need my Sunday boots."

"Are you crippled, too?"

"No! I just don't want anybody to see me not dressed. It's not polite."

Clifford sighed. He was tired of waiting on brothers.

"Who just came in, anyway?"

"Aunt Alabama and Uncle Dennis."

"Anybody else?"

"Some other folks. I can't remember."

"The Taylors?"

"You mean Flor-*ence*?"

Connell raised his hand.

"Wouldn't ya like to know."

Connell grabbed Cliff's arm. "Tell me, you little turd."

Tears welled in Cliff's eyes.

Connell suddenly felt awful. An hour's sleep in the barn hadn't been nearly enough. He let Cliff go. "I didn't mean that. Just get me my clothes, will ya?"

CHECK, ALABAMA, AND SEVERAL OTHERS were in the sickroom. Alabama was pale in the face and clutching a bedpost with bloodless fingers. Check rose and said, "Come with me." People moved aside to let them through. Check stepped into the dining room and pointed Alabama into the only remaining chair.

Alabama said, "I'm sorry, Check. I'm not feeling well."

Check cupped her chin. "You aren't looking well either."

Alabama took Check's hand in hers. She kissed it. "I'm fine. We need to worry about you."

Check's face relaxed a little. Tears came in her eyes. Alabama stood and embraced her. She said, "He's going to a better place."

Check put her hands on Alabama's waist and pulled back to see her face. "Any place without this pain would be better. I'm sorry about the smell. I can tell . . ."

"That's only part of it. Don't feel bad for me. I've seen much worse." She added, "It wouldn't affect me if I weren't with child."

Check's eyes widened. Both women smiled. They embraced again, drew back, and patted each other's cheeks. Just for a moment, Check felt relief. Then, from the hallway, a female voice called, "Oh, Connell! How handsome you look! In spite of your tribulations." The voice was too high, too loud. Check's and Alabama's smiles fell. Check's eyes narrowed. Alabama's rolled.

Suzanne Taylor was often affected and attention-seeking. And always too enamored of her social position. She was a Ross on one side, a Vann on the other. And Check and Alabama disagreed about her. Check thought Suzanne couldn't get over being a Ross. Alabama thought she couldn't get over being a Vann.

BY EVENING, THE HOUSE AND its porches were crowded. Dennis, Bell, and the Benge men and boys had taken up posts in the hall. Except for Glad, the carpenter, most of Fort Gibson's business community were seated, hunkered, or standing around. That included, to Hugh's discomfort, Willow's husband, Harry Watson. Hugh had looked for Willow when Harry walked in, but he'd come with other men. Some of whom had overflowed onto the back porch, where they could throw ashes and butts into the grass, talk a little louder, and stray off the subject of death.

Alabama was overseeing the food in the dining room. Sending Lizzie back and forth to the kitchen. She greeted everyone. Made certain their plates were filled when they left. Suzanne didn't particularly like that. She planned to be the mother-in-law of the oldest son of the house; Alabama's position should've been hers. She made do slicing pie, flattering people, and plotting a comeuppance.

Check, Connell and Florence, Hugh, Doc Howard, and some of the Indian womenfolk were in the room with Andrew. Connell and Florence were holding hands. Hugh, on a straight chair in the corner, was balancing Otter on his good leg. Propped beside him was a cane Doc Howard had brought. Check was over the bed, her eyes riveted to Andrew's face, her ears to his breathing. She wasn't aware of anyone except him. But she knew that the moment he died, she'd need the others. She was thankful for them. She just couldn't be distracted.

The hands, neighbors, and some fullbloods were on the front porch and lawn. When dark descended, Puny rode in. He found Clifford first, and asked him to tell Connell he was there. Connell excused himself from Florence and walked to the hitching rail. He told Puny, "Ezell and Lizzie are in the kitchen. Come in the front." He walked towards the front porch, and Puny followed. The crowd parted.

Puny first nodded to everybody in the sickroom who'd meet his gaze.

He mumbled something to Check that even he couldn't hear. He touched the footboard with the tips of his fingers. Hoped Mr. Singer could feel him reaching out. Willed that in his head. And Andrew's eyelids suddenly fluttered. Puny took that as a sign. It went straight to his heart. He began to feel warm. He was in a room filled with white people and Indians. And with dying. Puny hoped Mr. Singer would pass fast, without more pain, suffering, or medicine. He sent Andrew another thought: "I hope you see yer pa first thing." He turned away from the bed. Connell walked him through the front door.

Puny settled with Nannie and Coop at the edge of the porch. Bert and Ame were in that huddle, and Jenny found them shortly. She was carrying Paul. She handed him off to Coop, as her mother was already holding Joe. Then Coop and Nannie exchanged children, and Jenny went back to the kitchen, taking Bert with her. They returned with Bert carrying a large, heavy basket filled with cornbread, boiled eggs, and potatoes. They passed food to other families, then served their own group. They went to the summer kitchen for another round for the Indians on the ground. While setting boiled eggs over the potatoes in the basket, Jenny said to Ezell, "Puny took two handfuls of cornbread. He ain't getting enough to eat." Ezell paused kneading dough. She went back to it, harder.

An hour later that night, while everybody was busy being themselves and helping each other, Andrew took a deep breath. He looked Check clearly in the eye. And died. His eyes didn't close, but Check saw him leave. She understood before anyone else. And those few moments seemed like a wide-open space of eternity. They were the last private ones she and Andrew would ever have. In her estimation, the last intimate ones she'd ever have with anyone. Somebody coughed. She turned and said, "We've lost him." She shut his right eyelid. Did the same to the left. Her finger lingered on that lid. "The pain's gone," she said.

One of her Benge cousins put an arm around Check's shoulder. Dennis had come in. He said, "Maybe I'll read a little scripture." Several people in the room didn't believe in the Bible's heaven, and Dennis didn't see the occasion as a time to convince them. He chose a psalm. Read verses about green pastures, sheep, and fertility. His voice was strong.

When it was heard outside, some of the Indian men got up from the ground. They started a slow dance to a low chant.

After the scripture, Dennis prayed at the foot of the bed. Then all except the fuller-blooded Indians filed through, said goodbye to Andrew, and extended condolences to Check, Connell, Hugh, and Clifford. That procession went on until Check and Hugh had to sit because they could no longer stand. After the last person, Check asked for basins of water and fresh linens. Connell brought her a suit of clothes. Then Check shut the door, and she and her Benge cousins prepared the body. Andrew hadn't made water in a day. Hadn't taken solid food for several. Except for the smell of the disease, the work wasn't distasteful. Check's cousins handed her rags and towels as she needed them. And she found comfort in washing Andrew. Her hands lingered on his limbs. Her fingers on the hairs of his chest.

It was the custom of the day to lay the body out on the dining room table. But the table was filled with food, and Check found the custom repugnant. Earlier, the men had broken Hugh's bed down, and while Check and her cousins were at work, they left for the barn to gather sawhorses and planks. Connell led the group, and claimed the sawhorse in the far stall as his own. The saddle and blanket he settled on a stall wall.

In frontier fashion, the Singer hallway was the width of a trot. Once the sawhorses and planks were arranged in it, some of the women unfolded black cloth over them. During those preparations, Dennis entered the sickroom with a medicine bag in his hand. He said to Check, "A Creek medicine man named Fox handed this to me. Says he's married to a Cordery. Says you put the concoction in the mouth and sprinkle it on the chest to take care of the odor." He held up a black feather. "This gets waved over the body. There's a Creek incantation to make it work. He's offered to come in and say it for us. But everybody has to leave the room."

Check opened the bag and sniffed the contents. She handed the bag to a cousin, who did the same, and who handed it to her sister to whiff. They all agreed it smelled like bark; they weren't sure of what tree. One of the Benge women said, *"I know him. Fixed an abscess of my tooth with some kind of root."* She handed the bag back to Check.

Check shook it like its weight would provide a clue to its contents and effect. She asked Dennis, "What's his name again?"

"Fox."

"Not reassuring."

"Maybe it's different for Creeks."

"He's married to a Cordery?"

Dennis nodded.

"Is Sanders here? We could ask him."

"His boy says he's gone visiting his grown children."

Check said, "That's too bad. How 'bout Bell?"

"He's gone into town to order the casket. Fox was with Nannie Cordery. And Sanders' boy came in and got me."

Check handed the pouch back. Said, "Let me think on it."

After Andrew's body was dressed, his eyes covered with dollars, and a strap laid on his pillow, Check washed up alone in the winter kitchen. She wanted to stay there, not come out, speak to anybody, or walk back into the sickroom where Andrew, or rather his body, was still laid out. She scrubbed hard with lye soap. Felt like more of her skin than dirt was flaking off. Thought she could endure the rest of the night only by setting her jaw like her father's. She'd never expected to draw on his strength at that particular time. But, then, she hadn't, until recently, with the exception of wartime, expected to outlive Andrew. She had thought she'd most likely die in childbirth, or through some misfortune. White people lived longer than Indians. Everybody knew that. She dried her hands, clenched her teeth, and opened the door.

She gave her approval to the makeshift table, thanked the men who'd constructed it, and moved to the front porch. There, by lantern and light through the windows, she thanked the hands, greeted the fullbloods, and looked for Nannie Cordery. She found her against the wall at one end of the porch, Paul asleep in her lap. Check kneeled and touched her child's face. Said, "I'll have Cliff come get him." She touched Nannie's shoulder. Nannie touched Check's cheek. The two were like that, looking at Paul, when an Indian stepped out from the dark. He was short and sinewy. A feather was woven into his hair. Three medicine bags and a string of shells hung around his neck. He was shirtless, but wore a leather vest and leggings. He said something Check didn't understand.

She put her hand on a board and stood. "I don't speak Creek."

He switched to Cherokee. *"I make the smell go away. To the Breath Master, he goes fresh."*

The last thing Check wanted was to get into a conversation in Cherokee with a Creek in front of an audience. She said, "ii, ᎬᎥ," and let it go at that.

Fox jumped onto the porch, touched Paul's head, and followed Check inside. Two of the men in the hall nodded to him. He nodded back. Check opened the door to the sickroom. The Benge sisters were still in there with Andrew's body. They and Fox exchanged rapid-fire Cherokee. Check caught some of that. Then the sisters stepped towards the door. Eliza Benge whispered to Check, *"Can't hurt."* Check stayed in the doorframe after they left. But when Fox nodded and said something else she didn't understand, she backed away. He said something more and closed the door. Then he closed the windows and curtains. A few minutes later, he opened the door and motioned to Check. When she walked in, the room smelled of pine candles and forest grass after rain. Only that.

The men moved Andrew's body to the makeshift table in the hall. Dennis paid Fox, then left with Alabama, taking half the food for the reception at their house after the burial. When the last of the crowd dispersed, Ezell and Lizzie covered the remains of the spread with cheesecloth. Any food that could spoil was set atop ice brought up from the springhouse. Check went to bed on her cot in the sickroom, and Hugh, on his new cane, escorted Cliff and Otter upstairs. Connell and Nash sat down in the hall and watched the body.

It was well known that every now and then, a laid-out person would twitch or sit up. And a man in the Saline District had lived fifteen years after his eyelids were weighted with dollars and his chin strap buckled in place. Neither Connell nor Nash thought there was a chance of that. But occasionally a stray cat did wander into a laying-out and jump on a body. One had licked Nash's cousin's face when he'd died a couple of years back. The cousin had hated cats his entire life. The whole family saw it as an act of revenge.

Various People Pay Their Respects

EZELL SLIPPED INTO THE SICKROOM where Check was asleep on the cot. She cleared her throat. That didn't work. She cleared it again. Knocked the cot with her shoe. Check's eyes flickered open. Ezell said, "Wez surrounded by Indians."

"I beg your pardon?" Check rubbed an eye with her fingers.

"I didn't mean nothing by that, but look out the window." Ezell drew a curtain aside. On the porch and lawn were clusters of Indians. All were awake, many wore blankets.

Check said, "That's why we kept some vittles. Let me get presentable. Then let them in the house."

"Sweet Jesus. Theys must be fifty of 'em." Ezell suggested they feed them outside, but her employer's back was receding by then.

Check was brushing her teeth when she realized the Indians couldn't get from the front door to the food without passing Andrew's body. She went to the dining room, where Ezell was pouring melted ice from a pan to a bucket. She said, "They won't come past Andrew. Open the windows so they can come in them. But first open the front door. Let them see he's laid out in the hall. Don't want them to think we're inviting them in through the windows for no cause."

Ezell frowned. Threw a dish towel over her shoulder.

Check said, "Give them plates and spoons. And close that hall door before you let them in. Nobody can eat looking at a body." She left the room.

Ezell mumbled, "They'll steal them spoons."

AFTER THE FULLBLOODS WERE FED, Check washed her hair and bathed. She was at the dressing table in her real bedroom upstairs, feeling the relief of being clean and braiding her hair, when she heard Connell say, "Why, Mr. Forecaster!" His voice was unusually loud. Then she heard talk, followed by praying. If she stayed quiet on her bench in front of her mirror, Connell would take care of Forecaster. She listened for more conversation. The talking was going on too long. She was beginning to reckon that she herself was going to have to tell Forecaster he wasn't preaching the service when Clifford entered her room without knocking. He said, "The janitor's here."

"Thank you, Clifford. I hear him. Sit over there in the corner."

"Why? What'd I do?"

"You came into my room without knocking. I'll call you when your punishment's over."

Clifford pouted. But moved to the corner. "Don't forget about me."

"I couldn't if I tried," Check replied.

Forecaster had on a white shirt and a shiny black coat. He held a straw hat in one hand, a Bible in the other. Check stopped on the stairs above him, two steps off the floor. She said, "Why, Mr. Forecaster, how nice of you to come by."

"Miz Singer, you have my deepest condolences." He dropped his chin like he was praying. His bald spot was as shiny as his coat.

"And we certainly appreciate them. Don't we, Connell?" Check glared at him over Forecaster's head.

"Yes, we do, Mama." Connell hadn't slept since his nap in the barn. He was too tired to do more than agree.

Forecaster looked up, smiled, and just waited. Check hadn't figured on him being that smart. She said, "We missed you last night."

He jerked a little. "I waz preparing my sermon."

"On a Monday? How hard-working."

"Not for next Sunday. Fer the funeral. I reckoned I'd bone up. Haven't never spoke over somebody laid out."

Check went down one step. She glanced at Andrew's body, felt thankful it was covered by cloth. She laid her hand on the banister as close to Forecaster's arm as she could bear. "Oh, how thoughtful. I guess in all the confusion nobody thought to tell you that Mr. Singer's dearest friend and my relative, Mr. Bushyhead, offered to do the service. Andrew and

Dennis were like brothers. And we're related to the Bushyheads, Adairs, Martins, and both of the Rogers families in so many different ways it's hard to keep track."

That was partially true. But also something of a lie, designed solely to confuse the white janitor into thinking about political implications before he pressed further. Check hoped Andrew, if he heard, would forgive her. She continued, "So, it's only natural in these situations to keep the services in the family. Or families, as the case may be." She caught herself before she said, "It's the Cherokee way." She was thankful she had. Connell had perked up, and seemed to be listening.

Forecaster scratched his head with the hand holding his hat. "I didn't think of all that."

"It's true, nevertheless. But we're so glad you're here. Won't you come have something to eat?" Then Check realized the fullbloods had consumed every last morsel on the dining room table. She added, "I was just going to the kitchen to ask Ezell to make me some fresh eggs and biscuits. I'd so like for you to join me. You, too, Connell, if you want."

Connell mumbled that he'd already eaten and needed some sleep. But Rob Forecaster was delighted. He didn't have to deliver his first funeral sermon over, of all people, Mr. Singer. He could polish it, and save it for somebody else. Plus, he had a chance for a meal with Miz Singer. He could fill his stomach, and maybe win her favor.

The Funeral

WHEN GLAD BROUGHT THE CASKET, the hands unloaded and carried it into the house. Overseen by Check, they lifted and settled Andrew's body inside. Then they gathered 'round while Connell read from *Leaves of Grass*. Most of the men had had minimal schooling, so thought they were listening to scripture. When Connell finished, they said, "Amen."

By the time Check had set a picture of herself and the boys on Andrew's chest and closed the lid, other hands had hitched horses to the wagon and brought it up to the house. Bert, Ame, and two more hands were assigned to guard the buildings, livestock, and ferry. The rest helped Glad and Connell carry the casket to the wagon or fell in behind the lifters before they went to their horses and mules. When the box was loaded, Check and Connell boarded the buggy and sat Paul between them.

Connell picked up the reins and pulled out towards the cemetery. Hugh was behind them, driving the wagon, Clifford and Otter on the bench with him. Ezell and Lizzie were crammed in the bed with the casket and four hands. Others were mounted, most two apiece. The party was trailed by a flock of Indians afoot, and moved at the pace of a horse's clop. As the procession turned into the road, the Corderys joined up. Further towards Fort Gibson, the Benges folded in.

The line of mourners could be seen from a long way off. At the edge of town, Negro eyes caught the parade. Seeing Lizzie and Ezell in the wagon, several people came out from behind shacks and walked parallel to, and a little back from, the party. One bold girl, a friend of Lizzie's, wiggled in between horses and Indians, and walked near the left rear wheel.

The Bushyheads' house wasn't directly on the route. Their buggy, and the Gulagers', met the party at the intersection of the road from the fort. Marty Gulager was Granny Schrimsher's third surviving daughter, and Granny was with Marty and her husband. They'd left Puny and Bell behind at the Bushyheads' house. Bell could easily guard it on his own, and he and Dennis had urged Puny to go on. But Puny resisted with the excuse of protecting the post office. His real intention was to go later, by himself. He needed to avoid Ezell, and wasn't practiced at death. He also couldn't tell what Indians and white people were likely to do next.

The Taylors' front lawn was on the route. They joined in two buggies, one for Nash and Suzanne, the other for their daughters. Behind them were Doc Howard and his wife. On horses were town men, including Teddy Brewster, the blacksmith; Cox, the saddlery owner; and Major Percival, a retired officer. Mr. Spencer, Clifford's schoolteacher, was afoot, and had a gaggle of students with him. Cliff jumped off the wagon to walk with his friends.

As they moved out of town and up a low hill, the Martins stood clustered at the side of the road with the Adairs and the Foremans, their cousins. Their men were dressed in suits and shirts with high collars, some with ruffles. Their hats were stovepipe, derby, and cowboy. At the crest of the hill and the entrance to the Cherokee National Cemetery, Hellfire Jack Rogers' descendants and Rich Joe Vann's grandchildren were waiting on handsome horses and in brassy buggies. The funeral party climbed towards them slowly, a breeze cooling their backs. A cloudless sky spread out before and behind them. The wildlife disappeared into the weeds and the trees. By the time they reached the crest, assorted Rosses from Park Hill had fused with the Rogers and Vann contingents. When the procession turned into the cemetery path, they joined its tail.

The graveyard was high in prairie grass, too new to be populous. Most graves were poor Indians', marked by smooth sandstones. But one of Foremans was under an etched piece of granite; so was a Meigs child. And the stone of Mary McSpadden, Check's first cousin, had been erected three years in the past. The mounted mourners and those in buggies tied their horses to a few saplings, tilted northeast by the wind. They stood in groups made of cousins and kin. The walkers sat on the ground. The men of families still devastated by the War wore patched Confederate or Union jackets and hats. The women wore long dresses; some of fine dark material, others of homespun cotton. All wore scarves draped over their shoulders. Their hair was braided or loose, depending upon their marital status.

The men closest to Andrew in life dug the hole under Check's supervision. She had the earth moved and the casket laid in so that his head faced east, the direction morning prayers were sent to the homeland. She made that choice for her grave, not for his. After the men shoveled dirt back in, Connell, Hugh, and Clifford threw the last clumps on the mound, and Connell and Clifford packed it down.

Check was past thought or feeling. But if Andrew's spirit was hovering, he would've found his funeral party confounding. And wondered how he, a white Yankee merchant turned farmer, had died in such a strange and foreign land. For after the ground was packed, the son of the most famous Cherokee preacher prayed over his grave, first in the native language and then in English. Ceremonial smoke floated from small fires set by family groups. On a spot southeast of the bare earth, a few men and women danced to a chant. Others in the party included white frontier entrepreneurs, former slaves, and more than one man who'd escaped from the law in the United States. But mostly the mourners were a large group of mix-blooded people who shared a common history. They were neither Indian nor white, but both. And uniquely American.

THE SEARCH FOR GOLD

George Hops a Ride

GEORGE SIXKILLER'S INDIAN NAME, ᎭᎶᏒ, suited him. He moved in fits and starts, scampered from place to place, popped up everywhere, and faded into the woods when he wanted. He'd been rambling around between Tahlequah and Manard, but within sight of the Military Road, when the Rosses' horses and buggies passed on their way to the funeral. As soon as George saw them, he figured he was missing out on something everybody else was in on. He quickened his pace, took a shortcut through an orchard, and trotted down the thoroughfare in the same direction the Rosses had gone. After a while, he slowed and stepped to the side of the road to take a leak in the weeds. He was tucking himself in when he saw some mules and a wagon coming from the direction of Tahlequah. George was never one to walk when he could ride, and never one to be alone when others could enjoy his company. So he waited at the side of the road until the wagon was on him. He waved to the Negro driver, and said in English, "How 'bout a ride?" The driver ignored him.

That sort of irritated George. Any Freedman would've stopped and picked him up. That Negro was uppity. But during the night they'd been together at the bawdy house, George had adjusted to Puny, so he swallowed his pride, trotted alongside the wagon, and asked the driver where everybody was going.

"White man name of Singer died."

George said, "I knowed him! Can I catch a ride?"

The man said, "Do what ya want," but didn't slow the mules.

George pumped his arms to get up speed, jumped onto the sideboard, and bounded into the seat. When he caught his breath, he said, "Whatcha hauling?"

"Strawberries. They ain't fer you."

Strawberries were the delight of the tribe. As tots, children were told the Creator had made them especially for Cherokees. These were the first of the season. George licked his lips. "Who they fer?"

"The mourners."

George looked behind him. Bright-colored cloth covered bushel baskets. He said, "I helped take the bullet outta Hugh Singer's leg."

The Negro cut his eyes around. Pushed his straw hat back on his head. His smile revealed even, white teeth. "No fooling? You waz there?"

"Course I waz. Sanders Cordery's my friend. Him and I carried Crow Colbert's body into the Creek Nation."

The man's eyebrows raised up. "My name's Hank. Reach back there and get us some berries. We can eat whiles ya tells me about it."

The Reception

CHECK SAT ON THE BUSHYHEADS' porch with Alabama, Marty Gulager, Granny, and the Benge, Rogers, Adair, and Martin women. Fortunately, the porch was wide, long, and L-shaped, so that it extended across both the sides of the house fronting the river. Around the corner from Check's group, Suzanne Taylor was set up with her Ross and Vann cousins. Their efforts were concentrated on vying over describing the sights of Cincinnati, St. Louis, Philadelphia, and, in particular, New York City.

Below the porch, the yard was polka-dotted with bright quilts, baskets, and slings of food. Families and friends, milling from spread to spread, nibbled goodies, caught up with each other's news, and sprinkled gossip around. Children ran all over the lawn, and at the edges, three circles of boys and girls were on their knees shooting marbles. Other children pitched balls and horseshoes. The young men and older boys passed around ropes and showed off their tricks. Most of the marriageable girls and their slightly younger sisters watched them. Family men hung on the wagons that hauled the food. They talked politics, the new judge in Fort Smith, the crops, and the weather. The Negroes clustered around the post office dogtrot and porch. One of them had a fiddle, another a drum. Spread through the crowd were baskets of the Rosses' strawberries and pots of cream that Dove and her sister had churned that morning. It was a warm, cloudless, and, for those not directly affected, happy afternoon in the Cherokee Nation.

Hugh spotted Willow on a quilt with one of her daughters and one of her sisters. Willow was brushing a little girl's hair. Hugh thought the child was her granddaughter. On the next quilt over were three other Starr women and, around them, several children. Hugh was glad to see that none of the women's husbands, nor any of the Starr brothers, were with them. Harry Watson was in a group of men surrounding a wagon near the road. Hugh always kept an eye out for him. He also surveyed the lawn and the porch. His mother was safely encircled by cousins and friends. He looked back towards Willow's family. He didn't want to be seen staring, but hoped, if he looked hard enough, Willow would glance up. He had no doubt she knew about the bawdy house debacle. And, if she'd look his way, he'd be able to tell from her face how she felt about it. It seemed to Hugh that everybody had some judgment in their eyes. He'd been glad he'd stayed by his father's bed or with his little brothers most of the night before. That he'd had reason not to mingle with the men in the hall and on the back porch.

So Hugh was uncomfortable on the lawn at the reception. But glad Doc Howard had given him a cane. The crutches had felt like a badge of shame. He leaned on his stick and alternated between looking towards the Starrs' quilts and searching for Cowboy or Bob. They were about the only two men in the Nation he didn't feel embarrassed in front of. They'd been at the bawdy house, and had themselves been afraid. They'd carried Crow's guts to the stream. They'd given him good words to go on.

After what seemed like a long time but was only minutes, Bob Benge came to within shouting distance. Hugh called him over.

Bob said, "You happen to see Sarah anywhere?" He'd been sparking Sarah Foreman for over a year.

"Saw her a few minutes ago. She was braiding Betsy Adair's hair."

"Betsy's getting married?"

"Not that I know of. I think women practice."

Bob rubbed a rope he was carrying. "She needs to be practicing with me." He cleared his throat with a chuckle.

"See the Starrs over there?" Hugh nodded in their direction. "Willow Watson there on that mostly yellow quilt? You think you could get her away from the others and maybe bring her towards me? Just tell her I'd like to speak with her. You can play dumb from there."

Bob looked around. Everybody he knew was out on the lawn or up on the porch. A thousand eyes might see anything going on. He hadn't known Hugh was interested in Willow Watson; hadn't even known they knew each other. But Harry Watson sometimes cut his hair. When he did, his scissors and razor were fairly close to his neck. Bob raised an eyebrow. "That could be risky."

Hugh had already gotten Bob into one awful situation. He didn't want to press him against his will. But unless Cowboy happened by, he didn't have anybody else he could ask. And Cowboy could have the same reaction. Hugh sighed, and rocked on his cane.

Bob said, "I'll try. But I swear, Hugh, you git me into some shit." Then he lifted his hat and scratched his head. "Don't rightly know how to thread all them women."

"See the girl sitting next to her? That's her daughter, Birch. She ran her husband off a couple of months ago."

"What fer?"

"Drinking. Not working. She's a looker."

"Is it her yer after, or the mother?"

Hugh blushed. "I'm not after either one of them. I just want to talk to Willow. We're old friends."

"You can't be that old of friends. Ya just been here five years."

"Just go see if you can entertain Birch with a rope trick. Or take her some strawberries. Once you're there, I'll wander over."

Bob frowned. "What if Sarah catches me?"

Hugh shoved Bob's shoulder. "Sarah needs to mind her chicken yard. Fox could get her rooster."

Bob looked towards Birch. She was an attractive girl. And if her husband was shiftless, she might enjoy a few rope tricks. Bob cleared his throat. "Okay. But let's try not to get shot."

Hugh looked the other way. He couldn't bear to watch if Bob failed. He thought he'd get more chances with Willow if he could just get through this rough spot on the trail. His father's funeral gave him a sympathy edge he didn't want to waste. He knew his papa wouldn't approve of that, and felt a little guilt. But he also knew his father wouldn't approve of anything about Willow, so one more thing seemed like a twig rather than kindling. Hugh hooked Ross Meigs into a conversation while he waited for Bob to get established with Birch. Then he turned back around.

Bob wasn't with the Starrs. Hugh looked for Birch. She was there. But Willow wasn't. He surveyed the lawn. Neither Bob nor Willow were in sight anywhere. Hugh swore in his head. He didn't know what to do. He rocked on his cane and pretended to be interested in Ross's description of a tornado a few years back. But neither Willow nor Bob appeared, and after a while Hugh couldn't stand tornado talk any longer. He excused himself and limped over to a group of men throwing ropes. There, he stood and brooded. He held his neck stiff to keep from looking over towards the Starr women's quilts.

But not all the men and women at the reception were segregated into groups of the same sex. Some were sparking. They left the gathering in pairs and wandered down by the river or through the trees. And off one secluded path, so far away from the party that only an occasional high shriek of a child could be heard, Connell and Florence were deep in the woods, following a path laid down either by wild creatures or by Indians before their time. Eventually, they came upon a little stand of evergreen saplings that closed in a circle. Connell brushed a limb aside and said, "Let's go in here. I'm completely tuckered out." He tugged Florence's hand and led her to the center of the thicket, where the light didn't penetrate much. It was cool enough that moss grew in a blanket on the ground. Connell threw himself down. "I haven't had any sleep," he said. He held out his palm.

Florence was dressed in high-laced boots, a long skirt, and a blouse with ruffles. Her grandmother Taylor's cameo nestled between her breasts. Dark hair flowed down her back. Her cheeks were still chubby. She often sucked on the insides of her mouth to make them more fashionable. She did that, and then said, "I think I'll stand."

Connell winced and groaned. "Oh, baby. I just want you to be comfortable."

Florence crossed her arms. "I'm comfortable standing. We have to talk about last night."

"We can talk better if you're down here." Connell closed his eyes and reclined.

"Don't go to sleep, Connell. Look at me. I'm serious." Florence could feel herself beginning to cry. She blinked to squeeze out a tear.

Connell opened his eyes. "I know you are, baby. I'm serious, too. We're engaged." He propped up on his elbows.

"When do I get my ring?" Florence's lower lip was getting fuller, perhaps on its own, perhaps in contrast to her sucked-in cheeks.

"Soon, darling. As soon as I can find a suitable one."

"What's it going to look like?"

"Why don't you just sit down right here and tell me what you want it to look like." Connell patted the moss.

"I'm not coming down there 'til we talk."

"We're talking." Connell showed both palms.

"You know what I mean, Connell."

Connell, as exhausted as he was, knew he'd better get up. He put a hand to the ground and rose. He took Florence's chin in one palm, her hand in the other. "Darling, what's there to say? We love each other."

"Are you sure, Connell? Because Daddy would kill me if he knew what we did and we didn't get married."

Connell shook his head. He took a long sigh that he hoped made him appear older and wiser. He spoke softly. "Honey, what we did is natural. It's what happens between a man and a woman who truly love each other." He bent over and nuzzled Florence's neck.

"I've never done that before." Her voice quivered. But she tilted her head so that Connell could nuzzle more.

Connell realized he was in a situation where words weren't enough. He kissed Florence's earlobe and pulled the lower part of her body closer to his. Then Florence started a speech that, perhaps, she'd rehearsed. "Connell, last night was special. I just let you go that far because of your daddy. I don't want you to think we can do that again 'til we're married."

"It was special to me, too," Connell said between nuzzles and kisses. And he was telling the truth. He'd never gotten further than a fleeting hand on Florence's breast. But the night before, they'd slipped into the barn and she'd squeezed his penis until he had come. That had considerably dulled his pain, but had frightened her. He added, "You'll never know how much you've helped me, Florence. You've made the ordeal bearable."

Florence didn't particularly like the sticky stuff that had come out of Connell. But she knew it wasn't supposed to come out on her hand. It was supposed to come out inside her — or really, into a towel — until they wanted children. But a towel hadn't been available, because all of that had been unplanned. Done on the spur of the moment, only because of the stress of Mr. Singer's dying. An unusual circumstance. Florence told herself she was a compassionate person — the type of woman other people spontaneously turn to in grief. And it was only natural to comfort one's future husband. Besides, she'd just the day before heard a rumor that Hugh Singer had been using the whore at the bawdy house when all that awful business occurred. She didn't want Connell getting any ideas from his brother. The barn had been risky, but the cover of trees was perfect. And the moss could be useful. She thrust her pelvis forward. She said, "I'm just so sorry about your father."

Connell had his hand on his buttons, his mouth on Florence's lips, and his tongue in her throat in a blink. And within less than a minute their only impediment was where to accomplish their mission without mussing Florence's clothes. Between kisses and fumbles they debated that. Finally, because Florence's slips were easily lifted and her pantaloons just as easily lowered, they went at each other standing up. Fortunately, Florence, although a virgin, had ridden horses all her life. Connell, well endowed, slipped in inch by inch, with several questions about, "Is that hurting?" It was, just a bit. But Florence had been warned about that, and she was, in her own way, just as determined as her fiancé. He got in, and she loosened up. They rocked back and forth a little. Then he slipped out before he deposited any seeds in her furrow. He pointed and squirted in a direction that didn't muss either of their clothes. After they cleaned off with moss, they lay down, snuggled, giggled, and made promises. They both felt better than they had in months.

Poking Around at the River

LIZZIE AND JENNY HAD ALSO separated from the reception. They were walking along the rocky bank of the Grand. Lizzie was searching for any place a stash could be hidden. Jenny was imagining her future with Bert, including children. She was hoping to pry from Lizzie what it was like to be pregnant. However, neither girl wanted the other to know what she was doing. So both were being cagey, and they weren't making progress in either direction.

Lizzie pointed her snake stick and said, "Yuck. That's nasty."

A fish skull was nested in mud close to a large rock. A bug crawled out of an eye socket. Jenny said, "Jist a dead fish," and poked it with her stick.

Lizzie shivered. "That's a hex sign. Sure enough."

"No it ain't. It's fish bones." Still, Jenny looked away.

Lizzie stuck her stick under another rock and pried it from its resting place. It was maybe the tenth rock she'd done that way. Jenny was growing suspicious. Still, she was more interested in her own goals than in anything else. She said, "You gonna have another baby?"

Lizzie kept looking down at the rocks. She never thought about having another child. Her little girl was her raw, lost love. But she couldn't lay words on that. She cleared her throat. "Let's check under that one." She pointed her stick towards a large stone.

The two scraped mud from around the sides of the boulder, and from under it just a bit. In the effort, they pursed their lips. Then Jenny said, "I know wez looking fer sompthing. What is it?"

Lizzie had pulled in her feelings. She was focused again on her goal. "Jist sompthing I lost when I lived in town. Help me git this up."

Jenny shoved her stick into mud. She pressed down to lever the rock up, and Lizzie pulled on it from behind. It loosened with a sucking sound. There wasn't anything in its hole except worms, bugs, and larvae.

The two did that with two or three more stones. Then Jenny said, "Ever'body's eating strawberries and cream. We're out here digging and lugging muddy rocks. I'm going back." She jammed the tip of her stick into the earth.

Lizzie was afraid to be left by herself. "Jist go on. I won't hav'ta give ya nothing when I find it." She waved her stick.

"I don't care if ya do or if ya don't give me nothing. What is it, anyway?"

"I ain't telling. Jist go on back and eat strawberries and cream with those Indians. I don't care."

"Strawberries make me itch. If yer'll tell me what yer looking fer, I'll tell ya how to find it."

Lizzie was too smart to fall for that. She looked towards the river. When she turned back to Jenny, she said, "I had me a big ole sack of jewelry. When I got laid up with that baby, somebody stole it in the middle of the night."

Jenny scratched her ankle with her stick. "What makes ya think they brung it to the river?"

Lizzie started coughing. She managed to have a full spell, to have to sit down, and to get patted on the back before she came up with an answer. Finally, she said, "Ya can't tell nobody. But Puny waz there. He chased 'em down here. Saw 'em drop the sack in the rocks and jump off in the water, over there." She pointed to a big boulder.

Jenny didn't think that was true. But it could be. People were always stealing things. And they did cross the river at about the place Lizzie was pointing. It was also clear that Puny had spent time alone with Lizzie. Jenny said, "What kind of jewelry waz it?"

"Necklaces and earrings."

"Where'chu git 'em?"

"Stolen off a Yankee white woman." Lizzie's eyes expanded. "She and her Jayhawker husband come into the Nation from Kansas. They was planning on stealing Indian land jist as soon as the War waz over. She bragged about it to my mama. But Mama, she waz attached to Miz Singer's mama. And she wadn't putting up with none of that. So she stole her jewelry, and told me when I left to take it for safekeeping." Lizzie thought that sounded like a pretty good story.

And Jenny was only eleven years old; she didn't yet know that effective lying is part details, part truth, and part what the listener wants to hear. But she did know she didn't like thieving Yankee white people. And she knew, too, that Lizzie's mother had belonged to Miz Singer's mother. She also hoped that someday her own mother would come by some jewelry and entrust it to her. Jenny said, "I can show ya where it is. Cherokees know how to find anything lost." She was totally earnest.

Lizzie saw the sincerity on Jenny's face. And she knew Indians were mysterious folks who could do things other people couldn't. She said, "If yer'll show me, I'll do anything ya want." For a moment, she completely forgot she was looking for a gold stash rather than jewelry.

Jenny said, "It's a deal. Tell me what it's like to be pregnant."

Lizzie's face fell. She hadn't expected that. She'd just stopped bleeding. And she didn't yet know where her baby was buried. Her emotions on the subject were as raw as a skinned catfish. She couldn't trust what would come out if she spoke. She opened her mouth, but closed it. Tapped her stick on a rock. Then she looked off towards the river. She took a deep breath. "I had an easy time 'til the end. That's the hard part. Gitting the baby out and trying to git it enough to eat. Ya want to put off babies 'til yer full grown. Yer breasts gotta be big."

Jenny looked down at her chest. Little knobs were poking out under her dress. Her mind went to their milk cow's sack. She straightened her back, stuck her chest out, and looked down again. The knobs weren't any bigger.

Men Get Bad News

AS SOON AS THE FUNERAL party had returned into the lane, Puny had left the Bushyheads' house for the cemetery. He rode at a gallop, made good time, and, after a spell of heavy breathing on his horse, dismounted by the mound over the casket. He held the reins in one hand and picked up dirt with the other. He let the handful run through his fingers and scooped up another. He tilted his palm and shook a little dirt out. He said, "Mr. Singer, you waz always nice to me, and fair. I don't know how ya got yerself here. I don't know why I'm here neither. Following you, I guess. But we're a long way from home; on flat land, surrounded by prairie and Indians. I'm glad ya ain't hurting no more. I'll come out here again to see ya by and by." Puny looked around. He didn't know why Miz Singer hadn't buried Mr. Singer on the farm. The graveyard seemed lonesome. Puny looked to the sky. The horizon stretched forever. He looked in another direction. The sky there was just as wide.

Puny looked down at his hand. He saw his life in the remaining dirt in his palm. His mother was there. His father, too. Working in the post office had inspired him to write them a letter. He'd mailed it three days back. Hoped it'd get to them soon. He hadn't intended on spending his life across the country, away from them and his brothers and sisters. He'd intended to settle in Ohio. But one thing had led to another. He hoped his parents were still alive; prayed they were. They were older than the Singers, so they could be passed. But both of his grandmothers had still been kicking when he'd left home. He came from strong stock.

His mind traveled to Ezell. To the first time he'd seen her in the street. He felt like he'd been struck by lightning. That'd been the wondrous thing about it. He'd never felt that before, or since. And his only disappointment with their life had been not having a family. He'd thought it was him. The thought had grown to haunt him day and night. But clearly, he could father children. He was a complete man. It was Ezell. And Puny had been thinking on that. He'd thought about it while he'd lived at the bawdy house. He thought about it while he sorted mail. And while he smoked his pipe on the post office porch after poring over maps with Mr. Bushyhead. He'd come to a conclusion. He wanted to get his share of that stash. Work for Miz Singer until she got her feet under her. And then take Ezell back to Ohio. He had nieces and nephews. His blood would flow through them into the future. He looked to the horizon again and turned his hand. The dirt spilled. There was the little problem of persuading Ezell to take him back.

On his return ride to the reception, Puny spied first the Negroes clustered in and around the post office trot. A fiddler was standing with his foot on a log, a drummer next to him. Two or three couples were dancing a reel. A bushel basket was sitting on a stump. The fiddling and drumming wasn't loud enough to hear over the sound of hooves, but it bounced off the post office walls with beat enough for the dancers to be moving in unison. Puny's heart jumped in his chest. He was lonesome for African people. Wanted to get to them fast. And as he rode closer, he recognized Ezell as one of the dancers. She wasn't wearing her scarf. Her hair was loose and wild. In one hand she was flapping her skirt; her other hand was waving in the air. She was prancing around a tall, muscular man wearing red suspenders and a straw hat tipped back. That man's butt was wiggling. Puny pulled on the reins, stopped, and made a huffing sound as loud as a horse's snort. There he sat for a while, breathing hard, watching Ezell's hair, hand, and skirt, and the man's behind. It looked like it needed a good kicking.

Puny clenched his teeth. He willed Ezell to notice him. That didn't work. He willed somebody else in the cluster to look up. He jerked his horse's reins to make it prance to the side. He jerked the reins in the opposite direction. But not a head lifted. Nobody turned away from the dancing. Everybody was having a good time. Not paying attention to anything beyond the trot. Puny scanned the group for Lizzie. Even she was nowhere around. Finally, Puny spat, walked his horse to the hitching post closest to the Bushyheads' house, and dismounted there. He spat again. Then he joined a group of younger Cherokee men who were twirling ropes. Hugh was sitting in the grass watching Cowboy Benge show off.

Puny said, "Who's that black buck over there?" His head jerked.

"Where?" Hugh craned his neck.

Puny nodded towards the trot.

Hugh still hadn't seen Bob Benge or Willow, either one. He was tired of imagining what Bob and Willow could be up to. Tired of sitting out in public among people he felt sure were thinking about his dick being out at the bawdy house. Thinking about his getting Claudette killed. He wanted to go home. But there wasn't any way to do that. So seeing Puny was a relief. Though Hugh saw at a glance his friend was tied in a knot. However, seated, he couldn't see much else. He extended a hand and said, "Help me up." Once on his feet, he saw clearly who'd upset Puny. He said, "Never seen him before. Must've come with some of the out-of-town folks."

George Sixkiller was nearby. He appeared to be evaluating Cowboy's rope twirling, but was actually eavesdropping. He said, "I knowed him."

Puny said, "Ya do?"

"Sure!" George slung his hair like a dog shaking off water. "Name of Hank. Came back from Philadelphia with old Chief Ross after the War. Smart feller."

Hank's arm was around Ezell's waist. Puny growled.

Hugh bent down and picked up his cane. When he straightened back up, Puny's face resembled a thundercloud. Hugh said, "Don't worry too much. He probably lives over at Park Hill with the Rosses. It's a long way off."

Puny said, "I ain't worried. But I'm gonna beat the shit out of him jist on principle." His jaw muscles were working hard enough to knead dough.

And at that moment, Bob Benge appeared in the circle of men on the other side of his brother's twirling. He motioned to Hugh.

Hugh said, "Wait here. Don't do anything rash. I gotta relieve myself." He hobbled off.

Hugh followed Bob over to a trough. Then, past that, to where they stopped in the midst of horses tied to rails, tree branches, and each other. They were hidden by horseflesh and breathing horse smell. Bob laid a hand on a flank. He kicked a piece of wood on the ground. Hugh said, "Well?"

"I'd say give her some time." Bob's face was hidden below the brim of his hat.

Hugh looked up. A horse was giving him an eye. He felt like it was in cahoots with everybody else. He turned red in the face. He wanted to cry. Bob said something else Hugh didn't catch. He stifled the feeling rising in his chest. He couldn't be crying all the time. A lump stuck in his throat. A horse whinnied. Bob put a hand on his shoulder. Hugh shook his head. He couldn't speak. Bob said, "It's been a long day. I'm gonna get me some strawberries." He patted Hugh's back and walked off. Hugh laid a palm on a horse. It wasn't his. But the horse was warm and breathing. For a moment, he rested his face against its shoulder. Then he pulled himself together and hobbled back to the twirling.

Twilight

SOMEWHERE BEHIND CHECK, SUZANNE WAS too loudly describing a steamboat cabin with indoor plumbing. Closer by, Alabama, Marty Gulager, and Granny were chewing on the new Greek Revival–style house that Clem and Mary Rogers were building in the Cooweescoowee District. Below and in front of Check, a patchwork panorama of people were having a good time and getting on with their lives. She understood that, but resented their happiness. They seemed as removed from her as the leaves on the trees, as the stars in the sky. To keep her resentment from growing, she looked for her children. She spied Hugh first, leaning on his cane, talking to Puny. They were at a distance, side by side, looking towards the post office. Clifford was nearer, playing marbles with other children not far from the porch. Paul was asleep on Eliza Benge's lap, and Otter . . . Otter was temporarily missing. But Check had seen him not four minutes before. She looked for Connell. Scanned the lawn, and then bored in on individual quilts. She looked at the men around the wagons. Connell wasn't there either. She thought back. She hadn't seen him since shortly after they'd returned from the cemetery. And

Florence wasn't with her kin on the other arm of the porch. They must be together. Check pictured them strolling by the river, finding a rock to sit on, watching the water.

She laid her head back on her rocker, closed her eyes, and thought about Andrew. She wondered if he was watching, pictured the mound of dirt in the cemetery, recalled how devoid of feeling she'd been when the casket was lowered in. That wasn't Andrew in that box. That wasn't possible. Andrew was . . . well . . . he was somewhere. But not back at the cemetery, in the ground. He wasn't back at home, either. That sick, withered man hadn't been him. Check's thoughts drifted away from the last days of his illness to the earliest ones of their courtship. Even Andrew's accent had infuriated her father. She recalled a rage he'd gone into over the pronunciation of a word. What was it? She and Andrew had laughed about that word many times over. It was . . . It was . . . The word wouldn't come. And that made Check realize how exhausted she was. She closed her eyes. Within moments, her mind entered the twilight between wakefulness and sleep, where images arise and float away. She saw Andrew in a suit in her family's parlor . . . a section of railroad track in Ohio . . . her cousin John, smiling . . . her mother's silver-handled brush . . . an owl swooping down from a tree.

Check awoke with a start and a shiver. Twilight had come to the lawn.

A Surprise Attack

IT'D BEEN DARK FOR A while by the time Ezell and the hands started loading baskets of food into the wagon. But the Bushyheads' drive was torchlit for the occasion, and the horses stood patiently. Voices called out in the night, urging care on the road, cautioning each other about staying together, about keeping a lookout. Hugh walked up to Ezell. "ᎣᏍᏗ Benge left us a ham. I can't lift it with one hand. Will you give me some help?"

Ezell called to Lizzie, "They's two more baskets on the front porch.

I'll be back in a spell." To Hugh, she said, "Which one of the Benges is ᏔᏔ?"

"Martin. ᏔᏔ is Cherokee for Martin."

"That don't make sense."

Hugh laughed. "I know." He and Ezell were fond of each other. Most women were fond of Hugh. However, Ezell had wiped his butt as a baby; her weakness for him was rooted in that, not the usual reason. And in spite of the general prejudice against Negroes, Hugh could appreciate Ezell as a beautiful woman, and as a complicated one. He said, "Come with me. It's on a hook and a rope. We can haul it together."

They exchanged bits of gossip as they walked out of the light towards the post office. They were near that building when Hugh abruptly stopped. He said, "Wait a minute! I forgot. I'll be right back." He turned on his cane and limped off quite quickly.

Ezell started to yell after him. But, though it was dark, people were still calling back and forth in the distance, and she felt safe on the lawn. She sank to the grass and rested. Thankful for a moment of peace. The work of the past few days had been grueling. And she'd known Andrew Singer all of her life. She recalled him slipping her sugar cubes from his mother's pantry. Remembered him helping her with her numbers. Recalled him dressed in a coat and tie for her wedding. She felt real grief. And she was wondering how they'd all come to such a foreign place when a hand clamped over her mouth. Another pulled her shoulders to the ground. Suddenly, a man was astride her. Her scream was muffled.

The man whispered, "Baby, don't yell. It's me. I ain't gonna hurt ya."

Ezell recognized the voice and the smell. Panic left her. Puny took his hand off her mouth. But before she could speak, he kissed her. The kiss took a while. It was wet and full. And when it was over, Ezell struggled to regain her breath. When she finally spoke, she said, "You could've gave me some warning."

"I know, honey. I waz afraid. I've missed ya so much. I'll do anything if yer'll take me back." Hugh had given him those words.

And they took Ezell by surprise. She was uncertain how to respond. Puny grabbed her silence as a chance to kiss her again. He undid her scarf, grabbed her hair in both fists. He pressed his chest down even harder on hers. Spread her legs with a knee. Put a hand under her skirt. Then, kissing her all the while, he unbuttoned his trousers. Thrust into her, hard. Thrust again. Ezell's loins loosed up. Puny knew Hugh was guarding their privacy, and Ezell's mind sort of left her. They rocked back and forth.

Afterwards, they lay on their backs and stared at the stars. Took deep breaths and somewhat adjusted their clothes. Then Puny said, "Ya gotta let me back in my bed."

A bright star, maybe a planet, shone directly overhead. Ezell said, "That's gonna be kinda hard. Lizzie's in it."

Puny rose on his elbow. He fondled Ezell's breast with his free hand. "Can't ya put her somewhere?" There was a whiny tone to his voice.

"Well, I can't put her in the bunkhouse. She can't sleep in the big house. And she won't sleep on the porch after a skunk got her."

"She's in my bed. Ya won't throw her out? What kind of wife are ya?"

"What kind of wife am I?" Ezell scooted away. "Puny Tower, let me remind you *I* didn't put the girl in yer bed." Her voice rose. "You did that yerself."

Puny had made a misstep. Hugh had warned him about that. And he didn't want to lose ground he'd just recovered. He put his hand to his head and pinched his brow. "Yer right, darling. I'm sorry. I really am. We'll think on it, and come up with an answer."

The End of a Long Day

THE HANDS WHO'D STAYED BEHIND broke down the four-poster bed and assembled it again upstairs. But, either out of deference or ineptitude, didn't make it up. Check did that by lamplight, behind a closed door. Her hair was loosened and long over her shoulders. Across the hall, the older boys were putting the younger ones to bed. Most of their talk was muffled. But Clifford's voice was loud enough for Check to hear: "No!" And Hugh clearly said, "Don't be bothering Mama."

Check climbed into bed and thought about crying. But she was too tired for that. She fell asleep like a rock thrown into water.

IN THE CABIN, EZELL AND Lizzie were still wide awake. Ezell was reinvigorated by her visit with Puny. Lizzie was too young to be out of energy. They sat in bed, talking the way women do privately. On the subject of Hank, Lizzie said, "That man's got a butt on him!"

"Don't I know it. Can dance, too."

Lizzie had left with Jenny before the dancing began. But had come back while it was still going on. "Ya think Puny saw ya?"

"Know he did. And it worked." Ezell didn't go into detail. She was too prudish to mention marital relations. And no longer felt threatened by Lizzie or had any need to make her jealous.

Lizzie giggled. "Did ya tell Puny he waz married?"

"That subject never came up." Ezell giggled, too.

"Ya oughta make 'im crawl. At least 'til we find the treasure."

"He ain't gitting back in easy. And I done told him I ain't throwing ya to the wolves."

"Serves him right," Lizzie replied.

"You can say that again, girl." Ezell pushed Lizzie's leg with her toes.

Lizzie giggled. Then she sat up. "We're hav'ta get us an arrowhead."

"Cherokees haven't used arrows fer years. Ever'body knows that 'cept you."

"I know it! I was owned by Cherokees! But we still need an arrowhead. That's what Jenny said."

"Will an Osage one do?"

"I don't know. I reckon. Didn't think to ask that."

"Tell me more of what she said. Ya waz mysterious when ya got back." Ezell slid off the bed, went to the trunk, and lifted its lid.

"She said ya hang the arrowhead by a string, twirl it around in the air, and say this little saying. It'll point the way to whatever's lost."

Ezell drew a ball of string from the trunk. She tossed it to Lizzie. Then she held up an arrowhead between her thumb and forefinger. "Puny found this when he dug the garden."

"Wow!" Lizzie dropped the ball, jumped off the bed, and took the arrowhead to the lamp. "This'll be perfect."

Ezell picked up the ball and sat down in her rocker. She plucked her scissors from her sewing basket and cut a length of twine. She asked for the arrowhead back and wrapped the string around it at the notches. She held it by the string, jiggled it a little, and made it swing. Lizzie reached for it and moved to the other rocker. She swung it, too. They talked about Puny, and about finding the gold. They talked about the Creek medicine man making the smell of sickness go. In that single act, Fox had converted them to Indian magic.

The Problems of Orphans

FOUR DAYS AFTER THE FUNERAL, Sanders returned to the bottoms. George was still hanging around. He and Coop fished at the ferry in the afternoon. It being Saturday, they brought Bert and Ame back with them to the Corderys'. The group, including Nannie and Jenny, spent the evening around the fire. As they picked their teeth with fish bones, they relived Andrew's death, funeral, and reception for Sanders' benefit. And for their own enjoyment. Each offered an exaggerated perspective on everybody's actions and antics — except their own. They speculated on where Connell Singer spent the afternoon of his father's burial. And commented extensively on Ezell, the strawberry-wagon driver, and Puny. Eventually, Jenny said, "Ezell and Lizzie is looking fer gold." She was sitting rather primly on a log.

George said, "Ain't we all."

Coop said, "They won't find it."

Ame asked, "There's gold 'round here?"

George started talking big about stashes. Jenny glanced at Bert. She was waiting for him to ask George a question. He didn't. So she said, "I told Ezell and Lizzie how to find the stash with the arrowhead trick."

Nannie said, "That don't work."

"It worked fer finding my tooth!"

"Your tooth warn't lost. It waz over there on the ground." Coop jerked his chin.

"Well, I didn't know where it waz. And the arrowhead pointed the direction."

"Ya wouldn't have found it if ya hadn't stepped on it." Coop snickered.

Jenny threw a fish head at her brother. It bounced off his shoulder. He threw it back at her. Then he threw another that she quickly returned. Their tossing and teasing went on until Sanders said, "I'm gonna call Judge Parker down on ya both."

Bert had been waiting to talk like a man on a serious subject. The new judge fit that ticket. He said, "Does anybody know anything about him?"

"Hates Indians," George said.

"How ya know that?"

"Wants to make Indian Territory into a state. That's the talk at the inn."

"What's wrong with that?" Bert asked.

George looked up into the sky and didn't reply. Most everybody else studied the fire. Bert waited. A pop came out of the flames. He looked at Ame. Ame shrugged. None of the Indians changed expression. Finally, Bert said, "I guess I said sompthing wrong."

Sanders reached for a stick. He scratched his back with it. "Not many people 'round here trusts the United States government. Seems to be made up of thieves." He tapped the stick on the ground. Glanced at Bert out of the sides of his eyes. The boy was a little crestfallen. Sanders added, "Course, ever'body's got their own take on that. I actually got a first cousin named after that Jackson son of a bitch."

George said, "You ain't telling the truth."

Sanders said, "Ask Bell. His brother."

Bert wanted to recoup his position. "The night Mr. Singer died, Sheriff Rogers told me he thought me and Ame might be kin to some Indians 'round here. Maybe even him. According to our mother, we've got Rogers kin up thaterway." He nodded north.

Coop said, "Everybody's got Rogers kin. Yer probably jist dirty."

George said, "Hold yer arms up, we'll see."

Bert said, "I ain't any dirtier than you." But raised both his arms.

All the Indians except Jenny broke out laughing. She said, "Not like yer giving up!"

Bert lowered his arms fast. Brushed the hair off his face in a jerky motion.

Coop said, "Ya gotta take yer shirt off." He giggled.

Bert was doubly embarrassed. And he wasn't used to Indian teasing. Or had any idea why George had told him to raise his arms. Mortification ran up his throat like a hot fire. It propelled him into a standing position. He said, "Let's go, Ame." He snatched his snake stick and rifle. He walked off fast. Left Ame sitting.

The group chewed on his departure, but not for long. They hadn't meant to hurt his feelings. They told Ame to tell him they were playing. Trying to see if his armpits were as hairy as whites'. They sent him to catch up with his brother.

THE NEXT MORNING, SANDERS WOKE, stretched, and went off to the milking lot to relieve himself. While he was there, he petted the new calf and dodged a head butt by the cow. When he came back to the square, Nannie poured him a cup of ground okra and coffee. She told him Jenny had left to bathe as soon as the morning turned gray. She'd been broody. Said she wouldn't be back for most of the day. Sanders said, "Ever'body's milk's clabbered this morning."

Nannie nodded towards Coop and George, asleep on a tick. "Not ever'body. Some folks is dead."

"How 'bout some side meat?" Sanders picked Joe up and set him on the back of his neck. The baby played with his hair.

Nannie said, "How's Nannie-Berry?" She was his other wife.

"Clabbered, too. Mad at Jay."

"He's a handful." Nannie threw a piece of meat into a skillet.

"Yep. Boy's gonna break his neck trying to break horses. His daddy could do anything with a horse. Don't think Jay takes after the Berry-hills. He ain't got the touch."

"At least he's got an interest." Nannie glanced towards the tick.

"They's interested in sleeping."

Nannie shoved the side meat with a metal fork. "Jenny's sweet on that boy."

"I figured." Sanders lifted Joe off his shoulders. Set him on the ground on his feet.

"He's sweet on her, too."

"How ya know?"

"Bolted."

Sanders took two or three sips of coffee. Then he said, "Them boys is probably my aunt Peggy and uncle Alex's great-grandchil'run."

"Did Bell tell 'em that?"

"Don't know exactly what he told them. But he figured it out. Good friends with their granddaddy when they waz boys. 'Members their mama being born. She were named after Aunt Peggy. She sent 'em here. That Rogers kin he were talking about, that'd be Aunt Lucy's brood. I remember their grandfather myself. Ellis were his name. We rested with all them fer a couple years at the end of the Trail. They waz already out here."

Nannie turned her frying meat. "Ain't ya got Sanders kin over in Tahlequah?"

"Yeah. They lived 'round here 'fore the War."

Nannie lifted the meat out of the skillet. She put it in a gourd with some cornbread and handed it to Sanders. She thought about her brother off somewhere. Tried to picture his face. It came up, looking like it did when he was a child. She couldn't pull up his looks as an adult. She said, "We better take 'em in."

Sanders chewed. He and Nannie mostly saw eye to eye. There was no need to say he agreed.

Nannie broke some eggs over the skillet. They watched the boys sleep and Joe totter around. After they finished eating, Nannie said, "You wanta go over and ask 'em boys to come back? Or ya want me to do it?"

Sanders replied, "Sounds like sompthing a woman would be particularly good at."

Hearken, O Brown Arrowhead

THE JANITOR-PREACHER HAD NOT WON over Check during breakfast on the morning of Andrew's funeral. He'd confirmed her deepest suspicions. Nevertheless, the Singers were going to church because Suzanne and Nash Taylor had invited them for dinner. Check was less interested in the hands' souls than Andrew had been, and the men themselves were even less interested than she. Ezell begged off going, to catch up with her work, and Lizzie volunteered to stay and help. So the family rode off alone in the buggy and on horses that Sunday morning.

As soon as their dust settled, Jenny slipped into the kitchen. It was empty. There was a tin of biscuits on the table. She sat down and helped herself. She was munching and crying when Ezell came in from slopping chickens. She said, "Lord, child, you're too early. We still gots work to do." Then she noticed Jenny's eyes.

"I wanta live with the Singers." Jenny teared up more, but kept chewing.

"Course you do. Ever'body wants to live like the Singers." Ezell stuck the slop bucket under the sink. Jenny was on her last bite. A tear ran down her cheek.

Ezell sat down at the table. She suddenly got gentle. "What's wrong? Ya can tell me."

Jenny had a little sense of drama. But was too miserable to use it by design. She flung her arms around Ezell's neck. She sobbed sincerely.

Ezell had acclimated to young females' crying. She made soothing noises and patted Jenny's shoulder. Pretty soon, Jenny pulled away, wiped the back of her hand across her nose, and said, "Can I have some honey?"

Ezell rolled her eyes. But she got up, went to a shelf, and pulled down a jar. She said, "I guess ya want some butter to go with it." Jenny nodded and picked another biscuit from the tin.

Jenny told Ezell about how George got Bert to put his arms up in the air, and about his leaving. She said she'd been to the ferry, and that Bert wasn't there. Then Lizzie came in. Jenny had another biscuit while she told the story all over again. Lizzie gave her opinion on how to make up.

So a few minutes later, Jenny went back to the ferry. But she returned in tears again, as Bert wasn't there. Ezell said he was probably at the bunkhouse; he'd gotten locks to secure the ferry's cables, and he'd want company on his day off. Jenny couldn't hunt him over there; he'd be embarrassed again in front of the men. So she helped with the chores. And after they were completed, the three females took off walking the road towards town.

Loose dust was under their feet, a breeze stirred the air. They each carried a stick for the snakes. Ezell had freed her hair. Jenny's mind was still on Bert. Their conversation turned back to men. Lizzie said, "You can't trust one no further than ya can throw him. Jist 'member that."

Ezell said, "That's the way the Lord made 'em."

Jenny's brow furrowed over that advice. She'd never paid much attention to the Lord. But Lizzie, enjoying showing she'd learned her lesson, took Jenny's silence as a sign of the need for more instruction. When they turned onto the path to the Grand River, she said, "They'll try to sweet-talk ya. That's for certain. They's got honey dripping from their mouths. They can't do enough fer ya. And all they's want is to get their sticks into ya." She poked her snake stick straight out in the air. Thrusted it in a jabbing motion.

Ezell produced a loud, "Hum-um." She worried about Jenny and Bert, and was glad to hear Lizzie voice her opinion. Lizzie needed practice saying it, and Jenny needed to take it up. Ezell hoped they'd both remember the words in the future, when they needed them. And she suddenly felt uneasy about giving in to Puny so quickly. Maybe she shouldn't have done that. But it seemed right at the time. She ran her fingers through her hair. Reminded herself she and Puny were married. Theirs was an entirely different situation. It was her bounded duty to satisfy her husband. That was what the Lord said in the Bible. She wasn't exactly sure where.

Lizzie's preaching continued down to the riverbank, as though they were in church instead of out under the sun, with the smell of furrowed ground in the air, and the sound of the breeze rippling through the corn stalks and leaves. They'd been planning the trip for two days. Neither Lizzie nor Ezell was particularly greedy. They'd agreed if they were going to use Cherokee magic, they needed to let Jenny in on their secret and split the gold with her. When they got to some rocks, their minds turned to their mission.

Jenny pulled an arrowhead hung on a string from beneath her dress over her head. She said, "I'll tell ya what to do and we can spread out." The other two also pulled stringed arrowheads from around their necks.

Jenny moved her feet apart, held her arrowhead at arm's length, and swung it. "ᏇᎶᏞᎤᎫ! Ꭷ! ᏃᏆᏋ ᎾᎥ ᎲᎥᎯᏓ ᎠᏣᏩᏳ," she began.

"Hold on here!" Ezell interrupted. Lizzie said, "Wait, girl! We can't follow ya. Do it in English."

Jenny pulled her arm in. "I don't know if it works in English." She frowned.

"It's gonna hav'ta," Ezell said. "We can't talk that gibberish."

"It's not gib — or whatever. It's Cherokee!"

"Never mind. Jist tell us the English words."

"All right. But I ain't making no promises. It might not work in English."

"We understands that," Ezell said.

And Jenny, relieved for a way out if the gold didn't turn up, said in a voice reminiscent of Check's, "Okay. Say it after me three times. Then we'll see if ya can remember it. 'Listen! Ha! Now ya have drawn near to hearken, O Brown Arrowhead; ya never lie about anything. Ha! Now I am about to seek for it. I've lost my gold, and now tell me where I can find it. For it is mine. My name is Jenny.'"

Ezell said, "What's them 'Ha!s' all about?"

Lizzie said, "Do I hav'ta say 'My name is Jenny'?"

Jenny put her hands on her hips. "Are ya gonna ask a bunch of questions, or are ya gonna do what I tell ya?"

"Wez jist trying to understand what wez doing," Ezell said.

"Yer not supposed to understand. The arrowhead's supposed to understand. That's what's important."

And so the instruction went on. The two initiates learned how to swing the arrowheadS properly, and got the hang of the formula. They agreed to pursue their own paths until the sun hit a particular point in the sky. Then they'd meet back at their starting place.

All three, following the motions of their own arrowheads, spread out in different directions. And Ezell and Lizzie came back at the appointed time, although empty-handed. They sat down on a rock and waited. After a spell, they got up and walked the riverbank in opposite directions, keeping in sight of each other. Then they met back at their spot and called Jenny's name. They sat some more, then walked to the road in opposite directions again, keeping one another in sight. They met again on the road and talked over their options. On the far side of the river, the sun hit the treetops.

No Respecters of People

FLORENCE TOOK THE OCCASION OF Sunday dinner to announce that she and Connell were engaged. Everyone was surprised, including her intended. Nash, having not been asked for her hand, stopped with his fork in midair. He set it down on his plate full of roasted chicken and wiped his mouth with his napkin. Paul and Otter were eating in the kitchen with the help; a laugh from Paul floated into the room. A rooster crowed outside. From the foot of the table, Suzanne piped into the silence, "If you'd given us notice, we would've bought dresses when we were in St. Louis."

Check took a long drink of iced tea. She set down it carefully. Said, "That's delightful. But we have to respect your father. We'll be observing mourning for a year." Only Hugh, sitting between Florence's sisters, had the presence of mind to say, "Mama, you and Papa provided a wonderful example of wedded bliss. As have you, Mr. and Mrs. Taylor. I'm sure no young couple in the Nation has had better models." He raised his goblet.

"Here's to the bride and groom. May you have a long, happy, and fruitful marriage."

By then, Connell had gathered some thoughts. He was glad everything (well, not *everything*) was out in the open. He smiled at his brother for the first time in weeks. "Thank you, Hugh. We'll do our best."

The ride back home was silent. When the party arrived at the barn, a couple of hands took over the horses, and Cliff asked his mother, "Are her sisters gonna be part of the family?" He asked Connell, "Is the janitor conducting the service?" Check threatened a swat, and Connell didn't answer.

Hugh said, "A wedding's a complicated thing, Cliff. All that has to be worked out. Stick with me." He steered Clifford away from the others, around the house, and off to the kitchen.

Check went straight to the study, slamming two doors behind her. She sat at her ledgers, drumming her fingers until Connell knocked and came in. Before he could sit, Check said, "I like Florence, but she's rather sudden."

Connell took a cigar out of his pocket. "Well, yes, ma'am, she's high-spirited. I like that in a woman."

Check's eyebrow cocked. "I don't like surprises."

"Florence didn't mean any disrespect. She's just excited." Connell shook his head and sat. He hadn't recovered either. But he felt the need to defend Florence. And he calculated her announcement meant he'd be getting more of what he had gotten in the woods. He put the cigar, un-lit, between his teeth. Thought of thrusting in the thicket. The thought expanded into a vision. He was fumbling for a match, diverting his eyes from his mother, and trying to get his mind back into the room when a knock came on the door. Connell looked over his shoulder. Check said, "Come in."

Hugh's head, shoulder, and cane appeared. "Anybody know where Ezell and Lizzie are?"

"Have you tried their cabin?" Check replied.

Hugh left the doorway, called out "Have ya tried their cabin?," then turned back to his mother. "Yes," he said.

"Who's out there?" Check asked.

"Mrs. Cordery. She's looking for Jenny."

Check said to Connell, "It's really you I'm irritated with. You could've given me some warning. We'll continue this in a minute." She rose.

Hugh had moved to the back porch. Nannie was in the yard with a basket on her arm. She and Check greeted each other. Nannie said she'd been to the ferry. She wondered if Jenny was minding the children or playing with Clifford or Lizzie.

Check said, "We had the little boys in town with us for most of the day. We just got in a short while ago. Haven't seen anybody. But I'm sure they're around."

"If ya don't mind, send Jenny home when ya see her."

"I'll be glad to. But let me get you something first. We're still loaded with canned goods. We can't eat it all, and the cellar's full. Maybe you'll take some off my hands." She descended the steps and walked to the summer kitchen.

Nannie left with her basket full. When she was well into the potatoes, Check turned to Hugh. "It's hard to be poor, Hugh. War and luck are no respecters of people."

Darkness Falls

BY THE TIME EZELL knocked on the back doorframe of the Bushy-heads' house, she'd secured her hair in a green scarf. Lizzie was behind her, trying to look small. Ezell called in the door, "Miz Bushyhead?"

Dove came out of the kitchen, wiping her hands on her apron. "What'd'ya want?"

Ezell said, "I'd like to speak with Miz Bushyhead."

Dove looked the pair over. They'd been helpful during the reception, but were taking good jobs from Cherokee women. "The Bushyheads are on the front porch. I ain't calling 'em in. If ya wanta talk to 'em, go 'round the side of the house."

Ezell raised her chin. "We'll be glad to, Dove. Thank you so much." Lizzie mumbled. Not even Ezell heard what she said.

Alabama and Dennis were chewing on plans over strawberry pie. The baby and Mary and Clem's new house had given Alabama a desire to expand theirs. And Dennis saw an addition as a way to keep up with his in-laws, as well as a celebration of his fatherhood. They were knocking out walls in their conversation when, over Alabama's shoulder, Dennis spied Ezell and Lizzie. He was surprised. "Why, it's Check's cook."

Alabama set her plate down and turned around. When Ezell and Lizzie stopped at the steps, she said, "Ezell, is Check here?"

"No, ma'am, Miz Bushyhead. We waz jist taking a Sunday walk. I waz wondering if ya seen Jenny Cordery anywheres."

"Sanders' little girl?"

"Yes, ma'am."

"No. Have you, Dennis?"

"Can't say as I have."

Ezell said, "Ya happen to see Puny?"

Alabama paused like she was trying to avoid a spider's web. Dennis said, "He was over at the post office a while ago. Talking to a fellow about trading saddles."

Ezell and Lizzie looked towards the post office. Puny wasn't in sight. A silence arose in the group. It made Alabama even more uneasy. She said, "Ezell, is there something you need to tell us?"

Ezell looked towards the river. Dusk was settling in. She looked back at Alabama. "We waz walking with Jenny Cordery this afternoon. We broke up, and she waz supposed to meet us again. But she ain't showed."

"Where was she supposed to meet you?"

"At a rock on the Grand."

Alabama said, "You're sure she knew to come back?"

"Oh, yes, ma'am." Lizzie nodded vigorously.

Dennis felt out of his element. He said, "If you'll excuse me . . ." and started to rise.

Alabama interrupted. "We may need you here, Dennis."

. . .

A SHORT TIME LATER, CHECK was back at her desk. Clifford sat in front of her, in tears. He put a thumb under a suspender. Popped it against himself. He winced and cried some more. Check adjusted her glasses and waited. She waited longer, looking at the bookshelves beyond Cliff's head. Finally, Clifford said, "School'll be out in just two weeks. I already know ever'thing they're studying."

Check focused on him. "How do you know? You haven't been over there to find out."

Clifford sniffled, and wiggled in his chair. "Mr. Spencer told me."

"Mr. Spencer told you that you already know everything they're studying?" Check tapped the end of her pencil on the desk.

"Yes, ma'am. At the reception."

"I see. And what are they studying?"

Cliff wrapped a foot around a leg of his chair. "Reading, writing, arithmetic. Just the usual stuff."

"I see. And you already know all of that?" Check tapped the pencil again.

A knock came on the door before Cliff could answer. He jumped to open it.

Connell stood in the frame. "I'm sorry to bother you, Mama. But Uncle Dennis is here. He's brought Ezell and Lizzie with him."

"Well, thank God." Check had cooked the supper: side meat, and wild onions with eggs. She got up and followed her boys into the parlor. There, she found Dennis, Ezell, and Lizzie. The two women looked as though they'd been crying.

Check said, "Dennis, it's nice to see you. You, too, Ezell and Lizzie. What's going on here?"

Dennis said, "It seems as if Jenny Cordery has gone missing."

"Nannie was by here a couple of hours ago. Maybe she's found her."

"That could be. She could be at home." Dennis nodded to Ezell and Lizzie. "Her own home's the one place nobody's thought to look. That's probably it."

Check and Ezell exchanged a glance. Check said, "Connell, ride over to the Corderys' and see if Jenny's over there."

Clifford said, "Can I go with him?"

The corners of Check's mouth turned up. "Only if you'll go to school in the morning."

IT WAS DARK. CONNELL SANG loudly. Clifford, holding on behind him, wished he'd shut up. But Connell kept singing until they were in the middle of the Corderys' site, and he'd determined nobody was home but the dog. He told Cliff to slide off, dismounted himself, and tied the horse to the drying rack. He unhooked a lantern from his saddle, lit it, and poked his nose in the door of the cabin. Found a bed, a pallet, a baby cradle, a table filled with pots and pans, a couple of cane-bottom chairs, and a spinning wheel. Pegs held clothes on the walls, and an apple crate held knives, spoons, gourds, and plates. Although the fireplace was outside, opposite the door was a mantel and, below it, a small black kettle.

Connell and Cliff found the cow and a calf in the lot, the chickens in a scrub tree inside a pen. But Sanders' horse was nowhere around. Connell bent to the campfire; it held hot embers. He stood up and yelled, "Hey, Sanders!" No sound came back except that of the cow and calf moving around in the lot. Connell said, "They're not anywhere around here."

Clifford said, "Maybe they're bathing at the river."

"They wouldn't do that at night." Connell swung the lantern around and looked at the ground. "No sign of a scuffle."

Clifford said, "Do you think they've been killed?"

"No, idiot. I think they're looking for Jenny."

"Do you think something's happened to her?"

"Evidently," Connell said. He bit his underlip. He longed for a cigar.

Clifford started crying.

AFTER CONNELL AND CLIFFORD LEFT for the Corderys', Ezell motioned Check to the hall and then to the back porch. She said, "They's two things I didn't tell Mr. Bushyhead. One's that Jenny and that ferryman is sweet on each other. And the other's that we all waz looking fer a stash of gold."

Check said, "I don't see how those facts pertain."

"Well, maybe she's run off with the ferryman. Maybe they took the ferry and eloped into the Creek Nation." Ezell hoped that wasn't true, but it was better than other possibilities.

Check frowned. "I doubt that."

"Stranger things have happened."

"Well, he's a solid boy. And wouldn't leave his little brother behind. They're all each other has ever had. And if they've run off for the purpose you think, he wouldn't take the younger boy with him."

Ezell said, "I wouldn't be too sure 'bout any man's way of thinking." She touched her scarf.

Check ran her tongue around her lower teeth. Ezell had a point. She said, "Nannie went to the ferry this afternoon. I wonder why, now that you mention it."

Ezell raised both eyebrows.

"Okay. I'll send Hugh down there." Then Check shook her head. "No, I'll send Hugh to see if the younger brother is at the bunkhouse. I'll go to the ferry myself. Get me a lantern while I get my pistol."

Check walked to the ferry swinging the lantern, singing slow words off key and loudly. Bert woke up. His new puppy was whining, not barking. And Bert recognized the voice as female, and didn't reach for his rifle. He watched the light swinging towards him. It took him a moment to comprehend that Miz Singer was approaching, singing, "My Old Kentucky Home." He blinked hard two or three times, stood up, and pulled a quilt around his hips.

Check stopped singing and walking. She swung the lantern in a wide arc. "Bert!"

"Yes'um, Miz Singer. What can I do fer ya?"

"Have you seen Jenny Cordery?"

"No, ma'am. Seen her mother. She brung me some vittles and asked me the same thing. Is sompthing wrong?" Check was still thinking on how to answer when Bert appeared in the lantern light with the quilt around his shoulders. The puppy was dancing at his feet. He said, "What's going on?"

"It seems Jenny's run off. Or is missing. I don't know which." Check bent down and scratched the dog's head.

Bert looked downriver. Trees concealed the bend. A path thrown by the moon zigzagged across the water. Beyond the stripe of moonlight, the far bank was hidden by night. The river had enough force to suck all their lives into everlasting dark. Bert turned back to his employer. "Let me fetch my shirt and a lantern."

SOCIETY IN THE NATION WAS as stratified as it was in the United States. The hired help sitting in the parlor with their employer and the national treasurer would've made everybody squirm. The group was adjourning to the summer kitchen when Connell and Clifford returned. They ate strawberry pie to help them think. Lizzie, Ezell, and Bert were standing. Check, Dennis, Connell, and Hugh were in chairs at the table. Clifford sat by himself on a cot in the corner, sniffling between bites. They were digesting what Connell hadn't found when Dennis said to Check, "This pie's as good as Alabama's. Don't tell her I told you."

Check said, "It's Suzanne Taylor's. I won't breathe a word."

Dennis snorted. Silence returned until Hugh said, "What do we need to do?"

Check said, "Ezell, tell everyone what you told me about hunting for gold."

Ezell was behind Dennis. He turned in his chair. "What's that, Ezell?"

"When Jenny disappeared, we all waz looking for the stash that's hid somewheres between the Grand River and the fort."

"That's just a legend. There's not any gold around there." That was Dennis.

Connell said, "Did you all go off in different directions?"

"Yes. And Jenny headed in the direction of the Bushyheads' house. That's how come us to ask y'all about her." She was talking to Dennis.

"Did she go down towards the river?" Check asked. All minds turned to drowning.

"No, not really. She went more north. Towards the fort."

"There's not any gold at the fort," Dennis said. "How come her to think that?"

Ezell and Lizzie looked at each other. Neither wanted to confess to the arrowheads. Lizzie said, "She jist got it in her head. That's the old story. Ever'body thinks it."

Dennis turned back to the table, satisfied nobody was on to anything except rumor. He took his mind off the stash. Returned it to the situation at hand. But he didn't have a solution. He said, "There's nothing we can do until daylight."

Check said, "We need some sleep. It could be a long day tomorrow. Hugh, you go back to town with Dennis. Ride shotgun in the buggy for him."

Connell said, "Let me go and we can take horses. The buggy's not fast enough if we get into trouble. A hand can bring it around it the morning."

That's what Connell and Dennis did. Everybody else went to bed. In hers, Check convinced herself it was most likely that Sanders and Nannie had taken it in their heads to visit Tomahawk and Mannypack. Had rounded up their younger children and gone visiting. It was just like Sanders to leave unexpectedly. She also reminded herself that children were safe in the Nation. The whole tribe indulged their own and everybody else's. Cherokees' love of spoiling their offspring hadn't been diminished by removal, war, or hardship; if anything, Check thought, those disasters made the spoiling worse. She punched her pillow and rolled to her side. Surely, white intruders, the real source of violence in the Nation, wouldn't be interested in a child. They came to Indian Territory from Arkansas, Kansas, Missouri, and Texas, running from the law. Their crimes were theft, robbery, and murder for greed. A little girl with no money or possessions wouldn't be noticed by outlaws. Or so Check concluded. But when she slept, she was restless. She dreamed, not of the Grand River, which was relatively gentle. But of the Arkansas; of its strength, its roar, its treacherous sand.

Check Starts Her Search

CHECK AWOKE FROM A RESTLESS night and thought first of Jenny. Fears and theories tumbled in her head until another thought intruded.

She'd not awakened thinking about Andrew. She had every morning for months; every day since he'd told her of the pain in his stomach; every day, long before the doctor's diagnosis. Check's mind shot back to an image of Andrew pushing away from the table, a full plate of food in front of him. She saw the grimace on his face, the flare of his nostrils. She felt some guilt. But knew she couldn't do anything about the past, couldn't do anything about that particular illness. It wasn't like setting a broken arm, fighting a fever, curing a cough.

Check was forward-thinking by nature. Finding that child should be a concern, and was a distraction she needed. She imagined where Jenny could be. The rivers were present dangers. So were snakes. They were thick, and mostly cottonmouths. Check pictured Jenny on the path between her farm and Sanders'; she always carried a stick. And if she'd been bitten, somebody would've heard her scream. Not the past year, but the one before that, a hand was struck in a field near one of the swales. All the way in the kitchen, Check and Ezell heard his yells. He was laid up for a week. But he was a grown man. A cottonmouth's bite could kill a child, even a hardy one. A wave of revulsion rippled beneath Check's nightgown. She laid a hand over a breast. Those snakes were everywhere, and they ran in pairs. The image of two coiled together propelled her out of bed. But not before she checked where she was setting her feet.

She bathed in the bowl in her room, dressed, and went out the back door. The hands were dispersing from breakfast. The younger Vann boy was walking towards the ferry, carrying a sack and a cup. Check couldn't recall his first name. She called out, "Vann!" He spun around and reversed his direction. When he got to her, she said, "Jenny Cordery's gone missing."

Ame jerked. He raised his eyebrows.

"Do you know where the Corderys live?"

"Y-y-yes'um." He stuttered a little when nervous, and these were his first words with Miz Singer. He shifted from one foot to the other. Some coffee slipped over the lip of his cup.

"I want you to take a horse over there. See if anybody's home."

"Y-y-yes, ma'am!"

"You do ride, don't you, son?"

"Oh, oh, yes'um. Whenever I can!" Ame turned and started towards the barn.

Check said, "Take Bert's food to him first. But quickly. And get back to me as fast as you can."

Ame turned on his heel again and headed towards the river.

By the time he reported back that the Corderys weren't home, Check had Clifford's bag packed for school and Hugh had brought the buggy up to the house. Cliff was near it, whining to 'Wassee that nobody liked him. That he was going to run off to Texas. Hugh heard him. He said, "What's wrong, partner?"

Cliff looked to the ground. Hugh put a hand on his shoulder. "Fess up. It's just me."

Cliff's lip trembled. "She's making me go to school with Jenny missing." He pulled his cap down to his eyebrows.

"Jenny's been a good friend to you?"

"Yeah. For a girl." Clifford looked at his shoes and stockings. He was beginning to hate his knickers.

Hugh recognized his little brother had developed a crush. He winced in sympathy. Put both fists to his hips. "Partner, when we find her, I'll bring the buggy to town and let you know first." He added, "I promise," and tapped Cliff on the shoulder. Suddenly, Cliff grabbed Hugh around the waist. He sobbed. Clung to Hugh's leg. Fortunately, he picked the good one.

Clifford's face was still red when Check came out of the house. She carried a flour sack and a pistol in one hand, Cliff's bag in the other. She handed the bag to Hugh, slipped the pistol into the sack, and patted 'Wassee on the muzzle. She climbed in the buggy and scooted over. Clifford and Hugh climbed in, and Hugh took the reins. During the ride, the conversation was about the crops and the weather. Check made sure they stuck to that, to avoid discussion of Jenny. She knew Clifford was upset. Any talk about her would make it harder to make him stay at school without a fuss. She hated abandoning him there. Especially so late in the year. Especially with Andrew so recently buried. But Cliff had to learn he couldn't shirk his duties because things went topsy-turvy. Check felt firm about that.

She came out of the schoolhouse swiping her eyes with a handkerchief. She said to Hugh, "It's hot for so early in the season. I've worked up a sweat."

"So I see." He extended a hand to help her into the buggy. He added, "I guess Cliff's still a little tender."

Check spread her skirt over the bench. Said, "He's got to get tougher. I'll drive." Hugh lowered his head and lifted himself in. Check made a clucking noise and turned 'Wassee and the buggy south. They settled into a rhythm. She said, "Life's not easy. Children have to harden to survive."

Hugh spread his hurt leg out as far as he could. "I'm glad we weren't born a hundred years earlier. You would've had us walking the creeks barefooted in the winter."

"Nothing wrong with that. If folks hadn't believed in it, they would've raised puny children. Everybody would've died on the Trail."

The Trail was a difficult subject, even for Hugh. But he was always amused by his mother's promotion of ancient customs. "I'm mighty glad you and Papa let us take the train. That was generous." He grinned.

Check cut her eyes around. She looked stern. But Hugh was lifting her spirits. She said, "I told Clifford you'd pick him up Friday afternoon." She flicked 'Wassee on the rump with the reins. The buggy flew down the road towards the bottoms at a speed that caused Hugh to sit upright and hold tight. But when they approached the intersection of the Military Road, Check slowed the horse. Instead of turning west towards home, she turned east. Hugh said, "Where're we going?"

"Doesn't Tomahawk Cordery live between Manard and the bayou? I thought we'd see if Jenny's over there." Check flicked the reins.

'Wassee sped up. Hugh wedged his cane between his legs and gripped the dash. The buggy shook. The dust was rising. Hugh was thinking maybe his mother was trying to toughen him up, when he saw someone ahead in the road. He yelled, "Don't run over that old man, Mama."

Check pulled on the reins. "I'm not about to." She slowed 'Wassee almost to a walk. "Who is it? Can you tell?"

"Somebody who's afraid for his life, I suspect."

"Be serious, Hugh. I know him. But I can't call him."

The man was wearing a red shirt and a black hat with a feather in the band. He was pudgy and carrying a sack in one hand. Something was sticking up over his shoulder. Hugh said, "We know him. He's the well guy."

"That's it. Turtle Smith." Check jiggled her reins. 'Wassee picked up the pace a bit. When they got to Turtle, Check pulled to a stop. "ᎣᏏᏲ, Mr. Smith. It's Mrs. Singer. You remember my son, Hugh?"

Turtle responded in rapid Cherokee. He smiled.

"Well, it's so good to see you. The water in our well tastes wonderful," Check tried to say. But it came out, "I feel good to see you. The wood in our well tastes good."

Turtle chuckled and tipped his hat. Not only did Mrs. Singer not know what she'd said, she was lying. Her water tasted like sulfur. Like all the water in the bottoms. It perplexed him to no end. He responded in rapid Cherokee again. And Check and Hugh nodded like bobbers over worms nibbled by perch. Check said, *"Yes, I am in agreement."* Then she tapped 'Wassee on the rump and they parted. Not a moment too soon, in her estimation. She said to Hugh, "They just do that for fun."

Turtle walked down the road, his belly shaking with merriment.

Visitations at the Bawdy House

CHECK STOPPED THE BUGGY UNDER a tree by the creek forty yards or so from Tomahawk's cabin. Hugh tied 'Wassee while Check reached below the seat and pulled from the flour sack a corn husk doll. Its hair was horsetail, its skirt red cloth. The only feature on the face a protrusion of husk for a nose. Next, she brought out two jars of pickles.

Mannypack waved, but silently watched the Singers cross the field until they were halfway to her. Then she said, "ᎣᏏᏲ! Found Jenny?" Check shook her head. When she got to Mannypack, they embraced. Check pressed the doll to her. "This is for your little girl. It was mine long ago in Tennessee."

Mannypack was the great-granddaughter of John Lowrey, a negotiator of treaties and another of Check's great-uncles. Her father was a judge from the Flint District. So, though only a young woman, Mannypack wasn't intimidated by Check. She was delighted by her. And the doll was, after a fashion, a family heirloom. She hugged Hugh, too. Then led them into the site and invited them to sit on logs. She gave the doll to Minnie and took the pickles into the cabin. She brought out two gourds, one filled with water and the other with strawberries.

They settled quickly into talk about Jenny. Check shared all she knew. And Mannypack told them George Sixkiller had appeared at their site the previous night, searching and bringing the news. He headed back to the bottoms, taking Tomahawk with him. Check was disappointed. And Mannypack said, "It's not like she's a boy." Everybody expected Cherokee boys to disappear. That was their nature.

Check said, "Has anybody searched down at the bawdy house?"

"Nobody'll go down there. It's haunted." Mannypack didn't look at Hugh. But embarrassment climbed his neck until he felt like he'd fallen into a fire. He said, "Y'all got the perfect spot on this bayou." He peered at the trees like he was interested in scenic vistas.

Check said, "Haunted? By who?"

Warmth crawled up Mannypack's neck, too. To Hugh, she said, "We like the spot. There's a pool over there fer bathing and washing. And I can catch fish, and cook 'em up minutes later." She gazed up at the trees like they were a rainbow, suddenly revealed in the heavens. Check looked at her hands. Mannypack eventually added, "I won't go down there, so I don't know fer sure who's haunting it." She picked Minnie up and settled her on her lap.

Check cleared her throat. After a moment, she said, "I suppose it could be any number of people. Did Jenny know it's haunted?"

"I'd say probably not." Mannypack inspected Minnie's ear.

Hugh said, "I guess we better be getting back. People'll think we've gone missing, too."

Check said, "Mannypack, which way's that bawdy house?"

CHECK HAD ENVISIONED THE HOUSE looking like a picture she'd once seen in a book. A clapboard building with shutters. Porch and steps filled with women, buxom and heavily made up. But the house looked lonely. It was surrounded by trees, dappled by shade, silent, and peaceful. A couple of squirrels scampered across its porch. One ran up a post supporting the roof. Check said, "This is a nice house. It should have a family in it."

Hugh cleared his throat.

"Well, come on. You can show me around." Check had already disembarked from the buggy. She held her pistol in her hand and was starting towards the porch. Hugh groaned. Check stopped and turned. "Does your leg hurt you?"

He didn't answer. He knew his mother wasn't concerned about his leg. Knew, too, she couldn't be deterred. He was getting out of the buggy when, beyond the house, a noise arose from a thicket. Check raised her pistol. Hugh grasped the edge of the rig and drew his gun. They both stood still, listening for unnatural sounds. They heard insects and birds. Hugh said, "Probably a wild pig." He holstered his gun and grabbed his cane from the buggy.

Check called loudly, "Jenny?"

The sound that returned was the screeching of squirrels' nails on the roof.

Check reached the porch first. All the doors she could see were shut. She tried one to the room on the left. It creaked open. A shaft of light fell onto the floor. She stepped inside. Saw two pallets, a table, dirty dishes, and a couple of chairs. Clothing hung on the rungs of the ladder to the loft. A coal oil lamp was on the mantel. Check said, "Is this the way you left it?"

Hugh hobbled in. The clothes hadn't been on the ladder, nor the pallets on the floor. But Hugh didn't feel like discussing that with his mother. He said, "I don't really remember. It's been a long time."

"It hasn't been that long. You're still using a cane."

Hugh sighed. She'd poke him until she prodded out every last piece of information she wanted. It'd probably be easier to dish it up then and there. "Well, if you need know, this was the drinking room. The other one's where ever'body played cards. There were whiskey barrels all over this room. I don't know what happened to 'em." He walked over to the northeast corner and looked at the stains on the floor. He said, "This is where the woman and I were shot." Then he pointed to a spot on the floor in front of his mother. "See that? That's probably where Sanders attacked Colbert. But somebody shot out the lamp, and I was already down, so I can't swear to it. Are you satisfied?"

Check tucked her pistol in her skirt pocket. She was glad to finally get that information. She needed time to digest it. "I won't be satisfied until we find Jenny Cordery."

Hugh looked around. The lines of his face deepened. For a moment, Check saw in him a lighter version of her mother. The similarity softened her. She said, "Do you know how come Sanders thought to have that lamp shot out?"

Hugh was surprised. Beyond what he'd just said, he didn't know his mother knew anything about that night. He shook his head.

"Well, listen. This is something you should remember." Check rested a hand on the table. "You've heard of Chief Doublehead. He was a fierce fighter, but also mean and crazy. He murdered little children for no reason. He cooked and ate the adults he killed in battle. He did whatever he wanted. And everybody was afraid of him. Finally, he sold our land to the whites. Of course, it wasn't his to sell. But he sold it anyway. And he pocketed the money.

"That was the last straw. Alexander Sanders, Hellfire Jack Rogers, The Ridge, and James Vann banded together to assassinate him. Vann — Rich Joe's father — got too drunk to go. But the rest of them found Doublehead in McIntosh's tavern at Hiwassee. Rogers distracted him with conversation, and Alex Sanders shot out the lamp. In the dark, The Ridge shot the chief in the head."

Check had been in the tavern as a little girl. Been told the story there by one of the old Benge men who had known all the participants. That memory flooded back to her. She added, as much to herself as to Hugh, "They all fled, thinking Doublehead was dead. He wasn't. His friends slung him over the back of a horse and rode away with him. But word got out that he was alive. So Alex Sanders and The Ridge tracked the horses to a schoolhouse where a missionary was hiding Doublehead in a loft. Sanders and The Ridge climbed the ladder, and Doublehead attacked them with a knife. The Ridge tackled Doublehead, and Alex

Sanders shot him in the hip. But the chief fought on until Sanders wedged a tomahawk in his head so deep it split it in two. To pull it out, Sanders had to step on Doublehead's face." Check wiped her mouth with the palm of her hand. She looked directly at Hugh. "Sanders Cordery is Alex Sanders' nephew and namesake. The Ridge later fought for your grandfather at the Horseshoe. That's where he earned the name Major. He was the uncle of General Watie, who Sanders and your uncle Ruff fought under during the War.

"Our lives are shaped by our history, Hugh. We're all family. All connected. And the elders don't leave us just because they've died. They're still with us, guiding us in what we do. You are a Cherokee. You'll never be alone."

Hugh had always known of Chief Doublehead. But his mother painted a picture of his assassination like she'd been there. He was seeing the tomahawk being wrenched from the chief's head when Check looked deeper into the room. She saw braves in headdresses of white feathers and deer tails. Their faces and chests were covered with war paint. Their legs clothed in buckskin. They carried rifles. They were her father's men at Horseshoe Bend. Check shook her head. Her cheeks, lips, and chin quivered.

Hugh saw his mother's face tremble. He knew she'd seen something in the room. He was afraid it was the dead chief. Afraid it was Claudette's ghost. Afraid it was tomahawk-wielding Alexander Sanders. He was chilled to the bone. His heart thumped with fear. He said, "Mama, let's get out of here."

But Check wasn't frightened. She'd seen visions all of her life. And always took comfort from the dead Cherokees around her. She used their strength to steady herself. "Recall what I just told you, Hugh. We have to check the loft." She nodded to the ladder.

Hugh ran a hand down his chest, put the other on his gun. He walked over to the hole in the ceiling and yelled, "Jenny!" A jaybird screeched. They both jerked. Check said, "You can't get up there. I'll do it." She put a hand in her pocket, drew out her gun, and handed it to him. She said, "Fools fall and shoot themselves all the time. Hold the ladder."

Jenny wasn't in the loft.

The Noise in the Thicket

THE TWO MEN IN THE trees south of the house waited for the sound of the buggy to die. Then Jake said to Sam, "Goddamn! Yer so clumsy ya practically shouted where we waz!" He hit Sam on the back of the head and knocked him forward.

The former postmaster stumbled over a log. He fell on a hammer in his belt that he'd been trying, without success, to use as a tomahawk. He massaged his thigh, looked up, and pouted. "Why'd ya go and do that? Ya hurt my leg."

Jake walked on. "Now, why d'ya suppose they come down here?"

"Who cares? People go where they wanta." Sam got up, realigned the hammer in his belt, and kicked the log. "Maybe Singer wanted to show his mama where he jerked off."

"Right," Jake said over his shoulder. "Yer dumber than dirt. Now they'll know wez here. We hav'ta move."

Sam caught up to Jake. "They don't know a damn thing. All they knows is somebody's been living here." They climbed the steps together.

"Well, don't ya think somebody'll come look to see who it is?"

"They ain't come yet. Fer the life of me, I can't figure that out. Ya'd think somebody woulda been down here in all this time." Sam was truly puzzled. They'd camped by the river the first few days they'd been out of jail. After that, they'd taken up residence in the bawdy house. They'd been alone there for a week, and hadn't heard the gossip about the ghost.

Jake peeked in the room. "They didn't take nothing."

"Ain't nothing to take. Wez living like Injuns."

"You just wish ya waz living like Hugh Singer. What's his mama's name?"

"Miz Singer."

Jake punched Sam's back with the heel of his palm. "I knowed that, ya idjit."

Sam rubbed his shoulder. "Most her mail's addressed to Miz Andrew

Singer. But she gits official-looking letters from the tribe. They's addressed to Cherokee America."

"Goddamn Injuns got strange names."

"Yeah. What's it to ya?"

"Nothing. I'z jist going loony hiding out here like a sceered rabbit. I
say let's hightail it outta this Nation." Jake looked towards the trees.

"We can't do that jist yet." Sam spit off the porch. "I ain't walking off
empty-handed."

Searching

ON THE MONDAY ANDREW DIED, Turtle Smith, the well-witcher,
had been in Granny's kitchen at the inn, eating ꮬꮎꮧ ꭰꮧꭶꮻꮕ and
ꭻꮼꮀ for breakfast. He was wearing a red long-sleeved shirt and a
leather headband. Around his neck was a tobacco pouch. On his right
ring finger a big black stone. Turtle was accustomed to eating well and
was short in the legs, so was pudgy for a fullblood. His pappy's daddy
had actually been a white man from a village close to Liverpool. But
that didn't count to Turtle, or to anyone. "Fullblood" referred to habits.
Turtle's turned towards the old ways, and he was dark. But some light
Indians were fullbloods, too. And some dark Indians were practically
white people. It was confusing to anyone who wasn't a Cherokee, but not
confusing to Granny or Turtle.

Granny told Turtle that Dennis wanted to see him. And the two of
them chewed on the national treasurer's motivations. They both hoped
he wanted a well. Granny hated that her daughter's water tasted like sulfur, and enjoyed the idea of her rich son-in-law lining Turtle's pockets.
Turtle was too Indian to keep good track of money, but Granny kept his
books and he liked her looking after him. Turtle said, *"I'll go see* Dennis
when I get around to it." He licked his lips and pulled a sassafras twig
from his pocket. It was whittled into a flat plane on one end. He pressed
the plane against one of his teeth.

Granny said, "*When you go, if ya think of it, ya might mention to* Alabama *that I've been cogitating on piecing a new quilt.*"

Turtle ran his twig around a couple more teeth, thinking about Granny wanting fancy scraps from her daughter's fine clothes. He said, "*I'll take a sack.*" Then he added, "*You want anything else,* T∂?" ("T∂" means "pumpkin.") He winked. Granny said, "ᏍᎶ ᎠᏞᏚᏏ," which means "hard terrapin." It was, perhaps, an endearment. Or perhaps a question.

TURTLE GOT AROUND TO VISITING Dennis a week later, the morning Check saw him on the road, and the same morning the concerted search for Jenny began. Sanders and Sheriff Rogers organized the party. Bell and Connell led the group combing the white part of Fort Gibson. Puny and the town's remaining Negroes took their quarters. And Sanders, Coop, Tomahawk, George, and other friends took the rivers and the woods. Dennis's area was the old buildings around his house and the fort. He'd searched the barracks and was headed to a pile of logs salvaged from a newly demolished cabin when he saw Turtle walking towards him. Dennis waved, called, and greeted him warmly. He took Turtle to the house and asked Dove to serve them up food. Alabama was out searching, too.

A half hour later, Dennis and Turtle sat on the porch steps, picking their teeth, talking about Jenny Cordery. Turtle was of the opinion that whites had taken her. Dennis agreed that was a possibility. But he thought it more likely she'd fallen in one of the rivers or had been bitten by a snake. Turtle agreed the snakes were bad, and told Dennis a couple of snakes-in-the-well stories. They'd been putting off talking about the point of the visit until everything else was discussed. Eventually, Dennis said, "*I've been hoping you could find me a well.*"

"*Every well around here's likely to have* sulfur *in it.*"

"*I don't want more water.*"

Turtle angled his eyes towards his host and squinted. He didn't much like Dennis's beard. It made him look like a white man. Turtle gazed back out over the lawn.

Dennis said, *"Old fort records say that in the 1830s there was a well started around here and never finished."*

Turtle moved his sassafras stick to the other side of his mouth.

"I was hoping you could find it."

"Were it witched?"

"Don't know. But it's likely."

"If it weren't witched at the start, I can't find it."

"It seems to me they would've witched it. Surely they weren't so ignorant they'd just start digging."

"They were dumb enough to pick this spot for a fort." The military had chosen such a mosquito-ridden location that, until the cane was cut, droves of soldiers died from malaria.

"Chouteau had the good spot." Dennis jerked his head towards where the Verdigris flowed into the Arkansas, a mile above where the Grand came in. There, seventy years earlier, the French-American trader had built a post and shipyard.

Turtle reached behind his head and pulled his witching stick from its quiver. He flexed his wrist. Shook the stick around in the air. *"Could take a while. There's a lot of water around here. Stick might find that confusing."*

Dennis recognized they were discussing the price of the service. *"I'll make it worth your time."*

"I know you will. Reverend Bushyhead's son's not a stingy man."

Dennis understood the price had just gone up. *"Naturally, I'll need some results,"* he retorted.

"Do you have to have the same old well? Could I just find you some water?"

Dennis shook his head. *"No, I need it to store potatoes."* He tried to look sincere.

Turtle got off the step with a grunt. It was obvious Dennis was lying. But Turtle couldn't imagine why. He held up his sack. *"Granny's thinking about piecing a new quilt."*

"I'll see what Alabama has. She's been sewing dresses for somebody's baby."

"Well, if she don't have anything left over for her mother, I'll stop by Marty's on the road back."

Dennis reached for the sack. *"I'm sure she'll find something."*

"She might like some silk. Any little scrap'll do." Turtle held his stick in the air. He said something to the sky in a high-pitched, nasal voice.

Dennis couldn't completely follow. He did, however, recognize the ancient formula for finding water. As he watched Turtle follow the stick through the yard, he offered up a prayer to the Christian God for his success. He also offered up a prayer for Jenny.

The Criminal Element Coming In

COX, THE SADDLERY OWNER, WAS outside his place, repairing a saddle on a sawhorse with a round log back when Connell walked up and said, "Sanders Cordery's girl is missing."

Cox stopped working. "So I heared. I hope the wolves didn't git her."

Wolves hadn't crossed Connell's mind. He touched the cigar in his pocket. "She'd have to be down for that."

"Not if there's a pack. Back during the War, a pack stole a child off a porch right up the street." Cox pointed with a tube of glue. "Broad daylight. They was starving, like everybody else. Federal officer's little boy. Pulled him to pieces. Wife went mad. Started walking the streets in her nightgown. Don't know what ever happen to them. She shoulda never been here anyways."

Connell's stomach turned over. He brought out his cigar and put it unlit in his mouth. Sucked a little flavor. Got a comforting taste. To chase the wolves farther away, he took the cigar between his fingers and pointed with it. "Mighty fine saddle."

"Shore is. Belongs to Major Percival. Look at them little fleur-de-lis." Cox pointed with his little finger. Connell stepped closer and squinted. Cox said, "Mighty fancy. That costs a fortune."

"Wonder where he got it?"

"Came from France. Across the waters." Cox raised his eyebrow.

Connell stuck the cigar back in his mouth, still unlit. Major Percival had never taken up with a woman. A French saddle confirmed the suspicion shared by every man in town. Cox set the glue down. Pulled a strap tight on the saddle. Checked a buckle. "That's got her. I'll come help in a few minutes. The major needs this saddle this morning. Going to Fort Smith to meet the new judge."

"He probably won't be any better than the last one."

"Gonna run a bunch of marshals in here. Been hiring right and left. Would help on sompthing like this."

Connell didn't share Cox's views. And was alarmed by the news. He thought Cox, a white married to a Cherokee, needed a different attitude. "This is the Cherokee Nation. What we really need is for the US government to protect its borders. Let us protect ours."

Cox looked away. "I didn't mean nothing contrary. There's jist a lot of criminal element coming in. It ain't safe."

Connell liked Cox. And didn't want a fight. He said, "I need to get back to looking for Jenny."

At the River

BERT WAS IN THE MIDDLE of the river crossing with a ferryload of Creeks when Nannie came around the bend on the sandbar, holding Joe by the hand. She was plodding like a broken-down cow and carrying a sack. Joe was dragging a little limb. Bert asked one of the Creek men to help him pull the rope. Hurried the crossing, got the Creeks, their children, dogs, chickens, and calf safely on land.

Bert walked the cove stones towards Nannie and Joe, watching his feet as he went. At the point where they were again in sight, he glanced up every few steps. He wanted to run and hug Nannie. Only the day before, she'd brought him food, and told him to pay no mind to fools around a fire. Now she was closed in and walled off, her face drawn and dark. When he got to her, he said only, "ᎣᏏᏲ! Miz Cordery." Nannie squinted. Bert looked away. Added, "I been watching the river. Nothing's come down." Nannie blinked three times. Joe made an animal sound. Bert bent and picked him up.

Walking towards the ferry, Bert told Nannie what he'd learned from Ezell and Lizzie. She told him Sanders and the boys were searching the woods and cane. She had taken the sandbar. They fell into silence. Bert watched his step again, not wanting to fall and drop Joe. He couldn't imagine losing a child. But did know about losing a mother and father. He figured, either way meant the same cold ashes, the same empty space. When they got to the landing, he suggested they sit on the bank in the shade. They stared at the river together.

Endurance

IN 1838, WALKING INTO BITTER wind and blowing snow in the Arkansas Territory, Sanders was carrying his little sister when heard a scream. He turned. His mother was down. Sprawled from a fall. The child she'd been carrying was on the ground wailing. Sanders called to one of his brothers, handed their sister to him. Knelt by his mother. She was sobbing, her head in her skirt. Behind her was a path of pink footprints. Sanders' brother set their other sister down and picked up the dropped one. Sanders took off his shirt, tore it in strips, and bound his mother's feet. He lifted her in his arms and started walking. When he tired, he handed her to his older brother and took the child he was carrying from him. Another brother held an older little sister's hand. Only their youngest brother, crippled from a blowgun accident, walked alone. Their father had died of a fever the year of the treaty.

Sanders remembered the weight of his mother while searching for Jenny. His breath caught. His throat tightened. She'd been a slight woman and, by that far into the Trail Where They Cried, close to starving. But she was the weight by which he judged all others. Not the month spent in the holding pen before the march, not hand-to-hand combat, not the winter at Fort Davis, not defeat, not the death of his first wife, not the ashes of his home, not the walk to and from the refugee camp — nothing, nothing at all, matched the hardship of that journey with his mother in his arms. If he had to, he could look for Jenny night and day, without sleep or food. He could go on and on. Endurance was the lesson Sanders had learned from life. In the end, only it carried hope. He bent close to the back of his horse. Guided him under a limb. Straightened up. Called, "ᎠᏫᏫ," his pet name for Jenny.

Raising Buckaroo

AFTER VISITING THE BAWDY HOUSE, Hugh dropped his mother at the Bushyheads' and went in the buggy to town, intending first to meet up with the other searchers. But he couldn't sweep from his mind the deaths of Claudette and Crow, or the picture of Buckaroo, seen by every man in the room, limp as a dead snake, the arm of a rag doll, a leaf of wilted corn. Hugh felt sick to his stomach. But below that, didn't feel anything except pain above his left knee. Lost in humiliation and ache, and worried about the future of his pal between his legs, he drove past Harry Watson's barbershop. Two men were on the bench in front. Inside, a man draped with a white cloth was in Harry's chair. The men on the bench could just be jawing; somebody always was in front of the shop. But they also could be waiting on Harry to cut their hair. Hugh turned at the corner and circled the block. This time, he stopped at the shop. He asked the men if they'd seen Jenny Cordery. They hadn't, but had theories. While listening to those, Hugh determined that both men needed haircuts, and he drove off promising to look where they suggested — places that dropped from his mind like pebbles sink to the bottom of a rainwater barrel.

Soon Hugh was beyond Fort Gibson on a road that wove through the pastures and orchards. Like most Cherokee families, the Starrs lived on adjoining farms. The closest to town belonged to Willow's daughter,

Birch, and the husband she'd driven away. Hugh couldn't remember his name, and didn't try hard to, because the husband was spilt milk. The next farm belonged to Willow's mother. Some of her boys were living with her. Hugh didn't want to get caught by them, or by old Mrs. Starr; but if he did, he could say he was searching for Jenny. And while the Starr boys might be difficult, he doubted Mrs. Starr was all that concerned about her daughter. The family had a reputation for loose ways and wildness that, from Hugh's point of view, came in handy as long as it didn't rise to the level of armed robbery. He reminded himself that Tom Starr and his brothers were in the Canadian District. It was the more peaceful branch of the family that was settled by the stream, growing apples, pecans, strawberries, and corn.

Hugh drove 'Wassee to a stand of trees close to Willow's orchard, tied her to an elm, and took a familiar footpath until he was close to the house. With a stiff leg, he couldn't bend over well enough to hide behind a bush. So he hid behind a tree and peeped out. The house was clapboard, recently built by the white barber. A porch ran across the front; at the windows, curtains flapped in and out. No horses or wagons were in sight, but someone could've easily walked over to visit. Women rarely traveled any other way. So Hugh leaned on his cane and thought over the situation. If anybody was there, he could say he was looking for Jenny. If anybody came up while he and Willow were — Buckaroo moved a little when Hugh pictured that — he could say he'd stopped in to get a drink of water. Hugh gripped Buckaroo, gave him a little tug. Told him to get ready. Then he realized his alibis might sound unlikely with the buggy hidden by a stand of trees. He was thinking that through, with one hand on Buckaroo and the other on his cane, when Willow walked out of the house, swinging a basket. She was headed towards the chicken house. Hugh wasn't much of a chicken man, but he knew it was a strange time of day to be gathering eggs, and probably meant that Willow was fixing to bake. He'd get the buggy, drive it around, and have a conversation out in the open, like he was hunting a lost child. As things developed, he and Buckaroo might get a straight shot.

Hugh drove the buggy right up to Willow's porch, and had his good foot on the ground when she came up from the chicken house. Hugh found the sight of her lovely. She was a good twenty years older, but not yet wide in the hips or fat in the stomach. She wore her braid down her back, had high cheekbones, was dark, and had on a red dress. The color set her skin off flawlessly. She looked as tasty to Hugh as a fine loaf of newly baked bread. And Buckaroo agreed; he moved again. Hugh grabbed his cane and tipped his hat. He smiled in a way that made his eyes twinkle, the skin around them crinkle. Willow smiled, too. Her teeth were strong and white; stray strands of hair floated around her face. She shifted her basket to her left arm, placed her right hand in it, and brought out an egg.

Hugh was looking down to make sure his bad leg was planted right when the egg hit the side of the buggy. Slime slid down leather his parents had paid a lot of money for. He looked up. Willow had her hand in the basket again. She brought out another egg. Hugh said, "Please, please, hold up. I swear, I'm sorry." Willow lifted her arm. Hugh said, "Please, please, don't. I'm an asshole. I know it."

Willow said, "Say that again. I couldn't hardly hear you." He did. But she kept the egg in hand. Then she walked towards him saying she wasn't in the mood to be made a fool of, didn't like people getting killed for no good reason, and didn't like Buckaroo flopping around out in public. She wanted to know what Hugh had to say for himself, how long he'd been up to that kind of behavior, and why he couldn't appreciate the gifts he'd been given. Somewhere in the middle of that, Hugh reminded her that she was married. That got the egg thrown on his boot. She pitched another at the side of the buggy. It landed a little to the left and below the first one. Hugh realized then his best hope was to get out of there before 'Wassee got spooked and the buggy soaked.

He drove into town fast, and straight to the saddler. He asked Cox to get the egg off the buggy and boot. Cox said, "Didja git in a fight with a chicken?" and laughed.

"Had a little misunderstanding with a child. Parents don't raise children right anymore." Hugh couldn't turn red in the face because he was already crimson.

"Whose child were it?"

Hugh didn't know many children. He rubbed the back of his neck.

"Actually, I broke up a fight between my brothers. I don't want Mama to know. She has enough on her plate, and she'll wear 'em out."

"She will at that. And I wouldn't blame her." Cox bent down to touch the stain on the buggy. "I don't know if I can git her out, but I'll try."

He applied soap and cornmeal. He rubbed, and applied again. He recommended saddle soap when the stains were dry. The boot was old and scuffed, but the blemish on the buggy was still apparent. Hugh hoped to goodness it'd disappear after a saddle soaping. But he didn't see any logical reason for egg throwing at all. And he drove to the Bushyheads' with his face getting blacker and his mood bluer.

However, he knew he couldn't show up looking any different than he'd looked before. To erase the debacle from his mind, he turned his thoughts to other women. He pictured Florence's younger sisters, April and Eva. But neither of them appealed to him. And he didn't want to have to put up with what Connell was going through. He wanted a woman he could slip around to. A woman who wouldn't try to pin him down. A woman who would teach him all she knew. That is, if he could get Buckaroo back into riding condition. He looked down at the front of his pants. Under his buttons, his best friend lay like a dead fish. Hugh felt sick about that. But when he got to within sight of the Bushyheads' house, he decided Buckaroo had a sense of self-preservation, and that he'd better just lay low himself.

A White Man's Continent

HUGH HITCHED 'WASSEE TO THE Bushyheads' post so that the egg-stained side of the buggy would be facing away from his mother when they left. Then he went around front, and found her, Dennis, Alabama, Bell, and Nash on and around the porch. By then, the sun was hovering near the trees across the river. Hugh reported what he knew — or, really, what he'd made up — and the rest of them brought him up to snuff. They were discussing what to do if Jenny wasn't found that night when Alabama said, "Shouldn't Sanders be here before we make a decision?"

"He won't come back 'til he finds something, one way or the other." Bell said that.

Check said, "Will he know to come here?"

Bell looked off towards the river. "He knows this is the gathering spot. But ya know Sanders. Goes where he wants."

Nash had been leaning against a post. He straightened up. "I can take the stagecoach to Fort Smith first thing in the morning."

Check removed her spectacles, pulled a handkerchief from her pocket, and wiped her lenses. Bell pulled a tobacco pouch and papers from his pocket. He started rolling a cigarette. Alabama lifted a scrap of cloth from a sack, held it to the light, and inspected it. Dennis opened a pocketknife and began cleaning his nails. Only Hugh didn't have anything to do. He said, "We don't know that'd be effective."

"Hugh, if the criminal element has taken her, we need as many men as we can get." Nash looked at Dennis. "You said yourself, Dennis, that's a possibility."

Dennis flicked some dirt off the end of his knife. "I said Turtle thought maybe the invading whites got her. Personally, I suspect she's fallen in one of the rivers." He hesitated, then added, "Or into a nest of cottonmouths." He shivered.

Out on the lawn, a foal knelt and rolled over on his back. Everybody, other than Nash, watched like they'd never seen a horse do that. Finally, Nash positioned himself between the porch and the lawn. He squared his feet and shoulders, faced his neighbors directly, and gestured with his right hand and arm. "Look, I know this is unpopular. But I have three daughters. If somebody has taken this child, we need help. Everybody in the bottoms and Fort Gibson has searched all day. Nobody's turned up anything. Judge Parker has a passel of new federal marshals. I say let's get them to help us. That's all I'm suggesting." He looked straight at Bell. He said, "I'm sorry."

Bell blew smoke rings reminiscent of the Plains Indians' signals. Nash looked to Dennis. Dennis folded a small blade into his knife and opened a larger one. Nash looked to Check. She found another dirty spot on her glasses. The merchant shook his head. He started walking off. But after a few steps, the sound of hooves caught everybody's attention. In a moment, Puny came around the corner of the house.

He swung off his mount, shaking his head. "She ain't here in our part'a town. So I rode out to Manard. None of them folks seen an Indian girl they ain't seen before. It's like she's disappeared off the face of the earth."

Everybody shook their heads, blew out hard, or looked down. Except Nash. He was exasperated. And that the Cordery girl wasn't at Manard didn't surprise him a bit. He didn't understand why Puny wasted precious time riding over there. He said, "Puny, I need my mail."

Puny was startled by that. He looked to the others. Nash said, "Come on. I need to get back to the store."

Puny saw there'd been some kind of disagreement. But he didn't have a hint of what it was, and it didn't matter. He said, "Yes, sir," and turned towards the post office, reins in his hand. But he and Nash stopped after a few steps. An Indian had walked out of the woods. He was slowly crossing the lawn, looking at the foal and his dam until he passed them. Then he looked at the ground until he got to the gathering. He stopped about five feet away from Dennis. Nodded to where he'd come from. *"Water that way. Thirty feet down."*

Dennis didn't want the well discussed, and thought Turtle should've known that. He felt irritated, but couldn't say so. He said, "Puny, open up the post office for Mr. Taylor."

Nash had no idea what the fat Indian had said. And he was tired of people who wouldn't speak English, answer when spoken to, or use good sense. But they all bought from him, and some of them were probably kin to Suzanne in ways he'd never figure out. He said, "Let me know how I can help," and headed off faster. Puny followed, leading his horse.

As they moved away, Check mentally rehearsed, and then said, *"He won't let those girls speak Cherokee. Suzanne neither."*

Alabama said, *"If Suzanne wanted to speak Cherokee, nothing could stop her."*

At the post office, Puny went for a package stowed in the room on the other side of the trot. Nash waited at the counter, letting his mind wander to places he didn't often let it tread. During the War, his store had been looted by Confederates. His old house was raided. His furniture burned for firewood. Then the Federals came. They arrested him, Suzanne, and the girls. Took them, and the rest of the Ross family, to Fort Leavenworth, Kansas. Imprisoned them there. When they were released, he moved his wife and girls to his brother's home on Staten Island. He came back to Fort Gibson to sutler for the Federals' 3rd Indian Regiment. Nash was originally from New Orleans, and had seen more of the world, north and south, than had his neighbors. Beneath his storekeeper's mask, he harbored few illusions. And when Puny set the box on the counter, Nash let go of his tongue. "They're deluded. They think they can squat in the middle of the goddamn country with states all around. They're practically as white as I am. But they think they're something else. This is a white man's continent, Puny. You know that as well as I do. We can't live cut off. The law will come to this Nation, mark my words. It'll soon be part of the United States of America. And we'll all live to see it!"

Puny did what his father had taught him. He said, "Yes, sir."

Comfort Food

BY DARK, CHECK WAS ON her own back porch in her rocker. Ezell and Lizzie were on the planks, their legs dangling off. Paul was asleep in his cradle. Otter curled in his mother's lap and put his thumb in his mouth. Check moved it out. He put it in again. Check gave up and kissed his head. She said, "For all Nannie's been through, losing a child's a terrible thing." Lizzie's chin dropped. Ezell slipped an arm over her shoulder. Check hugged Otter closer. Her thoughts moved to her own dead infant, then to locating Lizzie's baby's grave. She'd ask Sanders, and take Lizzie there as soon as they either found Jenny alive or found her remains. Check thought again of the rivers. Bodies washed up all the time. She thought about how long Jenny could last without water if she were alive. Three days? Four? They'd already lost one.

The outbuildings were shadows. Tree frogs and crickets chirped. Lightning bugs popped on and off. Beyond that music and flickering, the bottoms were still. The Arkansas River roared in the distance. But the women heard horses before they saw riders. Check tilted her head towards the gun at the sash. Whispered to Ezell, "Move that rifle over here." Ezell got up and laid the gun between Paul's cradle and Check's rocker. She lifted Otter from Check's lap and walked him inside by the hand. She came back out for Paul. Check settled her rifle over the arms of her rocker.

Before the horses stopped, Connell shouted, "Mama, don't shoot." Puny yelled, "It's us! It's us!" They dismounted, tied the horses to the rail, and came to the porch. Connell removed his hat, ran his fingers through his hair. Puny twisted his hat in his hands. Connell said, "She's in one of the rivers. She can't be anywhere else."

Check was standing by then, holding her rifle by the barrel. Ezell and Hugh had come out of the house. "She knows to stay away from the rivers," Check said. "A child of Sanders' wouldn't wade into either channel."

Connell said, "How d'ya figure that, Mama? They bathe in the Arkansas, don't they?"

"The Corderys bathe in pools trapped by sand."

"Mr. Taylor thinks we should call in federal marshals."

"I know. That's not going to happen."

"He's pretty strong on it, Mama."

"I don't care. The United States is looking for any excuse to come in here and run us over. They've already run us across the continent. Don't forget."

"I'm not, Mama. But what if intruders have taken her? There's nothing we can do."

Check looked down at her rifle. After a moment, she said, "It's not likely a judge would send marshals in here over something as minor as a missing Indian child. Ezell, see if you can rustle up vittles for these two." She sat down and laid her rifle on the planks.

As Ezell headed for the summer kitchen, Puny picked up a snake stick from the porch and went to the pump. He sniffed two buckets on the platform for fish guts. Both were clean. He pumped water into each and carried them to the tub in the thicket of scrub. He filled the buckets twice again. Around the tub, he looked for the jar where Ezell kept the soap. Found it where it'd always been. He removed his clothes and soaped up.

He had one arm back in a sleeve when he thought better of putting the dirty shirt on. He tossed it into a bucket and walked back to the pump. He left both buckets there, and went, shirt in hand, to his horse. He threw his dirty shirt over his saddle. Pulled from a saddlebag a clean undershirt he'd worn at the bawdy house. He slipped it over his head. He didn't have a mirror. And couldn't have seen in the dark if he had. But by running his palm over his chest he could tell he didn't look half bad. He stuffed his dirty shirt in the bag. Walked towards the kitchen with a spring in his step.

Ezell was alone and looked up as he came in the door. "I'm guessing yer'll want biscuits to go with this. They're not ready." She pulled a piece of ham from a skillet.

"Whatever ya have. I'm starving."

Ezell forked three pieces of ham onto a plate. She piled on beans, saying, "I'll take Connell his food. Then ya can fill me in."

When she came back, she closed both the heavy door and a gauze-covered one that had gone up against flies and mosquitoes. Starlight streamed in the west windows. A lantern lit the room. The corners were shadows. Ezell said, "Lizzie's making a cot up for ya. It's in the hall where Hugh slept when he couldn't manage the stairs."

"I don't want anybody to go to no trouble. I can go on back to the post office."

"You can't ride alone at night. Ya got no more sense than a chicken without a head."

"Maybe not. But I've got more than a chicken's appetite. Are them biscuits done?"

Ezell took biscuits to Connell, and when she returned, Puny told her his share of the day's events. She told him about losing Jenny while looking for gold. They sat shoulder to shoulder, ate biscuits, and speculated on likely reasons for the child's disappearance. The whole thing was up-setting. And, naturally, they could feel each other's distress. And wanted to soothe it. The little cot in the corner wasn't sturdy enough for com-forting, but luckily held a small quilt. Puny spread the quilt on the stone floor. Ezell undid her scarf and hung it on the back of a chair.

A Stranger Land

PAIN SHOT FROM JENNY'S SHOULDER. Ran ragged jabs up her neck. Thumped behind her eyes. Migrated down her side, through the center of her body, into her leg and toes. She twitched. Jerked. Was still. Eventually, she drifted into a deep, thoughtless nothingness that lin-gered, without dimension, sensation, or color. But sometime on, she felt a caterpillar in her mouth. She worked her lips to spit it out. Lay with her tongue protruding from her teeth. Nothingness returned.

Later, sounds came from afar. Barking and howling. Scratching. Jenny shut her eyes tighter. The sounds filled her ears. Trying to scream, her jaw dropped. She lapsed into blackness. The noises disappeared. She slipped into a land she'd never visited. Foreign and dark. But she was beyond fear.

Morning

THE SECOND MORNING OF JENNY'S disappearance started out hot. And, for Alabama, got worse after breakfast. She threw up in a bucket, and brushed her teeth at the pump. That didn't make her feel any better. She dragged herself to the study and eased into a chair. Dennis was at his desk, his left hand atop a tomahawk-head paperweight. He rocked it a little as he spoke. "I saw Sanders at sunup this morning. He looks like a ghost. Won't stop for rest." Dennis peered at his wife. "You don't look much better yourself."

Alabama hadn't slept well. And was in no mood to be criticized. She almost said, "Whose fault is that?" Instead she said, "When are you going to Tahlequah?"

"As soon as I can. I have to have these accounts done when the chief returns." Chief William Potter Ross had been in Washington for two months and was due back any day. He might already be home.

"Do you think he'll send help?"

Dennis let go of the tomahawk stone. "If he's back, he will. But I don't see it doing any good. She's already been missing for a day and a half. The child's dead. She's probably been eaten by gars." The alligator gars in the Arkansas River grew to be as long as buffalo.

"I don't think she drowned."

"Why not?"

Alabama leaned back in her chair. Her nausea was easing off. "Just a feeling. She was closer to the Grand than the Arkansas. It's slow by comparison. If she could swim, she'd have a chance of getting out."

Dennis doubted Jenny could swim. The surrounding lakes were too snaky for swimming. The bayou was too far away for practicing, and also too snaky. The Corderys lived next to the Arkansas; nobody could swim it. The temporary pools were too shallow for learning. Dennis thought Alabama was grasping at straws. But she was pregnant; that would be expected. He said, "Well, at least Check said there're living people in the bawdy house. I'll tell Willy when I see him. He promised to take it off our hands if we could get the ghost out."

Alabama felt relieved about that. But didn't feel well enough to think about who to ask to smudge the place. She said, "Did you hear the wolves howling last night?"

"No, I was knocked out."

"They were loud. I got worried about Turtle sleeping on the porch."

Dennis tapped his tomahawk stone with his middle finger. He was still irritated at Turtle for mentioning a well in public. He said, "Turtle's fit as a fiddle. Was up and out before me."

Eureka!

TURTLE WAS BY A CORNFIELD near the Grand when he saw a dark man riding a horse at a gallop. He shouted, "ᏇᎷᎲᏉᏞ, ᏇᎷᎲᏉᏞ, ᏇᎷᎲᏉᏞ," and waved both hands over his head.

Puny was on that horse. But he didn't hear Turtle's shouts or see his hands. He was rushing to open the post office before people who hadn't gotten their mail the day before started lining up. He didn't want to get fired from his job, and was a little sore in the shoulder and hip from sleeping on the kitchen floor. However, aside from those worries, Puny was in high spirits. Not only had he twice relieved his tensions before sleeping; he and Ezell had agreed on adding another room onto their cabin for Lizzie. Before long, he'd be back in his own bed. So he was more thankful than achy when, over the sound of hooves, he finally heard shouts. He pulled on the reins. To his west, a man was coming through the corn, waddling like a frightened chicken. Waving his arms. Wearing a red shirt. Puny recognized the well-witcher. He held his horse to prevent him from rearing.

Turtle said, "ᎤᏏᏉᏞ ᏣᏆᏒ." He said the same thing again. Then he said it again. By that time, he'd waddled up close to the horse.

Puny said, "I don't know whatchya saying. Do ya need a ride?"

Turtle's head shook as hard as a tree in a storm. He said in English, "I need your rope! Come on!" He started waddling back to where he'd come from. Puny followed a few feet behind, his horse crushing the corn in its way. They went through the field into weeds until Turtle stopped in a circle of trampled vegetation. He threw his arms out. Said, "ᏇᎲᎴᏉᏞ!" Talking Cherokee again.

Puny jumped off his horse. "Listen! I can't speak Cherokee!"

Turtle smiled for an instant. ("ᏇᎲᎴᏉᏞ" means "listen.") He turned serious again. "Wolves here! See!" He looked to the ground. "Tracks! A pack!"

Several animals had been active in the spot. Weeds were mashed.

Dirt was scratched. The end of a piece of wood stuck out of the ground. Puny said, "Yeah, I see."

"Heard them this morning. In the dark. Came looking when light broke."

Puny kept scanning the ground. "Okay. So what's the importance?"

"The wolves were after something. That's why they howled and howled."

"Jenny!"

"ii! But no blood, see?" Turtle threw his arms out and waved them around.

Puny caught on. "She's in a well! And you've found her!"

"Found a well. Maybe her. We need the rope."

Puny and Turtle kicked away enough dirt to fully uncover a plank. Puny tied one end of his rope around one end of the wood, and tied the other end to his saddle horn. He mounted and backed his horse away. The board eased out of the ground. Turtle held its other end so it wouldn't fall into the hole. After that, they scraped away more dirt, and shifted another plank to the other side of the opening. The third plank was easier to move than the other two. They could tell there were other boards concealed under dirt, but moving three planks left a wide enough hole.

Puny said, "Hold my reins. I'll climb down."

Turtle replied, "My well."

"May be, but getting down and getting back up ain't gonna be easy."

Turtle grunted. He looked off towards the river. He spat.

Puny had never had any luck convincing an Indian of anything. And if the old man failed, he could pull him out of the well. He climbed back in the saddle and held the horse in place.

When Turtle was a boy, his favorite play had been swinging on a rope over the Hiwassee River. Letting go, spreading his arms wide like an eagle, dropping into the water. And going down the edge of the well, he felt like that boy all over. With each grip, he braced his feet against the wall and saw his father and mother, his brothers and sisters. The dark had swallowed them all; his mother in a pen, one on the Trail, the rest afterwards. He called to them softly. And, as they were never too far away from Turtle, they all came together. They tightened his grip. Steadied his muscles, his back and hips. They whispered in his ears. They kept him from falling.

At the bottom of the well, Turtle crouched and felt the ground. The dark was too black to see. The smell like the grave, musty and dense. Turtle sniffed. He caught human odor. He patted around. Touched cloth. A leg. He shouted, "I've got her. Throw me yer shirt."

Puny slid off his horse, pulled his shirt over his head, and threw it in the hole. He said, "Be careful, now." He gripped his thighs and peered into the well.

Turtle tied his shirt and Puny's together to make a sling. Then he ran his fingers over Jenny's whole body, pressing for the recoil of pain. She whimpered. Moaned when he touched her shoulder. His hands flew to her hips. He lifted them and slid the shirts under. He tied the sling to the rope and yelled up, "Pull her real easy."

Puny backed his horse up a step at a time. Turtle steadied Jenny's head until the bundle of girl and shirts rose out of his reach. Then he stood below with his arms spread to catch her if the sling gave way. When Puny dropped the rope again, Turtle tied a knot his daddy had taught him. He stepped in it and, on the way up, thanked his mother and father, his sisters and brothers.

When Turtle was safely out of the hole, Puny turned to Jenny. He stood to block the sun from her face with his shadow. He said, "Can't tell if she's alive or dead."

"She's alive. Out of her head. We need Fox."

But Puny's mind went instead to the Bushyheads. He said, "Stay low. Don't let anybody see ya. Mr. Bushyhead wants to keep this well hidden. I'll be back with his wagon and Miz Bushyhead. She doctored me." He mounted and rode off like a prairie on fire.

Puny returned with Dennis beside him on a horse. They stood around Jenny, blocking the sun from her face and talking about the rescue, until Alabama appeared in the wagon. Then the men lifted Jenny onto a pallet of quilts. The child groaned, opened her eyes, and closed them again. Alabama tried to reassure her with words, and then climbed in with her. Turtle took the reins. He turned the wagon towards town.

As soon as they rolled beyond earshot, Dennis said to Puny, "We've got to cover this place up." Planks were scattered. The weeds were even more trampled and smashed.

Puny said, "Let's git the planks back in place. We can throw dirt from the cornfield on 'em."

Dennis's religious upbringing and Princeton education made it impossible for him to see Puny as a lesser human being. He said without hesitation, "Smart thinking." But he couldn't keep his mind from turning to gold. With some effort, he got on his knees and peered in the hole. "We're going to need some lanterns and shovels, and maybe some picks. Did you ask Turtle what's down there?"

Puny's mind had been entirely on Jenny during the rescue. But he knew the well she'd fallen into was the same one Dennis had been trying to locate. He said, "I didn't wanta arouse too much suspicion. He couldn't see nothing no way. The sun were too low to shine in the hole." Puny grabbed his shirt from the ground.

Dennis looked up. The sun was higher, but the hole was illuminated only about three feet down on the west side. He said, "About noon we could probably see pretty far into her."

Puny, tucking his shirt into his pants, looked into the sun. "Yeah, but we'd be out here in plain view."

Dennis put a palm to the ground, rose, and dusted off his trousers. He said, "ᏔᏔ Benge plants this corn. He won't be over here. We'll cover her up and keep our fingers crossed. Did you tell Turtle to lie about where he found her?"

"Didn't put it directly that way. Told him ya don't want nobody to know where the well is."

Dennis bent over and picked up one end of a plank. Puny grabbed the other. Dennis said, "Let's hurry, then. They'll have to go slow. We can catch them before they get into town. We need a good lie about where she was. Turtle'll go along with it. Fullbloods are naturally deceptive."

Puny looked around. "We could say she was in the cornfield."

"No, she could get out of a cornfield."

"How about some sorta Indian trap? Don't y'all still make traps?" They hoisted another puncheon plank.

Dennis frowned. "Yeah, we do. But I didn't come from a trapping family. People gave us food. Daddy was the preacher."

Puny smiled. "Well, then, maybe ya shouldn't be lying."

Dennis was too preoccupied thinking up a believable story to indulge in self-irony. And by nature he was prone to taking himself seriously. He said, "Come on, let's grab some dirt. We're not lying. We're protecting our interest."

Visiting Doc Howard

DENNIS AND PUNY CAUGHT UP with Turtle and Alabama before they got into town. The Indians talked rapid Cherokee and spoke to Puny in English. Then they all resumed the trip. At the doctor's office, the men moved Jenny into the parlor and laid her on a table. While Dr. Howard examined her, Dennis and Alabama agreed that gathering Nannie and telling Check was woman's work; sooner done, the better. Alabama took Dennis's horse. The saddle was western, and, until reaching the edge of town, she kept her legs to one side and covered them with her skirt. Afterwards, she threw her right leg over the horse and galloped. If she were going to ride like a lady, she might as well have taken the wagon.

She found Check and Hugh at the farm. They all hurried to the stable. Hugh and a hand harnessed mules to their wagon. Alabama and Check harnessed 'Wassee to the buggy. Hugh turned the wagon towards town, and the women turned toward Sanders' home site. There, they collected Nannie and Joe, and all headed for Fort Gibson. On the way in, they passed Check's mules and wagon tethered to the school's hitching rail.

At Doc Howard's, they left Joe on the porch with an Indian woman and went in. The doctor was a tall white man with a mustache and beard. The hair on his head was parted in the middle, the mustache styled with wax into wings that resembled little horns. He wore a monocle on a ribbon, but kept the lens tucked in his vest pocket most of the time. The fullbloods called him ᎻᏬ ᎠᎭ, in honor of the funny piece of glass and in acknowledgment of the fact that he attended so many deaths. Someone told him the name meant "medicine man," so he was pleased every time he heard it. He had no idea it meant "one-eyed owl."

Dr. Howard drew the monocle out of his pocket and carefully placed it on his eye. He squinted at Alabama and Check, knowing Nannie wouldn't speak to him. He dealt with that problem all the time. "Well, ladies, the good news is that she's alive. And I think she'll slowly get better."

Alabama touched Nannie's elbow. *"You stay with her. We'll get the lay of the land."* Check said, "Doc Howard, maybe we should let Mrs. Cordery have some time with her daughter. Is there someplace we could go?"

The doctor widened his eye. The monocle dropped to his chest. "Of course." He opened a door and let them precede him onto a side porch. A flock of Indians was perched there, so he walked out into the backyard. Check and Alabama followed until they all stopped at a well. The doctor fingered his mustache. "She's in a coma. I'd say middle deep. Most people come out of those. Might take a while. I need to get water down her. Try to get her something mashed up to eat."

Alabama said, "Any broken bones?"

"Her left shoulder was dislocated. Maybe broke. Hard to tell. I moved it back into place. I'll tie it to her, to keep her from moving it."

Check said, "We're going to need to take her back to the bottoms. Hugh's bringing our wagon around."

Doc frowned. "She's safe here. And I'd like to watch her. She can't be moving that shoulder."

"You can bind it. Or we'll pack it in mud and straw," Check said.

"Mud and straw?" The doctor's fingers dropped to his monocle.

"Yes, I've done it myself. It'll be fine. But whichever you think is best."

The doctor looked off towards the porch. There were fifteen Indians on or around it. When he'd arrived from St. Louis, he'd had no clue what he was getting into. He said, "I sort of wish I could have her here to observe. She's had a concussion. She's likely to come out wild. Or go deeper in. Concussions are puzzling. I could tell you some tales."

Check said, "I'm sure of that. And you were so kind to Andrew, and to Hugh, too. But her mother will want to care for her in the bottoms."

Doc Howard tapped his palm with his monocle. He bit his underlip. He was used to people caring for their folks at home. Everybody did that. But the girl was in a bad way. And he'd seen those Indian home sites.

Alabama knew the doctor well enough to read his mind. "Don't worry. Mrs. Singer will check on her every day."

Check said, "I certainly will. The Corderys are our neighbors. Mr. Cordery, as you know, saved Hugh's life. I'll watch the child like a hawk."

The Rescue Story

The Corderys and most of the Singers went to the bottoms. The rest of the searchers gathered at the Bushyheads' for gossip, food, and a celebration of the rescue. When new people showed up, Turtle retold his story of witching to find Jenny. The stick had tugged him. Led him so fast his legs nearly buckled. Pointed up. Nearly shook his arms loose. It'd found Jenny in an eagle's nest on a tree limb hanging over the Grand River.

Nobody believed that. But neither was anybody foolish enough to ask a fullblood a question he clearly wasn't going to answer. So they nodded, ran their tongues around their teeth, and tried to imagine what the old Indian had been up to. Some of the searchers were from families who'd walked the Trail, some from Old Settlers' families, and one or two from Treaty Party families. They represented all sides of the Cherokee civil war, and they'd all been forced to take one side or the other in the United States' civil war. White people, like Nash and Cox, were there, too. When evening brought yearning for more stories, it was hard to choose a safe subject. They settled on the one thing they all agreed on — the savagery of the Osage Indians.

Bell was old enough to have memories of Osage battles. He started in

English, but lapsed into Cherokee to describe how a warrior, down on the ground, shot a bullet up an Osage's horse's nose. The horse reared. Snorted blood. The Osage was thrown. Trampled by the horse before he could tomahawk a Cherokee woman and baby.

At the end of the story, several people exclaimed some version of *"That skunk got what he deserved."* But Nash whispered to Puny, "Why'd he change languages, ya reckon?" They were on the edge of the porch, a little away from the group.

Puny'd been thinking about the well. He might be a rich man by midnight. And he'd had a little nip. He said, "Delicate subject."

"How ya know that?"

"I knowed what he said. Talking about scalping white people."

Nash ran his hand over his hair. "You understood that?"

"Mostly. The Singers talk it some."

"I didn't know that."

"Yeah. Hugh talks it pretty good. Connell's been practicing."

Nash looked across the crowd at his future son-in-law. He seemed to be enjoying himself. Nash said, "Where'd you get that whiskey I'm smelling?"

Puny said, "Found Sam's stash under a plank in the post office. I'll give ya some, but yer'll hav'ta bring yer own cup."

Eagles or Wolves?

CHECK WAS STILL AT THE Corderys' when Sanders and Coop came in. After visiting Jenny in the cabin, Sanders disappeared. When Check realized he'd been gone for a while, she asked Coop where he went. Coop shook his head. "Didn't tell me." Joe looked up, said, "Gone."

Check went back to washing Jenny's clothes in the kettle. Cliff, who Hugh had rescued from school, was with her. He and Coop began pitching ball. Check swished the clothes some more. Then pulled them out of the water with a pole and spread them on the drying rack. It was growing dark; she was thinking about going home. Then she heard horses. Nannie emerged from the cabin with a rifle. They heard Sanders yelling. The Creek medicine man was riding behind him. Check changed her mind about leaving.

Sanders said, "Can ya tell Fox what Doc Howard said?"

Check wasn't sure how much English Fox understood. She talked in slow Cherokee. Nannie chimed in. Soon Fox went into the cabin and closed the door.

"It's getting dark. Won't he need some light?" Check asked. She didn't appreciate a closed door unless she shut it herself.

"He'll ask if he needs it," Nannie said.

Check was figuring on how to prolong her visit when Sanders' stomach growled so loud that everybody looked at him. He said, "I been fergetting ta eat."

Coop said, "I'm hungry, too." Clifford echoed that.

Check said, "I'll go to the house and bring back some food." She hoped to make the trip both ways before Fox left.

But Nannie said, "My job. I'll throw in potatoes and hog meat." She headed off to behind the cabin.

Unless from a shoat, wild hog meat made the hairs on the back of Check's neck bristle. But she looked at the closed door. Fox would come out. She picked up a stick from beneath the kettle, moved it to the chimney hearth, and fed a fire there. Nannie came back with potatoes in her apron and a pig shoulder under her arm. She laid the shoulder on the stump, and threw the potatoes in at the edge of the fire. As she cut meat off, she handed it to Check to toss in the skillet. Sanders took his horse to the lot, and the boys followed him.

Before they returned, Fox came out of the cabin. He squatted near the hearth. Nannie was squatting there, too, poking the meat. Check gathered her skirt and sat on a log. Nobody said anything for a spell. Then Nannie handed Fox a piece of pork on a stick. He said, "*She's been frightened by wolves. Won't come back to us 'til they're gone.*"

Nannie handed a stick of meat to Check, who tested its heat with her fingers. Alabama had told her in private, "It's a miracle the wolves didn't get her," but she'd heard the eagle's nest story also. She said, *"I was told an eagle took her."*

Fox arched an eyebrow. He held out his elbows and flapped them. Check nodded, reminding herself she'd spoken Cherokee fluently as a child. She added, *"That story seemed strange to me, too."* She bit into her pork. It was milder than she had expected.

When Sanders and the boys returned, Fox repeated the diagnosis. While the rest were still eating, he got up and wiped his hands on a barkless log. He touched his medicine pouch and the feather woven into his hair. He said something in Cherokee, too fast for Check to catch. Sanders responded, "ii."

Fox went back inside the cabin and closed the door. Check had the same reaction she'd had before. She was brimming with curiosity when a loud, high voice floated into the air. The group turned towards it. Nobody ate during the chant, but Clifford got up and sat down closer to Check. She rubbed the back of his neck. When the chanting ended, Fox opened the door. He walked to the center of the foundation square. Sung in a high, loud voice. When finished, he said in slow Cherokee that he'd told the wolf spirit to go. Promised it baby chicks and kittens to eat if it did.

Later, when Check put Clifford to bed, she whispered that Fox had medicine like white doctors did. Told him to remember that when he became a physician. Cliff whispered back that he wasn't going to be a physician. Check realized then she hadn't told him her plans. Decided she was forgetful because of Andrew's death. Forgave herself, and looked to Otter's bed. Otter was soundly sleeping. So was Paul. She put her fingers to her lips. She kissed Cliff's forehead.

Check unbraided her hair at her dressing table in the light of the moon and the stars. She'd heard the eagle's nest story from Doc Howard, who'd heard it from Puny. It didn't make a lick of sense. Wolves really were a more likely explanation, but Jenny hadn't been bitten. So that didn't make sense either. Check took up her brush, and resolved to get to the bottom of the mystery. Then her thoughts moved to herself. She'd appreciated Jenny's disappearance. It had actually excited her. She thought about feeling guilty. But she was genuinely sympathetic to the Corderys' troubles. And Jenny had given her someone other than Andrew to dwell on. It was natural to want to keep her own loss at bay. She likened it to Fox's trying to keep the wolves away. She wished she could chant. Went to sleep thinking about chants she'd often heard as a girl. How soothing and settling they were.

Down in the Hole, Up in the Sky

DENNIS WAS DOWN IN THE hole Turtle had found. Puny was in the weeds on the ground. Dennis called up, "Drop it slowly. I can't see a thing."

"It's coming. I can't see nothing, neither." Puny was tying a lantern to a rope.

"I just hope I'm not in a nest of cottonmouths." Dennis wouldn't move until the lantern was in hand.

"Snakes won't be down in a hole this deep."

"I hope you're right." Dennis's fingers twitched. He felt disadvantaged by all the years he'd spent away from the Nation. Cottonmouths weren't studied at Princeton. And in the California gold fields, rattlesnakes had been the threat. The two reptiles were entirely different creatures. Even Dennis knew that. He grabbed the lantern and undid the rope.

The hole was more like a mine than a well. The shaft was five feet across. On the east side, it opened into a room where a man shorter than Dennis could stand barely stooping. Dennis set the lantern on the ground. Went down on his hands and knees.

Above, Puny stretched out on his stomach and hung his head over the hole. He wanted down there, too. But agreed it wasn't safe for them both to be underground at the same time. And somebody had to pull Dennis up. A horse couldn't do that without direction, and they hadn't yet come up with another solution.

Puny said, "Have ya found anything?"

"Not yet. I'll let you know when I do."

Puny rolled onto his back. The night was clear, the moon a quarter. The Milky Way an arc of haze. The stars in the millions. Close by, the horses grazed. The Grand hummed. The Nation seemed perfectly peaceful. No wolves howled in the distance. Puny listened to faint sounds Dennis made below ground. He stared at the sky. He noticed a large bird fly over. But he couldn't tell what kind.

New Life

DENNIS AND PUNY WEREN'T SUCCESSFUL at the well. But Dennis was bloated with confidence that he was on the brink of real wealth. In his study the next morning, he pressed two ten-dollar gold eagles into Turtle's hand. *"There's no way we'll be able to pay you for finding the Cordery girl. I want to give you extra for it anyway."*

The old Indian smiled. *"If anybody happens to ask, there's an old eagle's nest in a tree across from the shelving rock where the boats tie up."*

Dennis twirled his mustache. Turtle's lie delighted him. *"And how did you think to search there?"*

Turtle looked to the beams of the ceiling and said in an eerie tone, *"The eagle spirit came to me in a dream."* He lowered his head and glanced towards Dennis. *"He's pissed off about them boats."*

The two were giggling aloud, their faces crinkled and flushed, when Alabama entered. She handed Granny's scrap bag to Turtle. *"Tell Mama I'll come see her soon. We've had a lot of excitement. And I've been feeling poorly."* She hadn't told her mother she was pregnant, and didn't want her to hear it from an acquaintance. Too, she was leery of mentioning her inconvenience to a fullblood male. Most were skittish about being around a woman with child.

And Turtle's eyes did narrow. *"The squirrels run in your stomach?"* He slid his gold pieces into the scrap bag and gave the sack a shake.

"*Why, yes. Sort of.*"

Turtle nodded. "*Happens to many young women your age. Will clear up on its own.*" He picked up his quiver and left with a chuckle. He liked new life springing up.

On the Military Road

IN AUGUST OF 1838, TURTLE'S mother died of whooping cough in a stockade holding pen in Georgia. It was a few days before her detachment began their walk, but she hung around the pen, and when the journey began, floated over the heads of her husband and children. She stayed attached to them, drifting easier than they walked, and when her young one died in the snow, she gathered him to her. They moved as a family together, one above, one below, until they got to Indian Territory. Then the spirits dispersed, played, and nosed around, reuniting with the ones on the ground in times of need and when they were trying to pass over. But Turtle was his mother's only remaining child on earth, so she didn't laugh, play, or hunt; she minded Turtle's fire. And was always on the lookout for whites around him. When she saw two men hiding in a ditch beside the Military Road, she understood their intentions. She was determined to thwart them. She called to Turtle.

But Turtle was musing on recent events. Enjoying finding the well and the missing child in a single stroke. Savoring being the center of attention. A hero. He didn't hear his mother at first. She called louder. Turtle's head jerked. He caught a sound he found familiar. But was it on the ground? Or in the sky? He couldn't tell. He was sniffing the air when Sam Garrett and Jake Perkins popped up from a ditch at the side of the road. Jake said, "What'cha doing, Injun?"

Turtle sucked in a deep breath. Turned his eyes to his path. Kept walking.

Jake said, "Stop. Ya need to talk to us."

Turtle walked on like the men were weeds waving in the gully.

Sam stepped into the road. "Don't ya understand English, Injun?"

Turtle kept walking.

Jake said, "Well, I believe this is the well-witcher." He and Sam fell in alongside Turtle.

"Must be. He's got a stick in that quiver. Normal Injuns carry arrows," Sam contributed.

"I heared that stick can find jist about anything it sets its mind on," Jake said. The news that Turtle had witched the missing girl had spread like fire through dry timber. It was the talk of two districts. A bayou fisherman had brought the gossip to the bawdy house early that morning. Jake stepped in front of Turtle and put a hand on his shoulder. Turtle shook his hand off. He stepped around Jake.

Sam said, "Don't be so unfriendly. That's the most famous piece o' wood in the Nation. Finds water, missing chil'run, gold, and silver. We'll be needing to take it. And we want'chu to come with it." He reached for the stick.

Turtle's gun was in his quiver. If he could reach it, he could defend himself. He elbowed Sam in the ribs. Started his waddling run. But Sam and Jake were younger and quicker. Sam grabbed Turtle's collar. Jerked his witching stick from the quiver. Jake kicked Turtle in the back of a knee. He crumpled. Jake and Sam jumped on top of him. The three scuffled in the dust. They rolled over, fists and arms swinging. Sam's hammer punched him in his gut. He pulled it out of his belt and slung it. Granny's sack opened. The breeze caught swatches of Alabama's material. They fluttered in the air over the tussle. Turtle's mother blew them into bushes on the side of the road.

Jake jumped up and stomped Turtle in a kidney. He stomped him again in the other one. Turtle went still. Sam grabbed the stick from the middle of the road. He said, "Don't kill him. Let's git him in the ditch. Somebody could ride by any minute."

Jake snorted and cussed. They had a short argument about how to move Turtle. Should they drag him or pick him up? They decided on rolling. Sam took Turtle's quiver off his shoulder and stuck the stick in it. They rolled Turtle like a log into the ditch. Jake picked up Sam's hammer. He shook it.

Sam held up his hand. "Don't! We need him. Could be him, not the stick."

"The son o' a bitch won't help us. He don't even understand English. If we don't kill 'im, he'll bring the savages down on us. I value my hair." Jake ran fingers through it.

Sam held his breath and then blew out short puffs. "All right. But be quick."

Jake got down in the ditch in front of Turtle. He raised the hammer. Brought it down softly. Tapped Turtle behind the ear. Sam said, "Why ya doing that fer?"

"Jist taking aim." Jake stuck his tongue to the corner of his mouth. Drew his arm back and swung. The blow made a cracking sound. He held out the hammer to Sam. "You take a turn. We're in this together."

Turtle Is Discovered

IT WAS MIDDAY BEFORE DENNIS rode down the Military Road towards Tahlequah. He'd tried, as an excuse to take the buggy, to get Turtle to ride with him as far as Manard. But the old Indian had said he liked walking, and told him, *"Wheels fly off rigs."* Dennis interpreted that remark to mean "Real Indians don't ride in buggies." So he was stuck on a horse. His insides felt waggled, and he was certain his saddlebags were wrinkling his shirts. If he hadn't been thrilled about finding the well, his mood would've been sour. As it was, he was making the best of a bad situation by riding slowly to pamper his gut, and by distracting himself with thinking about how best to mine the hole. He figured, realistically, that he and Puny would need several nights to discover where the gold was buried. He would lay out the floor of the well in a grid, and explore every inch under lantern light. He'd be able to tell from bumps and dips where the earth had been disturbed. Dennis had learned a few useful skills in the California gold fields; and he liked to work smart, rather than hard.

He was musing on finding the stash when he spied a bright piece of blue cloth stuck to a bush at the side of the road. He pulled on his reins. Two other scraps were stuck to other scrubs. They looked vaguely familiar, and completely out of place. Dennis dismounted, plucked a piece of cloth from a bush, and rubbed it between his fingers and thumb. He studied the ground. Ten feet behind his horse, the dust was marked. Dennis examined the pattern. He followed an odd trail and footprints going off to the side of the road. There, in the ditch, he found Turtle's body.

GRANNY WAS COMING BACK TO the inn from her pigpen when she saw her son-in-law riding in with something draped over the back of his horse. It wasn't like Dennis to ride a horse, and that drew her mind first. Then she noticed a look on his face she'd seen before — but not since the War. She set her slop bucket down. When she straightened up, she saw Turtle's red shirt.

Granny wasn't the lone person to see it. Everybody on the porch saw Dennis ride in, and so did the Indians hunkered under the trees. George Sixkiller was one of them. He jumped up from throwing dice in the dust and pocketed his winnings. He rushed to help pull the body off the horse. He and some of the men from the porch carried Turtle into the inn. When he came back out, he saw Miz Schrimsher crying with her head against Mr. Bushyhead's shirt. Mr. Bushyhead was patting her back.

An Indian woman led Granny away. And Dennis pulled a handkerchief from his pocket and wiped his brow and his neck. Motioned George off the porch. He said, "Are you the boy I've seen with the Corderys?"

"Yes, sir. George Sixkiller. Proud to meet'chu, Mr. Bushyhead." He saluted Dennis.

Dennis had never been a soldier in any war, but he liked respect. He'd seen George at Andrew's funeral reception; pointed out as who'd helped Sanders take Colbert's body into the Creek Nation. He figured if Sanders trusted the kid, he could, too. He said, "I want you to take my horse. Tell Sheriff Rogers I found Turtle Smith in a ditch by the Military Road. Tell him to look where scraps of cloth are stuck on bushes. After that, see if you can find Sanders. Tell him the same thing." Then Dennis remembered Alabama. He added, "No, go to my wife next. Tell her to come over here to see to her mama real quick." In his experience, his mother-in-law was stoic. He'd never seen her break down. Never seen her even fret. So Dennis didn't know what else to say about that. But before George mounted, he said, "Tell my wife, too, that Turtle's been murdered. And that we've got to act before the US government gets to us."

Coming Together

ALABAMA WAS IN HER ROCKER on the front porch, sewing, when George came around the corner of the house. He pulled up at the steps. Jumped off Dennis's horse. Said between gasps, "Miz Bushyhead, yer mama needs ya."

Alabama stood. Her material fell to the planks. "Is she alive?"

"Yes'um. But she's had a go-to-pieces. Ya gotta go to her."

"Where's Dennis?" Alabama looked at his horse, stricken.

"At the inn. Turtle Smith's been murdered."

Alabama let out a strong breath. Nothing had happened to her mother or her husband. She pointed to the mare grazing the lawn. "Lady's my horse. My buggy's at the stables. Tie the foal to keep him from following. I'll get some clothes and a gun."

George brought the buggy around, and they rode towards the bottoms with Alabama behind until the intersection of the roads. She turned east and flicked Lady's flank with the tip of her whip. She flew fast, and soon came upon Bell in the road, his horse tethered to a tree. She slowed Lady to a walk and stopped.

Bell took off his hat. "ᎣᏏᏲ! Alabama."

"ᎣᏏᏲ! What's happened here, Bell?"

"Dennis found Turtle's body in a ditch. Seems he were carrying some scraps in a bag."

"He was taking them to my mother for a quilt."

"Is that one of 'em there?" Bell waved his hat towards a bush. That scrap was yellow.

"Yes. That's my old drapery. From before the War. Where's Dennis?"

"Still at the inn, I reckon. The stagecoach come by a few minutes ago. The driver said Dennis sent someone to tell the Lighthorse Patrol. Trying to stop the murderers 'fore they get to the Line." The Indian Territory–Arkansas border was called the Line all over the Nation. The Lighthorse Patrol was the tribe's national law enforcement. Bell added, "And 'fore the damn marshals run us over."

"Do they know who to look for?"

"I been thinking on that. No stable citizen would kill the well-witcher. That's plumb crazy. And, of course, Turtle's a hero." Bell looked at the ground. "We've got us three sets of tracks. One belongs to Turtle. So that makes two killers working together." He reached behind his back. Brought out the hammer he'd stuck in his belt. "Turtle twere killed with this. I'd say we're looking fer two white men on the run without guns. They most likely would be Sam Garrett and Jake Perkins." Bell scuffed up some dirt with his boot. He looked up. The lines of his face were hard-set. His eyes squinty and flinty. He tapped the hammer against his thigh.

FROM SANDERS' SITE, GEORGE RODE to Tomahawk's. He threw himself off the horse near Mannypack, who was sitting on the ground feeding Minnie mush. He gasped, "Where's Tomahawk?"

She pointed her chin towards the bayou. "Yonder past the trees, fishing. What's going on?"

"I gotta round up all the men. Turtle Smith's been murdered. Mr. Bushyhead wants us to track down the killer before the federal marshals come in."

Mannypack stood. She yelled, "Tomahawk, bring yer butt home!" She turned to George and said, "Who kilt Turtle?"

"Don't know. A white, probably. Twern't shot, twern't knifed. Head waz bashed in."

Mannypack's father had devoted his life to the Cherokee courts. She understood Turtle's murderer had to be captured quickly. Dangerous as he was, he wasn't as menacing as the US government. Judge Parker had announced his intentions towards Indian Territory. His federal marshals were howling to get in. A whole country of white people would follow them. She said, "I'll pack his ammunition and enough food fer ya both."

SANDERS HAD BEEN IN THE woods, hunting weeds that Fox needed for Jenny, when George arrived at his home. It'd taken a while to locate him, and he made up for lost time by riding fast. He slowed briefly when he saw a patch of cloth stuck on a weed. He increased his speed again, and kept riding hard until he got to the inn. He tied his reins quickly, and jumped the steps.

A sandstone fireplace faced the door. Over it, several kettles hung on chains, and over the mantel was a buffalo head and two sets of antlers. The walls were logs. Stuffed chairs, end tables, and benches clustered in front of the hearth. A long dining table and more benches ran along the west side of the room. There wasn't a soul to be seen. Sanders turned and looked out the door. The Bushyheads' horse and buggy were hitched; Bell's horse just beyond them. Sanders stood and listened. A female voice came through the ceiling's puncheon. The kitchen door opened. Bell said, "In here."

Dennis handed Sanders a dipper of water. He drained it, dipped up more, and drank that, too. He wiped his mouth with the back of his hand. "Who done it?"

Bell said, "Not sure. But we think it were Sam Garrett and Jake Perkins."

Dennis said, "They used a hammer. Must've been lying in wait." He sat down at the table.

Sanders said, "A hammer?"

Bell said, "I took their guns. Told 'em to telegraph me and I'd send 'em."

"He never heard from them," Dennis added.

"Ya got anything else?" Sanders asked.

"Three sets of tracks," Bell said. "One of them's Turtle's. All boots. No bare feet. No moccasins. And it tweren't robbery. Dennis gave Turtle two ten-dollar gold pieces for finding Jenny, and they weren't stolen."

Sanders took that like a blow in the stomach. He said, "I can't repay ya."

Dennis waved his hand. "Turtle did me a favor nobody knows about. It was mostly for that."

Bell said, "And they didn't take the big ring on his finger. But they did take his quiver and witching stick."

Sanders placed a hand on the table. Studied the grain of the wood while he thought. "Ever'body in the district knows Turtle said he witched to find Jenny. Them two could've been fool enough to believe it."

Dennis picked up a biscuit. Before he bit, he said, "They sure don't want that stick to witch lost children. Puny told me, while they were in jail, Sam told him and Jake that Turtle's stick could find gold and silver."

Bell said, "That's what they're after."

"Then they'll stay 'round here," Sanders added.

The Bushyheads' Private Conversation

IN A BEDROOM UPSTAIRS IN the inn, Dennis said to Alabama, "Sanders and Bell figure the killers will stick around. I'm going to Tahle-quah to stop the Lighthorse Patrol. Keep this from reaching Judge Park-er's ears. Our story is Bell has mounted a posse. And we're looking for a Cherokee. You keep the inn closed. Can't have outsiders picking up gossip. How's your mother?"

"She's resting. But, Dennis, she's taken this hard. I can't get over it. Even when Daddy died she wasn't this upset." Alabama's brow rippled.

"Well, they've known each other a long time. Evidently."

"I suppose so. But it's peculiar. You wouldn't think they would've been that close."

"He probably took a lot of meals here. Liked your mother's cooking." Dennis squeezed Alabama's shoulder.

"I guess. But Mama's not one to break down. I've seen her amputate a man's arm on the kitchen table and turn around and cook dinner."

Dennis had never heard that story. He said, "You have?" His biscuits turned over.

"You knew the inn was a hospital at the first of the War."

"Yes, but I never thought of the implications. Was it on the same kitchen table that's there now?"

"Of course." Alabama's voice rose a little. "That was the operating table."

Dennis burped. Knocked his chest with his fist. Said, "I need to be going."

Coop Spreads the News
to the Singers

CHECK, CONNELL, AND HUGH WERE in the potatoes when Coop tore across the backyard towards the ferry. Connell said, "He's sure in a hurry."

"Maybe there's a change in Jenny," Check responded.

"You'd think he'd come tell us. Why would he go to the ferry?" Connell said.

"Bert's worried about her," Hugh said.

Connell looked puzzled. Hugh added, "He's sweet on her."

Connell's eyebrows shot up. He considered that momentarily. Then he said, "There's nothing wrong with these plants except lack of water."

Check looked at the sky. It was a clear, breezy day. Her skirt flapped.

Connell held his hat on his head with his hand. Hugh was bareheaded. "Maybe it'll rain later," Check said. The last rain had been on the day of Andrew's death, about a week and a half earlier. Everybody was beginning to worry about weather.

They started towards the house, walking rows, Check in the middle. Out of habit, she scanned potato plants for bugs. Hugh said, "Cliff may be sweet on Jenny, too."

Connell said, "That's impossible."

Check said, "It is?"

"He's just a child. So's she. Besides, it's not suitable."

Check agreed with that. She said, "Remember Missy Simpson?"

"Vaguely," Connell replied.

Hugh said, "Why, sure you do. Back in Tennessee. She was that dirty little blond-haired girl that lived in that shanty with five or six brothers. You mooned around her like a sick puppy. Didn't Papa whip you for that?"

Connell mumbled. Tilted his hat down over his brow so his mother and brother couldn't read what was in his face.

They walked on a few more paces. Check said, "I suppose one or the other of you should have a talk with your brother."

Both Singer boys stopped. Connell said, "What do you mean?" to Check's back.

She stopped and turned. "What do you think I mean?"

Hugh said, "He's been around bulls all his life. Nobody needs to tell him anything." His cheeks were crimson.

"Did your father not talk to either of you? Or did he just say he did to make me feel better?"

Connell's cheeks were hotter than Hugh's. Irrationally, he wondered if his mother knew what he and Florence were doing. His eyes widened at the thought. "He did. But Clifford's only eleven."

"Well, then, don't say anything to him. But if he gets some girl in a family way, I'm coming after you two." Check walked off, holding her skirt down against the wind, leaving her sons in the potatoes.

Neither Connell nor Hugh had gotten more from their father than to respect women, stay away from brothels, and try not to touch themselves. The instructors at the Male Seminary had been even less enlightening. Abstinence was their sole prescription. And both Singer males were dwelling on their own predicaments. Hugh hadn't had a lump in his pants since the egg-throwing incident. That worried him more every hour. And Connell had been thinking about the pleasure of coming between Florence's legs. To convince her, he needed a way to keep her from getting pregnant, and he didn't know who to ask about that. But he did recall his conversation with Hugh in the barn. And he did want his brother to know he was finally tilling Florence's field. He said, "Made a little progress with Florence." He bent down and picked up a clod of dirt to hide his smile.

"Got the dirty deed done? Good for you."

"Yelp." Connell threw the clod. "Just need to keep any little Singers from coming 'til after the wedding."

"Mama's not going to let you marry 'til mourning's done."

"Yeah. That's sort of a problem." Connell thought their mother was far enough ahead in the field that they could start walking and their voices not be overheard. He took a step forward, and Hugh followed a couple of rows over. Connell added over his shoulder, "You know anything about keeping babies at bay?"

Hugh bit his lip. Connell didn't know about Willow — at least not to his knowledge. She used some sort of salve she swore by. But he didn't know what it was made of. Claudette always had a bucket of lard handy. But Hugh didn't want to talk about that. He said, "I hear tell you can use a pig bladder."

"How?" Connell stopped and turned.

"You tie it on to your . . ." Hugh almost said "Buckaroo." The word came out "Bong."

"Bong?"

"Dong!"

Connell tried to envision that. Didn't much like what he saw. "Anything a woman can do?"

"I think they've got this salve. I don't know what it's made of." Hugh took a few more steps. He added, "But you can do it in their mouths just as well."

Connell started walking again, to keep even with Hugh. "Are you kidding?"

Hugh felt a burn rise from his collarbone. But for the first time since the egg-throwing, Buckaroo jumped. Hope flooded his chest. He stopped. Looked off into the blue of the sky. He suddenly felt alive. A smile crept onto his lips, into his eyes. He glanced at his brother. "Yep. One hole's as good as another . . . I hear tell . . . I wouldn't know."

Connell rubbed his jaw. "I'll be damned."

Hugh hooked both thumbs in his belt. Buckaroo squirmed again. Hugh's heart leapt. The sun was warm, the air breezy, the dirt smelling of life. He said, "Just be careful she doesn't swallow it. It can get down to the baby-making place."

Connell tried to imagine the route it would take. He couldn't quite picture that. But he guessed it made sense. He said, "Okay. Good to know." He headed towards his mother, not paying attention to anything around him for thinking of Florence's lips, mouth, and throat.

SOME MINUTES LATER, CONNELL, HUGH, and Check were at the edge of a field behind the summer kitchen. Their talk was about laying a pipe from the river to the potatoes. Their arms were moving up and down, widely motioning in air, when Ezell yelled, "Miz Singer! Miz Singer!" They turned. Coop was running towards them. Ezell was behind him, her skirt held up in her hands. By the time Ezell caught up, Coop had told them about Turtle's murder.

Check said to him, "You need to alert the other ferry owners. Connell, help Coop saddle The Bay." She paused. "No, wait. Connell, saddle the horse and bring him around. Hugh, take Coop to the study. Ezell, get him some vittles."

Coop had been in the Singers' house only on the night of Andrew's death. And he was in such shock over getting to ride The Bay again that the hallway and pictures passed in a blur. He was still trying to take everything in when Hugh pulled a chair away from the sideboard and turned it towards the desk. He said, "Have a seat." He took the chair next to it.

Check came in and shut the door. She had a gun, belt, and holster in her hands. She laid them on the desk and sat down. "Coop, I'm going to tell you something you don't know. Hugh, you don't know this either." She picked the gun up, pointing it towards the ceiling. "This belonged to my little brother, Ruff. After my father's death, he came with our mother to the Nation. And he fought with Sanders under General Watie and Colonel Adair. He was killed young, before he had children. I came by his gun when we first moved here. Your father gave it to me, Coop. He gave me Ruff's gun — even though it's valuable — because they were friends and it belonged in our family. He did that after he'd lost nearly everything he owned. I'm giving you Ruff's gun because you're getting too old to go around unarmed, particularly with murderers on the loose. It's yours to keep. Take good care of it." She lowered the gun and shoved it, the belt, and the holster across the desk. She added, "It's loaded. Nothing's more dangerous than an unloaded gun."

Coop was about fourteen. His eyes were as large as eggs. His mouth opened in an oval. He didn't reach for the weapon. Hugh nudged him. He said, "Say 'Thank you, Mrs. Singer.'"

"ᏪᎥ, Miz Singer."

Check smiled. "Take them. And tell me, Coop, what does your father think about Mr. Smith's death?"

Coop was on his feet by then. Guiding the gun belt into the loops of his pants. "Don't know. He don't say much. And he's gone off to the inn."

"Did he give you any instructions?"

"Same as you. Go to the ferries. Make sure whoever done it don't escape to the Creek Nation."

"Anything else?"

"No, ma'am. That waz it."

"Do we know who we're looking for?"

"No, ma'am, I don't. George told Bell and Miz Bushyhead first. Then come to us and waz going to Tomahawk's. Bell told him to round up a posse."

Check tapped her fingers on the desk. "I can't think of anybody ignorant enough to kill a well-witcher. Nobody with land or a family would do that. It has to be an intruder."

Hugh said, "Did George say how Mr. Smith got murdered? Was he shot or knifed?"

"Beat in the head with sompthing," Coop said.

"Hum." Check's brow crinkled. "That's peculiar."

"That's what Mama said," Coop replied.

Hugh asked, "How come?"

"Well, almost everybody's armed with a knife or a gun," Check said. "A white would use a gun. An Indian would use either one. Mr. Smith was a knife Indian, wasn't he, Coop?"

Coop tried to picture the well-witcher. "I think so, Miz Singer. I never saw no gun on him."

"Neither did I," Check said. "Of course, that doesn't mean he didn't have one somewhere. But most fullbloods around here are knife Indians."

"Maybe it was a Negro," Hugh said. "Puny's 'bout the only one toting a gun in the Nation."

"That's a good point," Check replied. Then to Coop, she said, "Are you aware there's a new federal judge over in Fort Smith?"

"Oh, yes'um. Daddy says he's trying to open the Nation so white people can steal it."

Check nodded. "That seems to be the case. He's hired a new pack of marshals. Any excuse, he'll send them in here. Tell the white ferry owners that a Cherokee killed Turtle. But that we're detaining any man without a woman. Do you understand what I'm saying?"

Coop picked up the gun and holstered it. "Yes, ma'am. Yer saying I should lie to 'em. I can sure do that."

Jake and Sam

THEY WERE IN THE BAWDY house, trying to decide what to take with them. Jake grabbed an armful of clothes. "I can't believe ya waz dumb enough to leave that hammer. Why didn't ya pick it up?"

Sam grabbed a skillet and a pot. "Don't matter. We got a gun now." He had Turtle's stuck in his belt where his hammer had been.

"It do matter," Jake said. "How'd'ya think we could've made them traps without no hammer?" They'd split whiskey barrels apart. Nailed them back together to make traps for fish and small game.

"We still got the traps. We ain't going fer."

"Well, where are we going? I ain't going back to the sandbar." Jake looked around the room. He was sad to leave it.

Sam said, "We can't go thaterway." He jerked his head. "Oldest Cordery boy lives there. Want to stay away from them Corderys."

"Well, we can't go thaterway." Jake jerked his head towards the river. "Unless we catch a boat."

"Stick won't do us no good on the water." Sam nodded towards the quiver on Jake's back.

"We gonna hav'ta take a shovel with us, too." Jake jerked his head up and back. He was trying to indicate the rear of the bawdy house, where tools lay under the trot.

Sam held up the pot and the skillet. "We don't have nothing to carry this crap in. We gotta figure out where we're going. Come back and git it."

"Now wait a minute. Let's git smart here." Jake dropped their clothes on the floor. "Ain't nobody been 'round here but the Singers and that fishing guy. If we leave and take ever'thing, then ever'body'll know it waz us waz living here. But if we leave all this stuff, when people come by, they'll think somebody's still living here, and not know it's us."

Sam lowered his arms. "Run that by me again."

"Now look, put those things down." Jake stepped over the clothes. Took the skillet out of Sam's hand. Threw it into the fireplace with a *clang*. Sam set the pot on the table. Jake draped an arm over his shoulder. "Look, we jist leave this stuff here. Go about our bizness trying to find stashes. Come back ever' evening. Sit out there acrost the bayou. Scout out the house like wez Indians. When we see the coast is clear, we come in, sleep upstairs, pull up the ladder. Come down ever' morning 'til we find a stash or figure out the stick don't work. Anybody comes looking around will think whoever's living here jist ain't at home. Jist normal people. Going 'bout their bizness. Jist have to live that way fer a few days."

Sam said, "Beats living on the river or in the woods."

"A damn sight better." Jake slapped Sam on the back.

"Where's His Woman?"

EARLY THE NEXT MORNING, ALABAMA opened the door of the inn to five fullblood young men. Four were over six feet tall. The fifth was short, pudgy, and wearing a shirt. The tall ones were bare-chested, wore feathers in their hatbands, and blankets over their shoulders. All five had long, straight black hair. The pudgy Indian's was tied back with a bandana. Alabama said, *"The inn's not open."* Put her hand on a sign. It said in both languages, INN CLOSED DUE TO SICKNESS.

The tallest man said, *"We came for our grandfather."*

Alabama blushed. *"Of course. How stupid of me. I'm sorry. Please come in."* She opened the door wider.

None of the fullbloods moved.

She said, *"I'll bring food and water."*

When Alabama returned with a tray holding a pitcher, glasses, dishes, and cake, she found the short and the tallest fullbloods inside. The tallest had his hat in his hand. The short one was the image of Turtle. Alabama said, *"Please, refresh yourselves."*

The tallest said, *"G.V."* He picked the pitcher up, drank, and handed it to the pudgy one. Then he picked up a piece of cake. The three others came in, picked up cake, and passed the pitcher around. Alabama said, *"I'll just put this tray on the table."*

The tallest said, *"Who killed our grandfather?"*

"We don't know. We're rounding up a posse. You'll want to talk to Sheriff Rogers."

The pudgy one said, *"Where's my grandpappy?"*

"*His body's in the springhouse. I'll show you where.*"

Alabama led the group through the kitchen, out the back door, across the yard, and into the woods. They crossed a creek on a narrow bridge and walked a little further, to the mouth of a cave fitted with a rough wooden door. She said, "*We laid him out in there. Just in front of the ice.*" She inserted a key in a lock on a chain.

The men exchanged looks. Then the tallest said, "*I'll go back and get the horse.*" The rest nodded.

Alabama knew the young men could stand in the woods all afternoon. Not say a word and be perfectly comfortable. She looked around, found a fallen log, and sat down. She said, "*We were fond of your grandfather. He was a wonderful man. He saved a girl's life.*"

The young men grunted, pleased with the praise. One of the blanket wearers said, "*Where's his woman? We'd like to see her.*"

Alabama said, "*What woman?*"

The pudgy one said, "Granny."

Crumbs

THE FRONT ROOM OF THE inn filled up with men, both mixed-bloods and fullbloods. Three of Turtle's tall grandsons were present. So were George, Tomahawk, Coop, Hugh and Connell, and Cowboy and Bob Benge. Puny, elbow to elbow with Sanders, was the only man in the crowd not a Cherokee. Bell was in front of the hearth, giving assignments. He heard footsteps on the porch and stopped. One of Turtle's grandsons opened the door. Dennis came in. He announced, "I've called off the Lighthorse Patrol. The story is we're looking for a Cherokee. We think he's around here."

Turtle's tallest grandson, Muskrat Smith, said in a deep voice, "*Mix-blooded Cherokee!*" His eyes flashed like a panther's. His jaw clenched. Nobody shuffled their feet. Even Dennis didn't move. The boy added, "*Fullblood wouldn't kill a man with a hammer! Use a knife or a gun!*"

Everybody relaxed. Bell went back to assigning places to search. Dennis eased into the kitchen. He'd ridden since dawn. Every spot on him hurt. He put his hand on the small of his back and rubbed it. He glanced around for something to eat. Saw a tray of crumbs. He licked his thumb, captured a few, and put them to his lips.

Sanders slipped into the room behind him. He grunted.

Dennis turned. "Guess everybody ate everything up. I'm starving. Where's Alabama?"

Sanders raised his eyebrows towards the ceiling.

Dennis cleared his throat, lifted the tray, and captured more crumbs. "Guess her mother's not any better?"

Sanders pulled a chair away from the table. He turned it around and sat down, straddling its back. "Granny's gone off in her wagon to the Smiths.'"

"That's mighty nice," Dennis said. "But somebody needs to be cooking." Alabama had sent the help home when the inn closed.

Sanders said, "Dennis, why don'tcha have a seat. I got sompthing to tell ya."

Dennis said, "Is there something wrong with Bamy?" He looked alarmed and stayed standing.

"Nothing serious. But yer wife's had a little fainting spell."

Dennis sat the tray down. "She's in a family way. Nothing's happened to the baby, has it?"

Sanders scratched his head. "I don't know fer sure. But I don't think so. Alabama got up from her faint and had a fight with her mother."

"A fight?" Dennis's eyes widened.

"Yep."

"What are you not telling me?"

"Well, I can't swear to what waz said. Bell and me jist heard it through the ceiling."

"And?"

"And, well, I don't think yer wife knew her mother waz Turtle's woman."

Dennis's eyebrows jumped above his glasses.

"Bell thought somebody should tell ya."

The Avoid-Killing Lectures

CHECK BELIEVED IN HARD WORK as a remedy for grief. That included supervising work as well as performing it, and she'd neglected spring cleaning while Andrew was dying. By midmorning, she had Ezell, Lizzie, Clifford, and Otter at the clotheslines, beating rugs with swatters. Puffs of dust and lint flew up. They drifted on the breeze towards the bayou.

Lizzie said, "I don't see nothing wrong with bare floors."

Ezell said, "Bare floors ain't polite."

Lizzie's swat made a dull thump. "I'm glad I ain't white."

"Ya don't work for white people."

"They didn't get these rugs from the Indian side of the family." Lizzie swatted again. The rug cleaning went like that until Check, who was on the porch overseeing the beating, minding Paul, and shelling peas, looked off into the distance. Five horses turned towards the Corderys'; three horses turned towards them. Check tipped her pan of peas; a few dropped to the planks and rolled. She rose and shouted, "The men!"

By the time the riders were on them, the women and children were clumped close to the hitching rails. After the general greeting, Connell said, "Here's the situation. We sent men to Tahlequah on the theory they wouldn't have gotten any farther than there towards the Line. We rode towards the Grand. Nobody on any of those farms had seen anybody but themselves. Then we circled back through Fort Gibson. Checked it over as well as we could without telling people who we're looking for."

"Who are you looking for?" Check asked.

"Sam Garrett, the postmaster, and Jake Perkins. He's another white man," Hugh said and rubbed his leg.

Puny added, "When I waz in jail, they waz talking 'bout Turtle having a stick that could witch stashes. Turtle waz kilt with a lot of money on him. It waz in a sack of quilting scraps. They didn't check the sack. And they didn't take a ring, neither. But they took his quiver and stick."

Hugh said, "Turtle's grandson says the quiver had a gun in it."

"So Turtle was a gun Indian?" Check was surprised.

"Yes, ma'am." Hugh added, "They're armed."

"Is that who's down at the bawdy house?"

"That's my guess. If they are, they'll stick around at least a couple of days, looking for the stash." Hugh grasped the rail and wiggled his left foot. It was the first time he'd ridden since being shot. He felt an ache he hoped to shake.

"Did you talk to the stagecoach driver?"

Connell said, "Uncle Dennis told him. Said we were looking for a kidnapper and murderer. Not to take anybody suspicious-looking out of the Nation."

Ezell said, "Did they kidnap Jenny?"

"No," Puny answered. "But murder's so common, Mr. Bushyhead wanted to get his attention."

Ezell said, "What are ya gonna do?"

Puny said, "We need some food. Miz Bushyhead's mama's gone off burying Mr. Smith. And Miz Bushyhead's not feeling up to cooking."

Check said, "Nothing's happened to the baby?"

Connell answered, "No. Uncle Dennis says the baby's all right. Can we get something to eat?"

THIRTY MINUTES LATER, CONNELL, CLEANED up, slipped into his mother's study. Check was at her desk. She pointed her quill towards a plate of food on the sideboard. Connell's stomach growled. But, to tease his mother, he said, "I thought you and Papa didn't approve of eating anywhere except at the table."

"That is a table. Tell me everything you know."

Connell picked up a chicken thigh and bit into it. "Hugh, Puny, and I are going over to the Corderys'. Plan out how to approach the bawdy house."

"Who's in charge of the planning?"

"Bell. He's the sheriff."

"I know that. Stop gnawing your food while talking. You're not going to starve. And they're not going without you." Check removed her glasses and rubbed her eyes. "I take it you're planning on killing them?"

Connell waited until he swallowed. "I don't think we need to talk about that."

"I do. What if you're wrong? What if somebody else killed Turtle?"

"We're almost positive we're right." Connell picked up the plate and a spoon. He shoveled in a load of beans, rested the spoon on the plate, and picked up a glass of water. He moved to a chair in front of the desk. Set the glass on top of a ledger.

Check put her spectacles back on. "'Almost' isn't good enough if you're going to kill a man, son." She thought she'd already taught Connell that.

"Mama, we won't kill 'em unless we find Turtle's gun and quiver on them. That's what we've agreed on." He dipped up applesauce.

"So, you have to capture them first?"

"Well, yes, I guess we will." He took a big drink of water.

"That won't be easy."

"Probably not." Connell thought on what to eat next. He settled on a drumstick.

"Then, after you capture them, you'll have to kill them in cold blood."

Connell laid the drumstick down. He'd been excited by the events. And between them and his relationship with Florence finally feeling like he was becoming the kind of man that would make both of his parents proud. But his father was dead, and his mother clearly working herself towards a lecture. He winced and waited.

Check placed her palms on the desk. Studied the veins on the backs of her hands. "Connell, you know your grandfather Morgan was a famous soldier. So was my first cousin, John Hunt Morgan. My brothers, your uncles, died in battle. Your great-grandfather, Joe Sevier, was a Revolutionary War hero. His father, John Sevier, is remembered mostly as the first governor of Tennessee. But before that, he ruthlessly slaughtered Cherokee families — men, women, and children." She looked up. "Killing runs in our veins, Connell. We have to be extra careful. And, listen to me here — spilling blood for the first time makes spilling it again easier. You can't keep a dog from sucking eggs after he's swallowed one."

Connell saw his mother's face darken. And was shocked by what she'd said. He'd never put that together. And he'd never heard his great-

great-grandfather spoken of with anything but respect. But, first and foremost, he didn't want to worry his mother. And he knew how to disarm her. He laid his plate on the desk, put his hands on the arms of his chair, stood, and squared his shoulders. He said, "Mama, I was following you until you got to the egg-sucking part."

Check glared. Connell threw his hands up. "Mama, I take your point. I'm gonna try to leave the killing to somebody else."

A FEW MINUTES LATER, CHECK had Hugh in front of her desk. She thought maybe she'd gone too far with Connell. And Hugh had, in her estimation, grown extremely sensitive since getting shot. She took a softer approach. "I'm sure all of this riding has been hard on your leg."

"It pains me a little." Hugh, too, was cleaned up. He'd filled his stomach before his interview.

"Tell me about your aunt Alabama. I forgot to ask your brother."

Hugh looked down at his leg. He rubbed it. "I think she's all right. Maybe a little embarrassed."

"I can't imagine Alabama doing anything embarrassing." Check smiled softly.

"No, of course not." Hugh rubbed his leg more. He hoped he could keep rubbing until his mother changed the subject. Connell had already told him he was going to get lectured on not killing anyone. He didn't have a problem with that. The last thing he wanted was to get in another position to get shot. But he didn't want to discuss with his mother what was wrong with his aunt Alabama.

However, when she set her mind to it, Check could outwait any fullblood. When Hugh finally looked up, she was still smiling in an unnatural way that seemed spooky. He saw he wouldn't get out of the study without an account. "It seems Granny Schrimsher was particularly close to Turtle Smith," he said.

"Close?"

"Yes, ma'am. Close."

Check hoped that didn't mean what she thought. But Hugh was still rubbing his leg. And he seemed red in the ears. "I see," she said, trying to imagine Alabama's mother and the well-witcher in . . . a situation she didn't want to envision. She tapped a letter opener against the top of the desk. She looked out a window.

"I guess you've known for a time. So I don't need to tell you more," Hugh said.

Check didn't know if she should feel thankful for that. Or irritated with Hugh for withholding information. She decided to be thankful. She didn't want to discuss Granny Schrimsher's peccadilloes with Hugh any more than he wanted to discuss them with her. "Yes, of course. I just never mentioned it to you boys. Wasn't appropriate." She waved a hand to shoo an imaginary fly.

"That's what I thought. But evidently, Aunt Alabama didn't know it."

"I see, well . . ." Check had no trouble imagining that. She changed the subject. "So, tell me the plans for the posse."

"I don't know them. Bell and Sanders are in charge."

"That's good, Hugh. They've had to kill a lot of men already. They know how to do it. When you get into things like killing, leave it to experts."

Hugh smiled broadly. "Well, you know me, Mama. I like to shirk whatever I can." He stood up and walked to the side of the desk. He took his mother's head in his hands and kissed her on the forehead. He strode out the door, limping only a little.

The kiss startled Check. And she felt like she hadn't delivered enough of her lecture. But maybe she'd said enough. Hugh had been shot. In her experience, people who'd been on the receiving end of a gun were often less likely to be itching to pull a trigger. She hoped that was true of Hugh. Although she did recognize he had to do his duty. Whoever murdered Turtle had to be tried if they were a Cherokee, or killed if they weren't. The US government had to be kept on the other side of the Arkansas line. Why else had all those people walked so far in winter? Left their crops, homes, and improvements? Left their ancestors' graves? Their sacred mountains?

She thought again of her parents' home. She remembered the soldiers; their stories of chasing runaways. Her father had been unusually silent during those reports. Her mother was never around. She'd taken food to the holding pen every day, driven in a wagon by Lizzie's father.

Sometimes Check went with her. But her mother never let her go into the pen. From the wagon, she watched her mother and Handcock go in. Saw only a few heads at the opening. Saw her mother return each time with longer lines etched in her face. Listened each time she was told they should be thankful for their home. Check understood fully only after her parents were dead that they would've done better to have migrated with the tribe. To have shared the common fate.

She had no intention of making the same mistake. She would do her part. Join in. Fulfill the proper role of a tribal member. She opened a right-hand drawer of the desk and drew out her revolver.

Sanders Lays Out the Tactics

HUGH, CONNELL, AND PUNY WERE perched on logs. Tomahawk and George hunkered on their heels in the dirt. Sanders stood in the center of the group. He, using a white gesture, pointed directly at the fire. "That there's the bawdy house." He pointed again. "The chimbley's this site, here. The cabin's Tomahawk's. The cow lot fence is the Military Road. The Benges got it. That foundation there's the river. The drying rack's the foothills. The Smiths got them."

Coop was against the chimney, greasing his new gun with lard. He looked up. "What's the stump?"

"Don't mind the stump. Pretend it ain't there."

Bell, who'd conceived the strategy, was near Coop, honing his knife on a stone. Nannie was in the door of the cabin. Behind her, Joe played on the floor. Jenny, still in a coma, was on the bed. Sanders continued, "Tomahawk, you'll start between yer site and where the Smiths are. But first get Mannypack and Minnie outta there. Jist ride up like normal, in case Sam and Jake are prowling. Tell Mannypack Jenny has woke up. Wants to see her. Put 'em on yer horse."

Bell interjected, "Say it loud. Whisper the truth."

Sanders continued, "Git on now. I'm worried 'bout that baby. If they'll kill an old man, they'll kill a child."

Tomahawk rose. "Nobody'll mess with Minnie without gitting kilt themselves. Mannypack's armed."

"But she don't know who we're looking fer. They could come on her friendly, and she'd take 'em in. Git on. You know when to start moving on 'em." The plan was to surround the bawdy house at a distance and hold their positions until dusk. Then move in slowly and flush Sam and Jake towards the house if they were hiding out. If they were holed up inside, somebody would sneak up on them. Sanders had taken that task himself.

He continued, "Connell, Hugh, Puny, take the mouth of the bayou and the sandbar. If people are down there, ask 'em to walk towards the bend. When we flush these two, there's a good chance they'll run towards you and try to cross the river. It's low. They might think they can find bars to jump onto. If they do, let 'em git in the middle 'fore you shoot 'em. With any luck, the gars'll eat 'em."

Puny's mind turned to slaves crossing the Ohio River. He'd never actually seen those escapes. But he'd seen the river. And had heard the tales told by people who'd survived. Shooting anybody in the back while they were swimming for their lives didn't appeal to Puny. His stomach turned queasy. He said, "Ya don't want us to capture 'em?"

Bell looked up. He was letting Sanders spell out the tactics because it was improper for a sheriff to explain how to hunt men down to kill them. But he also recognized his cousin was trying to make things clear to people who were green. He said, "Puny, an innocent man who ain't nit-brained or lit up won't wade into the Arkansas River. He'll stop and talk. Only a guilty man'll run into roaring water."

Puny's brow wrinkled. He burped.

"Maybe they won't run to the river. We can hope not," Sanders said and squatted. He drew with a stick in the dirt. "Tomahawk'll be east of his site. Bell'll ride straight into it. Being the sheriff, it'll seem natural fer him to be out riding in plain sight. George, I want you east of Tomahawk. This site here's due west of the bawdy house. I'll go straight east

from here. Coop, yer'll stay between me and whichever one of them" —
he waved his stick towards Connell, Hugh, and Puny — "takes the west
part of their territory."

Hugh said, "I'll take it. Connell, let's put Puny between us." He didn't
want Puny to kill anybody. If he did, there'd be no way to protect him
from the United States' law. Connell nodded; he felt the same way. But
Puny had worked past his image of runaway slaves. They were searching
for white men who had killed an old man. He felt cross. Didn't want to
be treated like a lesser human being. He said, "I'll do my part."

Judge Parker

IN THE SPRING OF 1875, when Judge Isaac Parker took a seat on
the notoriously corrupt bench of the US District Court for the Western
District of Arkansas, he was a little-known congressman from Missouri
who'd proposed several bills to abolish the tribal governments in Indian
Territory. Those bills were in violation of the treaties of 1866. In violation, too, of all other pertinent treaties in all other years. Nevertheless,
the judge considered himself a Christian. And he did hate other people's
crimes. At thirty-seven, he wasn't particularly tall, but still had his hair.
He wore his beard in the same style as Dennis's, but wider. He spent the
first weeks of his appointment replacing the criminals and drunkards
who'd been the deputy marshals. By late spring, he was raring to use his
new crew. In his chambers with two recruits in front of him, he said, "It
has come to my attention there's been a kidnapping and a brutal murder
in the Cherokee Nation."

Tom Rusk, a stocky man with a generous mustache, said, "Do we
know who done 'em?"

"We don't know who *did* them. But we think they're connected."

Bill Bowden said, "Who got kidnapped and murdered?" He was
clean-shaven and lanky.

"A young Cherokee girl was kidnapped. The fellow who found her was murdered."

Bowden said, "Don't they usually murder the kidnap victim, not the rescuer?" He didn't pretend to know much about crime. He was a Baptist preacher trying to supplement his income.

Rusk, a newly married cowboy, said, "Waz there a shootout?"

Judge Parker ignored Bowden's question. "I didn't hear anything about a shootout, Tom. The rescuer was killed on the Military Road between Manard and Fort Gibson. I want the two of you to go over there. Bring back whoever the Cherokees arrest. Their jail's at the fort. But give 'em a couple of days. Let them do the work for us."

"I need to preach on Sunday," Bowden said.

"You can go after church. Mike Reeve, the stagecoach driver, is our source. I've made him an undercover deputy marshal. Don't let anybody know he's working with us."

"I won't tell a soul who don't need to know," Bowden said.

"Bill, I'm saying you can't tell *anybody*. If people know Mike's our man, they'll stop talking around him. Folks trust stagecoach drivers. They tell them all sorts of things."

Bowden looked troubled. "Miz Bowden and I don't have secrets. I believe communication ought to be entirely open between a man and his wife. Can I tell her?"

Judge Parker drew his handkerchief from his pocket. Patted his brow. It crossed his mind that there were disadvantages to recruiting honest men as marshals. He said, "Bill, if one of your flock confesses a sin to you, do you run home and tell Mrs. Bowden?"

Bowden shook his head. "Well now, Judge Parker, we're Baptists. Baptists don't confess to the preacher. We confess to the Lord."

"It's a hypothetical. *Would* you tell Mrs. Bowden if somebody *were* to confess to you?"

Bowden frowned and scratched his head. "I don't rightly know, Judge Parker. I'll have to think on that."

Parker turned to Rusk. "Don't let him say anything he shouldn't."

"Yes, sir. Do we have the authority to shoot anybody we have to?"

"You have the authority to protect yourselves. Don't shoot anybody unnecessarily. And I want you to bring back somebody alive. The murdered man was a fullblood Cherokee." The judge held up a hand and counted off on fingers. "If the murderer is white, or a Negro who's not a Freedman, or a Creek, or a Choctaw, he's mine." He made a fist. "I'm going to try him as an example. Finally bring law to the Cherokee Nation."

Alabama Wishes She Were a Man

ALABAMA AND DENNIS WERE IN the main room of the inn, alone, in front of the hearth with a buffalo's beard, ears, and horns over their heads. Alabama said, "I'm going over there. I'll be all right." Her pistol was in her right fist.

Dennis had been assigned the inn because nobody thought he'd be any good at killing. But Bell had told him, "We need a man of importance to delay any marshals that might show." The rationale had pleased Dennis in two or three different ways, but he didn't want his wife out riding around. He replied, "I don't care, Bamy. You're not going."

Alabama looked up at the buffalo's head. Had a sudden urge to pull it off the wall. Stuff it on her husband's shoulders. She looked back at Dennis. "Are you giving me an order? Because if you are, I don't want to hear it. My father never in his life gave my mother an order."

Dennis looked to the head, too. He didn't like the right glassy eye that ignored him and looked towards the kitchen. He said, "Well, maybe he should have." It was a risky retort. He smiled a little.

The smile didn't help. Alabama's eyes had the same glassy stare as the buffalo's.

Dennis tried another strategy. "Honey, it won't do any good to go over and tell Marty what your mother's been up to. She probably knows already. The Gulagers aren't strait-laced people."

Alabama flushed. But she put her gun in her skirt pocket. She turned her face towards the door. "Marty better not know. If I'm the last person in the Nation to know, I swear I'll roast Mama when she quits grieving."

"I was under the impression you'd already roasted her." Dennis sat down. He waved his hand towards the door. "But don't let me detain you. If you want to ride out alone in the buggy and leave me without transportation, just suit yourself." He'd again loaned his horse to George. "If you happen upon those two white fellows who've been your tenants, just go on and kill 'em for not paying rent. It'll save everybody a lot of trouble." He drew a cigar and match out of his vest pocket. "Be sure to drag the bodies off the road, though. We don't want the US law hanging a Cherokee lady. Would look bad for our womanhood." He lit up and took a deep puff.

Alabama felt silly. She had since she'd fainted in the woods and Turtle's grandson had slung her over his shoulder and carried her to the inn. She didn't know exactly how she was going to regain her composure. She said, "I wish I were a man," and sat down across from her husband.

Dennis smiled. "I'm sort of glad you're not."

"If I were a man, somebody would have told me Mama was having relations with Turtle. I wouldn't have been caught off guard."

"Well, that's probably true." Dennis took another puff.

"When did you find out?"

Dennis, an expert politician, recognized a trap when he saw one. He shifted his weight. "This darn chair's not as soft as it looks. And I think I've blistered my thigh from all that riding."

"That's too bad. You haven't answered my question."

Dennis stared at the ceiling. Took a long drag off his cigar. If he told the truth, it'd look like nobody told him anything, either. If he lied, his wife would scalp him for not having told her. He thought: What would Daddy do in this situation? He knew the answer: Tell the truth. But he didn't see that advice as pertinent to his particular predicament. Life had grown more complicated since his father was alive. "Well, I've suspected it for a long time. But I didn't want to accuse your mother of something that's really none of my business." He sounded a little sanctimonious.

Alabama patted her foot against a plank. "I can understand that." It wasn't any of her business, either. She wished she'd never found out.

So Does Check

CHECK HAD FIRST DEPOSITED HER revolver in an apron pocket. But little boys were running up and hanging on her, so she took the gun out of the apron and put it in a bucket. She carried the bucket around for a while, but had to set it down to do anything, so she finally got Andrew's gun belt and holster, and put the revolver in it. She started to buckle it on, but realized how silly she'd look, so stuffed the gun, holster, and belt in the bucket. She huffed real hard, and left it all on the back porch while she did her chores.

Check recognized that Turtle's murder, like Jenny's disappearance, distracted her from her grief. She was thankful for that, but irritable. She again fumbled around inside, searching for a reason. What she turned up was a wish, much like Alabama's, that she'd been born a man. She'd wished that before, but only during childbirth. What she really wished was that she could unclasp the confines of the feminine role like she unclasped her corset at night. She had more power and freedom as a Cherokee woman than she'd had living in Ohio as a white. But in this crisis, that wasn't enough. She wanted to strap on that revolver. Ride with the posse. Protect her sons. Kill the killers herself.

Petulant about her position, Check stormed around the house and kitchen. She quickly made Ezell avoid her, and threatened Clifford with sending him back to school. He reminded her there were murderers loose, so she retracted the threat. But she had worked herself into such an itch that she asked a hand to hitch 'Wassee to her buggy and bring it around to the back of the house.

Clifford saw her put the bucket in the cab. "Can I go, Mama?"

"I'm going to tend the sick. You'd just be in the way, Cliff."

"I want to see Jenny, too." He ducked his head. Scuffed up dirt with his shoe.

"I'm not going to the Corderys'. They're busy over there. I'm going into town on errands. Then I may go to the inn at Manard. Depends on where your aunt Alabama is. She's not feeling well. She's having a baby."

"Is it coming soon?"

"No. But sometimes women get sick long before babies come." Check climbed in the buggy.

Clifford considered that information. "Do they get sick in the stomach?"

"Yes they do, son." Check flashed on Hugh's remark about the bulls. Wondered if Cliff knew more than she thought.

Cliff rubbed his stomach. "I've got a tummy ache myself."

"Are you pregnant, too?"

Cliff turned as red as a cockscomb. "No, Mama!" He dropped his hand to his side.

"Well, that's good. Just don't get that way. I've got enough trouble as it is." Check suddenly felt better. She tapped 'Wassee's flank with the reins and rolled off.

A while later, she arrived at the Bushyheads' house. Dove told her, "They's at the inn. And everybody in town's asking fer their mail. Where's that big nigger?"

That irritated Check. She said, "I believe he's out trying to capture the people who killed Mr. Smith. If I run into him, I'll tell him you asked about him."

From there, she drove to Nash's store. Nash saw her buggy through the window, walked out onto the porch and down the steps. He ushered her in the front door, and, after handing her order to Jim, he whispered, "This business about a mixed-blood killing Turtle Smith doesn't look good for our situation."

Check said, "It's awful anybody killed him. What have you heard?"

Nash's voice got even lower. "The fullbloods aren't taking this lightly." He arched an eyebrow.

"You think not?" Check's brow knotted.

"No. They hate ever'body anyway. They could take this as an excuse to turn on us. Suzanne's worried."

Check lowered her head. Ran her tongue around inside her mouth. Nash irritated her, too. She didn't agree with his assessment, and she figured Suzanne shared it. She looked up. "You know, I've often thought it must be difficult for Suzanne, living in this environment. I've wondered if she wouldn't feel more comfortable in a sophisticated place. Maybe St. Louis or Kansas City." She smiled. Batted her eyelids once.

Nash nodded. Suzanne liked to travel, but only to shop. And she'd never be somebody in St. Louis or Kansas City like she was in Indian Territory. Nash couldn't say that, exactly. He scratched his beard. "It's certainly safer almost anywhere east. But it'd be hard to go. Suzanne's a Ross and a Vann both, you know."

"Oh, of course. I'd forgotten," Check replied. "Well, her Vann blood will see her through."

Nash looked blank. Check replicated his look. Wondered if Suzanne had never told him why and how James Vann died. The possibility of that omission perked Check up. Almost made her feel better. But she recalled the seriousness of the situation. She said, "We'll all be safer when Mr. Smith's murderers are caught."

Shortly afterwards, she drove down the Military Road. Before she reached Manard, she saw Bob Benge on his horse under a tree in a pasture. Bob also saw her. He rode to the side of the road. His horse pranced when he stopped; he patted its neck. Check drove close, pulled 'Wassee up, and said, "Bob! How ya doing?"

"Just fine, Aunt Check. What ar'ya doing out here?"

"Visiting, Bob." She sounded a little offended.

"You're aware we've got a stakeout?"

"Oh, really? How's that going?"

Bob thought maybe Aunt Check was pulling his leg. But maybe she wasn't. He said, "Well, so far we haven't turned anybody up 'cept you."

"Humph," Check said. "That's a shame. But, Bob, it'll be better if the older men do the killing."

Then they heard a rumble. Bob looked around to find a place to move to. He turned his horse from the road. Check turned 'Wassee and the buggy to the north as far as she could. The stagecoach roared through. After the dust died, Check turned the buggy again, and Bob rode up next to her. He said, "Aunt Check, do ya want me to ride with ya wherever you're going?" He'd decided he better not tell her to go home.

Check said, "No. Don't leave your post. I've got a gun on me. Tell your mother hello." She flipped her crop and drove off.

When she pulled up in front of the inn, Alabama quickly disappeared from a windowframe, flew out the door, over the porch, and down the steps. She threw her arms around Check as soon as they both were on the ground. "Oh, Lord," she said, "I'm so glad to see you."

Check had decided to let Alabama tell her about her mother, so she wouldn't think the relationship was gossip among the menfolk. She said, "Alabama, what's wrong?"

Tears flooded Alabama's eyes. "You're not going to believe this. Mama had taken up with Turtle! I found out from a complete stranger. And he was just a boy!"

Check patted her arms. She'd come to comfort Alabama for many reasons. Not the least of which was that her own mother had done the same thing. And she'd never had anybody to discuss that with. She'd wondered for a long time what it was about fullblood men that made them so attractive to older women. She'd settled on the theory that it was their peaceful air and pretty skin. But it could be something else. She said to Alabama, "Let's go in. You've had quite a shock."

The Posse Spreads Out

THEY MOVED TO THEIR POSITIONS on foot, the way their ancestors fought. Even in the late wars against the Osage, Cherokees avoided horses because one could sound as loud as a horn, while a walking man could slide along unheard. Sanders had assigned Connell, Hugh, and Puny to the sandbar and mouth of the bayou because he figured none of the three could slip around in the woods without making a ruckus.

Tomahawk gave Mannypack his horse. After she and Minnie left, he piddled around outside their cabin, appearing unconcerned. He picked up his rifle as casually as if he was going to hunt wild turkey. He walked into the trees. Deep in, he took off his shirt. Hung it on a branch. He was wearing moccasins; his pants were the color of his skin. Standing still, he resembled bark.

Sanders and Coop walked a short way together. Sanders whispered instructions to run Sam and Jake towards him, not towards the Singers. He worried about men who'd never seen battle. And, like Check, didn't want the young ones killing anybody. He knew, even better than she, that the first slaying is hard, but makes the next ones easier. His first soldier had been a white man in a Federal uniform dotted with brass buttons. His face turned ashen. A button turned dark. Shot again, he fell backwards. His boots turned up. They fit Sanders' feet. He patted Coop on the back. Said, "Be careful, son." He disappeared into the woods.

George rode down the Military Road past the inn. He left Dennis's horse with Cowboy Benge at a bridge on the road to Tahlequah. George walked south through fields of corn, through pecan and apple orchards. He was bare-chested. When he crossed a stream, he stuck a finger in mud and painted streaks on his cheeks.

Connell, Hugh, and Puny trod through trees and cane to the sandbar. Connell told a family there that shooting was likely; suggested they move towards the bend. Hugh stayed near the washed-up tree where they'd been camping. Connell and Puny walked east, crossed a stream of the bayou on a plank, and came upon the dune Puny had once slept against. They kept walking until they got to the boat dock. Puny stayed near it, under the trees, and Connell went north until he crossed a bayou creek on a wooden bridge. He walked back towards the river, settled under a tree, and took his gun out of its holster.

Bell rode straight into Tomahawk's site. He yelled, "Tomahawk? Mannypack?" He dismounted, went inside their cabin, and dipped up a gourd of water. He drank it in the doorway, his other hand on the small of his back. When he remounted, he rode up and down the creek like an old man who couldn't remember what direction he wanted to go in.

Stash-Witching

JAKE AND SAM BELIEVED INDIANS were partial to stumps for stash-hiding. They were near the west branch of the bayou, in a cleared space spotted with tree remnants decayed at the roots and covering holes in the ground. They'd already pointed the stick towards several stumps. At the last attempt, it jerked in Sam's hand. Jake thought Sam was just overly excited. But they had a shovel and pick, and were anxious to dig something up. Jake said, "Let's have a look." He bent towards a hole at the base of the stump. He didn't get very close, because both men also held the theory that Indians picked stumps for stash-hiding because cottonmouths favored them, too. Jake said, "Hold her towards the hole. See if she wiggles again."

Sam pointed one end of the fork towards the hole. It didn't tremble. Jake said, "Point the other one."

Sam said, "This here's the one that were feeling the tug."

"Well, it ain't feeling it now. Go on, try the other one."

Sam tilted the other fork towards the hole. Both men watched like gawking could make it twitch. It didn't move a whit.

"Let me have it!" Jake reached for the stick.

Sam held it away from him. "Jist a cotton-picking minute. I'm not through trying."

"Ya haven't found a goddamn thing. Ya've had it all afternoon."

"Ya had it this morning."

"But I didn't know what I waz doing then. I got the hang of it now."

"That's ridiculous. It moved fer me. Be quiet. Let me slap my mind back on it." Sam closed his eyes and began humming.

Jake checked another stump for cottonmouths. It looked safe enough to make a good seat. He studied the sky to keep from jumping up and grabbing the stick from Sam's hands. A formation of ducks flew over towards the river. Jake was thinking about shooting a duck when Sam said, "Ooooooo." The stick was moving again. Jake thought maybe Sam was shaking it.

Sam followed the stick in a stiff, mechanical walk about fifteen feet to the south. He turned and walked another fifteen west. Jake decided he was going in a circle. But then the stick pointed down and shook. Sam looked electrocuted. He yelled, "This thing's a-quivering. I can't stop it."

Jake jumped up and ran over. The left fork of the stick was pointed towards a stump about two feet in diameter. Sam's arms were shaking all the way to the elbows. Jake said, "Shit, ya've hooked something. Put the damn thing down. Let's dig. Be careful." He pointed. "Lay the stick over there so it won't git broke."

Sam leaned the rod against a stump three feet away. He stood over it, to catch it if it moved while Jake retrieved the pick and shovel. Then the two started in on opposite sides of the remnant the stick had pointed to. Occasionally, one of them let up to wipe his brow. They soon grew sweat patterns on the backs of their shirts. Birds twittered in nearby branches. A pair of coiled cottonmouths, disturbed by shaking ground, slid off towards water. Neither Jake nor Sam noticed the birds or the snakes, the eyes watching them, or the gun pointed towards them.

One Down

SANDERS HEARD THE FIRST SHOT. Jerked to his right. Saw trees, weeds, and a flock of crows in flight. The second shot, he stiffened to get better bearings. Arched his ears to stretch his hearing. A small animal crackled the weeds. A mockingbird chattered. A horsefly buzzed by. Sanders sensed the direction of the blasts. He set off, close to cover.

Hugh, too, jerked at the first shot. Winced at the second one. Drew his gun. Stood stone-still. Breathed hardly at all. Presently, caught a thrashing in the woods. Pulled back his hammer. Grabbed his right wrist with his left hand to steady his gun.

When Puny heard the first shot, he jumped behind a tree trunk. When he heard the next, he ran towards the sound, staying near the bank of the bayou. He kept running until he couldn't proceed in what seemed like the right direction unless he walked into water or circled back to the bridge above the dock. He tried to decide which to do, looking one way, then another. He couldn't swim, but thought the bayou creek might be shallow enough to wade. Taking that chance could be fatal. But circling back to the bridge would send him in the wrong direction.

Connell was taking a leak when the sounds drifted towards him. Caught midstream, he thought: *Oh, shit, I've got my dick out!* Then he decided he hadn't heard shots at all; rather, a limb cracking. He shook off, tucked in, and listened. He didn't want to be ambushed from the woods, so he pulled his gun, slid behind a tree, and hunkered down close to its trunk.

George was too far northeast to hear shots. And Tomahawk, near a small herd of cows plodding past, missed them in that commotion. But Bell heard the gunfire. He dug his heels into his horse. Rode at a gallop.

At home, Nannie, trying to cuddle Jenny awake, heard faint sounds in the distance. She recognized them. Pulled her arms tighter around her child. Sang, "ᏅᎦᏅ-ᏛᏗ, ᏅᎦᏅ-ᏛᏗ, ᏛᏗ-ᏛᏗᎮ, ᏅᎦᏛᎪᏗ. ᏗᎦᏛᎪᏗ. ᏗᏩᎤᏁᎫ ᏛᎦᏆᎫ; ᎡᎫ ᎤᏁᎫ ᏛᎦᏅ; ᏗᏩᏍᏂᎷ ᏛᎦᎫᏗᏍ."

Coop heard the shots. Felt like they went off in his head. His ears rang. He wobbled and wobbled. Tried to steady himself. His target had run out of range. But Coop couldn't stop shaking. He bent over. Dropped his gun to the ground. Gripped his thighs. Thought if he could steady his legs, his hands would follow; if his hands stopped trembling, his legs would follow.

Sanders, in the trees on the west fork of the bayou, stopped often to listen. He knew warm air diffuses gunfire, so wasn't sure he was going in the right direction. He moved south to where he thought Coop should be. Not seeing him, he looked at weeds, bushes, and trees. Finally, he found a slim trail snaking through the woods. He ran it quickly to a clearing. Coop was in bright sun. Bent over at an angle. Looking down. Sanders gobbled. Coop twisted slowly. Flapped a limp arm. Waved his father to him.

The body was curled on the ground. Sanders said, "Git down." He dropped to his haunches. Pulled Coop's pants. Coop dropped, too. Sanders grabbed the body by the shoulder. Rolled it over. The eyes were open, the mouth gaping, the shirt bright red over the chest. Sanders said, "Ya got a clean shot."

Coop was still trembling. His face stained with tears. "Did I kill him, Daddy?"

"Yeah." Sanders blew hard. He wasn't happy, but was relieved. His boy wasn't the body on the ground; he was alive beside him, panting. Sanders said, "I heared two shots."

"I shot at Jake while he were running away."

"Hit him?"

"Don't think so." Suddenly, he added, "Daddy, I gotta do my bizness."

Sanders had seen a herd of men shit themselves during the War. He said, "I won't git in yer way."

Bell saw Coop scamper over and squat in the weeds. Then he saw Sanders and the body. He kicked his horse. Rode at a gallop. Dismounted fast for a man his age. He said, "By damn, ya got him."

Sanders was standing by then. He jerked his head in Coop's direction. "The kid got him. Nannie's gonna scalp me."

Two Down

JAKE SAW A WHITE SHIRT between a large, washed-up tree on the sandbar and the river. He stopped in a stand of cane. Crouched and listened for someone behind him. Didn't hear a thing except insects and birds. He rose slowly and peeked out. The shirt was Hugh Singer's. Jake figured Hugh was part of a posse. He figured, too, it'd be a long shot for a revolver. He crept out of the cane, trying not to rustle it. He slipped over to a sapling nearer Hugh. Wedged the barrel of Turtle's gun between the trunk and a limb. Pushed down to secure it. Closed his left eye. Took dead aim. Fired.

When Puny heard that shot, he was still on the bank of the bayou creek. He hadn't made a choice about wading in or circling back. But that shot sounded towards the river. And the quickest way to it was through the water. He plunged in, holding his gun over his head, praying the creek wasn't too deep. Praying the mud wouldn't drag him to the bottom. He saw those slaves escaping the South. Took courage from them as he sunk lower and lower. The water rose higher and higher.

Sanders and Bell were talking over Sam's body when they heard Jake's shot. They bent, fell to the ground. Coop yelled from the weeds, "That's the way he went!" He jumped up clutching his pants, waved an arm towards the trees to the south. "Somebody git him!"

Sanders rose out of the weeds. Extended Bell a hand. Said, "I'll git that son of a bitch!"

"I'm the sheriff. I'll git him." Bell turned towards his horse.

Sanders grabbed his shoulder. "Let me git him. Turtle saved *my* daughter."

"Now, goddamn, Sanders . . ." Bell started. But Coop yelled, "Ya two stop fighting! He's gitting away!"

Sanders was startled by a command from his son. And in the second he took his focus off of his cousin, Bell mounted, shied his horse out of Sanders' reach, and rode off. Sanders yelled to Coop, "I'll tend to you later. Stay here!" He ran after the horse.

Hugh knew what it felt like to get shot. And he didn't like that feeling. So when the bullet shattered the bark of the tree beside him, he'd dropped to the sand and crawled on his elbows. He peeked around a limb. He couldn't see where the shot came from. He waited, barely breathing. His leg hurt. The sand was warm. A line of ants wound in front of him. One carried a sliver of wood three times its own size. Under a piece of bark, a grubworm curled tighter.

Puny was soaked only waist high, but his shirt was drenched with the sweat of exertion and fear. He was wet all over, but still alive, and determined to get in the fight if he could. He ran on for a bit. Stopped to get his bearings. Through branches and leaves, saw a color that wasn't natural. Tried to remember if any of his side was wearing blue when he'd left them. Heard a piercing gobble. Not a wild turkey's. Puny had never heard anything like it.

Jake heard the gobble, too. He didn't know what it was either. But it was behind him, getting closer, and accompanied by the thrashing of a large animal in the woods. The thrashing and the unnatural shrieks were coming nearer. And nearer. Jake ran for the river.

Puny saw him leave the trees for the sand. He shot. Hugh didn't know who was shooting or in what direction. Behind the beached tree, he curled up like the grub. His leg pulled to his chest pained him more. But he could bear it. If he raised his head, he could get shot and never know his killer.

Jake ran east on the sandbar. The wallops of his boots slapping packed sand were swallowed by the roar of the river. Puny ran past Hugh's tree, chasing Jake. Hugh popped up. Bell broke out of the woods on horseback. He galloped past Puny towards the white man like an arrow being shot.

Jake's arms pumped with fear and effort. He turned his head. Saw the horse bearing down on him. Stumbled. Caught himself with a hand. Swiveled towards the river. Waded into the water towards a sandbar in the middle. The river was cold, the roar deafening, the sand too unstable for footing. Jake couldn't swim the current. He tried walking through it. It pushed back. Tugged at his pants. The sand sucked his left boot off, then sucked off the other.

Bell pulled his horse up. Jake, arms thrashing, head thrown back, was probably yelling. When his head went under, Bell smacked his lips. When it went under again, Bell waited, his hand on his thigh. When the head didn't come back up, he said, "Good riddance."

By the time Sanders made it to the sandbar, Bell, Hugh, Puny, and Connell were lined up on Hugh's tree trunk like chickens gone to roost. They looked fairly smug, so Sanders slowed and caught his breath.

When he got close to the tree, he said, "Bell, that's the last damn time I'm joining ya in a posse."

Bell was rolling a cigarette. He didn't raise his head. "I can't help it if ya can't keep up. I'm jist glad Grandma ain't here to see ya."

Sanders rolled his eyes and spat. He crossed his arms over his chest. Looked off east up the sandbar. "Are ya gonna tell me what happened?"

Hugh said, "The river took him."

Bell said, "Yep. It were awful."

Stripping and Covering Up

CONNELL, HUGH, AND PUNY WERE hunkered down around Sam's body, peering at it like it was a species of creature they'd never encountered. Maybe a cross between human and bear, or maybe a hybrid human and possum. Hugh was at the left shoulder. He put a knee to the ground, leaned in, and twisted to see the face straight on. The mouth was a grimace. The teeth patchy and brown. The eyes wide and yellow. The creases of the neck were filled with grime. Hugh said, "He's sure dirty."

Puny said, "Dirt shows on white people." Hugh glanced up and across the body at Puny. Puny added, "Other folks get dirty, too. Jist ain't as apparent."

"Stinks," Sanders said. He was holding Sam's left calf, tugging at his boot. Next to their lying and stealing, Sanders' chief complaint about whites was their smell.

Connell knew Sanders was thinking about the odor. Most Indians claimed whites' scent was so strong it'd stampede a herd of buffalo a day away. Connell raised his shoulder slightly. Sniffed his armpit surreptitiously. His grandmother had teased him about smelling white. With a whiff of his cologne, his mind went back to the body. "This should keep the marshals out of here."

Hugh put his hands on the ground. Stood and wiggled his left leg. "What makes you think that?"

"Well, one of 'em accidentally drowned while running from the sheriff. Nobody's guilty there. The other was killed by a child. Can't put a child in jail." Connell stood, too.

"But the story is that a Cherokee killed Turtle. How're we going to explain why two white men died for it?" Hugh left unsaid his more immediate concern. The one at home in a dress. He wished anybody but Coop had killed Sam. He saw his mother giving Coop the gun. Imagined her reaction when she'd learn how he'd used it. She wouldn't wail, but she wouldn't take it well. The gun had been for self-defense. And she was burdened enough as it was.

Sanders had tossed Sam's boot into the weeds. He still held Sam's leg in the air. Was pinching off a sock stiff with dirt. He said, "All of us jist need to hold our tongues. No predicting what the new judge'll do." He dropped the sock to the ground. He was as worried as Hugh. Was figuring on the channels for the truth to leak out. Bell had left to round up George and Tomahawk and to call off the stakeout. He, for sure, wouldn't say anything to anybody that would bring in the marshals. Neither would the other two. Coop had gone to fetch horses; he wouldn't see anybody to tell. But he'd need to be cautioned against bragging. Killing was a hard secret to keep. Everybody wants to spill those particular beans. And beans have a way of bouncing and rolling around. Sanders knew that from long experience. He dropped the left leg and picked up the right. He added, "We might not wanta let Nannie know Coop done the killing."

Hugh felt relieved to hear that. Connell did, too. Coop had told them all who'd given him the gun.

But Puny teased, "Sanders, ya ain't afraid of yer woman?" He stood up, took his hat off, and scratched his pate like he was puzzled.

Sanders pulled the right boot off the foot. Said, "Had a little falling out with Nannie-Berry. Need to stay 'round here."

Connell, Puny, and Hugh exchanged rapid looks. Hugh's eyes lit up, welcoming company with a female predicament. And the fact that Sanders was undressing a body wasn't nearly as interesting as him actually saying something about his wives. They all cocked their ears, waiting for more information. But Sanders added only, "Help me git his britches off. He needs to be naked."

What They Told the Women

CHECK AND ALABAMA WERE IN the kitchen at the inn when they heard hooves. They wiped their hands on sugar sacks. Headed through the main room to the porch. Dennis was already outside, his hands on the railing. He was talking to Bell, who was still on his horse. Bell didn't dismount, and was riding away by the time the women reached Dennis's side.

He reported, "The killers are dead. We all can relax." He pulled a cigar out of his pocket and stuck it between his teeth unlit. Check and Alabama wanted to know who killed the men, where everybody was, and what were they were doing with the bodies. But Bell hadn't told Dennis any details, and Dennis hadn't asked.

Dennis lit his cigar and sat down in a rocker. Check and Alabama stayed standing, their arms folded beneath their breasts. Check fought an urge to tap her foot, to scold Dennis like she would one of her boys. But she'd seen how quickly Bell had ridden off, so fought that urge by pursing her lips. But both women wished one of them had been on the porch instead of Dennis. They said that to each other in glances and arched eyebrows. Then, out loud, Alabama said she'd better go tell her mother what little she knew. Check decided it was time to visit the sick and disabled.

Not much later, she drove 'Wassee at a full canter down the Military Road towards the bottoms. The sun shone in her eyes. Blinded her most of the way. The orb hit the tops of the trees only when she turned onto the road through her fields to Sanders'. As potato plants passed in a blur on the sides of her buggy, she began to relax. The real danger had passed. Justice had been served. The marshals were unlikely to invade. And the problem had been solved with the concerted effort of several people. The way a tribe is supposed to work. That, Check felt, was the difference between Indians and white people. Or, one of them.

When she got to the Corderys', she told Nannie and Mannypack that Turtle's killers were dead. Then she pitched in to help with their work. She'd just dumped the water they'd used bathing Jenny when she heard horses coming. Connell rode in with Hugh behind him.

Connell was surprised to see his mother with her sleeves rolled up, her skirt damp in spots, and holding a pan in one hand. Before his feet hit the ground, he said, "Mama, what are ya doing?"

"Never mind about me. Come give me a hug." Check set the pan on the stump.

Connell wrapped his arms around her. "You're not sick, are ya?"

Check pulled away. "Of course not! We bathed Jenny and she fought us. She's getting stronger. What happened?"

"I'm not supposed to tell."

Check squinted. She was saying "We'll see about that" when Hugh dismounted.

Hugh said, "Mama, what are ya doing here?"

"You sound just like your brother. I'm visiting! Decent people visit their neighbors."

"It's okay with me." Hugh held up his hands.

"Well, then, give me a hug."

Hugh did as told, looking over Check's head at Connell. Connell said, "Mama's been doing a good deed."

At that moment, Nannie and Mannypack, Minnie on her hip, emerged from the cabin. Nannie said, "Where's my men?"

Connell walked to the kettle. Looked in to avert his face while he lied. "Bell and Puny are rounding them up. Might take a while. Got a lot of ground to cover." He looked up and smiled. "This stew smells good."

"Well, what'd ya do?" Mannypack asked.

"We didn't actually do much. Just watched the river. It was boring," Connell responded.

Mannypack had heard the shots. She said, "Uh-huh," and shifted Minnie to her other hip. "I guess that must be disappointing."

"Well, you always want to be of some help if you can." Connell smiled again. Tried to look charming. He figured Mannypack wouldn't contradict him, especially in front of his mother.

But Mannypack said, "Yer an unlikely group of men to be doing good deeds."

And Check grunted. She'd have to pry the information out of her boys. She didn't like that one bit. They were too old to punish. She wished Andrew were alive for this phase of their rearing. Although Andrew would've objected to the entire situation. Would've spun like a small tornado. It was probably just as well he didn't live to see it. Check was shocked by that conclusion. Felt, also, a little guilty. But it was the truth. And she believed it was better to live without illusions.

Nannie didn't know the Singer boys well enough to tell if Connell was telling the truth. But it was clear to her the problem had been solved, and eventually Sanders would turn over the bucket about how. In the meantime, she was used to drips and drabbles. She went back inside the cabin.

In the next few minutes, George and Tomahawk straggled in, one at a time. They were followed by Bell. Puny, who stayed back to warn everybody off telling the truth, came in last. For each new arrival, Check dipped up water and said, "How'd it go?"

To a man, they said, "Not much to it." With each evasion, Check got more determined.

Later, the group gathered around the fire with gourds and terrapin shells of squirrel and bean stew. The food loosened some tongues. Taking their cue from Bell, each man talked about the part of the bottoms and the bayou he'd covered. That provided little information. Then Bell spoke again: "The most remarkable thing I ever seen down here were in the summer of '60. There were a powerful drought." He nodded towards Tomahawk. "Ya may 'member it, but ya waz young. People waz starving. Even the prairie grass died. The game fled to the rivers. Then they dried up. Ya could walk clear 'cross the Arkansas and never git yer feet wet. That river's mostly sand and gravel on the bottom. It shifts, but the current swirls and digs holes in the channel. Some of them holes is so deep that the water in them never dried up. The gars survived by staying down in them pools. That summer, I saw one that waz as big as a bull. And I think he were starving."

Mannypack asked, "Ya throw him any food?"

Bell said, "Well, yeah, I did. But only jist once." He ducked his head. Pulled his hat down over his brow. Puny and Hugh sucked wind through their teeth. George and Connell stared at the fire. Tomahawk at the sky. The women watched those little movements. They took from them that one of the white men had drowned in the river.

*T*o *the Spirits*

SANDERS HAD TIED SAM'S CLOTHES in a bundle around the pick and the shovel. He'd told Coop, "I want'chu to take these to the bawdy house. Round up anything there that belongs personally to them two. Dump it all in the bayou. Strew it around. Pick places where ya can tangle it in branches underwater. Or weigh it down with rocks. Leave the pick and shovel and anything else we might be able to use. Then wait fer me on the porch."

"Don't ya want me to come with ya?"

"We don't have a lotta time, Coop. We gotta split up the work."

"I kilt him — shouldn't I bury him?"

That offer struck Sanders as un-Coop-like. Coop would try any trick to keep from digging in the fields or garden. Had been known to get himself stung by a bee just to get out of turning dirt. But Sanders had too much to think about to wade the recesses of Coop's mind. He said, "No, son, it don't work that way. One person does the killing. The other does the burying."

"Are ya sure?"

"Course I'm sure. I've seen a lot of killing. I didn't bury Colbert. Think on it."

Coop looked off into the distance. A pink light lay on the hills behind Sanders' head. The light seemed eerie. Coop didn't want to ride off into it. He said, "I heared that bawdy house is haunted."

Sanders thought about saying, "Ya jist kilt a feller, and we're standing over him. His haint's probably over our heads while we're jawing." But he saw Coop shaking. He said, "These men been living at the bawdy house. They've been haunting it. There ain't nothing down there but evidence we gotta clean up." He put his hand on Coop's shoulder. He thought he should've kept Puny with him instead.

Coop liked the feel of his father's hand. He wanted to grab him around the waist. Cry into his chest. Instead, he sniffed and ran his palm across his nose. He pulled his stomach in, picked up the bundle, and secured it to The Bay. Then, together, they lifted Sam's body to the back of Sanders' horse. After that, Coop started to mount, then hesitated, trying again to delay riding into the eerie light towards the ghosts of the bawdy house. He watched his father tighten the rope around the body. He said, "Don't ya need the shovel?"

Sanders didn't want to answer that. Answering, in general, was against his nature. And he didn't want Coop to have to lie if he wound up being questioned. But he also felt the need to prepare his son for living in the world. He split the difference. "Can't have a fresh grave with the chance of marshals coming in." He put the witching stick between his teeth and his foot in the stirrup. He swung his right leg high over the body and settled into his saddle. Tucked the stick in his belt next to his weapons. Said, "Go on, now. Wait fer me. We'll go home together." He turned his horse and rode off towards the river.

IN THE WOODS, SANDERS FOUND a worn animal path and tracked it west. By then, darkness had moved in, and his horse had turned shy. Sanders talked to settle him, but the horse stayed skittish. So, at the first opportunity, Sanders turned south towards the river and broke out onto the sand. Between his legs, he felt the animal's breathing even out. He turned west again and rode closer to cover. The moonlight was so bright he could see where he was going without any trouble. He rode into a swampy place. Frightened a large animal that crashed through undergrowth and cane, spooking his horse again. Sanders tightened the reins. Said, "We're almost done, ᏒᏤᏪᏒ."

A little past the swamp, he turned again into the woods. He didn't go far, and from under cover could still see moonlight on sand. By that light, he untied the body. He dragged it from ᏒᏤᏪᏒ by the shoulders. Then he led the horse to a tree and tied him. He spread Sam's body out face-down. He said, *"I won't make you look in their eyes."* In a high voice, he sang a song to the wolf spirit.

IN THE OTHER DIRECTION, COOP came upon a stream, dismounted, and untied the bundle of clothes, the shovel, and the pick. He walked the bank with his load until he found tree roots growing into the water. He laid down the bundle, slipped out the shovel, and banged the ground to disturb any lurking cottonmouths. Then threw the shirt into the water. He used the shovel to pull it towards and under the roots. He did the same with the other pieces of clothing at different points along the bank.

When he was done, he remounted and forded the stream. He saw the bawdy house in the distance, came upon another creek, and stopped at it. The moon was full over the house, shimmering on the planks of the roof, hiding the porch, windows, and doors in shadow. The edifice seemed to Coop like a living, breathing presence. A head with a hidden face. The top of a body buried in dirt up to the shoulders. Coop stayed astride The Bay, afraid to get out of the saddle. And he was still sitting there, asking the rabbit in the moon for courage, when the barn owl flew out of the rafters and passed across the face of the moon. Coop and The Bay both saw the bird flying towards them. The Bay shied. Coop leaned forward and hugged his neck. The saddle horn poked him in the stomach. But he was too afraid to look up. He sat hunkered over, drawing reassurance from the smell and warmth of the horse. He waited for his father. Too frightened to go towards the house.

The Return of Harmony

BELL SPENT THE NEXT DAY in bed, perfectly peaceful, but too sore to move around. His daughter brought him coffee, food, and a newspaper, and tended to her grandchildren.

In the midafternoon, Granny returned to the inn from the Smiths'. As soon as she did, she sent her daughter and son-in-law packing. Alabama was glad to go. There was nothing to be said between her mother and her that hadn't already been spoken; and that, she was beginning to realize, was already too much. Dennis was also glad to escape. George had returned his horse; so he could ride, or tie it to the buggy and sit with his wife. The buggy was his preference. But Alabama's mood changed every time the wind stirred the leaves on the trees. Dennis would rather his insides jiggled to pieces than sit shoulder to shoulder with his wife. He threw his leg over his horse's back, and, for once, considered himself lucky to be in the saddle.

After the ferry closed, Bert and Ame visited the Corderys. They wanted the news like everybody else. But they were told the murderer had escaped. Nannie fed them, and after supper Sanders, Coop, and Ame took turns with a slingshot, aiming at a tin can in front of the chimney. The pebbles pinged and bounced. They retrieved them, and shot again and again. Bert didn't join in. He helped feed Jenny. She took food better from him than from her mother. That made Nannie feel like Bert was the path to recovery. She told him he was doing a good job holding Jenny's head, talking to her softly, wiping her dribble. Bert said, "Mama were sick. Took care of her."

Nannie hadn't gotten the story either. But Jenny was her sole concern. She'd seen too much stealing, war, and death to believe in a just universe or a loving god. However, she was a great believer in humans maintaining harmony. And knew her husband was, too. He had slept well after coming in. That told Nannie the story.

Secret Fears

CONNELL WAS ASLEEP. BUT HUGH heard his mother coming. He closed his eyes. Her hand tapped his shoulder. She whispered, "You're not asleep. Come with me." She disappeared through the door. Hugh sighed deeply, but got up and followed. A soft, wheezing sound from Puny floated up the stairs from the cot below. Hugh wished he'd thought to snore.

Check whispered, "Close the door behind you." She lit the candle on her bedside table. Her hair was below her shoulders. She wore a robe and a nightgown sprinkled with little flowers. She climbed on her bed and patted the spread. Said, "Have a seat, Hugh."

Hugh lay down, turned onto his back, and folded his hands on his chest. Check said, "Is there a particular reason you're awake in the middle of the night? Seems you'd be tired."

"Mama, did you get me out of bed to ask me why I'm not asleep?" Hugh cracked his knuckles.

"I thought your conscience might be bothering you. You might need to talk."

"No, it's clear, Mama."

Check nudged his side with her toes. Hugh added, "I swear."

"Don't play games with me, Hugh."

"I'm not. I just can't tell you."

Check let up. While listening to the sounds of the house, she'd realized it was Hugh not snoring. She feared he'd killed one of the men and was struggling with that. She wanted to help him. She liked the sensitivity he'd gained since being shot, but had to make certain he wasn't so tender he'd retreat from the world into guilt, silence, or bookishness. Indian Territory was too tough for a man to do that. She'd have to send him back east if he developed deep feelings.

On the other hand, she was annoyed about not knowing what'd really happened. Worried that whatever it was would bring in the marshals.

And below her concern for Hugh, she was irritated enough to wish he were young enough to spank. She sighed. Then she recalled the common wisdom about flies and honey. She swallowed. "I want you to know, whatever you've done, you're my son and I'll stick with you."

Hugh knew his mother wanted answers. And would revert to her usual self if she didn't get them. He rolled over towards her. In her nightclothes, with her hair down, she seemed fragile. Grief had etched new lines on her face. The shadows darkened them. A word caught in his throat. Came out as a groan. He swallowed, rolled over onto his back, and stared at the ceiling again. Check waited, not moving.

Eventually, Hugh said, "I didn't kill either one of those men. I promise. Don't worry." He sat up, slid off the bed, and walked out the door without turning. Back in bed, he listened to Connell's snoring. Thought about how his mother would react when she found out how Coop had used the gun she'd given him. He'd never known her not to uncover whatever she was interested in discovering. That worried him more than all the rest put together.

CHECK GAVE UP FOR THE night. Blew out the candle and laid her head on her pillow. To keep her palm from feeling its way to Andrew's empty spot, she intertwined her fingers. And, as her hands were in the right position, she tried to pray. But her lips stopped at "Our Father" when she heard her own father say, in a voice that seemed in the room, "Go inside. Don't watch through the window."

She was on her parents' front porch. Her older sister, Elizabeth, on her left, her little brother, Ruff, in front of her skirt. Her father's hand was on her shoulder, his thumb poking her back. Behind them, her mother cried, "Ꮒ! ᏒᎾᏞᏞ!" The hand lifted, the door slammed. And Check did look, with her mother and siblings, at the long line of Indians on foot, dogs, cattle, oxen, and wagons, guarded by soldiers on horseback. The procession passed the house. The people didn't look in their direction. Spoke so little that the whine of wagon wheels was the loudest sound Check heard. Until, suddenly, her mother wailed.

That cry came back to Check like lightning cracking a tree. She turned her mouth to her pillow. She cried. For Andrew, for Hugh, for Turtle, for Jenny. And after that, she cried for fear the US government would come again. And, again, destroy their lives.

The Stone with the Ring of Gold

AT BREAKFAST, EZELL AND LIZZIE grilled Puny like a fish hung on a wire over a fire. Their questions, the weather, and the stove's heat combined to make the summer kitchen feel sweltering. Little beads of moisture popped out on Puny's forehead. Rings grew in the pits of his shirt. He held the women at bay by saying, "I'm jist dying to tell ya. But I'm under orders from Sheriff Rogers to keep my lips shut." He said that more than once. Each time, it got a grunt, grimace, or "So you say."

A third biscuit swallowed, Puny stood and put on his hat. He truthfully claimed, "People swarm into town on Saturdays. They need their mail. I gotta go." His hand hit the edge of the gauze screen. He stepped away gingerly. But after he went, Lizzie left, too. And she slipped into the barn as Puny was tightening the front clench on his horse. She was so small, she didn't make noise. Puny was jerking the flank clench when she said softly, "I wants to know where my baby's buried."

Puny jumped. "Lord, Lizzie. You sceered me. Why don't ya give a person a warning?" He picked his handkerchief from his pocket and patted his brow.

"I want to know now."

Lizzie wore a dress made out of a burlap sack. She was flat-chested, and her feet were bare. She'd perspired at the stove, and there was a path of sweat down her neck. Puny couldn't recall why he'd found her attractive. But he felt a tug of responsibility for her, and she was, after all, another Negro. Too, Ezell had taken a liking to her. Puny appreciated how difficult that must have been. And he thought when they finally went back to Ohio, they'd probably take Lizzie with them. He knew where the baby's grave was. Sanders had told him the general location. And told him to look for a sandstone with a golden streak sticking out from the ground. He hadn't done that himself. But he thought he could lead Lizzie to it. He said, "I'll meet ya behind the barn."

They rode to the swale, Lizzie holding Puny's belt. He stopped when he saw the flat stone close ahead. He hesitated, thinking about whether he should get off and walk with Lizzie over to it. He didn't really want to do that. He wanted the whole thing behind him. Wanted to stay in good with his wife. To forget his own lust and desire, not only for Lizzie, but for the child. He shifted in the saddle. Said, "It's over yonder." He pointed. "Hop off."

Lizzie slid over the rump and tail to the ground. Hopped back quickly to avoid getting kicked. Puny shifted in his saddle again. When Lizzie was parallel to his leg, she said, "Where?"

Puny pointed. "Over there. Big flat sandstone. Got a gold streak."

Lizzie looked in that direction. She looked back up at Puny. He seemed like an uncle, or the husband of a friend. But someone who could be contrary and infuriating. She was still irritated over him holding secrets at breakfast. She said, "I see it. Ya don't hav'ta wait."

And Puny, so thankful that even his horse felt relief, said, "I'll get on to work, then." He turned his steed. Tapped his heels to its side.

Lizzie just stood for a while. The potato plants were dark green and high. Their tops rippled in the wind. The corn in the next field was higher still. Half the height it would grow, but also dark green. The breeze rustled through those leaves and stalks, shaking them like a rattle over a baby's crib. The swale was surrounded by scrub, with some clearly growing into trees. Her baby would feed those trees. Maybe they would grow into a forest. Reclaim the land, the entire horizon, spread every-where, in every direction.

Lizzie walked towards the sandstone with more feelings of hope than despair. When she got to the rock, sunlight caught the streak. Made it look like a band of gold wrapped around the stone. The baby. The earth. Lizzie's heart. She sank to her knees at the edge of the rock. She reached out and touched it. Fingered the gold. The stone was warm. She bent over, lay on her side in the dirt and weeds, and put an arm over the rock. She cried for a while. Her thin body shook. Then she heard a rustling that wasn't corn. She jumped up. The swale was a snaky place. She'd never been out there before. But everybody in the bottoms knew the kinds of places the snakes liked to nest.

Lizzie looked around for a stick, found one, and picked it up. She suddenly hated for her little girl to be out there. Surrounded by stinky, poisonous snakes. But she couldn't dig her up. Moving a body would bring a luck so dark she'd never overcome it. So she listened again for the snake. Mustered her loudest voice: "Come out where I can see ya. I'll beat yer ass to death." And because she knew cottonmouths move in pairs, she added, "And yer mama's ass, too."

But Lizzie didn't hear any more rustling except that of the crops. She tapped her stick against the ground and said, "Cowards." She turned around and started through the potatoes, hoping she'd live to see the day that snaky swale was cleared, the snakes run out, the ground turned over, and food grown there. She knew that was unlikely to happen soon, but she was planning to live a long life. She said under her breath, "I'll be back. I won't ever leave ya." And then, because she'd been so out of her head when she'd given birth, she started thinking on a name for her baby.

The Women's Plan

CONNELL TOLD HIS MOTHER HE had business in town. He was taking an extra shirt with him. There was a dance at the corner that night. He wouldn't dance, out of respect for his father, but she shouldn't worry or wait up. He'd stay at the Benges'. Or bring one of them back with him. He kissed Check on top of her head, a place she didn't much like being kissed. And that, in particular, reminded her that Connell was grown up, and could do almost whatever he wanted. He'd been even less forthcoming under questioning than had his brother. She didn't kiss him back; she tapped him on the thigh. And as soon as he left for the barn, she went hunting for Hugh. In the kitchen, Ezell told her he'd taken Clifford and Otter fishing. Hadn't mentioned where to.

Next, she asked if Puny had said anything interesting. And, disappointed with Ezell's answer, she took the breakfast slop to the chickens. She talked tough to the hens. They didn't pay any attention. They were busy pecking scraps. And that got Check to thinking about what scraps might be thrown to the men to loosen them up. She mulled on that more while she pumped and carried water to fill the chickens' tins. But she didn't arrive at anything she thought would prime the men's pumps. She went back to the house feeling glum. Not looking forward to a day that was turning hot and humdrum.

Lizzie returned from the swale, washed her face, hands, and arms, changed her dress, and went to the kitchen to work on the noon meal. She didn't want to talk to Ezell about her morning. So as soon as she crossed the threshold, she started in on the mystery of how Turtle's murderers had been killed. Ezell was still busting with the same curiosity. She fell into that line of talk rather quickly. Then both women turned to how irritating Puny had been. They extended their irritation to all the men.

So, after the hands came in for their meal, but before the cleaning up, the two cooks approached Check with a plan: none of the guilty men would get decent food until they served up what the women wanted. "Life goes both ways" Ezell was heard to say.

Check said, "It sure does."

Lizzie added, "You betcha."

Ezell's Advice

HUGH RETURNED FROM THE RIVER with a stringer of fish and two dirty boys. He sent Cliff to the house for clean clothes, and Otter to the kitchen for a pan. He drew water from the pump into buckets, and when the boys returned, told them to strip. He doused them, and they screamed with delight. Then he handed them soap, and poured water over them again. Afterwards, he gutted the fish on the pump's platform, threw entrails to chickens, cleaned his arms to the elbows, and washed the back of his neck. Then he tucked the pan under his arm, and entered the kitchen with it tilted in Ezell's direction. He said, "Lookee here."

"Whooee, he's a granddaddy." Ezell pointed to the largest fish.

"Bass. Caught him at the rocks on the bend." Hugh set the pan on the table.

"You let the little boys fish?"

"Cliff fished. Otter's more interested in making forts out of sand and rocks." Hugh pulled out a chair. Sat down at the table. Ezell took the pan to the sink, poured out the water, pumped more in, and added salt. She set the pan on the counter and covered it with an old flour sack. When she turned, Hugh was still there. He said, "You think we could have fish for dinner?"

"Don't see why not." She would have to burn his, and cook the others just right. She wasn't sure exactly how she would manage that. "You ain't going to the dance?"

"Can't dance in mourning." Hugh glanced up at a cleaver on a hook over the table. He'd never liked it hanging there, and had an irrational fear it would suddenly drop. Cut off an arm, hand, or finger. He usually envisioned the appendage as his. And the accident occurring when he was reaching for more potatoes, meat, or green beans.

Ezell looked at the stones of the floor. Hugh loved his daddy and missed him. But Hugh not dancing didn't sound right. She said, "I believe yer brother's already off to town."

"He's sparking. That's different. Florence expects attention."

Ezell thought Connell would dance a jig for Florence for the rest of his life. But, since shot, Hugh hadn't been off the farm except to bury his daddy, hunt Jenny, bring his mother the wagon, and ride with the posse. He hadn't had any fun. She said, "No cockfights tonight? Are they off-limits?"

Hugh looked at the cleaver. "They're sorta brutal for no reason."

"Horse races? Ya got that nice track."

Hugh put his hands on the table and started up.

Ezell said, "I made a pie this morning."

Hugh sat back down. He'd spied it and had lingered out of pie lust.

Ezell turned her back, reached in the drawer for a pie server. She was reaching for a plate when she said, "Puny Tower won't tell me nothing. Won't tell me what happen to those killers. Won't tell me what happen down there at that bawdy house." She turned around. "Whatever that was, ya might as well go on and hold yer head up. None of us gets out without sompthing bad happening. Think on Lizzie and that baby. Ya think I enjoyed that much?"

Hugh brushed his hair back with his hand. "I imagine not. You aren't guilty, though. I am."

Ezell cut a slice, slid it onto a plate, and held it out. It was against the plan, but she felt mercy, and would burn his fish anyway. "Here. There's redemption for us all. That's what the Lord says. Eat up."

The Perfect Time of the Evening

CONNELL ESCAPED THE FEMALES' FOOD plot for supper by taking Florence for a buggy ride on the road towards the Cherokee National Cemetery. Before reaching it, they turned north onto the ruts to the US Army's burial ground. At its entrance was a cabin. During the day, a soldier was stationed there. But it was late in the afternoon and a dance was in town, so the spot was deserted. The air was cooling, the breeze gentle, and the trees throwing shade on the ground. Connell spread a quilt under a cluster of elms at the edge of the graves. Florence pulled a picnic supper from a basket.

They talked wedding plans. And where they'd live after they married. Florence didn't want to live in the bottoms, and in all practicality, they couldn't bunk with Hugh. But the farm wouldn't run itself; and Connell couldn't ride in to work in the dark of the mornings, and ride home alone in the dark of night in the winter. They talked about building their own house, of sandstone, close to the Military Road. It would be expensive, but Florence's mother was a wealthy woman; and unlike her father and Check, didn't have to reinvest her money in running a business. They decided on a plan of Check supplying the land and Suzanne paying for the house. That was settled — at least, between them — by the time the sun dipped into the trees and the sky turned pink. And by then, too, Connell had brought out a bottle of port wine, and had confirmed in his mind they were far enough out in the country to be safe from company.

He scooted closer to Florence. Whispered in her hair. She giggled. They drank a little more port. Connell slipped his fingers to the buttons of Florence's blouse. The lump in his trousers had been hard for a while. Florence had noticed, and found it attractive. Connell kissed her neck. He undid the next two buttons. The top curve of Florence's right breast emerged. It was so soft and smooth that Connell couldn't resist. He kissed it. Presently, he swung a leg over Florence's skirt. Started work on her corset. He needed help, and Florence's smaller fingers knew its tricks. But once Connell's hand was inside, cupping her right breast, Florence put her hand over his. She said, "We have to be careful."

"Hum?" Connell kissed her neck again. Played with her nipple. Moved his leg further up her skirt towards her hip.

"I can't get in a family way."

Connell paused. He'd thought continually of Hugh's tip. Figured it was the time to mention it. He wasn't sure how. He said, "I got some information."

"From who?"

"A safe source."

"Who?"

"That's confidential."

Florence leaned away. She tucked her breast into her corset.

"Don't, baby." Connell wrapped his fingers around hers.

"Tell me, then."

Connell straightened his leg. Adjusted the lump in his pants. He reached in the basket for the port and held it up. Florence shook her head. He poured himself some, took a sip, and, while searching for an answer, tried to look like he was weighing whether it was ethical to reveal his source. He said, "Well," and examined his glass.

"Well?" Florence tied her corset strings into a bow. She started buttoning her blouse.

"Well, I read it in a book."

Florence stopped buttoning. "What'd it say?"

Connell looked to the horizon. The sky was filled with faint wisps. The sun almost down. "It said the best way to keep a family from expanding is to use another opening."

Florence looked down the hill to the gravestones. They stood in straight rows, and still white in the fading light. She couldn't imagine what the book recommended. "And that would be?"

Connell took another sip. He looked off towards the graves also. "Well, couples who really love each other, and who, you know, aren't in a position to start a family . . . maybe because they don't yet have a house . . . or because they're in mourning . . . and they can't get married solely because of that . . . they make accommodations." He sat his glass on a wooden tray. He rubbed the lump in his trousers.

Florence's eyes went to Connell's hand. She felt a tingle between her legs. She'd never really gotten a good look at Connell's equipment. She licked her lips. "What kind of accommodations?"

Connell moved his hand to his belt. Started unbuckling it. "Well, the woman kisses the man down below."

"Down below where?"

Connell slipped the leather out of the buckle. Undid his top button. "Down here. Where my hand is."

Florence looked off at the graves. Her brow knotted. "Kisses his trousers?"

Connell wanted to sound confident. "No, silly thing, kisses his you-know."

"His 'you-know'?" Florence fastened another button on her blouse.

Connell didn't take that as a good sign. "Baby, have some mercy on me." He rubbed himself again.

Florence said, "You mean, she kisses his cock?"

Connell was sort of shocked Florence said "cock." But also relieved. She understood. "Yes, his cock. Then that makes him expel his seed, and it's in the kiss . . . not in her you-know."

Suddenly, the graves came quite into Florence's focus. She pulled her chin in. Fastened her top button without looking down. She looked at Connell. Her eyes went to slits. "You've got to be out of your mind." She placed a hand to the ground and hopped up. "What kind of filthy book did you read that in?"

Connell's heart sank to his crotch. But he hoped to salvage something. He spread his arms and showed his palms. He widened his eyes. "One in my parents' study. You know there're a lot of books in there."

"You have a book in your house that recommends that?"

"Yeah, it's on a shelf with some books on breeding cattle."

"Breeding cattle?"

Connell realized that was a mistake. He buckled his belt and pushed up also. "There're all sorts of other books in there, too. I just didn't want to embarrass us by asking anyone anything."

Florence crossed her arms in front of her breasts. She tapped her foot. She was never going to kiss his cock. But she wanted some loving as much as Connell did. So she didn't want to tell him that. In fact, she thought she wouldn't tell him that until the stone house was built and they were married. She said, "I appreciate that. I'm just . . ." She looked down at the quilt. "I just have to trust you. You've got to always pull out, Connell. It's not my fault we can't get married yet. And if I get in a family way, we'll have to get married in spite of the mourning. That would set me off on the wrong foot with your mother. Can you understand that?"

"I do," Connell said. "I do, baby. You're the most important thing in the world to me." He stepped closer. Put his arms around her. "I want to do this right."

Florence looked around Connell's shoulder. It was now dark enough that they probably wouldn't be seen. But not so dark that the gravestones felt threatening. And the lightning bugs made the whole hillside look romantic. It was the perfect time of the evening.

3

JUSTICE

The Marshals Come to Town

THEY WERE HUNGRY. THEY STOPPED first at Nash's store. It'd have jerky, canned goods, and food out of barrels, and they'd been told the owner was a white man with sympathies towards the United States of America. Tom Rusk saw a boy on a ladder stacking a bolt of denim. He called, "Mr. Taylor in the store?"

Jim was afraid he'd lose his balance and tip the ladder if he turned around. He said, "You probably walked past him. Was on the porch." He pushed the bolt towards the wall.

Rusk looked out the window. Men were leaning on posts and lining a bench. Two were in rockers, hunched over a checkerboard. Rusk said, "Which one is he?"

Bowden said, "Can we git sompthing to eat first? I'm powerful hungry." They'd left out after church on Sunday, ridden hard, and had cooked supper and breakfast for themselves. Bowden wasn't used to campfire vittles.

Jim shoved the bolt farther in and descended. Once on the floor, he said, "Who's asking?"

Rusk pulled his vest aside, revealing his star. "United States deputy marshals. Ya wanta git Mr. Taylor fer us?"

"Could we git some food first?" Bowden asked.

Jim looked from one to the other. "Up to you. Whichever."

Rusk said, "Give us sompthing we can eat in our hands, and call Mr. Taylor fer us. He got an office 'round here?"

"Yes, sir. Back there. Will apricots do? We just got a batch in."

"That'll be nice," Rusk said. But Bowden whispered, "They sorta give me the squirts."

So when Nash entered his office, he found one marshal sucking an apricot and the other cracking pecans. He said, "Afternoon, gentlemen. I'm Mr. Taylor." They stood, and Nash crossed to the edge of his desk. "I understand you're federal marshals." He didn't like eating in the office, but could make an exception.

Rusk said, "That's right. I'd shake yer hand, but mine's juicy." He flexed his fingers. Bowden extended his paw. He said, "Bill Bowden. Marshal and preacher."

Nash smiled. "Well, what can I do for ya? Have a seat."

They both sat. Rusk said, "We're investigating a kidnapping and murder. They may be connected. Young Indian girl waz kidnapped. Then the feller who found her waz murdered. What can ya tell us 'bout that?" He looked around for somewhere to spit his pit.

Nash handed him a wastepaper basket and sat down at his desk. He didn't know why the marshals thought Jenny had been kidnapped. But didn't want to look ignorant. "Well, it's all been mysterious. The Indian who was killed claimed he found the girl in an eagle's nest."

Both marshals' eyes widened. Nash waved his hand. "Nobody believed that, of course. But the Negro who was with him backed up his story. Then the next morning, the Indian was murdered. Attacked with a hammer while walking home. A brutal killing." Nash shook his head. "The next day, the sheriff led a posse to find the murderer. But he gave him the slip. Indian law isn't always effective. That's a problem you're aware of, I suspect." Nash leaned forward in his chair and clasped his hands on his desk.

Rusk spit a pit. "We know it's lawless 'round here. But Judge Parker's gonna clean it up. I suspect ya know the sheriff?"

"Certainly do."

"If ya could take us to him, that'll be real helpful."

A short time later, Nash walked the marshals across the road and down a street to Bell's office. Bell was on the front porch in a cane-bottom rocker, talking to a fullblood who was frowning and making guttural noises. Bell was responding in a higher pitch. Nash didn't understand a word of the conversation, and it hadn't let up as he and the marshals neared. Nash cleared his throat. He cleared it again. Finally, he said, "Bell, I've brought somebody to meet'cha."

The strangers had not escaped Bell's attention. Nor had they escaped the attention of the Indian talking gutturally. That Indian had come to Bell complaining about a bad neighbor who was building fences where his cows were grazing. But as soon as it was clear the merchant and the strangers were headed their way, the two had started laying bets on who the men were. The irritated Indian bet they were railroad officials. Bell bet they were marshals. Bell said, "So I see. Glad ta meet'cha. Bell Rogers." He put a finger to the brim of his hat, but didn't get up. He'd promised himself never to ride hard again, but that hadn't made his pain recede.

The marshals introduced themselves, and Rusk said, "We're here on official business from Judge Parker."

Bell smiled. The fullblood pulled a plug of tobacco from a pouch on his belt and handed it to Bell. He spat in an arc and left.

Bell put his hands on the arms of his rocker and lifted himself out. He said, "I've been a little down in the back."

Bowden felt concerned. The sheriff was an old-looking fellow. He said, "Rub those joints with lard, and eat an onion first thing ever' morning. It'll fix ya right up." He'd discovered congregations appreciate preachers who do a little doctoring on the side.

"I'll think on that," Bell replied and turned into his office. He added, "Been awful dry lately. When's the last time y'all got any rain over in Fort Smith?"

Bowden scratched his head. "Been a while. That's another reason to lubricate your joints."

"That right? You fellows do much farming?" Bell sat down behind his desk. He motioned the marshals to chairs. Nash sat on the sill of an open window.

Bowden replied, "I'm a preacher of the word of the Lord when I'm not enforcing the law. Rusk here's a cowboy. But he's jist married a pretty little woman." He smiled.

Rusk said, "Bill, we don't want to waste the sheriff's time. What can ya tell us about the recent kidnapping and murder?"

Bell leaned back, trying to get some relief. "The murder warn't connected to the missing girl as fer as anybody knows. Mr. Smith — that's the murdered man — was kilt along the road. Beat to death with a hammer. Robbed of his gun and witching stick. He were a well-witcher."

"Somebody murdered the well-witcher?" Bowden's eyebrows went up.

"Shore did." Bell shifted his hips.

Rusk studied his hands. They were callused. He picked a piece of skin off a knot on his right forefinger and put the skin in his mouth. He said, "What about the posse?"

"I thought at first the feller who done it was a man I'd caught selling whiskey. I took his gun, and told him I'd give it back when he wired me from outside the Nation. Never heared from him. So it seemed like he were a likely suspect. I thought he might be laying out down at an old house on the bayou, not far from where the murder took place. I gathered a group and surrounded the house. Turns out I was wrong. Twasn't nobody there."

"Yer positive?"

"Yep. No sign of him, or his horse." Bell hoped Tomahawk had found Jake's horse. He'd told him what it looked like, and, if he found it, to give it to George, so the boy could finally have one of his own.

Rusk asked, "Was that man a white man?"

"The whiskey seller?" Bell replied.

Rusk nodded.

"Course. Nobody else sells whiskey to Indians."

Bowden shook his head. "That's not a fair thing to say, Sheriff Rogers." He looked rather mournful. "Lots of Christians don't approve of liquor themselves."

Bell said, "Yer right. I misspoke myself. I meant to say I've lived in Indian Territory since 1828, and ain't never seen nobody but whites sell whiskey to Indians. But I may have missed a couple."

Rusk reared back in his chair and clasped his hands behind his head. "Now, Sheriff Rogers, wez jist here to help ya with the investigation.

Judge Parker presides over this territory, and he means to see it cleaned up."

Nash saw the blood rise in Bell's face. He realized if the marshals insulted him things could get difficult. He moved away from the sill, positioned himself beside Bell's desk, and smiled. "Well now, we all want to get along. No use fighting when we're all on the same side. If a white man did kill Turtle Smith, then that would be Judge Parker's business. We understand that. But my understanding — correct me if I'm wrong, Bell — is that a mixed-blood might have done the killing. Isn't that the other theory?"

Bell looked up at Nash. "Well, we don't know who done the killing. But yes, the main theory we're working on now is that it were a mix-blooded Cherokee." He turned his neck back to a more comfortable position and focused his eyes between the marshals' chairs. "You understand, I reckon, that mixed-bloods — if they live with the tribe and are recognized by kin — are Cherokees, jist the same as fullbloods. My daddy hisself were a white man. It makes no difference, according to the law, Cherokee or white. But if it turns out the culprit ain't a Cherokee, I'll turn him over to Judge Parker when we catch him."

Bowden was confused. "What makes ya think a mix-blooded Cherokee did the killing? Did somebody see him?"

"No, the murder was unwitnessed. But a white would use a gun, and a fullblood would use either a knife or a gun."

"How'd'ya know that?" Rusk asked.

"Ever'body knows it. Common knowledge. That's why, at first, I thought it might be the white man I'd taken a gun off of. Then I figured it might be somebody who's jist a little confused. But really, we don't know who done it yet. We're still working on it. I'll let Judge Parker know if it turns out to be somebody other than a Cherokee."

Rusk's brow furrowed. He picked another callus. "The judge wants a hand in the investigation. Especially since it seems ya ain't making progress."

Bell rubbed his fist over his mouth. The gesture made Nash itchy. If the marshals seriously irritated Bell over jurisdiction, there'd be a lot of mad Indians around town. That'd be both dangerous and bad for business. Nash felt like he was balancing on a rail fence with his arms spread out. He said, "Why don'tcha question Puny Tower about finding the Cordery girl? None of that ever made any sense."

"Who's Puny Tower?" Bowden asked. He looked to Bell.

Bell was too exasperated to talk. Nash said, "He's the Negro who helped Turtle find the girl."

Rusk said, "Where is he?"

Nash said, "I suspect he's at the post office. Don't you think so, Sheriff?"

Bell scraped back his chair. "We'll go see."

The Marshals Question Puny

PUNY WAS ASLEEP, FLAT ON his back on the counter, his fingers clasped over his stomach. Saturday night, he and Dennis had dug in the well. On Sunday, he'd lugged and hauled sandstones for the foundation of the new room of his cabin. Sunday night, he spent several more hours in the hole. Had Dennis not turned up a gold piece in the corner, Puny would've been dead from exhaustion. As it was, he was pretty tuckered out.

Nash stepped inside the door. "Puny, folks here to see ya."

Puny jerked awake. He rubbed his eyes. "What'cha names? I'll see what I gots for ya."

"They're not here for mail." Nash stepped aside. Rusk entered the room, looking it up and down. Bowden stepped in behind him and smiled. He said, "Nice little post office ya got here."

Puny slid to the floor. "What can I do fer ya?" He didn't like the look of the stocky fellow.

Rusk said, "United States deputy marshals in the service of Judge Isaac Parker of Fort Smith. We want to ask ya some questions, nigger."

Puny rounded his shoulders to look smaller. He nodded.

"Did ya help rescue a kidnap victim last week?"

"Helped find a girl. Don't know that she were kidnapped."

"Tell us about that." Rusk put one palm on the butt of his gun, the other on a windowframe.

Puny shifted his weight. "Well, sir, she were missing fer a couple of days. Indian fellow jist come up on her. He wadn't part of the search party. Mr. Bushyhead hired him to locate water. He were a well-witcher." Puny kept his eyes on Rusk's boots.

"How'd'ya come to be involved in her rescue?"

"I just come up on 'em. I was riding in to work, that's all."

Rusk straightened up. "So, yer weren't looking fer her? Ya jist got lucky?"

"I were looking for her the day before. People needed their mail."

Bowden walked to the door to the other room. He noted the bed in there. Looked back to the counter where Puny had been sleeping. "Your bed ain't comfortable?"

"It's all right. I waz laid out in here 'cause I left the door open. Didn't wanta git knocked out completely. In case somebody come in."

"Where'd this well-witcher find the girl?" Rusk asked.

Puny felt his face getting hot. He kept his eyes lowered. "Well, I couldn't rightly understand him. He didn't speak English, and I don't understand much Cherokee."

"Where did ya first see them?" Rusk's voice got a little louder.

"Down close to the Grand River."

"So, the well-witcher waz witching fer water at the river? Do that make sense to anybody here?" Rusk spread his palms and surveyed his audience. His eyes were wide, his lips pursed. Nobody nodded. "How d'ya explain that, nigger?"

Puny shook his head and shuffled his feet. "Don't know, sir. Can't figure it out, myself."

"Well, nigger, ya can't be dumb." Rusk moved closer to Puny. "Yer the postmaster, ain't ya?"

Puny nodded.

"Ya carry a gun?"

Puny knew that the only people in the world who disliked armed Negroes more than Indians did were whites. His gun was hidden in the floor where the marshals would have a hard time finding it. He said, "Ah, no sir. I don't have no gun of my own. Guns shore are bad bizness for colored folks."

"Ya read and write?"

Puny nodded.

Nash felt uncomfortable. All his life he'd known men like Rusk who didn't want Negroes to have jobs above their station. "He hasn't been postmaster long. The former one got run out with the other feller. He's a fill-in 'til we find somebody else."

"What waz the postmaster run out fer?" Bowden asked.

Nash shook his head. "Never did hear. Did you, Puny?"

Puny shook his head.

"Waz he a white feller?" Rusk asked.

"Appeared to be," Nash answered.

"So, we got us an Indian sheriff who's run two white fellers out. And one of 'em fer sompthing nobody knows anything about? Then we got a dead Injun who warn't even shot. That's interesting." Rusk frowned.

Bowden added, "Yeah, that is interesting." He was smiling. When he wasn't starving, he enjoyed his job.

Dennis Intervenes

BELL HAD STARTED OUT WITH the others. But was detained by a man who wanted his brother-in-law arrested for killing his best dog. After that, he'd detoured to collect Dennis. They were crossing the lawn to the post office when the marshals, Puny, and Nash came out into the trot. As Puny was locking the door, Dennis boomed, "I'm Dennis Bushyhead." He'd learned a few white tricks at Princeton that had served him well since. One was how to shake hands. He walked towards the marshals with a smile on his face and a big paw extended.

Bowden smiled, too. "I'm Bill Bowden, and this here's Tom Rusk." Bowden started to put both hands on Dennis's, but Dennis stepped onto the trot, grabbed the back of the marshal's right arm near the shoulder, and squeezed it hard as they shook. He said, "Glad to meet you," and smiled wider. He turned to Rusk and did the same thing.

Rusk was a solid-built man, but several inches shorter than Dennis. He gripped Dennis's hand hard and showed both his upper and lower teeth. They were a little clenched. Dennis said, "My wife's kinsman, Sheriff Rogers here, tells me you're two of the new deputy marshals recently hired by Judge Parker. Looks like he's doing a fine job. I understand, Mr. Bowden, you're a preacher. Is that so?"

Bowden was massaging his arm. "Yes, I am."

"Well, now, my father was a preacher. I know what you're up against. Trying to spread the word of the Lord on the frontier is challenging. I'm sure you work from sunup to sundown. My father sometimes went without sleep two or three nights in a week." Dennis leaned into Bowden just a little. The marshal stepped back.

Rusk began, "We're here —"

Dennis interrupted. "I know you've heard about our recent misfortune of losing Mr. Smith, our well-witcher. He was a fine man. And a close personal friend of my mother-in-law, Mrs. Schrimsher. Perhaps you stayed at her inn near Manard last night?" He looked from one marshal to the other, squinting like he was concerned for their well-being.

Bowden said, "We slept on the ground."

Dennis shook his head. "I know the federal government doesn't pay their marshals all that well. I think that's a shame. Is Judge Parker going to address that?"

Rusk put his hand on the butt of his gun. "Now, Mr. Bushyhead, I'm supposed to be asking the questions 'round here."

Dennis tucked his chin in. Looked down and over the top of his glasses. "If you have a question, sir, you should ask it. Speak right up. Don't be afraid. Nobody's going to hurt you in the Cherokee Nation. I'll see to that. I'm the national treasurer. That's how I happen to know about your unfortunate pay situation." Creases appeared on his forehead.

Rusk said, "Is this here nigger a Cherokee citizen?"

"Mr. Tower?"

"Him." Rusk nodded towards Puny.

"He's a respected citizen of our community. He's our postmaster and neighbor."

"But is he an Indian?" Rusk smiled. "He don't look like one to me. But I know there's some nigger Cherokees."

Bell spoke. "If yer thinking about doing something to Puny, yer gonna need a warrant."

"Oh, no, sir. You're wrong there. A federal marshal don't need a warrant to take somebody out of Indian Territory ifin he's a murder suspect." Rusk whipped a worn book from his back pocket, flipped it open, and held his finger to a page. He read, "'No warrant necessary fer murder, attempted murder, manslaughter, assault with the intent to kill or maim, arson, robbery, defiling a woman, burglary, larceny,' etc., etc. See right there." He tapped the page.

Nash didn't like the turn of the conversation. And he'd thought they were leaving the post office only because Bell hadn't shown up. He said, "Puny hasn't done anything but help rescue a girl. He's not a suspect."

"Well, maybe that's 'cause the law around here ain't very effective." Rusk handed the book to Bowden and stepped back. He took his gun from its holster. Pointed it at Puny. "I ain't saying he done it. I don't know. But I bet he shore as hell can use a hammer. And evidently, he ain't a Cherokee. And even if he waz, if he's a suspect, we can take him outta here."

Puny raised his hands slowly.

Dennis said, "You're violating the treaties."

Rusk snickered. "That ain't a problem I'll lose any sleep over."

Bell said, "If ya take him back, ya git paid double for this trip, don't ya?"

Rusk said, "What's it to ya?" Bowden ducked his head.

Nash could feel sweat wetting his shirt. "Well, now, fellas, I think you're making a mistake here. This man hasn't done anything."

"Maybe that's true, and maybe it's not. We don't know. It's a mysterious killing. And we haven't got a chance to question him." Rusk liked the sound of his authority.

"Well, hop to it," Bell said. "You can use my office fer that. Ya don't need to take him to Fort Smith for nothing 'cept yer double pay."

Bowden felt embarrassed to be accused of greed. "What d'ya think about that, Tom? That seems fair. Let's take the sheriff up on that."

Rusk hesitated. He wanted the double money. But if he drew it for somebody who turned out to be innocent, Judge Parker would be mad. Rusk wanted to put his hand to his mouth, bite off more skin, and chew. But he'd look silly doing that while holding a gun on somebody. Besides, his best calluses were on his right hand. He said, "I better git some answers I like."

Florence's Planning Is Interrupted

CONNELL USUALLY DIDN'T SPARK ON Mondays. But he was in town anyway, and it'd been cloudy on Sunday. Florence wanted his opinion on where their wedding photographs should be taken. She was worried the afternoon light at the bottom of the staircase wouldn't be of any help to the photographer. She was posed there, asking Connell what he thought, when Nash came in the front door. Florence said, "Daddy, thank goodness you're home. I'm having a terrible time with this light. If I stand here, do you think it casts a shadow on my face?" She raised her chin. "Of course, I'll have on white. That'll give me more reflection."

Nash loved his daughters. But on some days, three were too many. He said, "I don't really give a damn, Florence."

Florence blinked rapidly, flushed to the top of her head, and called for her mother.

Suzanne had stepped into the parlor. She came back to the hallway. "What's wrong here?"

"The federal marshals have arrested Puny," Nash said.

"Why?" Connell asked.

Suzanne looked to Connell. "It must be a mistake. Hasn't he belonged to your family for years?"

"He's never been owned. And we pay the fee on him. They can't arrest him for no reason."

"Well, they have. Claim they're holding him for questioning about Jenny Cordery's disappearance and Turtle Smith's murder."

Connell sucked in air. "Where's Puny? And where's my hat?"

Nash took his own hat off and smoothed his hair. "At Bell's office now. But I think they're jailing him at the fort."

Florence stepped into the parlor for Connell's hat. Connell asked Nash, "What's Bell doing about it?"

"Apparently, there's not much he *can* do. He's kept 'em from taking Puny to Fort Smith. But I don't know how long that'll last. Probably only 'til morning." Nash wiped his brow with his handkerchief.

Suzanne said, "Somebody needs to tell Will." She was referring to Chief Ross, her cousin.

Nash said, "Dennis is headed to Tahlequah now."

Connell put his hat on and walked out the door ahead of Nash without saying goodbye. Florence was surprised by that, but flicked it out of her mind. She said to her mother, "Connell will take care of this."

Suzanne brushed a wisp of hair back from her face. She suddenly felt old. She recalled the beach at Staten Island. It had been cold. She recalled Fort Leavenworth. Roaches had crawled the walls at night. She said, "Don't bet on it."

Wolves in the Air

IN MIDAFTERNOON, NANNIE CAME BACK from hauling water to the cows to find Jenny crumpled on her side in an unnatural position. Joe was crying and poking her thigh with his fingers. Nannie looked Jenny over quickly. Called Sanders in from the corn. He rode out to find Fox. By the time the sun nestled on the trees in the west, Jenny was in the cabin again, and the adults, Joe, and Coop were eating in front of the fire inside the foundation. Fox was sitting cross-legged, slowly chewing Tom Fuller, a hominy and pork stew favored by Creeks and Choctaws.

Fox said, *"If you think that boy helped her, bring him back over."*

Sanders said, *"He runs Check Singer's ferry. He can't jist walk off."*

Fox rested his spoon in his gourd. He'd examined Jenny closely. She was skinny, but had enough water in her body. Her shoulder was in a sling, but she'd been better the day before, and he hadn't expected her to lose ground. He shook his head. *"Maybe she misses him. Love is powerful medicine."* He dipped cornbread into his stew.

Coop said, *"He'd come in a minute."*

"Ask Miz Singer."

Sanders said, *"Today it's love. Last time it waz wolves. I wish you'd make up yer mind. I may have'ta ask the white doctor. You Creeks can't be trusted."* He was teasing. But also frightened.

Fox said, *"Try him. I don't know what it is. I get only a picture of wolves in the air, up here."* He lifted his hand and cornbread a foot over his head. Some Tom Fuller dripped onto his thigh.

Sanders saw wolves over his head, too. And the image disturbed him. He wondered if feeding them Sam's body was coming back on him. He'd thought the offering would satisfy the wolf spirit that haunted his daughter. And also be a practical solution to a problem. But he'd lived through awful times. He'd seen lying, stealing, war, people herded like animals. He'd been naked in the cold. The memories went on and on. He knew in his heart it was impossible to please spirits. They did what they wanted.

Bad Food and Irritation

CONNELL WAS LATE FOR SUPPER. He ate at the study sideboard, complaining about his pork chop being tough, his beans being salty. Hugh hadn't liked his meal either, and was washing the taste out of his mouth with brandy. Check was behind the desk, eating a perfectly good piece of pie, as Ezell couldn't stand to ruin a pie. She said, "Puny was probably at the post office all that morning when Turtle was killed. A bunch of people would've seen him. You saw him yourself that afternoon."

Connell said, "I told 'em that. Tomorrow morning, we need to go through town. Find somebody who remembers getting their mail that day." Hugh had been mostly silent. Connell asked, "You agree?"

Hugh's brow furrowed. "I think the best person to have remembered getting their mail that morning would be Aunt Alabama. She's hard to contradict. And they won't believe anybody dark. Another possibility is somebody like Cox."

"I'm sure Cox is delighted to have the marshals in town." Connell recalled his conversation with the saddler when he was looking for Jenny.

"That doesn't mean he wouldn't tell the truth," Check said.

"Doesn't mean he'll help, either. He could urge the marshals to stay, even if they release Puny. That's the last thing we need." Connell studied his cornbread. Hard to ruin on a piece-by-piece basis, it wasn't too bad.

Check left her worries about Puny long enough to take some satisfaction in Connell's abandoned pork chop and beans. Beyond her assumption from Bell's remark that one of the killers had been food for the gars, she still didn't know what'd really happened to either of them. Had that one been shot? Thrown in? Drowned running? She didn't know. And she had no idea of the fate of the other one. If he'd gotten away, Sanders would have gone after him. That Sanders was at home was a sign both men were dead. But how? And who did the killing? She felt irritated. Her irritation was even more nagging than her curiosity. Her boys weren't showing enough respect. And she was going to take that situation in hand. Just because Andrew was dead, they weren't going to get away with whatever they pleased. She nearly said that.

But she did believe in more flies with honey — when she could remember that. So she said instead, "Of course, if everybody were filled in, perhaps we'd come up with a better story." She tried to smile.

Hugh said, "Mama, you raised us not to go against our word." He threw back his brandy. Connell swallowed too fast. Wound up coughing. Knocking his chest.

Check couldn't think of a retort to Hugh. She broke off a piece of crust with her fingers. She said to Connell, "If you'd chew better, you wouldn't choke."

Another Irritated Woman

ON HIS WAY HOME FROM Tahlequah, Dennis had spent the night at his mother-in-law's inn and was taking breakfast in her kitchen the next morning. He was hunched over his plate, and Granny was at the sink in front of him. She'd sent her help upstairs to make beds so she could have Dennis to herself. She wasn't happy with either him or his wife. But figured he had information on Turtle's death, and she could put up with him to get that. But she had no intention of asking him a direct question. And he'd been cogitating on how to bring the delicate subject of Turtle up. So the breakfast had mostly been silent, and Dennis had developed indigestion. He was thankful he'd taken the buggy. Gas on a horse was pure torture. He said, "I appreciate the bed last night."

Granny replied, "Warn't taken."

They were silent again. After a space, Dennis said, "The federal marshals are holding Puny Tower for Turtle's murder. He's Check Singer's hand. He's been running the post office. They know full well he didn't do it. But he's a Negro. So they can get away with pinning it on him."

Granny poured him more coffee.

"I went to Tahlequah to talk to Will about it. But of course he wasn't there." The chief wasn't yet home from Washington.

Granny said, "I could've told ya that."

"Looks like he'd be back by now." Dennis dipped his biscuit in egg yolk. He considered William Potter Ross an ineffective leader, and took any opportunity to complain about him.

"Stopped by Cincinnati on his way home," Granny said.

"How'd'ya come by that?" Dennis asked with his mouth full.

"I run an inn." Granny took her son-in-law's plate and set it in the sink.

Dennis had wanted another biscuit for his indigestion. He said, "I guess I'll get on home."

Granny said, "Tell Bell and Sanders they're welcome to free meals whenever they want 'em."

The Women Prevail

SOON AFTER THE HANDS WERE fed, Check started out in her buggy. Ezell was seated beside her, her hair tied in a dark scarf, her dress her Sunday best. Connell and Hugh followed on horses. Where the road split, they galloped towards town, and Check drove straight ahead to the Bushyheads' house. There, she, Alabama, and Ezell conferred on the front porch. They didn't have any disagreement, and, with their strategy laid, walked towards Bell's office with the intention of joining the men. On their way, they saw in the distance the two marshals sitting on the bench in front of the jail. The three women changed course and marched over, holding their skirts down against the wind.

Rusk and Bowden were complaining to each other about how long it was taking Bell to locate Puny's horse when they saw the women coming. With their skirts wafting wide, they looked like three big turkeys. Rusk didn't want to be pecked at, and felt like that fate could soon be his. He said, "We need to head 'em off at the pass." He rose. Bowden followed.

They met the women several yards away from the jail. Check said, "I'm Mrs. Andrew Singer. This is my friend Mrs. Dennis Bushyhead. You met her husband, our national treasurer, yesterday. This woman is my employee, Mrs. Tower. You've mistakenly imprisoned her husband, who is also my employee. We've come to get him out."

Rusk was just getting used to his new wife. And, in general, people of the female persuasion unnerved him. The woman who was speaking was small, but somehow sounded like a man. That made his eyelid twitch. He said, "Now, jist hold on a minute."

Check said, "I beg your pardon." She glared like Rusk was an egg-sucking snake.

He looked to the other two women. His eyelid twitched again.

Alabama said, "I was with Mr. Tower the morning Mr. Smith was murdered. He gave me my mail. And I spent the morning gardening next door to the post office. You've seen yourself how close those two buildings are. I saw him several times. Talking to several people." Alabama held both men with a tilt to her head that implied she existed on a plane a few feet above where they stood on the ground.

Bowden had a wife at home who could look that superior, although maybe not that attractive. He tugged Rusk's sleeve and jerked his head. Rusk said, "Excuse me. I need to confer with Marshal Bowden." The two walked behind the jail.

Check, Alabama, and Ezell stepped to the cell. Ezell bent over and looked in the peephole. She whispered, "Puny?"

"Ezell? Lordy. How'd you git here? Is Miz Singer with ya?"

"Shore is. Miz Bushyhead, too. We're gonna spring ya, or die trying."

Puny and Ezell fell to whispering. Check and Alabama sat down on the bench in front of the jail. They tucked their skirts tight to keep them from billowing.

Rusk and Bowden rounded the corner about ten minutes later. Rusk said, "We're interested in gitting to the bottom of this murder and kidnapping. If the nigger has an alibi, we'll release him." He started with his chest puffed out, but as he pulled the cell's key out of his pocket, it began to cave in.

When Puny stepped into the light, he shaded his eyes with his hand. Then he stepped behind the jail to get a little relief. When he came back around, Rusk said, "You better be at the post office if we have more questions."

Check said, "He won't be there. He'll be in the bottoms. You can come out there. Anybody can tell you the way." She added, "Let's go, Puny. I imagine you're quite hungry." She and Alabama turned and marched away. Puny and Ezell followed close behind.

By the time Dennis got home from the inn, the marshals had set themselves up in the post office and were sitting out on the trot. The place seemed like a good headquarters to them. Everybody came in there. That saved them the trouble of going out after people. And it gave them a free place to lodge. They would stay there, sleep in Puny's bed, and cook on his stove until they found a criminal to make their trip profitable.

Check Is Tricked

CHECK DIDN'T SEE HUGH AT breakfast the next morning. But thought nothing of that. He'd developed a habit of eating early with the hands, going to the fields, and staying. Connell had taken breakfast with her and the smaller boys, and had left for the potatoes rather quickly. If she squinted, Check could see him at a distance while tending her flowers. His head looked down like he was studying the plants. Puny was with him. Sometimes they disappeared and popped back up. That wasn't unusual behavior for men talking about soil, weeds, or insects. Check could track them, even when they were hunkering; their hats seemed to sit on potato plants. She figured Puny was avoiding the post office until the marshals left town. She thought that made good sense.

Ezell and Lizzie cleaned up after breakfast and ran Clifford back and forth with errands. Midmorning, Ezell sent him to the Corderys' with a pie. At noon, after the hands had eaten, Check popped into the kitchen and took her meal at the table. She asked if Hugh had gotten his. Neither Ezell nor Lizzie had fed him. She thought that was a little un-Hugh-like, but figured one of the hands had hauled his vittles to him. Both the men of the house and the hired ones ate dinner in the kitchen if they bothered to wash; if not, they ate outside in any shade they could locate. Hugh was probably into something dirty.

Shortly after the noon meal, rain came and forced everybody into the barn, kitchen, or house. Check spent time in the study, going over ledgers. After the storm abated, she went out the front door, studied the puddles to reckon how deeply the water had gone into the ground, and then walked to a rainwater barrel at a corner of the house. She had her head in it, checking the inches marked on the side, when Ezell softly came up beside her. She laid her fingers on the rim. Check jerked and raised up. Ezell said, "Come with me. Don't say a word."

Check was so surprised that she followed. Ezell led her to the tub in the little patch of trees behind her cabin. She turned and looked Check in the face. She was crying.

Check said, "Good Lord, what is it?"

"Puny's done told me sompthing he weren't s'pose to tell. It's got him and me worried."

A fist formed under Check's stays. Her eyes narrowed. "About what?"

"'Fore dawn, Hugh rode off to the Benges'. To git one of them to take him to the marshals. Tell 'em he's the feller who kilt Mr. Smith."

"That's ridiculous! Why would he do that?"

"Puny sez Hugh thinks it's the only way to get the marshals outta the Nation. They want extra pay. Won't go unless they take somebody with 'em. Hugh thinks, 'cause he's a Cherokee, oncet they git to Fort Smith, they'll let him go. But Puny says that they're bound and determined to try somebody for Mr. Smith's murder. And that y'all's arrangement with the federal government don't matter to 'em. They'll do what they please. Puny heared 'em talking about that when he waz in jail." Ezell stopped to let Check digest that information. It was a lot. And she couldn't tell if it'd sunk in. She added, "They don't care about y'all's treaties. They don't mean nothing to 'em."

Check's mind flashed on General Jackson, who'd refused to pay her father's soldiers after they'd won his battle for him. After Chief Junaluska had personally saved Jackson from a tomahawking in the head. Her father had railed about that all of his life. She said, "Where's Connell?"

"Puny sez he's done slipped off to tell the sheriff."

That statement didn't jibe with what Check had seen with her own two eyes. "He was in the potatoes all morning. He didn't ride out of here."

"He went down by the river. So as not to arouse suspicions."

Check's mind flew back. Fluttered all over the morning. The last times she'd seen Connell, she'd seen just his hat. She suddenly realized that Puny had been creeping through the potatoes, probably holding the hat up with a stick. Her temper flared so high it nearly choked her. She hated being tricked. She was going to wear Puny and Connell out if she ever got her hands on that stick. She started to say so to Ezell. But Ezell was used to reading Check's mind. She said, "Them men stick together. It's an honor thing. But Puny, he's scared. He knows what white people can do. He's seen more of that than yer boys have."

Check knew full well what whites were like. But she and Andrew had raised their boys without talk of broken treaties or hatefulness towards Indians. They hadn't completely agreed on the importance of treaties. Or on what breaking them revealed about whites. And she'd had reservations about that decision. But they had agreed they wanted their children to grow up grateful, rather than feeling like victims. And while they'd lived in Ohio, their neighbors hadn't been concerned with Indians; wouldn't have recognized one not dressed in feathers and war paint. There, being southern was the burden. But even in Tennessee, they'd raised their boys as whites. She hadn't prepared them to live as Indians. She had given them only stories.

Check felt like a fool. She said with force, "Go to the barn, Ezell. Have someone harness 'Wassee and bring her around." She marched to the house.

A Dispute with the Marshals

ALABAMA HAD BEEN WEEDING HER flowerbeds when Bob Benge rode up to the post office leading Hugh's horse, Hugh's hands bound to his saddle horn. Bob dismounted, pulled his gun, and loosened the rope. Alabama dropped her gardening fork, went inside, and woke Dennis, who was still sleeping after a long night in the hole. A few minutes later, they walked to the post office together. Bob had disappeared. Hugh was on the counter, his hands tied in his lap. Rusk said, "The post office ain't open."

Dennis said, "We're not here to get the mail. This young man's a Cherokee. You've no right to hold him."

Bowden said, "He don't look like an Indian to me."

Alabama said, "He is an Indian. We don't all look alike." She wished she'd inherited the good skin.

Dennis said, "We have twenty treaties with the United States government. Not a one of them gives you the right to remove a Cherokee from this Nation. Or to try him for a crime against another Cherokee. In fact, several prohibit it."

Rusk said, "Are ya some sort of expert on Indians?"

Dennis's mind flashed back to the day he left Tennessee. Except for low white smoke from the smoldering remains of holding pens, the day was sunny, the sky bright. His father, mounted in the distance at the front of the group, was leading the detachment. Behind him was a long line of wagons and horses. Dennis was towards the middle, seated on the top of a chest that was roped in a wagon. He was watching his father. Suddenly, above the trees beyond his daddy's head, a dark, spiral cloud arose. It spread. Floated over his father and towards the group. When it was directly over the whole body of travelers, thunder boomed from its center. The noise shook the trees. Christian Indians fell to their knees. They prayed and wept. The others raised their arms. Pleaded to the spirits of the forest. Dennis grabbed his little sister. Held her head to his chest. The entire party turned to clutching each other, seeing the thundering cloud as an omen of death. A sure sign they wouldn't survive their journey. Then the cloud floated on. It didn't release a drop of rain. The wood continued to burn. The white smoke stayed close to the ground. His father prayed in a shout. Then turned his horse west.

Dennis said, "I know something about Cherokees, if that's what you're asking."

Alabama said, "Hugh, tell them you're innocent of whatever they're holding you for."

Hugh hung his head. "Mrs. Bushyhead, I've told 'em that."

Alabama's left eyebrow flew up. "Mrs. Bushyhead?"

Rusk said, "We thought that waz your name."

"It is. There's been a mistake, Marshal. This boy's barely nineteen. He's probably trying to get the two of you out of here. That's my guess."

Dennis said, "What exactly are you charging him with?"

"The murder of Turtle Smith," Rusk said.

Dennis looked from one marshal to the other. He shook his head. "Don't touch him. I'm going for the sheriff." He turned.

But Bell appeared in the doorway. His gun was pulled. "No need, Dennis. I'm here." To Hugh, he said, "Get off that counter." Then he pointed his weapon directly at Rusk.

The marshal raised his hands but wagged his head. "Now, Sheriff, ya might wanta think about this. If ya kill a United States deputy marshal, Judge Parker'll run this territory over. The war here will make what's happening to the Apaches and Comanches look like a square dance. And y'all can't fight like them Indians can."

Dennis said, "Let's try to settle this peacefully."

But Bell shook his head. "Hugh Singer's a Cherokee citizen. If he's committed a crime against another Cherokee, that's my jurisdiction. I'll put him in my jail. I told ya to get down off that counter, Hugh. Mind me. Anybody else moves, ya get shot. Marshals, don't y'all take this personally, but I'm the law here. I'm taking control of the prisoner. After Hugh's in jail, we can visit 'bout what happens next. But in the meantime, you officers hand yer guns to Mr. Bushyhead. And Dennis, you take 'em." He said to the marshals, "Ya don't have to worry. He won't shoot ya."

Dennis took the guns. He emptied their chambers and dropped the bullets into his pocket. Then Bell said, "Dennis, you and Alabama take Hugh and put him in jail. Here's my key. When ya get him locked up, Alabama, you secure the key on yer person. Then the two of you get to yer house. I'll be 'round later."

Check Receives a Shock

MEANWHILE, CHECK HAD DRIVEN TOWARD town, determined to spring Hugh from the marshals. She knew they were set up in the post office, and almost went there first. But she figured she'd be on firmer footing taking Bell with her, and drove, instead, straight into Fort Gibson. There, she saw Hugh's horse tied to the hitching rail. She felt a surge of relief. She'd feared the marshals had already left with Hugh for Fort Smith. Feared she might not be able to resist taking off down the Military Road, with or without Bell.

A fullblood was guarding Bell's door. He was wearing a black hat. His legs were spread, his arms crossed over his chest. Check alit from her buggy and decided on a strategy for dealing with him while tying the reins. She marched up the steps, pulled herself to her full height of five foot two, and said, "*I want to see the* sheriff." She looked the Indian square in the face.

He stared about three feet over Check's head.

Check said, "*You need to move. I've got a gun.*"

He glanced down at her. "*Let's see it.*"

Check wished she hadn't mentioned it. Said, "*It's in my pocket.*"

He smiled. "*Mine's in my boot.*"

Check thought: *Fullbloods are the most irritating people on earth.* She said, "*Where's* Sheriff Rogers?"

The fullblood jerked his head towards the door.

"*Who's in there with him?*"

He looked over her head again.

She looked at his belt buckle. It was made from a turtle's shell. She thought about delivering a kick a few inches below it. Decided that would get her in trouble she couldn't handle. She said, "*Tell him* Check Singer *is at the* Bushyheads' *and wants to see him.*"

CHECK FOUND DENNIS AND ALABAMA striding their porch like hounds on the prowl. Dennis said immediately, "The chief's never around when you need him." Then they all sat down. Alabama told Check what had happened that morning. They were discussing what to do when Bell appeared. He told them Hugh was in his jail, and Rusk and Bowden on the bench in front of it. Dennis said, "We're going to have to try Hugh real quick."

"We can't have him convicted," Check said.

"He's not gonna be convicted. He's not guilty," Bell assured her.

"Well, then, will the marshals just stick around?" Alabama asked. "Since there's not a case against him, maybe we should let them take him to Fort Smith."

"Their prison makes mine look like a parlor. People die in that hole." Bell spat on the lawn.

Check said, "And that puts Hugh in the hands of a jury who thinks we're savages and wants any excuse to take our land."

Dennis said, "It would also establish a precedent for Judge Parker to try every case in the Nation. Our right to govern ourselves rests largely on a functioning judicial system. We'd lose that." His father had, at the time of his death, been the chief justice of the Cherokee Supreme Court.

"I was merely thinking out loud," Alabama said. "We have to examine the options. Hugh did this to get these people out of here. Every day they stick around increases the likelihood they'll sniff out that whites killed Turtle. If that happens, they'll stay around looking for them."

"And they won't find 'em," said Dennis. He handed Bell a cigar.

Alabama tilted her rocker forward. "What happens if they stay long enough for somebody to say, 'We took care of the killers'? People brag about that sort of thing."

"The particular people who took care of the killers won't be bragging." Bell spit the tip of his cigar into the yard.

Check saw her opening. "Who killed them? I have a right to know. Hugh's in jail."

Bell struck a match against a post. He lit his cigar and took a long puff. He couldn't think of any reason to withhold information. And Dennis already knew. He said, "Well, one of 'em drowned in the Arkansas River. Coop kilt the other one with a single shot."

Color drained from Check's face. Her jaw clenched. She clutched the arms of her rocker. The veins on the back of her hands popped up. Alabama, in the chair next to her, at first thought Check was having a stroke. When her lips moved but no words came out, Alabama feared that really must be the case. She said, "We need to call Doc Howard."

Check shook her head.

Alabama reached out. Put her hand on Check's arm. "What's the matter?"

Check didn't speak. She looked off towards the post office. The silence on the porch grew. Check's chest heaved, but still no words emerged. A tear formed and rolled down her left cheek. Alabama looked to Dennis and Bell. Dennis scratched his goatee. Bell's cheeks puffed up. He blew out air. He'd made a mistake. He looked towards the river. "I believe the gun Coop used were a gift." Without turning his gaze, he said to Check, "He put it to good use. Would've made yer father proud."

Check took a deep breath. Withdrew a handkerchief from her pocket and dabbed the tears on her cheeks. "That, I'm sure, is true. But we live in different times. At some point, we've got to stop teaching our children to kill."

Bell saw his uncle Alex teaching him to throw a tomahawk. Saw one hit a tree and stick. Saw one bounce off, chipping bark. Those lessons had happened in a world far away. Maybe as far as the stars. Their way of life wouldn't come back. So Bell agreed with Check. But he couldn't figure how Indians could stop killing until whites did. He didn't say that. And with Check still sitting there, lost in her thoughts, he, Dennis, and Alabama went back to working over the problem.

But eventually Check stirred. And when she did, she had the solution.

Forgive and Forget?

BOWDEN HAD SEEN IT AS a good sign that the sheriff considered the prisoner theirs to guard. But the sheriff had left without telling the marshals his plans, so they, too, were chewing on their situation. After considerable jawing and speculation, Bowden said, "I don't care what we do as long as I'm back for church Sunday morning."

Rusk said, "I do care. I keep telling ya, if we take him back, we git ten cents a mile fer him. That's a lot of money."

Bowden conceded the point. Preaching wasn't a full living. People paid in chickens, hams, and bushels of beans. The food was good, but the wife wanted a new dress occasionally. He said, "Well, then, let's take him outta here tomorrow."

"We gotta git our guns and him sprung first." Rusk tapped tobacco into a paper. He didn't know which irritated him more — the sheriff holding their guns, or that a woman was holding the key to the jail. He didn't want a hint of either floating back to Judge Parker. He and Bowden had already agreed on that. They both were fairly certain they'd lose their jobs.

Bowden said, "We could ask fer our guns real nice like."

Rusk rolled his paper, licked it, and lit the end. Bell had told them Mrs. Bushyhead was with child. He said, "You do the asking for the key."

"I can do that. She's a nice lady. Just high-strung 'cause of her condition. She'll want 'im to have a fair trial."

"I think we oughta take the Benge feller with us. That'll give us a suspect and a witness. We'll get paid extra fer him."

"Did he say he actually seen it?"

"No. Said ever'body knew it was a mix-blooded feller 'cause he used a hammer. Evidently, fullblood Indians don't know how to use hammers."

They'd moved on to talking about how to get their weapons back when they saw Bell crossing the fort square carrying a gun in each hand. He had another in his holster, so they reckoned those two were theirs. They got up, dusted off their pants, and met Bell under a tree.

Bell said, "I've decided to let ya take yer prisoner. I'll be over Friday morning to talk to Judge Parker." He handed Rusk his gun first.

Rusk said, "Didja bring the key?"

"Miz Bushyhead was indisposed. When she feels better later, she'll bring over food for ya and the prisoner. You can git the key from her then."

Bowden said, "We'd sure appreciate that."

But Rusk said, "We've got to git out of here by morning at the latest. If we don't git the key, we'll blow the lock off."

Bell scratched the back of his head. "Hell, I jist hand ya yer guns, and ya start threatening me. That's no way to show appreciation. I'm letting ya have him. I jist had to clear it with the tribal authorities. Gotta cover my rear end. Jist like ya do with Judge Parker."

Bowden said, "We do appreciate your situation." Then he added, "I'm feeling better about this whole thing. People need to see eye to eye and try to get along. Fergive and ferget, that's the Lord's policy."

Rusk said, "Bowden, this ain't a church service. It's an arrest."

Check Sets It Up

CHECK DROVE 'WASSEE LIKE BOTH of their tails were on fire. She was still upset about Coop, but had learned at her father's knee that it's better to shoot than to be shot. And Hugh's recent brush with the receiving end of a gun had returned that truth to her mind. She wasn't going to let Hugh get hanged. Even if she had to do the shooting herself. She left her regret in the dust, and sent her thoughts forward like an arrow.

Sanders saw her coming, arm raised, crop flicking. He turned to Nannie and Bert. "Check Singer's moving like a tornado." The three of them, and a man who'd come up from the river with a stringer of fish he was giving away, watched until the buggy stopped. Bert walked towards Check and extended his hand. He said, "Coop's minding the ferry fer me. Jist fer a few minutes."

Check handed her crop to Bert, alit, and said, "Fine. But I'll need you at the ferry tonight." She walked to the old foundation where Jenny lay on the pallet. She squatted, patted Jenny's hair, and recognized her turn for the worse. She looked up at Nannie.

Nannie said, "Bert's helping us some. Fox sez wolves around."

Check looked to the fisherman. He was squat, round-headed, probably a Creek. Certainly not a wolf. Those were back in town. She stood.

Nannie didn't want to say too much in front of Jenny. Knew she could hear. Said, "We appreciated the pie. It were tasty. Let me dip ya up some water."

"No need. I have to get home. The rain was a relief." Check patted her bun, turned towards her buggy, and took the crop from Bert's hand. She turned again, and said, "Sanders, I'm having a little trouble with an axle. Could you look at it for me?"

Sanders had been thinking Check was acting peculiar. Figured she'd cough up the reason out of the fisherman's hearing. He followed her to the rig. Got on his hands and knees. Looked under the carriage. There was nothing wrong with the axle. He looked up at her. "What seems to be the problem?"

"I'm not sure. Let me roll a little ways. See if you can hear it." She got in, rolled several yards, and pulled up the reins. Sanders walked to her and waited. Check said, "I was lying." Sanders smiled.

Check said, "Has anybody told you there're marshals in town?"

He shook his head slowly.

"Well, they're here. And they've arrested Hugh for Turtle's murder."

Sanders hooked a thumb in his pants. He squinted into the sun. Cleared his throat. Said, "We'll have to do sompthing about that."

"We've got a plan. We need help with it."

AFTERWARDS, CHECK DROVE AROUND THE swale towards the river. Coop heard her before he could see her. Thought he was getting a passenger until he saw 'Wassee and the buggy. Check pulled to a stop, stayed in her seat, and shouted, "Coop!"

"I waz jist tending the ferry while —"

"I've seen Bert."

Coop figured he and Bert were in trouble. He looked at his feet.

"Coop, please come up here so I don't have to yell."

Coop took in a deep breath. He hopped from the ferry to the rocks. Then hopped those until he stopped at 'Wassee.

Check said, "First, Coop, I want to say I'm sorry you had to kill that man. I didn't intend that. I gave you Ruff's gun so you could protect yourself. But I don't want you to feel bad. You did a good deed. Just try not to do another one. Killing gets habitual. You have to be on guard against that."

Coop looked towards the potatoes. He wasn't sure what "habitual" meant.

Check continued, "Later tonight, I want you to give your gun away."

Coop glanced up. Miz Singer looked dark in the face. He didn't want to cross her, but wanted to keep the gun. His mouth opened, his shoulders sagged.

"Don't worry. I'll replace it. Hugh's in jail, and we have to fix that. I need your help." She told him his part of the plan. Then she turned the buggy, smashing a few potato plants. She swore. Ruined potatoes were one more thing she was going to blame Connell for.

Connell had seen the buggy coming up from the river. He was waiting for his mother in a rocker on the front porch when she walked up from the barn. He stood for his tongue-lashing, ready to get it over. And Check did start in. "When did I get to be the last person around here to know anything? Tell me that, Connell Singer! Then explain why on earth you let Hugh do such a fool thing?"

Connell had been smoking a cigarette while he waited. He'd expected a lecture, but wasn't ready to answer questions. The plan hadn't been his. He'd tried every way on earth to talk Hugh out of it. But once Hugh made up his mind, he'd felt honor-bound to stick by him. Hugh was a grown man. He'd matured in a matter of weeks. Connell had told Bell what Hugh had done, but wasn't going to throw him under their mother's wagon wheels. So he took the Indian way out. He took a draw off his cigarette and looked towards the river.

Check was used to that trick. The more she said, the quieter Connell would get. And the more she'd sound like a jaybird mad at a stick. She marched up the steps. When she passed Connell, she said, "Make yourself useful. Bring Ezell to the study."

As Sweet as Strawberry Pie

AT TWILIGHT, ON THE BENCH in front of the jail, Bowden said, "That Miz Bushyhead's a fine cook." He knocked his chest with his fist and burped.

"She's a fine-looking woman." Rusk licked his fingers and picked another piece of cornbread from the basket. He was sitting on the ground, his back against a bench leg, watching the sky lose light.

"I try not to cogitate on any woman except my wife. That'll get a preacher in trouble." Bowden drew a match from his pocket, struck it on the bench, and lit a lantern.

Rusk didn't really think about women other than his new wife. But he liked to pretend he did. "Ya might as well be dead, then."

Hugh said through the cell's peephole, "Can I get more chicken?"

"I don't see why not." Bowden was really asking Rusk.

Rusk said, "Okay, but don't try anything funny." He got up, took his gun from his holster, and threw the key to Bowden. The preacher-marshal picked a leg and thigh from the basket, held the stump of the drumstick in his teeth, and undid the padlock. He opened the heavy door, removed the leg from his teeth, and said, "Have a thigh."

At that moment, the sound of a buggy floated in from a distance. Rusk said to Hugh, "Git against the back wall." Bowden shut the door and locked it. He then moved the lantern to the end of the bench close to the door. Both men stepped away from the light, one to one side of the building, one to the other. They drew their guns.

When the buggy rolled up, a voice called out, "Don't shoot me. I'm jist this boy's cook. I brung him a pie from his mother."

Bowden recognized the voice. He holstered his gun. "A pie?" He walked over and picked up the lantern.

Ezell said, "Yes, sir. She's too heartsick to brung it herself."

Rusk holstered his gun. "Ain't you the nigger woman we saw yesterday?"

"Yes, sir, I is. That's why I volunteered to brung it. His mama waz gonna git his brother to do it, but I wanted to thank ya personally for letting my man go. We ain't done nothing. Jist trying to get along with these Indians. It's kinda hard, ya know."

Rusk said, "You talk a lot fer a nigger. Let me have that pie."

"Yessir. I waz raised in the North. They didn't teach us no better."

Ezell handed the tin to Rusk. She added, "I got a message for the boy to go with his pie."

Bowden said, "What kind is it?"

"Berry pie. Strawberry. Will ya give it to him?"

Bowden said, "Well, sure. It's pretty big, ain't it?" He sniffed. "Smells warm, too."

"It is warm. I jist taken it out of the oven before I come. Now, can I tell this boy goodbye from his mama?"

Bowden sniffed the pie again. "Sure, shout it out. He can hear ya. You can bet he's listening to ever' word."

"Ya sure? It's kind of a funny message. He might not understand it."

"I can hear ya, Ezell." Hugh spoke loudly.

"Well, okay, Mr. Singer. Yer mama sends ya her blessing. ᏂᏆᏍᏬᎤ ᎠᏓᏪᏚ ᎠᏯᏂ."

"Hey! Now wait a minute! What'd ya say to him?" Rusk pulled his gun on Ezell.

She slid into the corner of the buggy. "Don't know what it means. It's a Cherokee blessing. They're a religious family."

"I'm gonna kill ya if yer lying to me!" Rusk's face contorted.

Bowden said, "Now wait, Tom. Hold up." To Ezell, he said, "Can ya say that again?"

Ezell was shivering. "I'm afraid to. Please don't shoot me. His mama's jist worried 'bout his soul. Indians got souls jist like other people."

"Nobody's gonna hurt ya. Tom, put yer gun away. It's always good to know other people's blessings."

Rusk said, "I can't wait to git outta here." He holstered his gun and spat.

Hugh yelled from inside the jail. "That's all right, Ezell. You can tell him. He's a preacher."

Ezell uncoiled from the corner of the buggy. She said in a loud voice, "ᏂᏆᏍᏬᎤ ᎠᏓᏪᏚ ᎠᏯᏂ."

Bowden said, "Well, now that's right pretty. What's it mean?"

Ezell said, "I told ya. I don't know."

Hugh said, "It means the Creator will rise up and help me. It's a standard blessing. Like, 'May the Lord bless you and keep you. And make his face to shine upon you.' Tell Mama I appreciate that. And that I love her."

"I will, Mr. Hugh. You take care of yerself. Don't let 'em do nothing to ya in Fort Smith. Mr. Connell, he'll be over to see ya on Friday."

"All right, Ezell. Don't worry. Hey, fellas, let me have my pie."

"Ya ain't gitting the whole thing. It's too much for one fella," Rusk responded.

Ezell turned the buggy back the way she came. Night had fallen, so she drove as fast as she could without being able to see well. A short way out of town, she saw the outline of a tall oak on the horizon. She flicked her reins. Hurried 'Wassee towards it. Two horsemen were concealed in the shade of its branches. One lit a match and held it high. The other one said, "Praise the Lord, she's made it."

Ezell pulled the buggy to a halt. Puny jumped off of his horse, flung Connell his reins, and climbed into the carriage. He threw his arms around his wife. Kissed her hard. When Ezell caught her breath, she put a hand to her breast. "Lord, man, a little danger gits yer blood rising."

Connell said, "How'd it go?"

Ezell took another deep breath. "Ain't no problem. Jist done it."

"What didcha say?"

"ᏔᏐᏍᏫᏌ ᎤᏝᏍᎭ ᎤᏲᎾ."

Connell smiled. He jerked his head towards the bottoms. "Y'all get on out of here."

Heart Problems

BOWDEN WAS DIZZY. HIS BREATHS shallow. Rusk, a heavier man and seated, was only having trouble focusing his eyes. The light of the lantern moved like leaves in the wind. He said, "I'm feeling drunk."

Bowden came from a family of teetotalers. "I'm not drunk. I'm sick."

"I'm not drunk either. I jist feel thaterway."

Bowden tried to reach the bench, but dropped to his knees. He grabbed the end. "I'm having . . . a hard time . . . breathing."

"I think it were the pie. There were sompthing in it." Rusk called to Hugh. "How ya feeling in there?"

"I feel fine," Hugh replied. "You men got a problem?"

Bowden clutched his shirt. "I'm having a heart attack. Rusk, help me. Jesus, have mercy." He fell over. His cheek smacked the dirt.

Rusk looked at Bowden. He was too shaky to get over to him. His chest felt like an anvil had hit it. He said, "Cathy, I love ya." He said that again. He slumped. Dropped to the ground slowly.

Hugh called, "What's going on out there?" Nobody answered. He sat down with his back against the door. His heart thumped so hard he could hear it.

Bred to Endure

DENNIS WHISPERED, "BAMY, I'LL DO that." He was going through Rusk's pockets.

She was going through Bowden's. "Don't be ridiculous. I undressed a lot of men when Mama ran the hospital."

Dennis shook his head and growled.

Alabama said, "I found it!" She pulled the key out and handed it to Dennis. He picked up the lantern and handed it to her. He fumbled with the lock and undid it.

Hugh slipped out. He looked down at the marshals on the ground. He inspected Rusk's face. "Did Mama kill 'em?"

Alabama said, "Mine's breathing. Is that one, Dennis?"

"Seems to be." To Hugh, he said, "Connell's got your horse. He'll be at our house by now. Give me a hug, son."

Hugh embraced Dennis, then Alabama. But said forlornly, "I have to leave."

Dennis pulled himself to his full height. Put a hand on Hugh's shoulder. "That's right. We have no other way to protect you. Or any of the rest of us. But, Hugh, I spent nineteen years away from the Cherokee Nation. I took it with me everywhere I went. You're a Cherokee. You have a tribe. You'll never be alone. Keep us in your heart. We'll keep you in ours. God be with you."

Alabama grabbed Hugh's arm. "We're used to long journeys, Hugh. We're bred to endure them. Go, quickly, darling."

The Leaving

CHECK PACKED HUGH'S CLOTHES BEHIND the closed door of her older boys' room. She couldn't stand any talk, any discussion, any questions. She was frantic to get Hugh out of Judge Parker's reach. And frantic because her sight didn't extend into the future. Would Hugh be killed on the run? Settle somewhere and never return? Build a life for himself, or wander from one thing to another? She threw shirts and trousers into his suitcase and into Connell's. Then she rushed to a small room across from the little boys', and grabbed her own bag from there. She filled it, too. Boots in first, then underthings, and personal items Hugh would either need or want — his shaving kit, a picture of Andrew, one of him and Connell, a bottle of cologne, his knife and its sheath, a small wooden horse she hadn't known he'd kept. She thought about packing a few books, but changed her mind, deciding Hugh wouldn't read. After she'd done all that, she realized he couldn't take suitcases away on a horse. She felt like she was losing her mind. Why would she pack all of that? She was as silly as quails running in circles. What she needed were saddlebags. They were in the barn.

She opened the door and yelled, "Clifford!"

Cliff was at the bottom of the stairs. He'd been told not to come up unless he was on fire. His mother loomed over him in lamplight spilled from his brothers' room. She didn't look like herself. She looked taller, and her hair had escaped her bun. Cliff took a step back before saying, "Yes, ma'am?"

Check sent him after saddlebags. Told him to hurry. While he was gone, she unpacked the cases she'd filled, and set to one side of the bed only what she could stuff into the bags. She repacked Hugh's suitcase and Connell's with the rest of his clothes and possessions. Wherever Hugh landed for a spell, she'd send them on a train.

THAT ALL WAS SORTED BY the time Hugh and Connell arrived at the ferry. People were waiting in groups around lanterns on the ground. Hugh went straight to his mother. She was composed; her hair in a braid down her back, his saddlebags at her feet. Check opened her arms to Hugh. He opened his. When he was in control of his voice, he said in Check's ear, "I'm sorry, Mama. Somebody had to do it. Best it was me."

Check pulled back. Held Hugh at arm's length. Her heart beat wildly. Her face was tear-stained, but hard. "Hugh, we live in a world not of our making. We do the best we can. Bert and Coop will ferry you across the river. Less than a mile in, there's a boundary pole for the Nations. Coop knows the way to it. Sanders is at the pole with a lantern. He'll lead you to his Creek friends. Tomorrow morning, head out early. Go somewhere beyond the reach of the government. Maybe Arizona. Or New Mexico. It'll be a long and dangerous trip. The Wild Indians are fighting for their lives out there. But it's more dangerous here."

Hugh said, "I understand. I'll be careful." He rubbed his thigh. "Bell's got my gun. Is he here?" He looked around.

"No, he can't be around when a prisoner escapes. But we have a gun for you."

Check called to Coop, who was on the ferry with Bert. He disappeared from the lantern light there and walked off the apron. He unbuckled his gun belt and held it out to Hugh. He said, "She's a straight shooter."

"Thank you, Coop. You earned it. But I really need it."

"It's yer uncle's. I'll have another one 'fore long." Coop looked to Check.

She said, "Y'all are just trading guns."

After that, Check pushed Hugh's arm, and nodded towards Puny, Ezell, and Lizzie. Hugh stepped over, laid a hand on Lizzie's shoulder. He said, "Behave yourself, will ya?" She nodded. He turned to Ezell. Put his arms around her. Whispered in her ear. Then he looked towards Puny. Puny shook his head. Hugh shook his. They grabbed each other. Squeezed, and let go quickly. Puny flapped a hand. Hugh croaked, "I'll see ya again."

Connell was next to Puny. He and Hugh also whispered in each other's ear. But they slapped each other's back so loudly, their whacks could be heard over Clifford's and Otter's crying. Hugh grabbed each of his younger brothers. Then he looked around. Check knew he was looking for Paul. She said, "Paul's asleep. I didn't know whether to wake him or not. It would just confuse him. But that was probably a mistake. I've had a lot on my mind."

Hugh said, "No, you're right, Mama. Tell him I'll see him another time."

Tears came into Check's eyes. "I don't want to lie to him."

"You won't be lying. I promise." He put his arms out to Check. She grabbed him and buried her face in his chest. Then she pulled back and held him at arm's length. "You need a head start." Her voice cracked. "They may be idiot enough to chase you." She let go of an arm and tugged his other sleeve. They walked towards the ferry together, Check's arm folded in the curve of Hugh's back, his over her shoulders. On the apron, Hugh put his mouth close to Check's ear. He whispered, "Ezell said the strawberries were poisoned."

Check shook her head. "Fox concocted something to knock 'em out. There's not a Cherokee word for 'narcotic.' Or if there is, none of us knows it."

The Next Morning

BELL SAID, "NOW, LET ME git this straight. I turn my prisoner over to you. You eat a pie. Take a nap. And let him escape?" His eyes were wide. He was on the Bushyheads' front porch with the two marshals, Dennis, and Alabama. The sun was shining and the air fresh. But both marshals groaned.

Alabama poured them more coffee. "You poor things. Do you think it was food poisoning?"

Rusk said, "I think she drugged us. Then her nigger hid off somewhere 'til we were out, and then sprung Singer." His head felt twice its normal size. He sipped coffee and rested his forehead against a porch post.

Bell scratched his cheek. "Well, I'm not too sure Miz Singer drugged you. She's a recent widow. She's in deep mourning."

Alabama twisted her brow into furrows. "She could've had some morphine left over from Mr. Singer's death. But you would've tasted it. Did the pie taste bitter?"

Rusk rolled his head against the post. That was as close as he could come to shaking it. Bowden's head was in his hands. He answered, "Naw. It was delicious. And we gave the boy half of it."

"He appeared to have cleaned his off," Dennis said. He looked perplexed. He hadn't seen exactly what Alabama had done with Hugh's part of the pie, so wasn't telling an outright lie.

Bell eased down onto a step. "Well, ya can bet he's long gone. He's had several hours. Probably in the Creek or Choctaw Nation. I don't have authority in them places."

Bowden said, "You don't think he's at his mother's? We need to talk to that cook."

Bell squinted like he was considering that. "Ya can if ya wanta. I'll be glad to go with ya. But I doubt it'll be very productive. My guess is Singer has hightailed it out trying to git away from Judge Parker." Bell stretched out a leg and pulled his knife from his pocket. He added, "Even if he's stayed, he won't be sitting on his Mama's back porch. Lots of rabbit holes in them bottoms. Fella could hide there forever. And if ya ain't accustomed to 'em, them cottonmouths are awful."

A shimmy ran over Rusk's shoulders. He sat up straight and rubbed his forehead. "Marshals'll be back in here. If Singer shows his face, they'll arrest him."

Bell studied his nails. "Well, that's why I think he's gone to one of them other nations. But I could be wrong. Yer welcome to stay. I can understand how ya wouldn't wanta tell Judge Parker ya lost yer prisoner."

Rusk's mind flipped between Judge Parker and the cottonmouths. Judge Parker bit only criminals.

Bowden lifted his head. He said to Rusk, "We need to leave right away. I hav'ta preach."

Bell opened his knife and cleaned under his thumbnail. "I guess we could not mention ya ever had him. Ya could tell Parker whatever ya want." He cleaned his middle fingernail. "Young fellas starting out in law enforcement naturally make a few mistakes. My advice, boys, is to jist learn from 'em, keep quiet, and go on." He gazed out over the lawn. It looked peaceful.

The Years That Followed

CHECK DIDN'T SLEEP THE NIGHT Hugh left. And though things settled down on the farm, she didn't sleep much for many nights afterwards. In exhaustion, she finally gave in to grieving. Not so much for Andrew, as she'd grieved him from the day he'd grown sick. She grieved for Hugh. And at times her sorrow overwhelmed her. But she was proud of Hugh, too. And every day when Puny returned from the post office, she met him, looking for a letter. There were a few. But Hugh was on the move.

In the years to follow, Check turned the events of the spring of 1875 over in her mind so many times that they were like a deeply furrowed field of fine-grained, sandy soil. Sometimes, even long into the future, she could be seen standing in the potatoes, staring towards the Arkansas River and the Creek Nation. When Sanders spied her, he kept an eye on her. If she didn't move for a while, he'd walk over. They'd talk about the weather, the crops, or the latest snake one of them had killed. When Check's mind was back in the present, Sanders would return to his corn.

Author's Note

The events in this book are entirely fictional. But I have some idea of the fates of the real people upon whom many of the characters are loosely based. Imagination can provide answers for others.

Check was based on the life of Cherokee America Rogers, who lived a long time and presided over a small empire of people and potatoes. She was "Aunt Check" to many, well loved, and generally got her way. She's buried next to her husband. Hugh's headstone is close by. Their home still stands.

Connell (Connell Rogers) became a wealthy farmer and an influential man in the Cherokee Nation. He remained on the land he inherited from his mother, served in the Cherokee Senate, and held several other offices in the tribe. He married a second time after his first wife died. Clifford did not become a doctor. His little brother Otto did for a while, but gave up medicine to grow potatoes. Paul became a cowboy.

Puny, Ezell, and Lizzie were not based on the lives of individual people, but on historical accounts of African Americans in Indian Territory, most of whom were former slaves. Scholarship on the relationship between Cherokees and African Americans is complex, fascinating, and still emerging. I like to think that Puny and Ezell got to go home to Ohio, and lived happy and successful lives. I suspect Lizzie stayed behind, happily married, had two other children, and continued to work for Connell after Check died. Also, far in the future, I think she may have been helpful to one of Jenny's granddaughters, Maud Nail.

Sanders Cordery was based on the life of Wilson Cordery. He gave up his wife on Braggs Mountain and remained with his Nannie in the bottoms (Nancy Hall Cordery). He spent some time in Judge Parker's jail, but got out alive. One of his granddaughters — my grandmother — told me on more than one occasion that he lived to be 102.

Jenny and Bert (based on the lives of Louisa Cordery and Albert Anderson) married. Their first child died as an infant, but they raised eight children to adulthood. Twice during their marriage they lived in the bawdy house. Five of their grandchildren were raised in it. That house was moved from the bayou to Fort Gibson, Oklahoma, a few decades ago and was later named the William Penn Adair House. It is currently in disrepair.

Sheriff Rogers, not a young man, died in 1876.

George Sixkiller was not based on the life of a single person. But many Indian boys like George died too young.

Coop (Anderson "Coop" Cordery) lived in the bottoms and on the bayou all of his life. In addition to working on the ferry, he drove the mail and farmed. He named his youngest son Connell.

Mannypack (Amanda Pack) died young. Tomahawk (Thomas Cordery) then married a white woman and had a few brushes with the law. He named sons Hugh and Clifford.

Bert's little brother, Ame (Amos Anderson), grew up to be a farmer. He married twice. His first wife was Tomahawk and Mannypack's little girl. Upon her death, Ame married a daughter of Fox, the Creek medicine man.

Four years after this novel is set, Dennis Wolf Bushyhead became the chief of the Western Cherokees. He was well loved and reelected three times, but never lost his interest in money. Alabama died many years before Dennis. She was older than portrayed in this book, and went by her first name, Elizabeth. She is buried in the old Cherokee National Cemetery within sight of Check's grave.

Granny Schrimsher may be best remembered through the life of one of her grandsons, Will Rogers. Her picture hangs in his childhood home mentioned in this book and in the Will Rogers Museum in Claremore, Oklahoma.

Nash Taylor was based on the life of Florian Nash. Mr. Nash remained a successful businessman, farmer, and community leader. He lived into old age. His house still stands, and is listed on the National Registry of Historic Places.

Judge Isaac Parker became known as "the Hanging Judge." His reputation still lingers in history. One hundred and sixty people received the death penalty in his court, and seventy-nine of those were executed. He extended his control over the Cherokee Nation as much as he could, but in later years somewhat softened his racist views towards Indians.

The gold stash was found — but not in the fake well.

In an attempt to destroy nonreservation Indians by assimilation, Congress abolished their tribal governments in 1898, and required those nations to submit to a general allotment of their lands and to the laws of the United States of America. The Cherokees were the last of the "Five Civilized Tribes" to capitulate. Oklahoma became a state in 1907. After that, the Cherokees in Oklahoma languished for decades without tribal rights, a chief, or a government. They slowly regained their autonomy and power, due in no small part to the efforts of Earl Boyd Pierce, one of Wilson Cordery's great-grandsons, who, as the Cherokee general counsel, fought tirelessly to reestablish the tribe. Today the Cherokee Nation of Oklahoma is thriving, and one of the largest employers in the northeastern part of the state.

The Arkansas River was tamed by the McClellan-Kerr Navigation System. It still goes around the bend, but without the roar.

Acknowledgments

Aside from my grandmother, to whom I have dedicated this book, I particularly want to thank:

Sequoyah, for the invention of his syllabary, which, in a matter of months, educated the Cherokee people in a written language, changed the course of Cherokee history, and contributed to the plot of this tale. Sequoyah could neither read nor write any other language, and his intellectual achievement is unique in human history.

Emmet Starr, the author of *History of the Cherokee Indians and Their Legends and Folk Lore,* which was first published in 1921 and is filled with tribal facts and genealogical information without which this book would have never been conceived nor executed. Before the internet was invented, I used Starr's rather complex genealogical tables for the "Old Families" of the Cherokee Nation to establish blood relationships among characters. Subsequent research might prove them factually incorrect in a few instances, but they are a primary source, and as fictional people have lives of their own, that possibility hasn't concerned me enough to check sources beyond Starr.

James Mooney, the author of *Myths of the Cherokee and Sacred Formulas of the Cherokees,* which was collected in two volumes in the 1880s for the Bureau of American Ethnology. My copy was reproduced in 1972 by Charles Elder, Bookseller and Publisher, Nashville, Tennessee, probably at Elder's own expense.

C. W. "Dub" West, author of *Fort Gibson: Gateway to the West,* who, again probably at his own expense, published 1,000 copies in 1972. I consider myself fortunate to own copies 188 and 189.

The Fort Gibson Genealogical Society, which compiled *Fort Gibson, Oklahoma Area, and the Old Illinois District of the Cherokee Nation,* published in 2000.

My cousin, Nancy Leeds McLemore, for lending me a helping hand, and Denise Chaudoin and Ella Christie, teachers at the Cherokee Charter School, Tahlequah, Oklahoma, for improving my dictionary Cherokee with accurate translations and advice. If there are any mistakes in the Cherokee, they are my own fault for not providing enough context.

Earl Boyd Pierce, the chief attorney for the Cherokee Nation from my early childhood long into my adulthood. Earl was my mother's first cousin and my grandmother's favorite nephew. He could talk about John Ross and John Ridge as if he knew them well and had seen them yesterday. While I was growing up, Earl fought and eventually won, before the US Supreme Court, the Arkansas Riverbed case, which awarded over $14 million to the Cherokee Nation and provided for me proof Indians don't always have to be victims. Novelists are sometimes asked whom they'd like to raise from the dead and invite to dinner. Earl would be on my list. I wish I'd paid more attention to his stories when I was young and dumb.

I'd also like to thank the following friends of mine who read and critiqued any of the numerous drafts of this book I've written over the years. That list includes my ex-husband, David Verble, who spent many a Friday night listening to me read aloud what I had written during the week; my college roommate, Laura Derr, with whom I exchanged chapters for her suggestions, first through snail mail and then electronically; my business partner, Judy Worth, who criticized the manuscript in helpful ways; my first cousin John Haworth, Senior Executive Emeritus of the National Museum of the American Indian, who has an encyclopedic understanding of Native American issues; and other readers, who probably doubted this book would ever be published, but nevertheless spent their time, energies, and minds to help me improve it — my aunt Barbara Haworth, and friends Bill Blackburn, Gretchen Brown, John Burruss, Lana Dearinger, Rona Roberts, Martha Helen Smith, and Sue

Weant. I'm sure I've left somebody out. I apologize. It's been a long, bumpy road, with many turns and several washed-out bridges.

Finally, I'd like to thank my agent, Lynn Nesbit, who is a legend in her own time for good reason. And Nicole Angeloro, my editor at Houghton Mifflin Harcourt, for her deep understanding of the book, her sense of humor, and her light, helpful touch.

A Conversation with Margaret Verble

How long did it take you to write Cherokee America?

So long that I almost can't remember when I wasn't writing it. I think I actually started putting words to paper about 1999 or 2000. But I'd been reading Cherokee history for over twenty years before that.

Why did you decide to include the Cherokee language in the novel?

First, it's crucial to the plot. Second, we (the Cherokees) are trying to save this language. We have a Cherokee immersion school in Tahlequah so we can pass the language down from elders to children. It's also possible for adults to take courses, both in classes and online. This is a crucial part of preserving Cherokee culture, and the Nation has put a lot of resources into it. I want to do my part. Third, Sequoyah's syllabary symbols are physically beautiful, and a breathtaking intellectual achievement. I want people to see them.

How is your own family included in the story?

Sanders Cordery was based on the life of my grandmother's grandfather, Wilson Cordery. Grandma knew him and told me about him. She said he walked the Trail of Tears, was six foot four, and lived to be 102. I'm not sure if she was right about his age — in his time, people were less than precise about age than we are now. But you did have to be strong to survive that walk, and the men in my family are tall.

Also, much of the story takes place on my family's allotment land in the Arkansas River bottoms outside of Fort Gibson, Oklahoma. I've been intimately familiar with that land all of my life. When I was a kid roaming it, I discovered my great-grandmother's headstone in a snake-infested cemetery in those river bottoms, and I've visited it again as recently as last summer. My great-grandmother is Jenny in the book.

What do you hope readers take away from Cherokee America?
I mainly hope they have a good time reading the book. I think literature should be good storytelling, and entertaining as well as instructive. It bothers me that so much of literary fiction is psychologically painful and sort of a chore to get through. People have choices. They don't have to read. If they do read, they should find it rewarding. And it's easier to absorb ideas under pleasurable conditions.

As for instruction, I want readers to learn some Cherokee history beyond the Trail of Tears story and begin to see American history in a way that's not so Eurocentric. I also tried to write a story where people care about each other and get along in spite of their racial, wealth, and class differences. We need more of that.

A FINALIST FOR THE PULITZER PRIZE

A debut novel chronicling the life and loves of a headstrong, earthy, and magnetic heroine

FINALIST
FOR THE
PULITZER
PRIZE

"Verble's voice is utterly authentic, tender and funny... vivid and smart... A wonderful debut novel."
— ROXANA ROBINSON

MAUD'S LINE

Margaret Verble

A NOVEL

HMH hmhbooks.com